CITY
DARK

OTHER TITLES BY ROGER A. CANAFF

Copperhead Road

Among the Dead (ADA Alex Greco Series, Book One)

Bleed Through (ADA Alex Greco Series, Book Two)

CITY
DARK

A THRILLER

ROGER A. CANAFF

Text copyright © 2022 by Roger A. Canaff

Published by Thomas & Mercer, Seattle

www.apub.com

Amazon, the Amazon logo, and Thomas & Mercer are trademarks of Amazon.com, Inc., or its affiliates.

ISBN-13: 9781542039543
ISBN-10: 1542039541

Cover design by Damon Freeman

Printed in the United States of America

For Adam Sheldon,
who embodied New York City and left us too soon,
and for Richard Malnati, mentor and friend,
and my last, fast connection to the island of my birth.

"If I get her in my sights, boom, boom. Out go the lights."

—Little Walter

"Man, I swear, I'd give the whole thing up for you."

—Lou Reed, "Coney Island Baby"

8:37 P.M. LOAD IS HIGH. LIGHTNING STRIKE, BUCHANAN SOUTH SUBSTATION; SECOND STRIKE: INDIAN POINT ENERGY CENTER—TWO ADDITIONAL TRANSMISSION LINES OVERLOADED.

8:55 P.M. LOAD IS HIGH. TEMPS REMAIN HIGH. LIGHTNING STRIKE, SPRAIN BROOK SUBSTATION, YONKERS; TWO TRANSMISSION LINES OUT, REPOWERING.

LOAD IS HIGH. REPOWER OVERLOADING ADDITIONAL LINES; CON ED TO REDUCE POWER AT EAST RIVER FACILITY.

9:19 P.M. FIVE PERCENT REDUCTION AUTHORIZED. LEEDS SUBSTATION TRIPPED; LONG ISLAND AND NEW JERSEY POWER SOURCES COMPROMISED.

LOAD IS HIGH. REDUCTION INCREASED TO EIGHT PERCENT. EXTEND CONNECTIONS TO LONG ISLAND LIGHTING SYSTEM AND NJ SOURCES.

9:27 P.M. RAVENSWOOD No. 3 POWER GENERATOR DOWN; ADDITIONAL SHEDDING NOT MITIGATING.

9:37 P.M. CONSOLIDATED EDISON POWER DOWN.

CITY DARK.

PROLOGUE

Wednesday, July 13, 1977
Henry Hudson Parkway
New York City
9:32 p.m.

When the lights went out, their mom, Lois, was driving, and Joe and Robbie were in the back seat arguing. That was normal, as Robbie was fifteen and Joe ten. And it was the last normal thing any of them would ever know.

Daylight had melted from the sky over New Jersey, fading from a dirty, yellow haze to a smoky blue. The air rushing in the open windows of their LTD station wagon gave little relief. For one, it smelled. As both boys frequently announced, pretty much the whole city smelled. The Hudson River smelled, too, as it slid by them to the right looking soupy and brown.

They were on the Henry Hudson Parkway, just north of where the map started calling it the West Side Highway. Up front, Lois had her elbow out the window. A cigarette deteriorated rapidly between two fingers, and from time to time she tapped on the butt with her thumb. It was a nervous habit; Joe knew it gave her a smelly, yellow-stained thumb. Lois didn't go in for feminine cigarettes like Eve or Virginia Slims. She smoked like a man and favored Winston Reds. It was a habit she'd picked up from the man who had given her the boys in the back seat, along with multiple black eyes and fat lips.

The song on the radio was "I Just Want to Be Your Everything" by Andy Gibb, who Robbie swore was queer. Robbie had run electrical tape down the "center" of the back seat to mark off his and Joe's respective territories, but Joe was convinced that Robbie had taken at least 60 percent, and Joe had just learned about percentages. It didn't matter much anyway. The heat was so bad, the tape had long since sweated off the vinyl bench seat, and in its place was a nasty, sticky trail of adhesive. Robbie scooped up a fingertip full of it, then reached over and stuck his finger in Joe's hair.

"Stop it! Gross!"

"Chill, crybaby. It's Fabergé Organics Shampoo. With wheat germ and honey. So now you've got wheat germs."

"Mom!"

"Guys, please," she said. There was exhaustion and a panicky edge in her voice, something Joe had started to notice with growing disquiet. "Both of you."

"Let me see that," Robbie said. He was looking at Joe's most prized possession, a Hostess baseball card of Reggie Jackson that Joe had found in a Ho Hos box. Joe had it cupped in his left hand. It seemed impossible for him not to gaze at it every few seconds.

"No way."

"Give it. You're gonna ruin it anyway; it's getting all smudged."

"Leave me alone."

"Whatever. It's just a Hostess card. Sucks anyways."

"You suck," Joe said.

Then Robbie pulled a trick and pointed to his right, shouting "Whoa!" as he did so. When Joe turned to follow his gaze, Robbie snatched the card out of his hand. Then he held it out the window, grasping it by a tiny piece of a corner between his thumb and forefinger as it fluttered in the wind.

"Robbie, no!" Joe cried.

Robbie smiled—a mean, toothless grin. Then the grin faded. Actually, everything faded in that moment. It got dark. Really dark.

"What the—" Lois started.

"Robbie, give it back!" Joe yelled, not yet noticing the change in the lights. Robbie, mesmerized, let the card slip from his fingers. "Noooo!" Joe was screaming now. "Mom! Pull over!"

His mother was pulling over, but not because Joe had asked her to. She was pulling over because everything to the left of them, the whole scene on the city side, was suddenly black. She eased the LTD off the highway and into a little pull-off area between the pavement and the river, a drop-off spot that allowed people access to Riverside Park up by 116th Street. By dark in the summer of 1977, that wasn't many people at all.

"Let me out!" Joe screeched. "Let me out. My card!" The car came to a slow stop.

"Joe, come back here!" he heard his mother yell, but he was already bolting up the side of the highway, dashing over broken glass, trash, and the occasional hubcap. He was desperately scanning the mess beneath his sneakers as he ran north, trying to see in the wash of headlights. But then, when the cars passed, there was no light above him, just the last weak glow in the sky.

"Joey, come back," Robbie called, catching up to him. "It was an accident!" Darkness threatened to swallow them completely in between the wash of headlights.

"Get back here!" their mother called.

"Help me find it—" Joe started. Another terrible minute or two passed, and then Joe's heart leaped. There it was, lying flat among some debris and cigarette butts. He held the card up, waving it triumphantly. His sense of relief was palpable, but then he caught sight of his mother. In her face, even from that distance, he saw worry and something like gnawing fear. Traffic was light, but cars were slowing down as the fact of the darkness set in, headlights glowing eerily down the highway like they were purposely moving in slow motion. Like for a funeral procession.

"*Move it, you two!*" Lois shouted. "*Something's going on with the power. Get back here!*"

"*Mom, I found it!*" Joe said as they reached the car. He waved the card in one hand, and Robbie made a swipe for it.

"*Give me that thing,*" Lois said. She glared at Robbie. "*You stand still.*" Then to Joe she said, "*Give it here. I'll hang on to it until you two can get along. Give it, Joe. Now.*" With an air of defeat, Joe handed over the treasured card, and Lois stuffed it into the back pocket of her blue jeans. From inside the car, the radio was no longer playing "*I Just Want to Be Your Everything.*" Gibb's high whine had been replaced by static.

"*What's up with the lights?*" Robbie asked. Joe looked toward the city through some trees. Some distance away, where the buildings were, he could see headlights shooting through the darkness, illuminating people on the street.

"*I don't know,*" Lois said. But to Joe she looked like she definitely did know, and he felt dread spreading through him as he studied her face. They had driven through frightening electrical storms about an hour earlier in Westchester. Now there was darkness around them, and dead static on the radio. It was like a scary movie.

Lois looked down at the two of them. "*Get back in the car.*"

CHAPTER 1

Thursday, July 13, 2017
Riegelmann Boardwalk, Coney Island
Brooklyn
11:50 p.m.

Seagulls were picking at something on the beach. Wilomena, pushing a noisy shopping cart along the boardwalk in the moonlight, strained to see what it was. Wilomena had a great eye for abandoned things. Where there were gulls, flocking and diving over a pile on the sand, there might be the remains of an interrupted picnic or party. It had been the perfect night for one, velvety and warm. That meant bottles for deposit. Maybe cigarettes. Maybe something better.

Her shopping cart had a dozen knotted plastic bags hanging from it. Some held useful things. Some, dirt. Some, water. She stilled the screeching wheels and went down the concrete steps. The tide was higher because of the full moon, and the surf was washing up close.

Gulls, all right. A dozen of them. There might not be much more than chicken bones and french fries, but it was worth checking out. She took awkward, dragging steps in the sand toward whatever they were cawing at and pulling apart.

She stopped when she saw two shoe-clad feet. She recognized the shoes. They were like new: soft-pink tennis shoes with nice white edges and beige soles. They had been way too small for Wilomena's feet. Lois, though, one of the newer people Wilomena had seen around the Coney Island strip since the beach opened, had lit up like Cinderella when she slipped them on, back at the Lighthouse Mission near the park. They gave out shoes every few days.

Passed out on the sand, Wilomena thought. *Lois, damn, you could drown out here.* She was about to kick at the feet to wake Lois up but then froze as the rest of the body drew her attention. Lois was wearing sweatpants, but they were pulled down and bunched just above the knees, exposing mottled thighs and the old woman's crotch. The skin seemed transparent in the wedding-white glow of the moon. She had a gray T-shirt on, the collar torn open, exposing one of her shoulders. Just below her face was a bra, skin colored for a white woman, wrapped around her neck. The eyes were nearly closed, but the mouth stood open, the chapped lips parted. Wilomena's heart started to thump. If a crab crawled out of that mouth, she was going to scream. That didn't happen. Instead, a gull landed on Lois's stomach, strutted across the T-shirt, and thrust its white head into the gray mound of her pubic hair.

Wilomena screamed.

CHAPTER 2

Friday, July 14, 2017
12:32 a.m.

"Lousy catch for you," Sedrick, the night-watch detective, said. "I hate these freak-show cases. Haven't seen one like this in the Six-Oh for a while." He was referring to the Sixtieth Precinct, the one that included Coney Island. Sedrick was thin and hunched over, his voice raspy and low. He was a silhouette in the dark, a streetlight corona behind him.

"My fault for answering the phone that late into a tour," Detective Xochitl Hernandez said, rooting around until she found a box of evidence gloves in a battered gym bag. She stuffed a few into the pocket of her khakis, then breathed in the salt air and glanced over toward the crowds, lights, and sounds of Coney Island. The heart of it was maybe a half mile down the boardwalk.

"Ha, yeah, right?" Sedrick said, gasping on the initial guffaw and coughing through the rest. "You're Zochi, right? From the squad?"

"I am," she said. Xochitl Hernandez had been given a first name impossible for most Americans to spell or sound out, and she had long ago started referring to herself, in spelling and speech, as "Zochi." Barely five foot two, she was compact with short black hair, aqueous eyes of a similar color, and lovely dark skin. "MLI been called?"

"Yeah. They'll be here in ten." MLI was the medical legal investigator, the arm of the Office of the Chief Medical Examiner that did the initial handling of the corpse at a homicide scene. No one, not even the crime scene investigators, touched or moved a body before MLI in most cases. "Crime scene should be right behind them."

"Thanks," Zochi said. "Let's take a look."

Behind them, three young patrol officers prevented onlookers from spilling onto the boardwalk. A few flashes from camera phones went off. Normally, that part of the beach was dark and empty late at night. There was a boardwalk but no amusement rides or hot-dog stands as far west as they were. Just high-rise projects. Zochi gazed out over the water as they stepped down to the sand. The surf was calm, lapping on the shore.

"Who found her?" she asked. "That woman back there?"

"Yep. Homeless. Goes by Wilomena. Pushes a shopping cart. She won't give us a last name, but you should follow up with her. The vic looks homeless to me also, but sometimes you can't tell. Especially in the summer, you get all types out here. Well, hell, why am I tellin' you?"

"Yeah, summer," she said, as if the word had weight, which, to Six-Oh detectives, it did. It meant far more work than the winter months. "Let's watch where we walk, in case this is the path someone took on the way out." She moved forward, carefully placing her steps. She viewed the body the same way Wilomena had, feet first, then moved her eyes slowly up the legs and torso to the bra around the neck. Her eyes moved back down, making a visual outline around the body. They stopped where the sweatpants were still bunched up above the knees. There was something in one of the deep pockets.

"You got a flashlight?" she asked. Sedrick handed one over, and she trained it on the bulge.

"Something in her pocket?"

"Looks like it." She handed the flashlight back and pulled on two gloves, then gingerly reached into the pocket. She drew out a worn brown or black leather folder, almost like a rectangular women's wallet. It zipped down the middle like a day planner, but the zipper was broken. What remained was held together by two rubber bands. Papers were stuffed inside; a few looked as if they'd gotten wet and dried out again.

CHAPTER 3

Bath Beach, Brooklyn
12:37 a.m.

Joe DeSantos had been walking for what seemed like miles in the dark. He made deliberate strides in a sweaty button-down shirt, slacks, and brown loafers. The streets seemed uniform, empty, and swallowed by shadows.

Now, though, his attention was drawn to the open door of a mid-'70s Chevy Monte Carlo, black with red interior and velour seats, across the street. Sitting in and around the car was a group of Black teenagers, illuminated by the interior lights and passing a joint around. He could hear music from the car—a song he recognized. But that seemed odd because the song was very old. It was "You Make Me Feel Like Dancing" by Leo Sayer.

He felt a flutter of hope, as if the darkness he'd been plodding through was finally breaking altogether. He smiled as Sayer's falsetto screech caught in his memory. One of the kids noticed him and ribbed his companion. The group seemed to brighten in unison, nodding and following him with laughing, sleepy eyes. They were dimly visible in the yellow glow of the car's dome light—combs and Afros, tube socks and short shorts. The song faded, and he heard a female DJ's voice, silky and echo laden.

It is 1977, it is JUE-ly, and the Big Apple is hot, honey!

He struck an aluminum pole, first with his left foot and then his nose. He cursed and rubbed his face, the collision reigniting his perception. It was a sultry night, stinking mildly of the avenues and the bay beyond them. He was on a street that was nearly silent. No old car, no kids. His eyes cleared, then darkened.

It's still with me.

His heart started to thud.

No. There's light, see? Relax, it's all around you. It's 2017, not 1977. That was a dream. Or a hallucination. Or something.

His gaze, suspicious and uncertain, moved over cars, stoops, and doorways, then softened as he took in window boxes, clumps of pigeon droppings, trash cans, and cracks in the sidewalk. All were laid bare by sodium streetlights and bulbs in windows. His eyes feasted on them.

You're in Brooklyn. You're a lawyer. And everywhere there is light. You can see, and you're not afraid.

He wasn't afraid, but now he felt hypervigilant and antsy. To the left was his house, ornate and empty. To the right was a bar called Greeley's. His addled but otherwise razor-sharp brain knew that the house—his bed—was the right way to go.

But Joe wasn't done drinking.

CHAPTER 4

Riegelmann Boardwalk, Coney Island
1:01 a.m.

By the time an assistant district attorney arrived, professionals were hovering around the body, including two crime scene investigators who snapped photos and momentarily bathed the scene in harsh light from various angles. Zochi recognized the ADA as the chief of the sex crimes unit in Brooklyn: a woman in her midfifties named Mimi Bromowitz. Mimi approached in slacks and a golf shirt, flashing a badge to a couple of patrol officers nearby. She was tall and wiry, athletic looking, with flat brown hair in a tight bun. Zochi, like many people, had mistaken Mimi for a lesbian cop at their first meeting. In fact, she was a lesbian prosecutor, married to a woman who was an accountant. Through IVF, they had twin boys.

When she recognized Zochi, Mimi nodded and waved, then kneeled beside the corpse as a man and a woman from the medicolegal investigation unit prepared to seal it into a white body bag. The bag seemed fluorescent in the moonlight. Zochi could see that the dead woman's face was still visible, only partly lost to the shadows below the zipper. She looked like she was cocooned in a sleeping bag, ready for bed.

"You the DA?" one of the MLI techs asked Mimi.

"I am."

"Want to see her before we zip up?"

"Just from the neck up, thanks." She studied the face and the neck, then said to no one in particular, "Do you see ligature marks?"

"We didn't," Zochi said, impressed that Mimi had picked up on those. "There's a bra around her neck, just like you're seeing, but I couldn't make out any markings."

"We'll see what the ME says," Mimi said. "Any obvious vaginal trauma?"

"No. Nothing inserted. No blood underneath her."

"Gotcha," Mimi said. Zochi followed her gaze as it lingered on the bra, still wrapped around the neck, then moved up to the head. The victim had a thin, angular face. Her cheeks looked crumpled and jowly, like the skin wanted to slide off either side. The nose seemed a little crooked. The eyes, like the mouth, were not quite closed, as if she'd been peeking at the person who murdered her rather than staring up at him. "Zip her up," she said, standing. "And how the hell are you, Zochi?"

"I'm good, Mimi, thanks. Why are you out here on this?"

"We're slammed," she said with a shrug. "I took the beeper tonight. I don't live far from here; we're over by Poly Prep." The "beeper" was a dated reference to actual beepers, which used to summon ADAs to crime scenes when they were on homicide duty back in the day. Now it was mostly cell-phone calls.

"I found this in a side pocket," Zochi said as they moved aside to let MLI work. "No other ID. No purse, nothing." In an evidence bag was the leather object, soft looking and ragged.

"Looks like a day planner. Or a wallet?"

"Day planner, I think. I don't know why she'd need one, but homeless people carry all kinds of things."

"Have you looked inside it?"

13

"Not yet. It looks like it's ready to come apart—rained on or in the water at some point. I'd like to open it and set things out, but not here."

"PSA can get you into the management office of that building," Sedrick said, walking over and sticking his thumb in that direction. "They'll wake someone up."

"That'll work," Mimi said. She looked Sedrick up and down. "You with the Six-Oh?"

"Nope. Night watch."

"Did you get here first?"

"We got here around the same time," he said, nodding to Zochi. "Guys from PSA—one heard a woman screaming and came over. It wasn't the vic screaming, though; it was another homeless woman who found her. Cart-pushing lady named Wilomena. She's back there with PSA still, but she's not talkin'."

"Is someone else coming out?" Mimi asked Zochi.

"Yeah, Len Dougherty from the Six-Oh. I texted him. He'll be here in a few."

"The wheel," Mimi said. "You're on that too?" The "wheel" meant the notification process that the responding detectives went through to get the police chain of command involved with a homicide.

"Oh yeah, they're chattering already. We'll see brass in a few minutes."

Mimi nodded and glanced over Zochi's shoulder. "Okay then. Back to Wilomena?"

CHAPTER 5

1:12 a.m.

Wilomena had little to say after an hour in police custody, although "custody" in this case meant she was seated on the curb with a couple of patrol officers who had asked her not to leave. They were from Police Support Area—or PSA—1. PSAs were commands that patrolled public housing units. There were a few such units, including some historically dangerous ones, in Coney Island. To Zochi, it seemed like a pretty cool gig for a younger cop, at least in the summertime. Rather than a typical squad car, PSA 1 responders tooled around in a marked NYPD pickup truck. For the moment, it was parked where Twenty-Seventh Street met the boardwalk.

Wilomena wore a dirty yellow housedress over a pair of long underwear. Her dark, fleshy arms were wrapped around her knees. She was staring out at the ocean, the south shore of Staten Island, and the distant lights of New Jersey beyond it. From time to time she would snap her eyes over to her shopping cart, as if someone might try to sneak off with it. To Zochi she looked forty or fifty and clearly homeless, or mostly so. In Zochi's experience, people like Wilomena could be much younger than they appeared.

"Wilomena, my name is Detective Hernandez," she said, sitting down. Mimicking how Wilomena was sitting, she put her arms around her knees.

"Yeah, I'm Donna Summer." Wilomena stared at the water.

"We know your name; it's okay."

"Not my last name. You ain't gettin' that neither."

"I'm not asking for it. Look, Wilomena—"

"It's Donna. Wake up!"

"Wilomena, come on, this is serious. As far as anyone knows, you were the first person to find her over there."

Wilomena frowned, jutting her lower lip forward, and shifted her eyes to Zochi.

"So what?"

"So did you know her?"

"Seen her 'round."

"What was her name?"

"Names, names, we all need names," Wilomena said, as if reciting verse.

Zochi cataloged this in her mind—the possibility that Wilomena was mentally ill, maybe delusional. That was far from uncommon in the city's homeless population.

"You know what I mean," she said quietly. "What did people call her out here?" Zochi's "call" came out *cawl*.

"Damn, you the smart ones! You got DNA, right? One hundred thirty pounds of it in that body bag just went by. *You* tell *me* who she was."

"It doesn't work that way. You know that."

"What do I know? DNA. Y'all know everything now."

"Nah, we don't. Listen, no one's gonna keep you here, Wilomena. It's a nice night; we're gonna let you get back to it. But I think you can help us. What was her name?"

Wilomena's eyes seemed to cloud over. She went back to gazing over the water, gleaming in the moonlight. The moon was taking on a yellow tinge as it descended in the west.

"Lois," she said finally. "Her name was Lois."

"Any last name?"

"She was trying to get over there," Wilomena said, as if she hadn't heard the question. She nodded toward Staten Island, and Zochi's eyes followed.

"Staten Island?"

"Yeah, over the bridge. She was trying to get bus fare. But it's a few buses you gotta take. The B64 to the B1. Then one or two more. It's like twice the normal fare, and she couldn't keep all the details straight anyway."

"Did you see her talking to anyone out here?"

"Nah. She was like invisible, yo. Like all of us."

"What was in Staten Island for her? Do you know?"

"Nope. She just talked about getting there."

"Wilomena, how long had she been out here? Do you remember when you first saw her?"

"Twenty questions," she murmured. "Two, three weeks maybe. Like since the Mermaid Parade."

"So she's not someone you've been seeing out here very long, then."

"Is two, three weeks very long?" She put exaggerated stress on "two" and "three." *Definitely not delusional,* Zochi thought.

"I get the point. So the name was Lois, huh?"

"That's her name, yo. Don't wear it out." Wilomena's eyes seemed fixed on the dark water and the blinking red-and-green navigation lights in the harbor. Zochi waited a beat before trying one more time.

"What was her last name, Wilomena?"

"No one needs a last name out here," Wilomena said. She shifted her eyes, surprisingly alert and cold, back to Zochi. "No one *rates* a last name out here."

CHAPTER 6

1:25 a.m.

On Sedrick's recommendation, Zochi had a PSA 1 cop call the after-hours line for the management of the building and claimed a desk in the office to take a closer look at the contents of the planner. The property manager, a small man with a tuft of gray hair shooting up from his head, sat in his bathrobe in a swivel chair in the corner. He looked thoroughly annoyed. Beside him, a bored-looking PSA 1 cop stood with his arms crossed next to the doorway. Next to him was Len Dougherty, the other Six-Oh squad detective Zochi had called in to assist.

"Whaddya seein', Zoch?" Len asked, Zochi's name swallowed in a yawn. Len was tall with a wide face and strong Neanderthal brows that shaded dark, steely eyes.

"DeSantos," she said without looking up. Her gloves still on, she had gingerly drawn a few of the items from the planner and laid them on the scarred metal desk.

"DeSantos is her last name? Was there ID in there?"

"I'm not sure if it's *her* last name or not," Zochi said. "But it's the name of the person we'll probably need to notify. I think we're looking for her son. Joseph T. DeSantos. He's a lawyer, or was one. Nobody I've heard of, though."

"What else? Why do you think Lois was his mother?"

"A couple o' notes," she said. "Folded up. They're on paper that's a lot newer than anything else in here. I'll go through it all tomorrow, but it looks like she started these notes to him and never finished. One starts, 'To my baby Joey,' and then there's a bunch of stuff I can't make out. One is folded, and on the outside it says, 'To Joe from Mom.' It's blank, though."

"There was a guy with that last name in the Bronx," Len said. "He was an ADA when I was in anti-crime up there. I never met him, but I heard his name."

"That would make sense," Zochi said. "I found this." She handed Len a stained, crumpled business card. On it was a small, neat logo with a blind-folded Lady Justice holding a sword in one hand and scales in the other. Below that was the name of a law firm, ABRAMS & DESANTOS, CRIMINAL LAW. There was a 718 phone number, a website, and an address in Queens.

Len did a quick search of the website on his phone.

"It's not coming up," he said. "Just a message asking if it's a domain name you want to claim. The firm must have broken up, but I know people who probably still know of it. I'll find him."

"How about tomorrow?" the property manager asked in a thick Russian accent. He grimaced at Zochi and Len like he was being held prisoner.

"We'll be out of here in a few," Zochi said, raising an eyebrow. "Relax."

"Any photos?"

"Nothing yet, but there're a few things kind of clumped up and an old plastic card or two."

Len squinted. "They must have been estranged, right?"

"Yeah, I guess, if she was out here homeless, dead on a beach."

"The witness—Wilomena—did she mention any shelters or what-not that Lois might have gone to?"

"Yeah, a few," she said. "The mission over on Nineteenth and a shelter not far from there. Let me bag this up, and we'll map it out."

"Tomorrow, maybe," the property manager grumbled.

CHAPTER 7

Friday, July 14, 2017
Greeley's Bar & Grill
Gravesend, Brooklyn
11:30 p.m.

"Joey D!" the bartender called out, using a nickname she had pinned on Joe DeSantos a couple of years before. "Wake up, babe." He was at the end of the bar, and she was behind it but on the side closer to the door. Joe had been there most of the day, at a few different spots in the bar, and was now planted on one stool, where he had been since maybe nine, nodding off since eleven.

"Goin'," Joe said, slurred so it was just one syllable. His head slumped forward so that he was staring straight down into his glass. "I know it's late. I'll go."

"It's not late," she said, walking over to him. Her name was Doris. Joe loved that a thirty-year-old bartender somehow still had a name like Doris. "Joe, there are cops here to see you."

"Cops?" He lifted his head and cleared his throat. "What cops?"

"Those two," Doris said. He saw her gesture toward a short woman and a tall man. There were two other drinkers at the bar, but both were watching highlights from an earlier basketball playoff game, and neither seemed to be paying attention.

"Detectives, good evening," he said as they approached. He smiled at Doris and opened his eyes wide, signaling that he was back to lucidity.

"Mr. DeSantos," the woman began, "I'm Detective Hernandez, and this is Detective Dougherty. Can we speak with you?" Her eyes narrowed on him.

Her male partner, Joe could see, was a big, kind of bland-looking guy with a wide face and suspicious eyes. Both, he figured, were gauging how bombed he was.

"Sure," he said, hoping he wasn't still slurring. The word sounded smooth enough exiting his mouth, but you couldn't always tell. "What can I help you with?"

"Mr. DeSantos, we're here because the body of a woman was found on the beach near Coney Island. I'm sorry to tell you this, but we have reason to believe she may have been related to you."

"Related to me?" He immediately pictured his ex-wife, but as far as he knew, she was in Florida with her new husband. "Related to me how?"

"We're not certain, but we believe she may have been your mother."

"My mother," he said in puzzled acknowledgment, as if the person they were talking about had never really existed. For Joe, that was mostly true.

"Her name was Lois," the woman, Detective Hernandez, said. Now an image swam up from the depth of his memory. He had a fleeting thought that what he was picturing most likely didn't match the person they had found.

"My mother's name was Lois," he heard himself saying. But it was like he was watching himself. He saw the reaction from the two cops and drew back into his head. A fog of alcohol still weighed down his thoughts, but it was receding.

"Do you know if she also used the last name DeSantos?" the male detective, Dougherty, asked.

Joe felt his heart start to pound. He shook his head. His eyes went from the woman to the man.

"Mr. DeSantos, do you recall the last time you saw your mother?" Hernandez asked.

Joe opened his mouth to answer, then shut it again. The truth—that of course he knew exactly when he had seen her last, the exact date and approximate time even—sounded too ludicrous to just spit out.

"She abandoned my brother and me as children," he said instead, although now the image of her in his mind, the last one he had formed from the back seat of their station wagon, was so clear that he could have described the shirt she was wearing. "I haven't seen her in forty years." *Jesus, almost* exactly *forty years,* he thought. *To the day almost. What's today? The fourteenth, fifteenth?*

"You've had no contact with her at all?" Hernandez asked.

"Absolutely none," Joe said, aware that he probably looked a little spaced out. He tried to push it back down, that last image, Lois surrounded by darkness in the hot, fetid air and looking at him with some weird mix of dread and sympathy. If she was dead, there was nothing he could do about it, except maybe try to avoid responsibility for the burial. But that didn't seem likely. "I don't know what to tell you, but I haven't seen her since I was ten years old."

"I'm sorry," Hernandez said after a moment. Joe looked closely at her. She seemed to accept this. Anyway, he could verify it.

"Do you know . . . what happened to her?" he asked.

"We're not certain. There were no obvious wounds, but suspicious circumstances. It looks like she might have been homeless. I'm sorry to be telling you this."

"Oh God," he whispered. His head was no longer spinning from alcohol.

"Does she have any other family you know of?" Hernandez asked.

"I have an older brother," he said. "He lives on Staten Island, not far from where we grew up. At least, that's what he tells me."

"What he tells you?" she asked.

Joe sighed. "I know this all sounds strange. Cold, even. The fact is, I didn't have a family for a good twenty-five years. My brother and I were raised by my uncle Mike, who was my mother's younger brother. He died when I was a senior in high school. My brother is kind of a mess. I didn't talk to him for a long time, but we've reconnected some in the last year or two. Not much, though."

"Do you remember when you saw him last?" Dougherty asked.

"Saw him? It's been a few months."

"Could we get his contact information from you?" he asked.

"Of course." Joe waved Doris over and asked for a pen. He checked his phone and then scribbled the cell number he had for Robbie. "The woman you found—did she have identification on her?"

"She had some personal papers," Hernandez said. "That and what I believe is a business card of yours. They're what led us to you. The note we found was to a Joe. A Joey, actually. Was that a name she used for you?"

Joe hesitated, trying to shake a deeply stunned feeling. "Uh, yeah, I'm sure she did."

"I'll have to examine the personal effects more fully. We can discuss it more later. I can't release them, though; they're evidence. I'll keep them safe."

"I understand. Has she been autopsied?"

"It's scheduled for tomorrow. We'll follow up, but they may reach out to you."

"I couldn't identify her," Joe said, his eyes going blank. "It's been too long."

"They'll get that," Dougherty said.

"I understand you're a trial attorney," Hernandez said. "And you were an ADA?"

"I was for years, in the Bronx."

"Did you handle homicides?"

"Quite a few, yeah, but it's been a while. I worked more as a defense attorney. That was mostly in Queens."

"We can connect you with victim services," Hernandez said. "Even if you know the drill, it can be overwhelming when it happens in your own family."

"She wasn't really my family, but thank you. Yes, I know the drill. I understand it's a homicide investigation. I don't think I can help, but I'll make myself available for whatever you need. I can't speak for my brother, but I think he'll cooperate also."

"We appreciate that," Hernandez said. "Here's my card."

When the detectives left, Doris walked over, cautiously it appeared to Joe, like she wasn't sure who he really was.

"They think they found my mother," he said, then related what the detectives had told him. He gave Doris about the same amount of backstory he'd given the cops. He wasn't being cagey. There just wasn't much to say, and what there was, he didn't feel like going into with anybody.

"Jeez, I'm sorry," she said. "You want a glass of water or something?"

"Or something." He held his glass up and tilted it.

"Joe, you should go home."

"I will. Just one or two more to settle me down." He flashed a smile, probably his best feature after his eyes. It was warm, inviting, and unassuming.

Joe's smile came easier when he was drinking, which was far too often. A hard-drinking trial lawyer in New York City was nothing out of the ordinary, and over a twenty-five-year career he had mostly maintained functionality. But the last few years had devastated him. His forty-sixth birthday, four years before, was one he had almost spent in jail after hearing from a divorce lawyer that his wife was leaving him. A cop who remembered him from the Bronx DA's office had prevented the arrest, so Joe had ended up in a cab instead of a squad car.

Professional failure mirrored that of his marriage the same year, 2013. His small law practice dissolved, and his partner, Jack, nearly sued him over a string of booze-fueled fuckups. Before that happened, though, they scored a terrific settlement in a products liability case. In the end, Joe's partner had been decent about money, and Joe walked away with plenty. Because of that, Joe was able to make one very smart purchase—a beautiful house in a great neighborhood. The bad thing was that Joe wasn't motivated to work much for the next year and a half. In fact, he didn't remember much about the next year and a half. Most of the leftover money disappeared quickly.

It was a combination of dwindling bank accounts and some character that got him moving again. Like in his early days as a prosecutor, he was back in government, this time for the New York State Office of the Attorney General. An old supervisor from the Bronx was now a bureau chief there and had hired him as an assistant attorney general in 2015. Given his age at the time—forty-eight—and his history, the opportunity was as much a lifeline as it was a job.

The work was a little weird. He was handling sex offender civil commitment cases, a new kind of litigation that was different from both traditional prosecution and anything he'd done in criminal defense. But he was back in public service in downtown Manhattan, working with a good group of people and a great boss. He had cleaned himself up and found something like a sense of purpose again.

But Joe was still drinking.

CHAPTER 8

Wednesday, July 13, 1977
Upper West Side, Manhattan
9:39 p.m.

"Can we make it to Uncle Mike's in this?" Robbie asked as their mother pulled away, joining the careful procession on the highway.

"Of course! It's just a power loss. Hopefully just a few minutes." Lois turned the knob on the radio, moving through static until she found a news station. There were reports coming in of a blackout in New York City. A major one, affecting all five boroughs and parts of southern Westchester. Joe watched with growing anxiety as she scanned the highway ahead.

One thing Joe did know was that the car needed gas, badly. His mother had said something about a station right off the Ninety-Fifth Street exit, but now as the exit approached, she wondered aloud if you could pump gas in a blackout. Joe and Robbie knew the question wasn't meant for them, but they looked at each other and shrugged anyway.

"Jesus, why the hell didn't I go over the GW?" he heard her mumble. "I could have put a gallon in right on the other side."

"The tolls," Joe said, assuming he was being helpful. "I thought we were saving money going through the city. The Staten Island Ferry is only two dollars."

"Know-it-all," Robbie said with practiced disgust. *"She just said that, like, ten minutes ago."*

"He's right," she said, shaking her head. *"Even if I had enough change for the turnpike, after the gas I wouldn't have made it over the Goethals."*

Joe wasn't sure what the Goethals was, but it must have been something requiring a toll. He had read a book once about a little troll that lived under a bridge and demanded money from people crossing it, so maybe it was a bridge.

A few seconds later, as if on cue, the car started to sputter. Lois spoke through gritted teeth as Robbie announced that they were passing the Ninety-Fifth Street exit.

"We can't get gas if the stations are dark," she said. *"Look, at the next exit there's a boat dock. Someone might have gas there, like in a can."*

"How long is it to the boat place?" Joe asked in almost a whimper.

"Like a mile. Just relax, okay?"

"Something's wrong with the car, Mom," Robbie said. His usual insouciant tone was gone. He sounded worried. It was really dark in the car now. Lois stole a look at Joe in the rearview mirror, and Joe's eyes started to tear up. His mother looked like she was about to cry.

Lois put two hands on the wheel as the sign for the Seventy-Ninth Street Boat Basin emerged out of the darkness. Joe saw the first dotted lines of the exit in the headlights. Lois drifted right, and the car stalled. She shifted to neutral and cranked the engine. It roared to life, then stalled again. That was it. She rolled off the ramp onto some gravel.

"Oh, dear God."

"We're out of gas?" Robbie asked, high-pitched with fright.

"Yes."

The southbound parkway at Seventy-Ninth Street exited onto a traffic circle that overlooked the Hudson River. From the exit, you entered the circle at a six o'clock position. If you kept going around, you would be at a nine o'clock position and on Seventy-Ninth Street, going east into the city. Or you could get back on the parkway southbound at a twelve o'clock *position. There was a little side road down into Riverside Park at around one o'clock on the circle. That road led to the boat basin, behind iron gates at the water's edge.*

As the car came to a stop, Joe felt clammy fear slip into his belly. All around them it was as black as pitch. The car's headlights cut a path of light straight ahead—three o'clock—toward the concrete wall at the edge of the circle overlooking the water. Across the river was New Jersey, still lit up and normal looking but far away and disconnected.

"Mom, what're we gonna do?" Joe asked.

His mother lit a cigarette and sighed. She turned off the headlights, which placed them in terrible darkness for a moment, then clicked on the yellowing dome light in the car. "I'll have to go looking for gas." She turned around to Robbie. "You need to stay here with Joe, okay?"

"What? Mom, no way! It's dark as all hell."

"H-e-double toothpicks," Joe said.

"Shut up."

"Robbie, please," Lois said. To Joe her eyes looked red rimmed and pleading. "Please, I need you now."

"C-can we leave the light on?" he asked.

"No, honey," she said. "The battery will go dead; you know that." She dug through her purse and produced a Bic lighter. "Here. Use it if you need it, but be careful with it. Anyway, your eyes will adjust."

"Mom, please," Joe whined. "Take us with you."

"I can't, baby. Everything we own is in this car. We can't leave it. Just give me a few minutes. I'll find help and get us a can of gas. Once we get to the ferry, it'll all be fine. I'll call Uncle Mike and have him meet us in Saint George."

"Where will you find gas?"

"I'll check at the marina," she said. "Or I'll walk up Seventy-Ninth to Broadway. There will be people out. Someone will help. I'll be back in fifteen or twenty minutes. We've got plenty of time. The last ferry leaves at *eleven thirty."* With that, she clicked off the dome light and opened the car door. When she closed it, the darkness was all-encompassing.

"Mom, no!" Joe cried.

"Joey, shush," she said. Robbie clicked the lighter on, and for a last moment Joe saw her through the flicker of the little flame. *"Be brave, both of you. Robbie, turn that off now. You'll get burned. Just let your eyes adjust."*

"Wait," Robbie said. *"Just for a second. Till our eyes adjust."*

She stood outside the car for a moment, leaning down into the passenger window. Joe felt like a shadow, fidgeting in his seat. Robbie sat still as a stone, which was not at all like him. It occurred to Joe years later that it was as if Robbie was trying to avoid being seen or sensed by something. Around them, the city at the river's edge seemed strangely quiet. The air, heavy and hot, lay on them all like a thick blanket.

"See? It's okay," their mother said. *"You'll be fine here. Just stay in the car, and I'll be right back."* She looked at them both one more time, from one to the other. Robbie was fingering the lighter. *"Robbie, don't use that unless you have to. And don't turn on the dome light either. If the battery is dead when I get back, what will we do then?"*

"Okay," he said, sounding dejected. *"Please hurry."*

"What if somebody comes?" Joe asked.

"I'll be right back. No one is coming to the park in this . . . whatever it is. You'll be fine." She paused and gave them a smile. *"I love you both."* Then she turned and was gone.

CHAPTER 9

Saturday, July 15, 2017
Bay Thirty-Fourth Street
Bath Beach, Brooklyn
11:57 a.m.

When Joe's ex-lover knocked on his heavy, ornate front door, he was sitting in a T-shirt and underwear on his bed upstairs, staring at Zochi's card. "Detective Xochitl Hernandez, 60th PCT," it read under a blue NYPD banner with the department's patch logo on one side and a detective shield on the other.

He had no idea how he had gotten it.

"Joey, open up!" she called. The voice was muffled but unmistakable, even after months of not hearing from her. She was known to everyone except her parents as Holly, but Joe loved her real name, Hallelujah. "Come on, it's almost noon!"

"Hang on!" The morning had started off weird, and now it was getting weirder. He set the card back on the nightstand and pulled on an old pair of slacks. He hurried down the wide hardwood stairs, running a hand through his hair in a vain effort to straighten it. Joe's house was mostly empty and in desperate need of a woman's touch, but it was a masterpiece. Tucked into a vibrant, mostly working-class neighborhood, it was redbrick, sturdy, and nearly a century old. To Joe its best feature was that it was within walking distance of a fishing boat he kept in a tiny private marina just underneath the Belt Parkway.

"Are you okay?" he asked, motioning her in. With her came her smell—perfumed, fresh, feminine—and Joe felt his heart skip. He glanced out the window. It was a hot, bright Saturday morning along his short block and the longer Cropsey Avenue. He had woken thinking about taking the boat out, just before the appearance of the mysterious detective's card next to his watch and wallet. And now here was Halle Rossi knocking on his door after all this time.

"Am *I* okay? What about you? Joe, I'm so sorry." She frowned up at him, the frown making her lower lip push up and purse. It was an adorable expression, the kind that got Halle noticed everywhere she went. She opened her arms. "Come here." They hugged, and now the feel of her body, the generous flesh of her arms and shoulders and the smell of her jet-black hair, had him feeling faint.

"What . . . what is this? I mean, it's great to see you, but . . ." Now her arms stiffened, and she pushed away from him.

"Oh, Joe." Her face darkened. It was a lovely face, heart shaped and inviting. She had strong southern Italian looks, thick brows, deep brown eyes, a large, well-formed nose, and a luxurious mouth with full lips. Her skin was pale and smooth, her body full and voluptuous. Joe couldn't help but take all of her in whenever she appeared. Now she seemed shy and tentative as she folded her arms across her chest.

"'Oh, Joe' what?" he asked. "Come in." She followed him through the foyer into the kitchen. He stopped at the fridge, wondering if there was something he could offer her. She was a coffee drinker, and he still didn't have a coffee maker. "Sit down, please. Tell me what's going on."

"You called me last night. This morning, really. You wanted someone to go with you to the morgue."

31

"The morgue?" His hand froze on the fridge door handle. He pictured the card on the nightstand. Slowly, he turned back toward her. "What about the morgue?"

"Jesus," she said with exaggerated awe. "You really don't remember, do you?"

"Remember what?" A feeling of defeat and fresh dread shot through him.

She shook her head and sat down at the bare kitchen table, crossing her legs. Below a Mets T-shirt, she had on gray yoga pants and cross-trainers. "I shouldn't even tell you."

"Please tell me. What happened?"

"Your mother, Joe," she said, and the sharp rebuke in her voice, that Italian edge, was gone. "NYPD found her on the beach, on Coney Island. I guess that was Thursday night. You called me last night. Told me you'd probably have to ID her. You didn't want to go alone." Halle used the term "NYPD" rather than "the cops" or something more civilian-like because she was also in the business. She had gone to St. John's University School of Law in Queens and had met Joe through an internship with Joe and Jack's law firm when she was a second-year student. The two didn't become involved until later, when Joe ran into her outside a courtroom one afternoon in Brooklyn. It was 2015, and Joe had just started working for the attorney general. Shoptalk that night turned into drinks, which turned into raw, wild sex at her place in Sheepshead Bay. At twenty-six, she was a little more than half his age.

"My mother?" he asked. Joe couldn't know it, but he uttered those two words in exactly the same way he had to Zochi and Len when they had found him at Greeley's.

"That's who they think it was. It looks like she was homeless. They . . . they think she was murdered."

"Oh God." Joe dashed back upstairs for the business card. A few flashes of memory were popping into his brain, but they were only images. He was picturing a small but sturdy female detective with big eyes and short black hair. Another guy with her, big guy with kind of a moon face. He pictured them at a bar, probably Greeley's, although he wasn't positive, sometime late. But that was it. He couldn't recall anything they had told him. His heart pounded. When he returned to the kitchen, he looked at Halle with a grim mix of guilt and frustration. "She was homeless? On the beach at Coney?"

"You told me they're not sure if she was homeless." Her voice started to break. "Joe, I hate this! I hate having to repeat this to you!" She started to cry, and he fell to one knee and took her right hand in both of his.

"I'm so sorry, Halle. I can't make this right, but I am so sorry."

"No," she said, forcing tears away. "No, don't be. This isn't . . . it isn't about me. It's just frustrating, you know?"

It's what broke us up, he thought. Of course he knew. His mouth was dry. It seemed as if he had just dreamed about his mother and brother, earlier while he was in the gray area between drunk and hungover, when sleep was fitful and thin. The anniversary of that night had just passed, and it had been haunting him all week long. "I'm sorry I called you in the first place. Afterward, I just . . . forgot."

"You didn't forget," she said, staring down at the hand he had taken. "You didn't make any memories of it. You were blacked out. Again."

He opened his mouth to speak but then shut it. The smell of her—Halle was playfully vain and girlish and traveled in an aura of her own scent—threatened to knock him over. It was a lovely and painful contrast to the aroma he normally experienced in his big hollow house: fried food and bleach.

"The thing is, it was a bad week," he finally said. "I knew it was coming; it happens every year. Then I had a big hearing on Tuesday, and my boss gave me the rest of the week off. It's no excuse. It's just . . . what happened."

"I saw that on a docket sheet last week," she said. "That pedophile, right? The one you got put into the psych hospital last year?" She still wouldn't make eye contact with him.

"Aaron Hathorne, yes. This was his twelve-month review of confinement."

"So he'll stay confined?"

"We're waiting on a final ruling. I think so, yeah."

"Well, that's good, I guess. But I mean . . . to celebrate *that*, you went on a three-day bender?" Her voice rose on the last word. The edge was back.

Joe sighed. "Two days. I didn't start drinking, really, until Thursday." His knee aching from kneeling, he stood and went to the fridge in search of grapefruit juice. He was hungover and thirsty. "I didn't get arrested. I didn't get thrown out of a place, at least that I know of. There are just . . . things I can't remember."

"Like two cops, Joe, telling you your homeless mother was found murdered on a stretch of beach?"

"I don't have a mother!" he snapped, shutting the fridge door hard with a juice carton in hand. "I didn't on Thursday night either, when whoever this woman was got killed."

"You told me it was an anniversary," she said, almost whispering. "The night of the blackout in '77."

"Yes, '77." *And a good fourteen years before she was born,* an inner voice chided him. *You never had the right to drag her into your life, no matter how hot for it she seemed, no matter what daddy issues she has.* "That was the last night she was my mother."

"Well, the police think she *was* your mother. So I guess the city thinks that too, and I guess you're responsible for her, right? You said last night you'd have to go to the morgue in Queens and ID her."

"I'm sure I said that, but it was stupid. I can't ID her; it's been way too long."

"Yeah, but you can claim her, right? Someone has to."

"Not really," Joe said. "I have to deal with the police. I don't necessarily have to deal with OCME."

"You know what happens if you don't? She ends up being buried by inmates. On that island out there."

"The potter's field, yes." He took a long swig from the carton and wiped his chin. "I know that sounds cold, but like I said, I don't have a mother. I'm within my rights to let the police ask what they want until they go away. I'm not a suspect."

"It just happened; you don't know what they're thinking. And you can't even tell them for sure where you were Thursday night. I know it's crazy, but God, what if they start focusing on you? I've seen what they can do when they want a case closed."

"I was probably at one of two bars," Joe said at lower volume, as if that could contain the shame he was feeling. "Greeley's, more than likely. I won't have any issue verifying that. Look, whoever killed her is probably someone she was involved with on the street. If they solve it, it'll most likely be within a couple of days. If it takes longer than that, it may just stay unsolved. Either way, at some point, yes, the city puts her out on Hart Island. I'm sorry, but that's where she belongs."

"What about your brother?"

"Robbie? What about him?"

"You said he was back in touch."

"Yeah. He's in Staten Island, but I haven't been over there in years. He reached out for money once, but otherwise we don't speak much."

"Will they talk to him? Detectives, I mean."

"If they can find him, I guess," Joe said with a shrug. "They'll tell him independently of me. I really don't care."

"Joe, come on."

"Come on, what? Why do I need this? Why do I need a five-thou-sand-dollar funeral bill for a woman who abandoned my brother and me in a station wagon forty years ago?"

"It wouldn't be five grand," she said. "I looked it up. You could have her cremated for less than two thousand." He was aware again of how devoted she had been to him, some pickled suit with a crumbling law practice. He burned anew with guilt.

"She doesn't deserve my involvement," Joe said. "And she certainly doesn't deserve yours. Thank you for looking into that, Halle. I mean it. But she doesn't."

"It just seems wrong. It's not my business, I know."

"I made it your business, so it is."

"She's your family!"

"She was once. She destroyed what was left of my family."

"She paid for that," Halle said. Her eyes were pleading, and he wasn't sure where this desperation was coming from. "Look at how she was found, out there like a stray dog. Whatever she did to you, she was punished for it. Life did that to her. She shouldn't have to pay again now."

Joe stared back for a long moment, then sighed. "I'll go."

"Good. I'll take you. I drove here. We can stop at my place, and I'll get changed. You might need to sober up anyway."

Halle's apartment in Sheepshead Bay was close to where she had grown up, a couple of miles east. While she waited in the kitchen, Joe found the remainder of an outfit. He was looking for his loafers, the ones he hadn't worn since Thursday. Normally he would wear boat shoes, but they were getting smelly. The damn loafers were nowhere to be found, though, so it was back to the boat shoes. He gave them a spray of Lysol.

"You don't have to do this," he said when he'd returned. "I'm grateful, but you really don't."

"What else am I doing today? We're still friends, right? Get cleaned up. You know this is the right thing to do."

It's also the smart thing, he thought. He couldn't express it to Halle, but the truth was, it would look odd if word got out in his professional circles—and it would—that his mother had been found murdered and Joe wasn't stepping up to claim her body. The circumstances really didn't matter. Going through the motions and making the arrangements were what a person did, at least when that person was a responsible adult and an assistant attorney general.

A responsible adult. That's a laugh. You have basically no reliable memory from around seven o'clock on Thursday until twenty minutes ago.

CHAPTER 10

Office of the Chief Medical Examiner
Jamaica Hills, Queens
2:15 p.m.

The identification process at the medical examiner's office had gone to video a few years back. There were still cases where the dead were viewed from behind glass—the gut-wrenching stuff of movies and television. Now, though, the identifying person was escorted to a small waiting room just off the main reception area of the office. A large monitor sat on a desk, and the face of the deceased was displayed via closed-circuit television.

Halle was in the reception area while Joe waited to view the dead woman. He had explained to a staff attendant that there was virtually no hope he'd be able to provide a positive identification. The staffer, a tired-looking older Black man with sad eyes, had simply shrugged. Joe didn't have to view her if he thought it was futile.

He wanted to, though. He was an attorney and had been in law enforcement for years. He had seen bodies in morgues and other places. It would not shock him. He also suspected that there might be a bit of closure in it. Even if he couldn't match the face that he was about to see with the last one in his mind, maybe this face would provide some final ending to a terrible, drawn-out story. He would rather have a last image of his mother to replace the ghost that still walked in his head. Maybe seeing what she had become would shut a door once and for all.

He settled in the chair before the monitor. The staffer asked him if he was ready. A second later the monitor lit up. The view was of a woman's head against a stainless-steel table. He took in the face, sunken and dreadfully pale. He blinked and wiped his eyes, then looked again.

Hollow cheeks. Long, thin nose, a little bent.

He was glad that Halle was not in the room as he stiffened in the chair. Joe DeSantos had no idea who the woman on the table was, but he was certain that he had seen her within the last two weeks.

CHAPTER 11

Bay Thirty-Fourth Street
Bath Beach, Brooklyn
3:10 p.m.

"Oh shit," Joe said as Halle's car pulled up to his house. Their time at the medical examiner's office had been brief, but traffic was terrible both ways. "Not him."

"Who?"

"My goddamn brother. I guess he found out." Robbie was around the same height as Joe but narrow in the shoulders and thinner. In pretty much every way he just seemed smaller. His hair was graying and covered his head like a thatched roof. His face had a sour, dull hostility to it, the corners of his mouth in a permanent frown. Dressed in an old T-shirt and blue jeans, he squinted in the sunlight and sucked on a cigarette.

"Oh, that's Robbie?" Halle asked. It was strange to Joe, Halle's emotional investment in his life. In the short time that they'd been together, she had learned more about him than had his ex-wife. The ex-wife, Judy, had met Robbie once or twice over the years, but she knew almost nothing about him and, at bottom, not much more about Joe himself. Judy knew only the broad strokes about Lois's abandonment and the boys' lives after, but Joe didn't blame her for that. He had become an emotional vault by the time they'd gotten together and had been unwilling to even consider another way of being. Their marriage had largely been a sham because of it. Halle, though, had pried that vault open in the space of a few months.

"Yeah, that's Robbie," he said. "I don't suppose you want to meet him."

"It's not a good idea," she said quietly. There was pain in her voice but also resolve. He nodded. The truth was, he had no interest in introducing her to Robbie. He just didn't want to leave her company. For one thing, the undeniable familiarity of the dead woman had been gnawing at him below the surface, almost to the point that he wanted to talk it out with Halle. It was best not to, though. There was too much weirdness swirling around as it was, and for all he knew, it was an illusion. Or maybe he *had* somehow recognized Lois, whatever the hell had become of her, in some unknown way that no one could explain.

Aside from that, his heart had been lighter all afternoon, while he and Halle were sitting in traffic, cursing at other drivers on the Brooklyn-Queens Expressway, and then huddling in the sterile greeting area of the OCME. A stop for lunch at a pizza joint in Bay Ridge had them laughing at old times, their first days of working together at the firm, before something more than friendship had entered either of their minds.

He missed her. It was a silly affair, something between playing house and a months-long fuckfest. He figured she had issues—unresolved hurts and inadequacies that had driven her to open her heart and her bed to him. Whatever had sparked it, he missed her. And he had blown it.

"The drinking," he said. "It has to stop. I wish I could tell you right now that—"

"Don't," she said. "You should stop, yes, but not because of me. Our time is up, Joe. Do it for yourself, though, okay?"

Our time is up. It sank through him like lead. Had his brother not been standing outside the car, smoking in the heat like some beach bum, he might have broken down in front of her. She was right, though; their time was up. It hurt, but his inner voice reminded him that Halle Rossi had been a lost cause anyway. He had turned her head for a while, but pretty, vivacious young women eventually leave broken old men, whether for another head case or just a better deal. Joe would have been no different. Booze just sped up the inevitable.

"Thanks again, sweetheart," was all he could manage. Damn near chilly from her overworked AC, he stepped out of the car and into the sunbaked heat of the avenue. He made eye contact with Robbie. Instead of acknowledging him, Robbie's eyes slid past him to Halle, still strapped in the driver's seat.

"Who told you about Lois?" Joe asked as she pulled away.

"Some kid detective in Staten Island. I didn't think they had detectives in Staten Island."

"Plenty."

"I don't think he does anything but tell people that a found body is related to them. Sounds like a great job." Robbie's voice was higher than Joe's and sharper, with more of the old Staten Island accent.

"Come in if you want," Joe said. He was already sweating, despite the chilled air of Halle's car.

"Why did she dump you?" Robbie asked, nodding in the direction she had gone.

"Why did she . . . what?"

"It's obvious. No kiss goodbye. That little talk you had. And now your face, ready to slide off your skull. She hit a nerve, didn't she?"

"I'm going in," Joe said. "Follow if you want. If not, goodbye."

"She looks too young anyway. This house is impressive, though. That might have kept her around."

"It didn't. Goodbye, Robbie." He turned away.

"Come on, man. I didn't come here to bust your balls."

"Funny way of showing it."

"I want to help with the burial."

"She'll be cremated," Joe said, turning back toward him. "It's cheaper."

"How much?"

"Probably two grand."

"Here," Robbie said. He walked over and fished out a wad of bills, counting out ten of them. "That's a grand. My half."

Joe looked at the bills but didn't take them.

"What is this? Why?"

"Jesus Christ, that's all you can manage? I have *mon-ey*. I want to help with the burial of our *mother*. Which part of that is harder for you to believe?"

"You being here at all is hard to believe. You want me to take that, really?"

"Take it and burn it with her. I don't care. I want to do my part."

Joe took the bills and stuffed them into a pocket of his slacks.

"Why go cheap, anyway? I'm working now. I could kick in more than that. I'm pretty damn sure you could, unless you're drinking it faster than you can make it."

"Everything I have is tied up in this house," Joe said. He could feel himself getting angry and also itching for a drink. He needed to get out of his brother's presence soon. "I'm working for the government. I don't have money to throw away. And if I did, it wouldn't go toward her."

"You know, I thought about calling before I came all the way out here," Robbie said. "I had to wait awhile till you came back, but I'm glad I caught you like this. It's always better when I just catch you. I get to see you off your throne. Fucked up, just like the rest of us."

Joe's fists balled up. He looked at his brother and forced calm into his voice. "Thanks for the money. Now get the hell off my driveway."

Joe was almost to his doorstep when he remembered where the missing loafers were. It was a typical place to deposit shoes, particularly after a hard night of drinking. Joe's driveway had a carport with an A-shaped vinyl covering supported by rusted '50s-era stilts.

Sure enough, between the left rear tire of his Buick and the side of the house, he found them. They were next to a pair of nice dress shoes that he had deposited after work on Tuesday. He stared at both pairs, feeling lucky that it hadn't rained since earlier in the week. The loafers he didn't care about, but the dress shoes would have been destroyed. They were yet another thing he was just letting slip, exposed to ruin if he wasn't more careful. He reached for the loafers and then felt his whole body go cold. There was sand in them and scattered grains on the concrete underneath.

CHAPTER 12

In his New York Department of Corrections photo, Aaron Hathorne looked innocuous enough: an older white man, clean shaven with longer-than-usual hair. His skin was pale, but the lighting used by the DOC was not to the standard of a fashion magazine. His face was a narrow, inverted triangle running from a high forehead down to a small mouth and pointed chin. The nose was a little crooked, as if perhaps it had been broken in the fifteen years he'd been in custody. Then again, Hathorne's corrections file didn't reflect much violence at all throughout his entire stretch in the DOC. For a notorious pedophile, he had done surprisingly easy time.

Maybe it's the eyes, Joe thought, studying the photo. Cold, dark, and alert, the eyes seemed to stare from the photo into the eyes of the viewer. Most men in DOC photos looked dully into the camera. Resigned, mostly. Oblivious, sometimes. A few seemed ashamed. Hathorne, though, a man who had been a respected, well-to-do pediatrician before his public disgrace and conviction, seemed as proud as an award recipient on a podium. *And there were a few times over the years he was exactly that,* Joe thought. A chill cut through him. Hathorne looked like he could rule a prison from the inside on cunning alone. Joe had seen a few guys like him, especially after coming to the Sex Offender Management Bureau, where psychopaths like Hathorne were targeted for the kind of litigation that the bureau handled.

Hathorne looked more menacing than most Joe had seen, though. There was iron will in his gaze, which also had a strange, woken glee behind it. Joe wanted to put the photo down, but the eyes seemed to hold him in place.

"Watch out for that one," Aideen Bradigan said from the doorway of Joe's office. He looked up, the spell broken. Aideen was also an assistant attorney general in Joe's bureau. "I hear he likes to sue people."

"I've heard that too," Joe said, setting the photo down and smiling. "It wouldn't be the first time I was dragged into court."

"We're not talking about your ex-wife, buddy." She grinned and slipped into a chair in front of his desk. Like Joe, Aideen had been a sex-crimes prosecutor in the Bronx before she joined the AG's office, and the two went back many years. Aideen was brilliant and funny and had a devilish prankster streak. Her lineage was solid Irish, but she looked Scandinavian, with blonde hair, peaches-and-cream skin, and sky-blue eyes. The running joke in her family was that a Viking invasion altered the bloodlines in County Donegal, the far north coastline inhabited by her ancestors. She was short and sturdy and carried herself with a broad-shouldered, tough-but-feminine swagger that radiated confidence. "He gathers intel also. Ben told me."

"How is Ben?" Joe asked, although he could guess the answer, and it wasn't good. Ben Bradigan was Aideen's husband, an NYPD lieutenant who was steadily losing his battle with a 9/11-related cancer. Aideen was leaving the office to care for him, and their children, full-time. The Hathorne case would have gone to her, but Joe had offered to take it from her as she prepared to leave state service. He was taking over more than his share of Aideen's cases, something she thanked him for repeatedly, although he didn't want or expect her thanks. They had always watched out for each other.

"Not great," she said. She shrugged, a slight movement of her shoulders, which was as much negative emotion as Aideen ever projected. "He's comfortable, though, for now."

"The kids?"

"They're tough, you know."

"Not as tough as you," he said. He tapped the photo with a finger, absently careful not to touch the face in the image. "You should have taken this one."

"Too late. I'm outta here." She got suddenly serious. "Really, be careful with this guy. Ben's got friends in the DOC, and they say Hathorne is a litigation machine. He goes after everyone involved in his cases. Judges, therapists in corrections, the detectives—everybody. And now with this coming down? He'll be as mad as a hornet."

By "this," Aideen meant the legal process under state law whereby a person convicted of a sex crime could be kept under supervision, either in a hospital or on probation, even though their criminal sentence had maxed out. The state's mental health office vetted prisoners like Hathorne who were about to be released, singling out those who could be shown to have a "mental abnormality." This meant a mental disease or defect that made it more likely that the person would commit another sex offense once released. If the mental state could be proven in court, the person could be remanded to continued confinement. The law called it "sex offender civil management." These were the cases that Joe and Aideen's unit handled.

In Aaron E. Hathorne, MD, they had a decent target. Hathorne was genius-level smart, socially skilled, and masterfully manipulative. His manner as a predator was gentle and unassuming, avuncular and soft spoken. From a wealthy and established family, he flew through medical school and graduated a year early.

Then, as a family practitioner, he sexually abused hundreds of boys. His MO was to move to a new community in upstate New York every two or three years. He lured families with small boys on the promise of reduced fees for medical care. Not unlike what predators on the level of Jerry Sandusky and Larry Nassar were doing at around the same time, Hathorne targeted single mothers and families in crisis. His practice flourished, and his name was widely praised. He was called a hero and written up in local newspapers and magazines. Hathorne's timing was almost perfect. Few predators like him ever saw justice during their active years, and he almost escaped it as well.

For nearly three decades, his image was that of a world-class physician choosing small-town life over a host of more exciting options and assisting the underprivileged in his communities. Where there were desperate parents with boys—particularly mothers on their own—there was something for Hathorne to exploit. His victims almost never came forward and weren't believed when they did. The fallout was terrible. Wherever Hathorne went, addiction, suicide, and unimaginable heartbreak followed. It wasn't until the late '90s that the first of his victims reported sexual abuse and was taken seriously. From early in 1973 until his multi-count felony indictment in 2000, he got away with it.

Interestingly to Joe, it wasn't the internet that brought Hathorne down. That engine of progress was still in its infancy when Hathorne was first investigated. Instead, it was a handful of remarkably brave boys and some good detectives. They brought about the indictment and then the weekslong, press-covered trial in Saratoga Springs, New York.

It *was* the internet, years later, that brought Hathorne to the attention of the New York State Office of Mental Health once his prison time had drawn to a close. Hathorne was quiet, a model prisoner in most respects. There was an Achilles' heel, though. Hathorne, who never drank or smoked and showed no other addictive tendencies, nevertheless became addicted to child pornography in prison. He found ways around corrections-imposed content blockers, and he mastered online platforms. He posed as dozens of different people: some were children, and some were public figures. He became involved, for a second time, with the infamous North American Man/Boy Love Association, or NAMBLA. He communicated and traded in foreign countries, as he was multilingual. Hathorne covered his internet traffic well from prison, but not well enough. He was caught in repeated violations of internet use as his release date approached. Now he faced indefinite confinement in a psychiatric facility.

"This should be a barrel of laughs, then," Joe said to Aideen. He flipped Hathorne's photo so that it wasn't staring up at him. Rain, turning to sleet, slashed against his office window. "Drinks after work if this weather lets up? I think a few of us want to take you out before you leave on Friday."

"Maybe. I'll see how Ben's feeling. He may be fine just hanging with the kids tonight."

"I hope to see him again soon," Joe said. "Please give him my best."

Joe wouldn't see Ben alive again, though. Aideen's and Ben's lives would become shrouded in hospital care and then hospice care, and Ben would be dead that October, just before the presidential election.

"I will."

"And thanks for the tip, Aid."

She offered a slight grin. "I'm always looking out for you."

CHAPTER 13

Aaron Everett Hathorne was in perfect health, right down to his hands and fingers, which suffered no arthritis, even though he was sixty-eight. It had always been that way; Hathorne had a brilliant constitution and was never seriously ill. He remembered one of the mothers of his child victims lamenting that fact to a judge during his criminal trial in 2000. Her son, whom Hathorne had victimized while he was practicing medicine, had died of leukemia. The mother, Hathorne remembered, had made quite a scene before the judge at sentencing, crying and carrying on about how unfair it was that he, Dr. Hathorne, was in such perfect health when her own son had died just before the trial. Hathorne remembered being amused by it. As if his health and that of the boy were somehow cosmically connected. As if God cared.

Because he had no arthritis, Hathorne had adapted very well to the screen keyboards on the so-called smartphones (sometimes borrowed, sometimes purloined) he used to communicate with the outside world. He had been at St. Lawrence Psychiatric Center for a year, but he had quickly identified and recruited two individuals to assist him. One was a family member of another patient, the other a staff member. These two individuals, separately and unbeknownst to each other, would bring things in for Hathorne or smuggle them out.

The staffer, easily bribed, had power and access. The family member was liked and trusted within the facility, so she was also valuable. An aging mother with a son confined as a psychiatric patient, she was a needy, stupid woman whom Hathorne could readily manipulate. It was as simple as pretending to understand what afflicted her son and then promising to help him in a way that the doctors apparently could not. Through these two people, Hathorne could obtain things such as additional computer hardware and concealed packages from his contacts on the outside.

A few of his contacts were ex-cons like him or undetected criminals. Some, though, were part of an ongoing legal and investigatory team Hathorne paid a pretty penny for. His family loathed him, but they were rich, and he still had access to a hefty trust fund. He paid for things such as practical goods and information and surveillance. So far, few things had proven more valuable than a simple smartphone, in this case an iPod Touch, with which he could connect to an internet signal. The hospital didn't allow this, of course, but Hathorne had devised a way to connect to a virtual private network, or VPN. He could explore the whole internet with the VPN, including its very dark side, and he could communicate with anyone he wanted. He still used regular computers for illicit communication at the psych center, but it was more difficult to get away with than it had been in prison. Hathorne was unimpressed by any of the St. Lawrence staff, be they educated or not, but they were head and shoulders above the idiots he had encountered in the DOC.

It was nearly midnight, and Hathorne was resting on the narrow bed in his locked room. The lights were out, and a thin sheet covered him. Silence blanketed the facility. He could crack the window above his desk in the corner and sometimes hear owls in the surrounding woods. He had to admit, SLPC was a pleasure dome compared to his previous accommodations.

His heart burned with hatred anyway. He didn't belong here. He had "done his time," to use that vulgar expression describing the odious power of the government. He had been caught, and he had paid for it. Maybe not as robustly as he deserved, because the government only knew about, much less proved, a fraction of the crimes he had committed. Regardless, why did the government get to say what were crimes and what weren't, anyway? He had needs. Children filled them, and he healed them in exchange. That was all over now. An actual child's touch was beyond his ability to secure. There were photos, though, and videos and stories. He had tapped into them from prison, gotten caught for it, and paid for those sins also.

And then it arrived: a short, neutrally toned letter from the Office of the Attorney General informing him of his status, now as a "respondent." After all of it—the trial, the sentencing, the years of drudgery and misery in upstate prisons—now they wanted to keep him confined even longer. And how? With some constitutionally twisted, punishment-in-disguise "public safety" law that only meant he would be demonized further, dragged through the machinations of the court system for a second time, and then confined to a locked hospital. Possibly forever.

Hathorne had fired off lawsuits against everyone involved, of course. His legal and investigatory team was handsomely paid and ready to work tirelessly for him. The case for proving he had a "mental abnormality" was strong, but it could be beaten. He was ready to stalk and sue everyone attempting to keep him confined. For a while, things looked as if they were turning in his favor. Ultimately, though, there was one man at the center of the effort who had made it stick. One man who had dredged up the old victims and set them up to testify so compellingly. One man who had arranged the cadre of doctors declaring him a danger with their interminable psychobabble. He was about to be released—the law had no choice—but then along came this one man and his pathetic crusade. One man, Hathorne was convinced, had snatched freedom from him. One undeserving, unhinged, stinking, sweaty drunkard of a state lawyer—Joe DeSantos. Now it was Hathorne's turn. He was going to put an end to Joe DeSantos, and so far the man was making it laughably easy for him.

The process had already begun, and he was continuing it tonight. Using his thumbs deftly, he typed out a message to one of his contacts. This contact was particularly valuable, and Hathorne had to handle him with skill and care.

Have you spoken with him yet?

While he waited for a reply, he turned his head toward the sliver of yellow light coming in through the door gap. A hospital attendant made regular rounds on his floor, but Hathorne knew when, even if they changed up the schedule, and he could hear the footfalls, in any event. There was no one around. He turned back to the dim white screen.

A single word moved across it.

Yes.

How does he seem?

Spooked. Good enough for you?

Hathorne grinned. Yes, that was very good indeed.

They were not using the iPod's built-in text program. Instead, to communicate with this contact, Hathorne had created something far simpler but equally effective. It was beyond "old school," as people said nowadays. In creating it, Hathorne had mimicked programs from the early days of computing itself. The program was his own creation, just a simple messaging application. There were no screen names, even, just eerie green text on a black square. His contact had been given an old laptop computer with the same program. Hathorne had loaded the program on to the laptop right there in the psych center and then arranged for the laptop to be smuggled out.

This contact, Hathorne knew, was not computer savvy. He knew only enough to leave the computer on during certain times, usually around midnight, and then wait. When Hathorne chose to reach out, the program would open and produce a simple ding to alert the user. They would communicate until Hathorne decided the session was over, and then the program would disappear.

The contact had no idea who Hathorne was, other than a person who, for a few small favors, would significantly enrich him when the favors were done. Hathorne knew the contact's name but never used it. In fact, to keep his mind ordered, he even banished it from his own thoughts as much as possible. He referred to this contact, in his thoughts and in his exchanges, only as Reaper.

He is guilty, Hathorne typed. Know that, and that he will pay. Soon.

What now? came the reply.

There will be further instructions. How are your circumstances?

My what? My life? It sucks. When do I get my money? I've done what you asked.

Soon enough. You'll be able to do whatever you want very soon.

There was a long pause and then: Really not sure this is worth it. Who are you, anyway? Who's the guy who gave me this computer?

I get orders from him through text messages, but I haven't seen him since.

> You'll know what you need to know when it's right for you to know. And it's almost right. You'll get what you want. Every bit of it.

> What do you know about me? What do I want, anyway?

Hathorne narrowed his eyes and stared at this for a few seconds. There were the distant sounds of a toilet flushing and a man coughing down the hall. Otherwise, the ward was deathly quiet and dark. His thin fingers hovered over the little device on his chest. He clicked his tongue and typed out, Light.

Then he turned off the program, and the word and the light vanished.

CHAPTER 14

Sunday, July 16, 2017
Bay Thirty-Fourth Street
Bath Beach, Brooklyn
2:45 a.m.

Joe lay in his oversize bed, sweat soaked and dry mouthed. He had just woken from a dream in which he was floating in black water, down a river in darkness, toward some loud, rushing sound he never reached. It was unsettling, but it hadn't scared him. What was scaring him was the sand in his shoes, the shoes he had, by all appearances, recently worn to a beach nearby.

Yes, and perhaps the same beach where a woman who is apparently your mother was found murdered by some guy with strong hands. She is a woman you have seen somewhere else, but cannot place.

She was there again, in his mind's eye, the discarded-looking creature at the medical examiner's office. The one he was never supposed to have recognized. He had seen no familial resemblance. He had felt no deep stirring, nothing that told him he was attached to the dead woman in any way. Still, he had seen her before, and not long before. That was undeniable.

I didn't kill that woman, he thought for the thousandth time, and then corrected it to *I didn't kill my mother.* He cursed himself for even entertaining the idea. *God, of course I didn't. Even if I wanted to, I couldn't pick her out of a lineup!* The internal dialogue went on, the warring voices in his head relentless.

Then why was the woman familiar? Who was she?

I don't know! I don't know, but there's an explanation. I didn't kill my mother. Why? Because I haven't seen her in forty years, and I haven't cared in probably thirty. I would have no reason. I would have no desire, no ability.

The dead woman is your mother, though. And she was someone you had seen before recently.

So what? At some point I saw a woman, somewhere, who got murdered near where I live. I did not know her by name, or by any other identifier. I told them truthfully that I did not know who she was. And if—if—I did go for a walk on a beach somewhere? So what? I live near a beach. That's it. End of story. I'm not a killer. Of anyone. The worst that happened is I took a walk, and I don't remember it because I was soused.

That wasn't really the worst, though. The worst was that he couldn't remember a goddamn thing about the night in question.

Blackout.

That's what he had experienced, and it was haunting him now that he was faced with these strange circumstances. It's also why Halle had been so upset. The true nature of the matter was that Joe didn't have a "true nature" when he was in a state like that. If he willed himself to reflect on it long enough, it chilled him to the bone.

Blackouts were an occasional consequence of drinking that he still hadn't gotten a full handle on, or at least that was the official explanation he gave to himself. It was deceptively easy to dismiss the problem; in two years of working for his former and now current boss, Craig Flynn, he hadn't missed so much as a morning meeting. He functioned, solidly, during the week. It was just weekends, and sometimes Thursdays, when he let loose.

Wrong. It's more than letting loose. You go way, way too far.

That was a reality he could not avoid, even with the cleverest distortion of thought. What Halle had said on Saturday morning was basically true: It wasn't that Joe had *forgotten* what the detectives had told him, along with most of the other events of the past weekend. It was that his brain hadn't *encoded* most of those events in the first place. That's what a blackout was—a failure of memory to encode because of the temporary loss of function to parts of the brain. There might be flashes of memory, things that made it into the vault when brain activity momentarily snapped back into gear, but most of it would be lost, never recorded.

It was a consequence of binging, both heavy and steady. Probably, he just hadn't stopped—other than maybe passing out for a few hours—until Saturday. That's when he had woken, his head pounding, to find a detective's business card that made no sense to him. Any functioning person acknowledging a bender like that would know it was time to make some changes, and a part of Joe's brain was making that argument.

There was a convenient counterargument, though, and one he still didn't recognize as classic drunk logic: *Okay, sure, so maybe most guys wouldn't let a bender draw out the way you still sometimes do. We'll work on that. But, hey, most guys haven't been as far down as you've been and come back so strong!*

That rejoinder—"But look where I am now!"—dominated whatever self-evaluation Joe put himself through. He would acknowledge, in the long run, that he needed to quit. He'd known that for years. But it was because he'd been so relatively balanced with liquor the past twenty-four months that he hadn't bothered to stay on the wagon.

He could get and stay dry for a few days at a time. He was doing his job, competently and cheerfully. His boss and his coworkers loved him. The judges liked him. These things were well and good, but they also marked the point where functioning alcoholics halted self-analysis. If he was killing his liver or his social life, the argument went, well, that was a reckoning he'd face later. The important thing—for now, at least—was that he could face the world and be dry when he needed to be.

Ah, but dry isn't sober. And you, Joe DeSantos, really need to get sober before something else happens that you don't have a memory of. This he could not argue with. For the moment, he did not believe that he'd somehow made his way over to a deserted stretch of Coney Island and murdered his estranged mother. Still, he had carefully cleaned his shoes and swept the sand away. And he was racking his brain for a memory of where he'd seen the woman's face before—for some explanation of the recognition that had flashed in his mind.

More foreboding, even, than either of those was the realization that he was allowing himself to fall deeper and deeper down a rabbit hole when he did start drinking hard. That process was going to hurt him if he wasn't more careful.

You or someone else, he thought, resigned to sleep remaining far away. *You or someone else.*

CHAPTER 15

Monday, July 17, 2017
Kings County District Attorney's Office, Sex Crimes Unit
Brooklyn
7:45 a.m.

"Thanks for coming in early," Mimi Bromowitz said as Len and Zochi settled into the two chairs before her desk. Zochi filled hers like she was made to sit there—a plump but lovely little woman with big dark eyes and hands clasped in front of her. Len looked gangly and oversize in his, legs parted like a split tree trunk. "Anything in terms of a suspect?"

"Nothing," Len said, shaking his head. "I hate it, but it's starting to look like a dead end."

"Oy, really?"

"You know how it is," Zochi said with a steep shrug of her right shoulder. "You hope for a great lead up front. We pounded the pavement. Didn't find one. We're not giving up, but . . . it's a shit case so far. Looks random."

Mimi sighed. She had gone over their DD5s from the remainder of the weekend. Both detectives had gotten overtime to work the case in its first forty-eight hours, a window of time that wasn't just the stuff of Hollywood.

With a case like the one involving Lois, a woman who lived on the fringes of society in the city that never sleeps, the window of opportunity closed fast on tracking a random killer. People without homes or considered "vagrant" weren't insulated the way nonmarginalized people were. Their patterns were less traceable. They could come in contact with an almost limitless number of people at all hours of the day and night, far more than what most would consider normal. New York was hardly unique that way; cities had served as bottomless pits for the disappeared since ancient Rome and long before. But more than most places, New York was an organism that churned and flushed away everything, like the estuarial waters licking around its edges.

"We found a few people who had seen her around," Zochi said. "Like Wilomena, from the reports. But no one really knew her. We went to a mission called Lighthouse not far from there. You know it?"

"I don't."

"It's well known to the Six-Oh," Zochi said, and Len nodded. "They give out food, clothes, and things. A worker there thought he had heard the name but didn't have anything else. There's also a flophouse on the other side of the amusement park." She looked over to Len, as if to let him finish the story.

"Yeah, that looked promising at first," he said. "An old lady runs it and tries to keep it clean. She recognized Lois's name for sure. She showed us where she stayed a few nights, all within two weeks or so of that Thursday night. But no ID, no personal effects left behind. We can't even find a photo of her from when she was alive."

"And the planner you found on her?" Mimi asked, still scanning the reports.

"Some receipts," Zochi said. "Too faded or water damaged to read. There were a few handwritten notes, like we talked about. That got us to Joe DeSantos, but I don't see anything that helps otherwise."

"Cameras?" Mimi asked. That was often the last question. When all else failed, she turned to video. It was everywhere.

"Shit, yeah," Len said. "We sat through hours of stuff. There are cameras from the projects on Twenty-Seventh that cover the boardwalk, and one street camera that looks out on the steps near where they found her. We saw footage of Wilomena going down there, but nothing much before that other than a couple walking along the boardwalk and different groups of kids from time to time. Almost no one went on, or came off, the beach after dark from that area, though. It's weird, because it's summer, but it was just dead out there."

"She must have walked onto the beach somewhere else," Zochi said. "But there's no telling which way she came from. I looked for prints in the sand, even, but the water was coming up. Didn't see anything."

"Okay," Mimi said. "You're right; it looks bleak so far. Hopefully there's foreign DNA on the body, or the bra."

"OCME's got both, along with the rest of her clothing," Zochi said. "We'll see."

"Anything else on the brothers?" Mimi asked. "The one you found, Joe DeSantos, is at the attorney general's office, down by Wall Street."

"We should find out how long he's been there," Zochi said. "He plays it off well, but the guy has a drinking problem."

"How bad was he when you found him?"

"Functional," she said. "But that's kinda the point. Guys like him have a lot of practice playing it sober. You can almost see the effort."

"She's right," Len said. "He put on a decent show, but that probably means he's a professional at it."

"Well, he's been at the AG's office for about two years," Mimi said, narrowing her eyes on a page from her own notes. "He was part of a law firm for a little while, but the partners split up three or four years ago. I don't know much about the other brother, Robert. He lives in Staten Island. You all should probably follow up. I'll reach out to Joe and see if I can get him in today. Can one of you come back for that?"

"Overtime," Len said, smiling. "I'm all yours."

CHAPTER 16

"You heard, right?" Craig asked when Joe picked up the phone. Joe had been sitting at his desk, twirling the detective's business card in his hand and vaguely fretting. For a horrified moment, he wasn't sure if Craig was talking about the discovery of Lois's body on the beach.

"Heard what?"

"You did it!" Craig exclaimed.

Joe jumped in his skin. *God, stop!* "Oh, you mean Aaron Hathorne?" Relief flooded him like a drug.

"Of course I mean Aaron Hathorne! The son of a bitch stays confined for another year. I figured the judge's chambers had called you by now. The decision came down this morning. Nice work, Joe."

"Thanks," Joe said. He smiled, grateful for the diversion. In any event, a compliment from Craig always got to him. "He refused to do his treatment homework all year, so really he did it to himself."

"Whatever. You kept him in there. That's big. If he'd been released after just twelve months, he would have declared victory, and the program would look shaky. This shows that the judges are still taking it seriously. Guys like him can't just dick around in sex offender treatment and walk away."

"Treatment isn't doing a thing for him. You know that. They mean well up there, but they're not getting to him."

"Of course I know," Craig said, as if this was not only obvious but also a little funny. "Whatever. They're *trying* to treat him. He needs to *try* to be treated. Otherwise, fuck him. He can spend the rest of his life in a hospital. It's a resort compared to what he deserves."

The case against Aaron Hathorne had been strong, but not a slam dunk. Joe found himself cross-examining nationally known psychologists and psychiatrists during the trial and dealing with Hathorne's aggressive investigation team as well. He was no longer close with his family, but he had a very deep trust fund and access to seemingly unlimited amounts of money. Still, the case against him as mentally ill and dangerous was one an upstate jury had taken little time to accept. Hathorne was stoic during the trial but visibly crumbled at the verdict. After he had awaited complete freedom for years, Joe's office snatched it from him under a new rubric.

The case had won Joe statewide acclaim in legal circles, and on top of that Joe had persuaded the judge to confine Hathorne to a psychiatric hospital rather than release him on intensive probation. The confinement was reviewable every twelve months, and Joe had just scored again by keeping him confined for at least another twelve.

"Who's your doctor again?" Craig asked, referring to the principal state psychologist who supervised Hathorne's treatment at the St. Lawrence Psychiatric Center in upstate New York.

"Gabe Seigel."

"Oh, good. He's a ballbuster. So you'll tell the victims?" By that, Craig meant Hathorne's victims, now adult males, a few of whom had worked with Joe and testified at the trial.

"Of course. This week."

"Excellent. How's the city?" Craig ran the bureau from Albany.

"Hot."

"Someday you'll learn. Nice and cool up here."

"Yeah, whatever."

"How are you otherwise?"

"Well . . ." Joe trailed off, sighed, and gave Craig his news.

"Oh, shit," he said after Joe had finished. Craig knew Joe's back-story and most of the details of his post-divorce life, including Halle. He didn't understand Joe the way Halle did, but he was a friend, and Joe trusted him with details he didn't easily share. "Man, I'm sorry about that."

"Thanks. I'm stuck with cremating her, I guess. And my brother resurfaced and wants to help."

"Oh, wow. Where's he now?"

"He's been back in Staten Island for a year or two. He actually brought money for the cremation instead of asking for it. That was a surprise."

"I hope you took it."

"I did, yeah."

"Will you do a service?"

"Shit, no."

"Yeah, I get that. Still, there are arrangements and stuff. Take some time off."

"You just gave me time off. I didn't use it well. Anyway, I'm fine. I'm meeting with a Brooklyn ADA this afternoon. That's about it."

"KCDA is involved? Do they have a suspect?"

"No, but I guess their office is involved early. I doubt it goes any-where. She was lost, Craig. Homeless, they think."

"I don't know what to say."

"There's nothing to say," Joe said, again uneasy and anxious. "Thanks for the good news on Hathorne, though."

"It's your good news. This is why I brought you back, Joe. You're a winner."

CHAPTER 17

Wednesday, July 13, 1977
West Seventy-Ninth Street and the Hudson River
Upper West Side, Manhattan
10:23 p.m.

"You know who's out here, right?" Robbie said, his voice purposely hushed. It had been maybe forty-five minutes since their mother had walked away, but it seemed like hours. The stillness was like lead; the heat of the night pressed on them.

"No one's out there. Shut up."

"Son of Sam," Robbie said, as if evoking a deity at a forbidden ritual.

"Stop."

"He's out here somewhere," Robbie said, looking over his left shoulder toward Seventy-Ninth Street. Whenever they moved, their sweat-soaked shirts made squishing sounds against the vinyl. Joe felt his heart pounding.

"The papers say he looks for guys and girls together," Joe said, not sure about the word "couples" but not wanting to use it, in any event. "Like, kissing and stuff."

"He looks for people in cars," Robbie said. "Like us. Just sitting here."
The air in the station wagon was impossibly heavy, the open windows making no difference. Not even insects made a sound. Every now and then a car

would enter the traffic circle, its headlights washing over them, tires spitting gravel into the darkness. "We've got to get out of here."

"But . . . Mom."

"She would have come back by now."

"She'll come back."

"Maybe not tonight, though." Even in the dimness, Joe could make out the sweat over Robbie's upper lip.

"Then what? What are we supposed to do?"

"We're supposed to go to Uncle Mike's," Robbie said, definitively, as if relating gospel. "Mom too."

"Then let's wait! We can't leave the car. That's what she said."

"She's gone." The certainty in Robbie's voice was black and terrible. "We can't wait any longer. If they tow the car, Uncle Mike will help us get it back. Right now we can't just sit here."

"Nooo," Joe said, aware he was whining like a baby. He didn't care. He folded his arms over his stomach and pulled his legs up. It was a fetal position he couldn't describe as such, but it was as natural as breathing.

"We're going," his brother said, opening the door and grabbing Joe's right arm. "Come on."

"We don't know where to go!" Joe cried, the yellow glow of the dome light flooding his vision. His arm being pulled from his body felt like his insides being torn open. Outside the car, he stiffened with the chunk of the LTD's heavy door as Robbie shut it. "The boat place," he said, his eyes adjusting. "It's that way, right?"

Instead of answering, Robbie jogged toward the edge of the traffic circle overlooking the path and the river. As Joe hustled to catch up, a big Chrysler approached, bathing them in light. The windows were open, and a long-haired man in the passenger's seat leered at Joe, his eyes huge and crazy. The driver leaned forward, his face glowing green in the dash lights, screaming something profane. They broke into laughter and sped away. A cloud of exhaust stung Joe's nostrils. Darkness reenveloped them.

"*Robbie, wait! I can't see!*"

"*Over here!*" *Robbie was standing at the concrete barrier that formed the edge of the traffic circle. To their left was a pathway that led down to the park, swallowed in blackness. In the distance were yellow and orange circles of light, bouncing lightly in the gloom.* "*The boats are right over there.*"

"*We can't walk down there,*" *Joe said, shifting his eyes to the path. Robbie looked over and smirked.*

"*Scared? Nervous is why there's new Soft 'n' Dri.*"

"*Shut up.*"

"*She's not down there anyways. She'd be back by now.*"

"*Maybe she needs help.*" *Joe stared at the boats, the forms of which he could make out now. They didn't look like a happy collection of welcoming vessels, though. More like secret little tombs guarded by torchlight. Through the gloom he could hear clanking chains and the low squeak of twisting metal.*

"*She's gone someplace else,*" *Robbie said.* "*We can't sit out here waiting for someone to grab us. We need to go where people are.*"

"*We can find a cop, maybe,*" *Joe said. He had seen something like that on an episode of* Baretta, *a show he might have been watching a rerun of that very moment at home if he wasn't stuck in this nightmare.* "*A cop could help us find her.*"

"*A cop? How?*"

"*You know, they'll put us in a cop car, and we can drive around until we see her!*"

"*Cops are gonna be too busy for that.*" *Robbie injected authority into his voice. He was doing his best to distance his tone from Joe's animated, hopeful one, something that Joe felt but could not articulate. Maybe it made Robbie feel better, like the strong older brother, but it made Joe feel like a baby.* "*Best we can do is hope the lights come back on. If things settle down, maybe we'll look for a cop. Come on.*"

He pointed through the traffic circle and east, to where there were headlight beams and red taillights sliding in and out of view every few seconds. But they looked tiny and woefully far away, on the other side of what seemed like an impenetrably dark space, a black field before the hulking shapes of buildings. That space, neither of them yet knew, was Riverside Park.

CHAPTER 18

Monday, July 17, 2017
Kings County District Attorney's Office, Sex Crimes Unit
Brooklyn
2:15 p.m.

"That song," Joe said, when Mimi asked if everything was okay. The two had exchanged pleasantries and small talk about Joe's work in the Bronx DA's office years back. Len was also present; they were getting started in Mimi's office when Joe trailed off. Mimi and Len exchanged glances as Joe fell silent.

"The song?" Mimi asked. She listened closer. Outside her office door sat one of the administrative staff members, an older woman named Helena. She played an easy-listening station through her computer most of the day. It was a sound that Mimi rarely noticed after a few minutes each morning, but now she could hear it, tinny and distant. The song was "Looks Like We Made It," by Barry Manilow.

"It was big that week," Joe said. "The week of the blackout. July 1977." He was clad in a simple dark suit and tie, and typical of a trial lawyer, he seemed both unemotional and comfortable in a DA's office. But now his brow was knitted, and his eyes darkened. "Wow. I swear, I really didn't think I'd react to any of this."

"Let us know if you need a moment," Mimi said.

"Nah, I'm fine, thanks." He sighed. "It was just a strange feeling all of a sudden. That song was big that summer. Do you know it?"

"My mother is a huge fan," Mimi said with a grin. "Of course I know it. I was fifteen the year of the '77 blackout."

"My brother was also," Joe said. "I was ten."

"It was a weekday, right?" she asked. "We were out of school, but I think I remember that."

"It was a Wednesday, yeah," Joe said, as if relating a dream. "It was the last time I saw my mother. July 13." His eyes met Mimi's, and she found them profoundly deep. He was composed, but the eyes were like windows to a shrouded interior. "It was hotter than hell that day. Then it stormed like you wouldn't believe. Then the lights went out. We were on the West Side Highway, going south."

"We?"

"My brother, my mother, and me. We were going to Arizona. It seemed like another planet. You remember that show *Alice*?" Mimi smiled. Len looked at him blankly. "It was a movie too. Anyway, she figured she could move us out there over the summer, get a job, and start us in school somewhere. She needed money, though. So the plan was to stop at my uncle Mike's place. He was a bachelor. Truth is, he was gay, but no one talked about that then. We were going to stop there for a few days, my mother was going to soak the poor guy for whatever money she could get, and then we were going to head off to Phoenix. But the lights went out."

"And you were in the car," Mimi said, not really a question. She could almost feel how scary that would be.

"Yeah. My mother lived through the '65 blackout, but that was a different world. We might have made it down to the ferry anyway, but we ran out of gas. It was right around Seventy-Ninth Street, where the boat basin is. She pulled the car off the exit; it sputtered and died. Then she told us to wait in the car while she looked for a can of gas. That was it." With this, Joe put his hands together in prayer formation and looked from Mimi to Len with an almost wide-eyed expression. "We just never saw her again."

"So the two of you made it to Staten Island on your own?" Len asked.

"More or less, but that's another story."

"Wow," Mimi said quietly, breaking the silence that followed. "I'm sorry."

"It's old business," Joe said with a shrug. "I did okay, I guess. My uncle was a godsend. He helped me get into Fordham, before he died. I was eighteen when that happened. Robbie—my brother, Robert—was twenty-three. He's still in Staten Island. He didn't do so well, but he's a survivor."

"No criminal record?" Len asked.

"No. He's kind of a scammer. Just being blunt. He's had a string of jobs like the one he has now."

"Which is where?"

"He's at a long-term rehab center near SIU Hospital in Midland Beach. Before that he was mostly in nursing homes, caring for the elderly. Except in his case, that meant ripping them off, too, from time to time. I've had to deal with the families of two or three of his victims."

"He got money from them?" Len asked. "How?"

"Personal effects, mostly. Jewelry, cash. It never reached the courts. I guess it couldn't be proven, but there were a few angry family members who tracked me down and knew I was a lawyer. I tried to make it right when I could. I sent money to a couple of them."

"Did Robbie know you were doing this—making restitution for him?" Mimi asked.

"I think he knows I did it, yeah. We've never really talked about it. It's hard to explain, but I think whatever I did for Robbie, he felt entitled to anyway. I wasn't sure if I'd hear from him again at all, but he reached out about a year ago. We've stayed in touch since then."

"Do you know why he reached out?"

"I'll be blunt again. Probably because he found out I had a government job again and some stability. To Robbie, that means a now-and-then payday loan. I heard from him after a long silence once before. It was when I started my law firm years back. At least this time he hasn't hit me up. We'll see how long that lasts."

"Detectives will have to interview him as well," Mimi said. "Any reason to believe he'd be a suspect in her death? I have to ask."

"I understand. No, I don't think Robbie would hurt anyone physically. He's slippery but not violent. And as far as money goes, whoever my mother was when she died, it doesn't look like she had any."

"No," Mimi said. "It doesn't."

"I wish I could help you more. I have a few old photos, somewhere. A box of stuff from way back."

"They might help," Len said.

"Okay. I'll look for them. We'll also claim the body, my brother and I, when OCME releases it. We found a place in Brooklyn where she can be cremated. We understand if it'll take time."

"I'll update you," Mimi said. "Oh, and the personal notes that Detective Hernandez found—the ones to a Joe, or Joey?—I may ask you to look at them at some point."

"Notes to me?" he asked. Mimi noticed a change in his demeanor. It wasn't suspicious, but it was odd. He seemed clueless about what most people would remember as a significant detail.

"They were found with the body," Len said. He hesitated for a moment. "With a business card of yours. We told you about them when we found you on Friday night."

"Oh, of course," he said, but his eyes were blank. Then he shook his head and sighed. "Look, I won't bullshit you. I don't remember much about that conversation. I drink; I'm not sure how else to put it."

"I kinda sensed that," Len said with a shrug. "Anyway, the notes were on paper that looked newer than the other items she was carrying around."

"And a business card," he said, sounding bewildered. "I swear I don't know how. I mean . . . I don't know where she would have gotten it."

"We don't know how or when she got it," Mimi said. "I know you're at the AG's office now. The business card is old, right? It was from a firm called Abrams & DeSantos."

"Yes, at least three years old." He'd been looking down, but his eyes snapped back to the two of them. "Jack Abrams was my old partner. The firm dissolved in early 2014."

"Have you been back to that office?" she asked. "I saw the address was in Kew Gardens, near the courts."

"Not in months. I had an appearance out there on one of my AG cases, but it was before Christmas."

They discussed a few other details, and Mimi looked to bring things to a close. "Thanks for coming in," she said, standing and offering her hand. "The detectives told you about victim services, right? I can walk you over there."

"They did," Joe said. "And I did this job, so I know how it works." He made eye contact with Mimi and Len in turn. "I thank you—on behalf of my brother also. But we're really not the victims. My mother was. For us, she was gone a very, very long time ago."

CHAPTER 19

Thursday, July 20, 2017
Sixtieth Precinct
Brooklyn
4:45 p.m.

"Hernandez," Zochi said into the phone, taking a gulp of coffee. She was at her desk in the Six-Oh squad room, buzzing with the usual elevated summertime level of activity.

"Zochi, it's Quinn." As usual, he sounded hoarse, like he'd just woken up. Dr. Adam Quinn was a forensic pathologist at the OCME. He was in his midfifties, built like a fireplug, and Zochi's image of a walking heart attack. He was thorough, though, and competent.

"Hey, Doc. You callin' about that old lady? DeSantos?"

"Yeah. I'm curious—when you saw the bra, what did you think?"

"I didn't think it killed her. ADA said the same thing."

"Bingo," he said with a chortle that turned into a cough. "Yeah, she wasn't strangled."

"More like someone wrenched her head back? Broke her neck?"

"You shoulda gone to med school. Yeah, that. Perp gave her a snap, then rotated the head back straight. Must have made a nasty sound."

"So then what? He wrapped the bra around her neck anyway? Or maybe he was doing something else. Maybe he was gonna use it but then changed his mind?" Zochi was just thinking out loud; they weren't questions that a medical examiner could answer.

"Don't ask me," he said. "They pay *you* to figure that out."

"Yeah, yeah. Anyway, the bra was wrapped, right? Like a loose knot? From what we saw, the cups were behind her head, against the sand."

"Yeah, that. Not clasped but sort of wrapped. Oh, and another thing: I don't think that bra was hers."

"Why not?"

"The size is just wrong. I know that homeless people wear what they can find, but I don't think she was wearing this. It's at least two sizes off."

"Okay," Zochi said, scribbling some notes. "Anything else?"

"Yeah, I'm gonna email you an image. You at your desk?"

"Yep." She waited a few seconds, then an email popped up. "Okay, I see it. The bra strap?"

"Yeah, see the letters?" Zochi expanded the image on her laptop. She could see them now. There were six small block letters written out along the back left strap of the bra. They spelled out F-W-Y-D-T-M.

"Okay, yeah, I see them."

"Do they mean anything to you?"

"Not a thing. Was there anything else unusual?"

"Nope. Nothing like it on any of the other clothing. Just that, whatever it is. I thought it was initials at first. You know, how people mark things, especially when they're in and out of shelter environments. You don't need six letters for that, though."

"Yeah, and it doesn't look like a name, right? Like, you can't sound it out."

"No. I mean, I'm not a linguist, but . . ."

"Neither am I," Zochi said. "I'm with you, though. I just see a jumble of letters. I'll make a note of it."

CHAPTER 20

Carole Miller, the young criminalist who had been assigned to examine the bra taken from Lois's body after it had been autopsied, carefully removed it from the sealed brown bag in which Zochi had collected it as evidence. Carole placed it on her "workbench," an immaculate white surface that looked more like an operating table. Wearing a surgical mask, goggles, long gloves, and a white gown, she moved her eyes and a penlight across the front of the bra, then the back. She studied the strange writing that the pathologist at the OCME had made a note of—FWYDTM along the back left strap. The letters had been handwritten with a black marker. They were small but easily legible block letters that fit inside the fabric space between the stitching at the top and bottom of the strap. It wasn't fancy, but it wasn't shaky or smeary either. To Carole, it looked like a person had taken care with the inscription.

She moved her eyes to the right strap. Along the same narrow stretch of fabric she encountered a rust-colored spot, maybe a quarter inch in diameter, about midway along the strap.

Blood.

Probably, but she wouldn't jump to conclusions. The next step was a Kastle–Meyer, or KM, test of the spot. If the splotch she was looking at was composed of human blood, she would know soon enough.

Within a few hours, Carole had her answer. She had a blood stain and a good one for analysis—not a smear or thin spatter. More like a single healthy drop. She cocked her head and studied the spot under a magnifying glass. The edges were clean. *Nice,* she thought. *Might not be a mixture.*

Mixtures were common. They were splotches of blood containing the biological material of more than one bleeder. This happened when victims struggled with their attackers, or when there was an explosion or a car crash that smashed shattered bodies together. This neat single drop didn't have that look. She marked the area, made a careful cutting of the affected part of the fabric, and prepped the swatch for DNA analysis. It would take time, but assuming that her instincts were correct, the dried blood spot would produce a singular genotype—the genetic blueprint of exactly one human being, far more distinctive than the most carefully captured fingerprint.

CHAPTER 21

"This is it," Joe said, setting the box at Zochi's feet. She was seated on a dark leather sofa in Joe's cavernous but sparsely furnished living room. The box was medium size, large enough to carry a drawer full of sweaters.

"This?" she asked. He nodded and took a seat across from her on a fat, sturdy ottoman that went with the sofa. Both were well made, but they barely filled a room that to Zochi seemed to need much more, including—desperately—a woman's touch. Zochi couldn't have known it, but Halle had felt the same way.

"That's it," he said. "It's everything I took from my uncle's apartment in Staten Island. I could have taken a lot more, but it was practical to travel light. I was on my way to college, and I had no idea where I'd even spend the summer."

Zochi gingerly went through the box, finding things she mostly expected: a high-school graduation cap with a little faux-brass "85" hanging from a tassel and plenty of Kodak-era photographs. There were some magazines and newspapers from historic events, such as Reagan's assassination attempt and the death of John Paul I.

In the photos, Zochi finally beheld Lois DeSantos in life. Death had left her face sunken and scarred, but otherwise it was the same person. In most of them, she had a cigarette in her hand or mouth. One series was taken on Christmas morning, presumably with Joe and his brother, Robbie, climbing over her to get to a present. A later photo revealed it to be an air hockey table. In the photos, Lois was in a housedress, seated beside a fake tree adorned with colored lights.

She had been attractive, Zochi thought, her hair parted '70s style down the middle, presenting a pleasant angular face. Her eyebrows were faint. Below them, the eyes were alert and intelligent. She looked gloomy and tired. In most of the photos, the smiles seemed forced, never reaching the eyes.

Zochi flipped through a few photos of Uncle Mike, who looked more or less as she expected. He was thin with sad eyes, a high forehead, and a pencil mustache. In a few of the photos he was with another man, or a small group of men, on a beach or at a table in an outdoor restaurant. There was only one photo of him with both boys, taken in a park in cold weather. On the back, someone had scrawled, "Mike, Joe and Robbie, Feb. '78." The rest of the photos were of just Joe and Mike; one or two were taken at a beach, and one was taken somewhere in Manhattan.

"These are nice," Zochi said. "None of your dad, though?"

"Not a one," Joe said, and Zochi sensed some feeling behind it. "That bothered me for a while. Lois didn't keep any, though, and Uncle Mike didn't have any. My father's been dead a long time."

"He died when you were a kid?"

"Yeah, I was nine. Robbie and I were born in Staten Island. That was home for my mother and her family going back two generations at least. My father was from Bayonne, but that's all I knew. We never met any of his family. Around 1970, he got a job in Danbury, Connecticut, and we moved there. He walked out on us when I was eight, so in '75. A year later, he was driving drunk with his girlfriend in the passenger seat and wrapped his car around a tree. Killed them both."

"Eesh, I'm sorry," she said. "That's some backstory."

"It's okay. Neither Robbie nor I took his death very hard. Mostly, the guy was an asshole. I don't think my mother felt anything when he died, other than the need to get the hell out of Danbury."

Further down in the box, Zochi came to a thin and faded amateur-looking magazine. On the mustard-yellow cover was a mimeographed drawing of an ashtray with a cigarette in it. A twirling column of smoke curled up to form the title and year: *LIT*, 1979.

"Oh, dear God," Joe said as she lifted it. "I haven't thought about that in years."

"It's like a school thing, right?" she said, looking it over. "Like a little publication."

"Our literary journal, yes," Joe said, putting a little flourish around the term. "That was from my sixth-grade year. My uncle must have had twenty copies. He sent them to everyone, like a proud parent. I haven't seen it since it came out."

"You made the journal," Zochi said with an admiring little turn-down of the lips. "Very nice."

"It was just a collection of stuff from the kids, some bad drawings and poems. A poem was my contribution." She thumbed through and found Joe's poem on page twelve in simple black type.

"For Lois," by Joey DeSantos, 6th Grade, Mrs. Benedetto's class

There was no illustration accompanying the poem, just five stanzas, all in the same black typeface with old newspaper serifs. Zochi mused for a moment about what her own thirteen-year-old daughter, Lupe, would say about such an effort. Lupe had a passion for design and was already creating professional-looking layouts with no more than an iPad. There was something Zochi liked about the simplicity of the printed words on the page, though. It came through raw and innocent.

In the mirror still I see
The scars, for what you did to me
The birds that sing, up in the trees
They're mute, for what you did to me.

A bright full moon, over the sea
It's dull, for what you did to me
A scrape I got once on my knee
Not kissed, for what you did to me

At night I think of your embrace
Through a flame's light I see your face
At the river's edge I made my case
But then you left, without a trace.

And so I go on, silently
A new life I've found separately
Happy for those who care for me
But still I wish . . . and I ask thee

Will you ever light the way for me?
Set out a lamp, so I can see
Chase away the night's eternity
For once, for what you did to me?

"Joe, you wrote this when you were what—eleven?" He took the magazine from her and held it at middle-aged distance to read without glasses.

"Well . . . yeah, I did."

"That's impressive. I mean, really."

"It was an assignment from a counselor," Joe said. "Not a guidance counselor but a therapist. My uncle had connections in the mental health community on Staten Island. He got me in to see, for a time, a guy who suggested I write something. I worked on it for a while. I think I had, like, thirty stanzas at one point. I had to narrow it down. I was never happy with that ending, but . . . that was it."

"Takes guts to put that out there when you're that age," she said.

"I didn't put it out there." There was a wistful smile on his face. "Uncle Mike did. It's the only thing he ever did that really made me angry. He showed the final product to my teacher, the Mrs. Benedetto you see up top. She went crazy over it and wanted to put it in the yearly magazine."

"They printed it without you knowing?"

"No. She was very nice. She gave me a choice on whether to publish it or not. My uncle and I had it out, though. I was pissed. Couldn't believe he showed it to her."

"So you showed it to him?"

"Yeah, I was proud of it. And it was the only thing that came close, you know, in terms of how I felt about it all. You can't say things like that, right? I couldn't, anyway. Not then."

"I couldn't now," Zochi said, looking the poem over again. "So your uncle couldn't help himself."

"I guess not. It all worked out. He and Mrs. B left it up to me ultimately, which was good. Empowering, I guess. I let it go forward. I was a little worried about how the other kids would see it, but most of them knew I was living with an extended family member and not my parents. I don't remember if they called me an orphan or not. I guess not, because no one knew where Lois was. Anyway, I got compliments on it. That was nice."

"Lois," Zochi said at low volume. "It must have seemed odd, referring to your mother by her first name."

"By that time," he said with a shrug, "Lois was all she was to me." They were silent for a moment. Zochi continued through the box until she reached two light-blue baby rattles at the bottom. Three inches long and made of plastic, they sounded like little castanets when shaken.

"These are cute," she said, holding one up.

"Oh, yeah, the rattles," Joe said. "There was one for each of us, Robbie and me. I didn't know they existed until after Uncle Mike died. I found a few things he had kept. I have a feeling he was going to . . . I don't know . . . *present* all that stuff to me, when he could. After he died, I found some of this stuff laid out in his bedroom closet."

"When you say 'present,' you mean . . . ?"

"Well, you had to know my uncle. He was uniformly cheerful, like everything was a breeze. And no serious talk, you know? Like everything just had to be peachy. He wasn't unkind, not a bit. He just . . . never got real." Zochi nodded. She could relate. "He started getting really sick around Christmas in 1984. It was AIDS, but I didn't know that until later. Robbie was long gone—we hadn't seen him in a year or more. So Mike ordered in Christmas dinner, just for the two of us. He was shivering a lot by then and couldn't get out of bed much. He made a big thing about Christmas dinner, though, and bought me a bunch of presents he probably couldn't afford. And he said we had to have this talk but that it could wait until I was eighteen."

"Which was a few months later, right?" Zochi asked, letting her eyes find his. Joe looked wistful, almost surrendered to some lulling memory. He was opening up. The part of Zochi that couldn't help but be a detective perked up. She listened closely.

"Yes, in April. I was on a senior trip overseas. My birthday was the eleventh. I was scheduled to get back on the seventeenth, but Mike went into a coma, and the tour company sent me back early. I got to the hospital in time to see him before he died, but he was out of it. We never spoke. I watched him die and then packed up what I could. Like I said, it seemed like he had laid some stuff out that he wanted me to have, I guess. I think he wanted to explain it, but . . . that didn't happen."

"I'm sorry for that."

"I am too," he said, with feeling. "He was getting sicker, that whole winter. I shouldn't have gone, but he wanted me to go. You know how when you're a kid you don't think bad things will really happen? Or if they do, somehow they'll be on your timeline?"

"Sure."

"Well, that was me."

"Maybe it was him too," she said. "The timeline thing. Maybe he thought he had more time."

"Maybe. I never knew what was going on in his head."

"The baby rattles," she said, "and the pictures. How did your uncle get them? I thought there wasn't much contact between your family and him when you were little."

"You're a good detective," he said, looking genuinely impressed.

She smiled. It *was* a good question.

"He got them from a suitcase my mother packed. It was in the station wagon, the one she ditched us in. We'd been living with Mike a week or two when he tracked the car down. After the blackout, the city towed it to an impound lot on the West Side. There were storage fees and a fine to get it out, so Mike just left it, but a decent guy over there let him take the luggage and the boxes out of the car. That was how my brother and I had coats and long johns a few months later. And let me tell you, that following winter was cold, no matter how hot the summer was."

"I've heard that," she said. She held up both rattles, one in each hand. "They're the same, you know. Your mother must have gone back to the same store when she was expecting you."

"Probably," he said with a shrug. "Staten Island was smaller then. Not sure what choices she had. It's weird, you know? I haven't seen those rattles in years. I never gave them much thought, but you're right— they're identical. As for Robbie and me? Nothing could be further from the truth."

CHAPTER 22

Thursday, July 27, 2017
New York County Superior Court, Part Thirty-Four
Manhattan
2:30 p.m.

The crime scene photos, ten by twelve inches, were old school. Not the pixelated wizardry of digital photography, no. These had been developed in a lab, on glossy blank paper swished around in a chemical-filled tray until the images floated up from shadows. For three decades they had yellowed in an evidence bin.

Their subject was a woman, still alive but beaten so badly that she was nearly unrecognizable. She was in the entrance of the elevator where she had collapsed, thirty-five years and six days before the hearing where the images of her were again relevant. In the black-and-white photos, the heavy scarred door of the elevator rested against her left thigh, unable to close. At the judge's request, Joe handed them forward. Judge Feldman sifted through them and grimaced.

"Why the hell were they taking her picture if she was still alive?" he asked in a loud whisper. He was looking down at the two lawyers—Joe and Joe's adversary—before the bench. "I know it was a long time ago, but still."

"They didn't know she was alive, at first," Joe said. "The responding officers had a crime scene photographer with them, and he started to snap photos when she gasped or coughed or something."

"Oh," the judge said. He shifted his eyes to the subject of the hearing, Evan Bolds, who sat calmly at counsel table with his hands in his lap. He was fifty-three, according to the file, and hefty. He had graying hair, a mustache, and small eyes that made him look a little like a walrus. Bolds had raped the woman in the photo after breaking into her apartment. She had broken free afterward and had run screaming and half-dressed out the front door toward the elevator. Bolds had followed and squeezed into the elevator with her just as the doors were closing. It was in the elevator that he had let loose on her, grabbing her by the neck, slamming her face repeatedly into the button panel, and beating her until it must have seemed like she was dead.

The issue today was not whether Bolds was guilty of the rape and attempted murder. In the steaming summer of 1984, he had been found guilty of both in a courtroom right across the street from where he was now. He had served almost thirty-three years—plus two years of probation afterward—for those crimes. The issue now was whether, as in the case of Aaron Hathorne, Bolds could be shown to have a "mental abnormality" and continued on supervision, even though his criminal sentence had maxed out.

"Are you sure this is the same guy?" Feldman asked Joe and his counterpart, a young lawyer named Ben Yang who was representing Bolds. Ben worked for the Mental Hygiene Legal Service, an agency that functioned like a public defender's office for people with mental illnesses.

"He looked different in 1983, Your Honor," Joe said.

Ben shrugged.

"Didn't we all," Feldman said. "All right, step back." He waited until the lawyers had returned to their tables. "Mr. Bolds, do you understand what's going on here?"

"Yes, Judge," Bolds said, speaking for the first time. His voice was almost walrus-like too, his words a little like pinniped barks. "They want to put me back, I guess."

"Well, not exactly. You were convicted of rape and attempted murder back in 1984. You've served your time for that, and it looks like you've been on probation now for almost two years. Your probation is about to end, which would make you completely free of legal supervision. What's happening is, the attorney general's office has filed a petition against you because they believe that you may have a mental health problem, and that you may reoffend sexually. So even though you're being released from supervision, they're seeking to put you in an institution or on strict probation. If they can prove their case, then one or the other of those things would continue until the state says you're no longer dangerous. Does that make sense?"

"Yeah, I guess."

"Do you feel like you're dangerous?"

"Dangerous? I don't go nowhere."

"Mr. Bolds's entire life revolves around his mother, who is in a nursing home, Your Honor," Ben said. "He lives nearby, and he's lived quietly for almost two years on probation without major incident. Other than visiting his mother, going to work, and shopping in the neighborhood, he doesn't go anywhere."

"Without major incident, yes," Joe said. "But Mr. Bolds's behavior around public libraries and parks near where he lives in Brooklyn has sparked—"

"No arrests," Ben interrupted.

"Don't speak over each other!" the court reporter barked.

"I apologize," Ben said. "But, Your Honor, the AG's office really can't point to much outside of speculation."

"He owns a panel van," Joe said. "He says he uses it for his job, making deliveries for some dry cleaners in Brooklyn. He was detained outside of a public library branch in Flatbush two years ago on a citizen's complaint. He was in the van, and it was found to have duct tape and various kinds of rope in the back."

"Mr. Bolds explained to police at the scene how those things were related to his job and various other tasks he does around his home. He was not arrested. There have been no probation violations either."

"I can read the file, Mr. Yang," the judge said. "And I understand your argument, but the probation officer himself has expressed concerns about Mr. Bolds. The PO believes he's got strange ideas about women and sex."

"My client tends to say unfortunate things, Your Honor," Ben said, as if accepting responsibility for a bad recipe. "But there's no evidence it's anything but fantasy. Anyway, the PO isn't a psychologist."

"Which is exactly why he's a candidate for this process," Joe said, seizing on the point with a sonorous pitch. "The Office of Mental Health has made an initial determination that Evan Bolds might have a mental abnormality. If Mr. Yang is right that he doesn't, then this process will clarify that."

"Oy gevalt!" Feldman said, raising his hands. He shifted his eyes to the sedentary, composed man at the table. "Mr. Bolds, did you understand my question before? Do you believe you're a danger to reoffend, sexually or otherwise?"

"Dangerous? Like would I hurt another lady?"

"Well, yes. Or anyone."

"Oh. No, I'm too old for that now. That's for the young guys."

"That's comforting," the judge said, frowning. He turned his attention to Joe. "Mr. DeSantos, Mr. Bolds seems . . . less than fully repentant, maybe. But he was released after nearly thirty-three years in custody, and they were mostly quiet years. He's done a couple more years on probation without a violation. Is he really a good candidate for this . . . civil confinement?"

"Well, it's civil management, Your Honor," Joe said. "We don't anticipate that Mr. Bolds will be confined again. But he's fifty-three, which is relatively young. He's demonstrated serious deficits in empathy and understanding regarding what he did, both back in the '80s and recently. The Office of Mental Health believes he's a good candidate for strict probation. We filed based on that."

There was more discussion and ruminating on Feldman's part, but at the end of the day this was a probable cause hearing, and he was bound to rule that the AG's office had made its case. Bolds would stand trial again, this time not for being a criminal but for having an identified "mental abnormality" and considered dangerous.

"Mr. Bolds, I find that the state has met its low burden for the purposes of this hearing. You'll stand trial for civil management on a date to be determined. In the meantime, I'll allow you to remain unconfined, but you'll be assigned to a new pretrial officer for checkups. Good day, sir. Next case."

CHAPTER 23

2:48 p.m.

"Really, Joe?" Ben asked as the two left the courtroom with Bolds a few feet behind them. Ben was a short, neat-looking guy of Chinese descent with black hair and dark eyes. Joe liked him. He was a straight shooter and a good litigator. "This guy? For civil management?"

"OMH gives my office permission to file. In real terms, that means we'd better file. Either that or the AG takes the blame if this guy snaps again in an elevator. I'm a soldier, and those are my orders. You know that."

"I get the politics, but this guy isn't Aaron Hathorne. Far from it."

"No one is Aaron Hathorne," Joe said. "I know this case sucks. It's a dog, and I've gotta walk it."

Ben shrugged and nodded. It was a sentiment all trial lawyers understood. He asked about some additional records on Bolds that Joe was supposed to bring, and Joe led them over to a bench outside the courtroom.

"Mr. Bolds, sit for a second, okay?" Ben asked. Bolds sat silently, his hands moving to his lap like it was a trained response. He stared downward.

Joe set out a couple of thick accordion files and thumbed through them while Ben looked at some messages on his phone. Joe produced the documents and then heard a loud crash. Across the hall, another courtroom door had flown open and struck the wall.

"Fuck you, Vera! This shit ain't over!" a young man screamed, stomping into the hallway and tossing court papers behind him. He then winged a cell phone down the polished tile floor of the hallway like it was a skipping stone. Three uniformed men from the Office of Court Administration, or OCA, took notice. One barked into his radio while the other two chased the phone thrower down.

A sobbing woman, visibly pregnant, walked out from the same courtroom a few seconds later and bent over to pick up the discarded papers. She was carrying her own fat file of legal paperwork and looked like she might fall over. Joe and Ben both called out to her. "*Miss, please!*" and "*Whoa, lady, hang on!*" were overlaid on each other. The two men gathered the papers and pointed her toward the elevator. In the distance, the phone thrower bellowed like a bear in a trap as he was subdued.

"Will they arrest him?" Ben asked, brushing his hands clean.

"Nah, not as long as he shuts up," Joe said. "If OCA had to collar every guy who acted like that in family court, they'd be doing nothing else." From the pile of paperwork on the bench, he pulled out the reports for Ben and handed them over. Beside the two men, Evan Bolds continued to stare like nothing remotely disturbing had just taken place. *That's prison,* Joe thought. *He's used to ignoring outbursts.*

"Mr. Bolds, let's go," Ben said. "I'll show you where you'll need to report next." Bolds rose, poised to follow him. He had an almost robotic air about him, something between an impeccably mannered child and an obsequious servant.

"Okay," he said. Ben and Joe shook hands, ready to part. Then Bolds turned to Joe. "Um, you have a good day too, Mr. DeSantos."

Joe looked back at him quizzically. Most guys in Bolds's position didn't talk to the other side's lawyer.

"You too, sir," Joe said. He winked at Ben and turned away.

Next stop was for a hot dog. It was almost three o'clock, and Joe hadn't eaten anything all day. He waited a solid minute for an elevator; the ones at 111 Centre Street were notoriously slow. A crowded one arrived, and Joe stepped in as he riffled through the Bolds file again. He frowned at the messiness, knowing he'd have to reorganize it at the office. He had done little with the case file since right after Lois's body had been found. It had been an unproductive week.

Booze filled, more like it.

The elevator came to a stop, paused for another aching moment, and slid open. The echo-laden noise of the courthouse lobby and some fresh air billowed in. Joe was about to pull his hand from the folder when his fingers brushed plastic. He fished out a small ziplock bag with something that looked like a postcard or a photograph inside. When he glanced at the thing in the bag, his breath caught in his throat. People were already pushing out behind him, forcing him into the tributary of the courthouse exit that fed the river of humanity that was Lower Manhattan. The thing in the baggie wasn't a postcard or an old photograph; it was an old, rather flimsy-looking baseball card.

Hostess.

Reggie Jackson.

1977.

CHAPTER 24

Office of the Attorney General, Sex Offender Management Bureau
Lower Manhattan
3:26 p.m.

The baseball card was still in the ziplock bag on Joe's desk, as if somehow keeping it in there would contain its effect. There were a dozen things he wanted to do with it, from clawing it free and sobbing with his face buried in it to burning it, bag and all. There was the fleeting, vague idea of having it "tested" somehow, for something, but that was nonsense.

Stop with the dumb ideas. Think. *Where did this come from?*

He tried to focus on when he had handled the file last, but that was maddeningly fuzzy. The fact was, he had gotten the case brand new from the Office of Mental Health right before his big hearing on Aaron Hathorne's case. That was the same week of the fortieth anniversary of the blackout and Lois's disappearance. The file had traveled with him upstate to the hearing—he figured he'd have time to look it over on the train—then back home, where it eventually made its way to the office. He'd been drunk more than sober during that whole period, though, and couldn't remember how much he had actually rummaged through it. His eyes crept back over to the baggie again, and he winced. It was a sick irony: he had no idea how this little prize had reappeared in a work folder and yet had the clearest recollection of when he'd last seen it.

She grabbed it after Robbie sent it flying out the window. He could see them again, Robbie and his mother, standing by the faded maroon LTD in the last of the light, their faces reflecting an orange tint from the Jersey side. Lois wore blue jeans, gray tennis shoes, and a sleeveless blouse—something pink, he remembered. He saw again the fear in her eyes, the awful weight of stress and uncertainty.

"Give it, Joe. Now."

He remembered the bullheaded, frustrated feeling of losing control over his favorite thing, especially after the miracle of finding it on the highway. Still, there had been security in it. That's what mothers provided. The card wasn't, for the time being, his to finger and twirl, but it wouldn't disappear either. His mother had it, and it was safe, away from his brother, away from the elements, away from the city. It would warm in her back pocket for a few hours. He just needed to remind her it was there before she put the jeans in the wash, wherever they ended up.

For a few seconds he was sure that he was going to cry—just let his hands fall into his lap, let the tears fall between his tie and his shoes. Then the grip of fear snapped him out of it. His mother's body had turned up on a beach near his home. There was sand in some shoes he had no memory of wearing on a night he had no memory of passing.

And now a simple case file had regurgitated a bittersweet piece of his childhood.

He dug back through the accordion file. That particular one was filled with older records on Evan Bolds, from his dismal performances in failing New York City schools in the '70s to the bloody elevator case in 1983. There was nothing else of Joe's in there, no other legal papers or personal stuff. He couldn't shake the feeling that he had dumped the contents onto the dining room table one night. It was a common habit when he was working from home: spreading out what he was focused on and pushing other things, like mail and canceled checks, aside. If that was the case, then maybe the baseball card had been swept back in? Okay, but that said nothing about how *he* had gotten it in the first place.

Did she give it to me somehow? Is that why I recognized her in the morgue? She approached me, maybe, when I was bombed out of my mind, and now I don't—

"Or did I find it on her?" he asked out loud. His eyes shot over to the closed door of his office. It was late July—the place was mostly empty—but still his heart thundered in his ears. He swallowed hard.

No, no, no. I didn't.

You can't remember!

Memory was impossible if he truly had been blacked out during some encounter with Lois. The darker truth was that Joe didn't understand what was happening to him at all.

Lois, he thought. His supple mind, having been on a quickening treadmill of tasks, subtasks, and ideas, now ground to a halt. *You're going to need to understand her—and what became of her.*

He felt cruel for lacking the slightest interest in doing so before this miserable afternoon. He was an attorney, an ostensible seeker of the truth. As a prosecutor, he had access to all kinds of investigatory knowhow and resources. Why the hell *wouldn't* he want to know what happened to his mother after forty years and such a dreadful end?

"Because she never tried to find out what happened to me," he said, whispering this time. Now he did cry. Pressing a thumb and forefinger to his eyes, he heaved softly and wept for the first time in years. Eventually, his left hand found the knob to the lower desk drawer. There was a bottle in there, probably two. He wouldn't drink all day in the office, but he needed to start. Now.

CHAPTER 25

Wednesday, July 13, 1977
West Seventy-Ninth Street and the Hudson River
Upper West Side, Manhattan
10:28 p.m.

A few cars moving from West Seventy-Ninth Street through the traffic circle provided a brief view of the path ahead, but it also shrank their pupils and dimmed their night vision. Then the traffic petered out and disappeared altogether. They were about to enter a short tunnel at the edge of the circle that went under the parkway and then east along Seventy-Ninth Street. In front of them was blackness; not even the other end was visible in the gloom.

Joe's stomach felt fluttery. Before the move, their house was on a rundown street in Danbury, Connecticut. It was dark at night, but there were house lights on all the time and tall streetlamps every half block or so. Neither boy had done much camping, so a complete absence of light was scary to begin with. This was much more ominous, though. Grown-up places, Joe knew instinctively, places with lots of people and big cities especially, shouldn't be so dark. Darkness like that wasn't natural. It only hid bad things.

Robbie clicked the lighter on, and a warm cone of light leaped up the curved wall of the tunnel. Mostly it illuminated graffiti—dirty words and other letters that Joe couldn't make out in a dozen spray-paint colors.

"Let's walk in the street," Robbie said, letting the lighter go dark. "I can click it on every few seconds, maybe."

"I can't see the other side," Joe said, his voice rising with fright. "Even with the flame, I can't see more than a little bit in front of us."

"Those cars up there," Robbie said, although the passing cars up the hill on Broadway weren't visible from inside the tunnel, "that's what we're aiming for."

"I can't see them!"

"Ugh, it's because there's a hill that goes up. Just walk straight, okay? We'll be out in like thirty seconds." They began to move forward, Joe close behind his brother. The air was hot, still, and fetid. Inside the tunnel it smelled mostly like pee, but there was a dankness underneath, like wet earth. They heard the rumble of vehicles passing overhead every few seconds. Robbie clicked the lighter on, and more garish graffiti appeared along the scarred barrel of the tunnel. Then there was a sound, a moan or a grunt, followed by a cough. Robbie lifted the lighter higher, then squealed and it clicked off, leaving them in blackness.

"Ow, my thumb!" Robbie said. "I can't keep it lit like that!"

"What's going on?" Joe asked, his heart in his throat. "I heard something."

Another few coughs echoed in the gloom.

"Hey! Who's there?!"

The voice was gravelly and deep. Joe felt his penis shrivel. He grabbed Robbie by the arm, and they both stood still. Joe stared straight ahead at nothing, praying for the glow of headlights, but none came.

"Who's there?!" It came out "hoo-ZARE," and the last word was a throaty scream. More hacking and phlegmy coughs were punctuated by a mumbled curse that Joe couldn't make out. The voice was closer now. Robbie took a step backward and almost tripped over Joe. Neither boy dared make a sound. Then there was a bad smell. The whole place smelled bad, but this was a distinctive fug—the clinging, almost food-like smell of body odor. Now there were shuffling and scraping sounds as the stranger moved along the pavement toward them.

"WHO IS IT, GODDA—" *The words devolved into throaty spasms, hacking, cursing, and coughing. There was a hock-spit sound, and Joe ducked as if expecting to be struck by saliva. The person was close to them now, his breathing audible.*

"Run!" Robbie said. "Run!"

"Which way?!" Joe cried as his brother pulled away from him.

"Away from him! Just go!"

Too afraid to cry, Joe bolted forward in the dark toward the sound of Robbie's voice. There was a terrible moment when he felt hot skin, like a hand or an arm, reaching out to grab him. The smell was sickening. He heard footfalls and Robbie cursing up ahead. Then there was a thump. Robbie must have struck the wall on the left side.

Joe staggered on. His eyes had adjusted, and he could see a few things outside the tunnel. There were spots of yellow and orange—candles in windows up high—and the dim outline of the buildings. They still seemed very far away. Behind him, the person in the tunnel sounded like he was throwing up. Echoes of it punched through the hot air.

Joe reached the outside. Headlights on the Henry Hudson Parkway lit up some treetops above him. They were in a park. Robbie was a few feet ahead of him, his hands on his knees. A car approached from the east, moving down Seventy-Ninth Street, but it turned onto another street running parallel to them and sped off. It had been bright again, but now it was even darker.

"What street is that?" Joe asked. "How far off is it? I can't see again!"

"That's Riverside Drive," a male voice said. It came from their left, off the street, where there were trees and bushes. Robbie stood up straight and peered in that direction. Joe made his way over to him, preparing to start running again. This voice was much different, though. It was a calm, civilized voice belonging to a perfectly reasonable-sounding grown-up. "How many of you are there? Boys? It's okay. You can tell us."

CHAPTER 26

Thursday, July 7, 2016
Saratoga County Courthouse
Ballston Spa, New York
9:57 a.m.

"You worried?" Joe asked his boss, Craig Flynn. Outside, it was a bright, beautiful summer's day, and Joe stared longingly through the window. The United Kingdom had recently voted to leave the European Union, and it was looking increasingly likely that Donald Trump would be the GOP nominee for president. In the vestibule outside the witness room, three corrections officers debated Trump's best choice for a running mate. Five months had passed since Joe had first laid eyes on Aaron Hathorne, in the ID photo on his desk, and Aideen had relayed her warning.

"Nope, 'cause I know you're gonna nail it," Craig said, hooking his hands behind his head. He grinned, the usual toothless, oversize one that seemed to stretch his face like taffy. Craig was a few years older than Joe, tall and slender with the toned body of an athlete, but bald and possessed of a long face short of handsome. The face itself was well shaped, but his features and ever-present oval glasses made him look a little cartoonish. This was particularly true when he made an exaggerated expression—a frown, a furrow of the brow, or, as in this case, a grin.

It was a look, in general, that Craig embraced. He knew he looked like a goofball, and he reveled in it. Part of it was that Craig Flynn enjoyed being underestimated. Of Irish descent, he had grown up poor but managed to obtain an Ivy League education. Like Joe, he had a quick mind and a masterful ability to remember facts, figures, and dates. He was opinionated and could have been called a bully were he not so kind underneath it all. It was no understatement that Joe was more grateful to Craig than to any other man in his life except for Uncle Mike.

"He's got polished counsel," Joe said. "His trust fund is still working for him."

"What, those white-shoe pricks with sticks up their asses? You'll wipe the floor with them."

"Gonna do my best, Skip," Joe said and smiled. A few lawyers in the unit affected a habit of referring to the chief the way that mafia soldiers referred to the bosses, calling them Skip or Skipper.

"You've got him," Craig said. "And remember"—he made one of those exquisite magnified Craig faces—"failure is not an option."

Joe's challenge at this dispositional phase of the process was to keep Hathorne confined rather than released on intensive probation. Although Hathorne's family expressed public disgust with him, they were ready to take him back, in a manner of speaking. On the grounds of their estate outside Saratoga Springs, Hathorne would be provided with a guesthouse and round-the-clock security that his trust fund would pay for. Given Hathorne's wealth, no level of therapeutic care was too costly or too exotic. The family would see that he complied with whatever was necessary, and they agreed to cooperate with any probation rules the court would order.

Joe had to overcome this effort—the family's pledge to sequester Hathorne in the interest of public safety. It was no longer a jury question but rather one for the judge alone. That judge—a small, humorless man named Lance Whitford who looked mole-like behind thick glasses and knew Hathorne's family through social circles—was Hathorne's last hope.

"Dr. Hathorne," Joe said, buttoning his suit jacket as he stood to begin cross-examination, "let's start with some things we can agree on."

"Certainly," Hathorne said with a polite nod. Joe narrowed his eyes and took a single wide step to his left. This moved him from behind counsel table so that he had a clear path to Hathorne.

"You weren't born Aaron Hathorne, were you?" Joe asked. He put minor but clear stress on the first syllable.

"I'm sorry?"

"You were born Aaron Everett *Hawthorne*, weren't you?" The *aw* sound was more apparent.

"I was," Hathorne said without rancor.

He's well prepared, Joe thought. *Because he knows where I'm going.*

"And it was you, as a young man, who changed the spelling, isn't that right?"

"It was me, yes."

"And there was an allusive purpose to it, wasn't there?"

"It was a decision I made, as you yourself alluded to, when I was a young man." Hathorne put a tiny stress on the word "allude."

That's right, Joe thought. *Play with me. You've been prepped not to, but you want to.*

"In fact, you made that decision in reference to a historical event, didn't you?"

"I don't recall every reason now, to be honest."

"The Salem Witch Trials of 1692," Joe said, his eyes narrowing on his subject. "The role of a man named John Hathorne, commonly known as Judge Hathorne."

"Is there a question?" Hathorne asked with an innocent look.

Snark. Just a touch. Here we go.

"Judge Hathorne's actions as part of the Salem Witch Trials," Joe said, looking down through reading glasses at a legal pad. He raised his eyes back to Hathorne. "Is it fair to say that those actions, in history and popular culture, are widely believed to have been sadistic and unjust?"

"They often are, yes."

"I mean, Judge Hathorne is reviled by many for his brutal interrogation tactics, his cruelty to the accused women, correct?"

"I have read as much, yes."

"Right. And Judge Hathorne's actions—his memory—that's what inspired you to change your name, wasn't it?"

"As I said, I don't recall every reason. If you're implying that I was a rebellious young man, I think the record is clear and that I've paid dearly for it."

"You're familiar with Nathaniel Hawthorne, correct?"

"Of course."

"He's no relation to you, though, right?"

"He is not."

"But you wanted to make a point, didn't you, Dr. Hathorne? A statement."

"I may have."

"You wanted to make a point of doing the *opposite* of what Nathaniel Hawthorne is believed to have done, correct?"

"The author Nathaniel Hawthorne published under the original spelling of his name as well. There is speculation as to why he eventually changed the spelling, but no certainty."

"Sir, that's why I said, quote, unquote, 'is believed to have done,'" Joe said. He was staying conciliatory but on the offensive. He slowed his speech. "The statement you wanted to make was based on the common belief, proven or not, that Hawthorne added a 'w' to his name out of shame. Isn't that right?"

"Whatever my reasons were, Mr. DeSantos, I'm sure you'll paint them in the worst possible light today."

Slipping from form. He's getting angry.

"Please answer the question."

"I don't remember entirely." He shifted in the witness chair.

"Nathaniel Hawthorne is *believed* to have been so ashamed of his ancestor's actions in the witch trials that he altered the spelling of his name to distance himself from that figure, correct?"

"I am not a teacher of American literature, but it's a theory, yes."

"Right, because that was your motivation, wasn't it? To make a statement about yourself that was opposite of the one Nathaniel Hawthorne made."

Hathorne's lead attorney, David Mullen, cut in then. "Your Honor, Mr. Hathorne changed his name when he was around twenty years old." Impeccably dressed and manicured, Mullen looked to be in his fifties. "What's the relevance now?"

"It's a dispositional hearing on the respondent's mental state," the judge said. "I'll allow it. But if there's a point, Mr. DeSantos, let's arrive there."

"Of course, Your Honor." Joe turned back to his witness. "You viewed yourself as more of a *Ha*thorne than a *Haw*thorne, didn't you?"

"At one time, I suppose I did."

"And this legal change to your name was a gesture you were proud of, wasn't it?"

"The level to which I felt good about it varied."

"Well, you wrote about it, didn't you, in internet chatrooms?"

"Probably."

"You boasted about it, correct?"

"Not sure how you'd define that."

"It was a goal to which I aspired from the time I began to read Hawthorne," Joe said, raising his voice a touch as he quoted Hathorne from a chatroom transcript that had been intercepted while he was in prison. "'Hathorne the judge was the kind of man I wanted to be. Hawthorne the effete, the abashed, the cringer was not.' You wrote those words, didn't you?"

Hathorne sighed. "I did, yes."

"Within the last year, isn't that right?"

"There is a certain amount of theater played in online communities. Bravado is tossed around here and there. I'd guess if you were trapped as I was in a cell with so little to look forward to, you might—"

"Answer the question, please," the judge said.

"Yes!" Hathorne snapped, his head turning toward the judge. Joe saw his jaw clench.

That's it, Doc. Let go.

"So you looked forward to those online sessions, didn't you, Doctor?"

"What if I did?"

"You can't answer a question with a question," Joe said. "You looked forward to these online sessions in which you bragged about taking on a persona widely considered to be evil, didn't you?"

"You judge me," Hathorne said, the utterance somewhere between a growl and a mumble. His head drooped.

"Excuse me?" Joe asked. His heart picked up a beat.

"You judge me," Hathorne said. His head was still low, but his eyes rose. "What is it *you* look forward to, Joseph DeSantos? Other than your next drink? Will you swear to this court that you haven't had one today?"

"Dr. Hathorne, you cannot pose questions," the judge said. "You must answer Mr. DeSantos's questions; that's all."

"Shall I repeat my original question, Doctor?" Joe asked.

"Drunkard," Hathorne said, nearly spitting it. His breathing became audible, an engine-like pumping of air through old lungs.

The judge spoke next. "Doctor, once again, I—"

Hathorne cut him off by slamming his open hand on the fine wooden frame of the witness box.

"You weak, pathetic sot!" The last word cracked through the air of the old courtroom, echoing up to the rafters. For a moment there was stunned silence. In his peripheral vision, Joe could see Hathorne's lawyers briefly close their eyes.

"I believe your point," the judge said to Joe, "has been made."

CHAPTER 27

Halle Rossi was in desperate need of a pedicure. With her own finger-nails, she was an artist, but her toes were a goddamn pain in the ass. In a red silk robe on her bed, she reached back and pushed the temperature button on the window AC unit down to sixty-eight degrees. A rush of cool air fluttered the hair, black and baby fine, around her face. She tightened the robe as she reached for her left foot again, a tiny glistening brush in hand. The color was Lincoln Park After Dark.

"Ugh, you *fucker*," she breathed. She could reach her feet well enough, but the act of brushing on nail polish was not something she could accomplish without getting it all over the place. She put the capped brush back in the bottle on her nightstand and lay back on her bed.

Queen size, the bed dominated her studio apartment. Halle was fond of saying that she had the smallest rental in the city, which of course she didn't, but it *was* unusually tiny, particularly for a seaside neighbor-hood way out in Brooklyn. She was born and raised in Sheepshead Bay, a little pocket of narrow streets and row houses east of the Coney Island strip, and she still lived there. After a century and a half of working-class life, it was pockmarked with a slowly evolving array of chain stores, pizza joints, Russian baths, churches, and synagogues.

Her parents still lived a few blocks away in a lovely house they had begged her to return to after law school, but she was twenty-six, and that was the last thing she wanted. She had no desire to be in Manhattan, though, as so many of her girlfriends and classmates did. She was a Brooklyn girl, and she loved her second-floor nook, one of four little apartments in a square brick building on a quiet street. What she loved most was the little rectangular balcony where she could stand and smell the ocean while she watered her plants.

The clock over the TV, opposite the bed, struck twelve and emitted a low clang. Under her thigh and just south of the crotch panel on her underwear, her cell phone vibrated, sending a little tingle through her midsection. *Whoo!* She scooped it up and opened it with her thumb.

Holly what up? It was her friend Ronit. Like everyone else in her life other than her parents and Joe, Ronit knew her as Holly.

In bed. U?

not even midnight come out

wtf no way. we'll hang tmrw

come on

gt bed

whatev

tmrw

She sealed the exchange with two red high-heeled shoe emojis. Then she turned toward her balcony door, which was a few feet to the left of the window that held the AC unit. Something was making a tapping sound on the glass of the balcony door. Or maybe it was a scratching sound; she couldn't tell.

The door was an unusually beautiful piece, with a lacquered wood frame and a full-length glass panel. It was the creation of the owner of the building, a red-faced Italian man who made wine in his basement and treated Halle like a granddaughter. She turned off the AC unit so that the room was quiet. At first, there was nothing. Then she heard it again, something between a tap and a scratch, like a tree branch brushing against the glass. Except there was no tree in reach of the glass. With a crook of her head, she sat up and swung her legs over to the floor. Seconds passed with just the hum of the refrigerator in the kitchenette. Nothing else.

She hooked her phone to its charger and went to wash her face before bed. The bathroom was through a narrow door to the right. An old wooden crucifix hung just next to it. Halle blew a kiss toward it as she approached the bathroom.

There it was again.

Scritch, scritch.

She turned and walked back toward the balcony door. The glare didn't allow for much of a view outside, but she could see her potted plants on the right side: a coleus, a heart of Jesus, and some impatiens, limp in the summer heat. She placed her fingertips on the glass.

Scritch.

She heard it for a split second, down and to the left. She looked in that direction but couldn't see a thing. She had some begonias on that side. Could be there was a bird on the balcony, some stray gull or an ugly blackbird. They might peck at the flowers. Or maybe it was a cat. It wasn't hard to reach her balcony. A cat could almost jump to it from the ground. She stood back, straining to get a view, but saw nothing. She paused and then opened the door a few inches. Hot, damp air rushed in, the kind that would frizz her hair in seconds. She poked her head out and looked down.

A big hand grabbed a fistful of her hair and slammed her face into the doorjamb. Too shocked to form a scream, she let out something between a cry and a moan. Her face felt like it had been split down the middle, her eye socket like a thin shard of glass had been jammed through it. Her left hand, still inside, splayed against the wall. Her right hand clutched the doorknob.

She felt the attacker's grip loosen, then close again around more of her hair. In a reflex, she yanked her head back and lost a clump, pulled from her scalp like patches of grass. In a ballerina twist she spun around and flung herself into the apartment, her hands reaching forward like a drowning person's. The red robe flew open, exposing her breasts and the rounded curve of her stomach, dwarfing the baby-blue panty triangle beneath.

She lurched a step forward. The attacker's big hand found purchase again, this time like pincers on her neck. She gagged and felt him draw close. She could almost smell him now, an earthy scent like wet cement. His other hand slid across her stomach. The sensation of spreading fingers over her body made her want to retch. Instead, she drew a breath to scream. He moved the gripping right hand around to her throat and choked the scream quiet. Then he pushed her through the door and bumped it shut behind them both.

Panic crawled up Halle's belly, a blooming sensation like she'd been plunged into cold water. The last thing she focused on was the ancient wooden crucifix—her grandmother's—the one that opened in the back to reveal holy water, two candles, and crumpled, yellowed directions for last rites. Crazily, she remembered in that moment how weirded out she and her grade-school friends had been when they first discovered that the wooden back slid open to unveil such creepy stuff inside: the vial, the curled paper, the thin, white candles.

She reached for the crucifix in those last seconds, her eyes like saucers. The man gripped her shoulder with his left hand, felt for her jaw with his right, and wrenched her head back as far as he could manage with a savage twist. There was a sickening series of snaps, like breaking wishbones.

Then the darkness around Hallelujah Rossi ate her whole.

CHAPTER 28

There was no headboard on the dead woman's bed, just a mattress and box spring pushed against the wall. She had a wealth of pillows, though, including an embroidered one with the names of twenty Brooklyn neighborhoods stitched over its surface. Above that pillow, on the yellowing plaster wall itself, was a message, written out in OPI's Lincoln Park After Dark nail lacquer:

HOLLY

FWYDTM

The letters were neatly painted, the width of the polish brush and maybe a half inch or more in height. They seemed to magnify in flashes as the crime scene unit snapped pictures. The duty lieutenant from the Sixty-First Precinct, a tall, lanky, mustachioed Black man named Goodridge, stood between the kitchenette and the bed and cursed under his breath.

"I hate this shit," he said. Beside him was a Six-One detective, the one most likely to catch the case. He was short with a pink face and a baby-fine buzz cut. His name was Brad Gallagher.

"What shit?"

"This shit. Clown car, freak show . . . what the fuck?"

Gallagher grunted something in reply. Outside the tiny apartment in the hallway, the neighbors were wailing like professional Sicilian mourners—another thing Goodridge had to deal with. It was making canvassing almost impossible. Everyone was hysterical, and so far no one had reported seeing a thing. They were also exchanging observations and stories and getting lost in each other's shock. The dead woman's landlord, in particular, was a complete mess.

Her body was splayed out on the floor. She should have been facedown, but her head was turned at a hideous angle to her body. The robe was still on, hiked up so that her backside was exposed, covered only by a blue thong. It was a grim example of the indignities of violence, even in death. The crime scene unit and MLI techs moved around the place like ants. It occurred to Goodridge that there had probably never been as many people in this space as there was now.

"No signs of forced entry on the door to the balcony," Gallagher said. He had sauntered away but was back. Goodridge sighed. She had been found by a friend who had keys and hadn't heard from her all day despite a slew of messages. The friend had turned both locks, including a dead bolt, to open the front door, so unless the killer had his own keys, that wasn't how he had left.

"Great," Goodridge said, rubbing his forehead with a thumb and forefinger. "Okay, so maybe she let him in and locked the door behind them. Then, after he greased her, he went out the back door. Just shut it behind him and jumped."

"It's possible," Gallagher said. "Or maybe he climbed up. There's all sorts of shit to climb up on back there. It wouldn't be hard to get to that balcony. Who knows? Maybe she called him up, like Rapunzel or some shit."

"You can't even spell 'Rapunzel.'"

"Whatever. I know the story. Look, it's obvious that he knew her, right? Writin' her name in fuckin' nail polish, holy shit. Gotta be an old boyfriend or some shit. You're right, though, this is weird. Those letters on the wall? What the fuck is that?"

"What about family?" Goodridge asked, ignoring the immediate question. "What do we know?"

"They're in Paris," Gallagher said, as if that were both weird and extra awful.

"Paris?"

"Vacation. That's what the friend said, the girl who found her. One of the neighbors backs it up too. Fuckin' A. So we gotta call someone over there to notify?"

"We'll let the command decide that," Goodridge said. He paused, his mind clicking back to something he remembered in conversation in the squad room. Those strange, seemingly nonsense letters painted on the wall—hadn't there been some other fucked-up case that had come down earlier that month in which a woman's neck had been broken in a similar manner? The head wrenched back? Something around Coney Island? His eyes lit up.

"That freak-show case in the Six-Oh a couple weeks ago—know what I'm talkin' about?" Gallagher thought for a moment.

"Old lady on the beach, yeah."

"Who caught that?"

"Ugh . . . shit, I know her. Six-Oh. She's like . . . a little fireplug. Zochi something. I can find out."

"Do that. And get her over here."

CHAPTER 29

Sunday, July 30, 2017
Marine Basin Marina
Brooklyn
7:45 a.m.

Another dream of floating down a river in darkness. Water was lapping against the boat, except it wasn't a boat—it was the family LTD. He was in the station wagon in the back seat, and Robbie was up front driving, but not really driving because neither of them was in control of the car. It just drifted along. It was hot. So hot. There was a sound that they were floating toward, a rushing, churning sound.

Joe woke up soaked in sweat and feeling like he'd passed out in a steam room. His breathing was labored, his mouth sticky and dry. He rubbed his eyes and felt the room tip slightly, then right itself. The confines were cramped. He was on his boat.

Jesus, how the hell did I end up here?

The interior of the cabin cruiser took shape around him. He was lying on the starboard bunk facing the rear sliding door and the stern. He swung his feet over to the cabin sole and stared pitifully at a group of empty bottles, clinking against each other as the boat rocked in the wakes of early departing fishing boats. He could hear men speaking in

Spanish and a few local guys barking back and forth about what they were going to catch.

How long have I been here?

He was clad in only a frayed pair of cargo shorts. The shirt he'd been wearing was in his lap, sweaty and balled up. He shook it out, then did a double take and held it up with both hands. It wasn't a shirt at all. It was a skimpy, mostly see-through black cover-up that Halle had left on the boat. She had worn it over a bathing suit most of the time, or thrown on after sex when they were down below the season before, the summer of 2016. He laid it aside and stood up, placing a steadying hand on the cabin top.

He was fishing a bottle of water out of the icebox when he saw Detective Hernandez and another cop he didn't recognize pause on the dock. Joe always backed in, so the dock was just a step beyond the stern platform, where he kept a couple of rickety wooden chairs and a little table. He thought about tossing the cover-up forward into the V-berth up front, but he left it where it was for the time being. He fished around for his boat shoes.

"Detective Hernandez?" he asked, sliding the glass door open.

"Joe, we need to talk," she said. Her face was grim, and the guy with her seemed jacked up. He kept his eyes glued to Joe, tracking his every movement.

"Let me grab a T-shirt," he said. "I'll be right out. Come aboard if you want; there's some shade here." Joe ducked back inside. Now he did stuff the cover-up into one of the drawers in the V-berth. He pulled on a white T-shirt. When he emerged, Hernandez had stepped aboard the boat and sat on one of the gunwales closest to the stern. The male detective stayed on the dock, his feet shoulder-width apart. He looked cautious, ready for anything.

"I'm sorry. I just woke up." His eyes moved from Hernandez to the male detective and back. "Is everything okay?"

"We need to know where you were last night, Joe," Hernandez said. "Holly Rossi was murdered."

After a few moments, the male detective, named Gallagher, seemed to tire of the sunlight and stepped aboard. He rested his butt against the gunwale on the other side of the boat from Hernandez and folded his arms. His eyes mostly stayed on Joe but slid about to various things around the boat—the old five-gallon fish bucket, some coiled dock line.

"You need to think, Joe," Hernandez said. "Think about where you were all night. This is very serious for you."

"I . . . I must have been here," he said, shaking his head for the hundredth time. "At least after some point." He was beyond bewildered. It wasn't really sinking in, though—not like it would in a few hours.

Halle.

Dead.

Murdered.

It would get in, though, and it would shatter him. In the meantime, he was a prime suspect. Underneath all that, still scratching through, was the image he knew he was projecting, sitting potbellied in shorts and a T-shirt like some piece of trailer trash, unable to explain his whereabouts because of a half dozen mismatched bottles behind him.

"That's not good enough," Hernandez said. She spoke low and smooth, but there was something blunt and steely underneath it. "I know you cared for her. Now something terrible has happened to her, and we need to figure out what."

"I just saw her," he said, aware of how spaced out he probably sounded. "I mean . . . for the first time in months."

"What day was that?"

"The day I found out Lois was dead. Saturday, I guess. The fifteenth. She went with me to identify the body."

"How did she know about your mother's death?" She was taking notes.

He sighed. "I had called her . . . a few hours before. I . . . I didn't *remember* calling her, because I was drunk, but that's what happened. I called her after you found me, you and the other detective."

"Detective Dougherty," she said.

"Yes, exactly. Anyway, I don't remember making the call, but she was at my house the next day, around 11:45 a.m. We spent a few hours together, went to OCME, and then had lunch. When we got home, my brother, Robbie, was there, waiting for me. She left. Robbie and I talked for a few minutes. He wanted to give me some money for the cremation costs."

"Did you see Miss Rossi again after that?"

"No."

"Did you speak, text, or communicate at all after that?"

"No."

"Why not?"

"There was nothing to say. It was over between us a while ago. She was just . . . being Halle. Being a really good friend." Now it was starting—just starting—to sink through him. This vivacious, funny, flinty, wonderful woman was dead. He squeezed his eyes shut.

"You're sure about that?" Gallagher asked. It was the first time he had asked a question.

"Honestly, I'm not sure about anything," Joe said, spitting it out without thinking. His head was spinning, his heart breaking. "I mean, look around. I've got bottles everywhere. I'm a sweaty, stinking mess. And you're telling me Halle's dead?" His breaths were coming faster and sharper. He was angry, he was sad, he was *pathetic*. He slammed his hand on the little table.

"Hey," Gallagher said, battle-ready rigid in the blink of an eye, "stay calm." Joe lifted the hand from the table and placed it in his lap with the other one. He sat before them like a chastened child, drowning in shame, fear, and budding grief.

Slipping through circles of hell, that's what this is. Just slid through four, now down to five.

"You'll have to come with us," Hernandez said. "We'll talk more at the precinct. I know this is awful, Joe, and I'm sorry. But you really need to think about what happened last night—where you were and why. Go ahead and gather your keys and such. We'll wait here."

You really need to think about what happened. And why.

This, he figured, was Hernandez's next move, after asking for the simple alibi he could not provide. At first she seemed sympathetic, just trying to help Joe clear himself. Joe couldn't help with that, though, so maybe she was starting to see things differently. Maybe he, Joseph DeSantos, deserved to be a prime murder suspect after all.

As far as they're concerned, maybe I did it.

Yes, as far as they're concerned.

CHAPTER 30

Zochi's neck and back ached. The day had been endless, beginning with the predawn search for DeSantos, and it wasn't over yet. It was nearly dark out, the last of the light fading in a baked sky. Joe had been in an interview room, just off the squad room at the Six-One, for more than ten hours, with just a few breaks. He had not cracked, and no arrest warrant had been issued. There wasn't enough evidence yet.

A little before 9:00 p.m., Brad Gallagher, the Six-One detective, walked Joe out of the precinct, releasing him with the usual "don't leave town." Joe nodded and padded off down the block like he was going to walk home, which maybe he was. Like most people who had been through the relative torture of an all-day interview as a murder suspect, Joe seemed enervated and a little loopy. He was sad, too, Zochi could tell. Really sad, like a part of him was dying as the reality of Holly's death sank in.

He's guilty. Keep your eyes open.

She was doing that, searching for the thing that would make her 100 percent on him as a suspect. It had been her job to break Joe during that long, hot day. The squad lieutenant had insisted that she stay in the room with him, and to his credit, Gallagher seemed to have no problem letting her lead the interrogation. Joe hadn't broken, though. He wasn't admitting anything, but he also hadn't tossed out something desperate and plausible, like "Oh, wait—I *do* remember where I was around midnight." Nothing like that. He made no excuses. He was drunk and blacked out all night; that was all he could offer.

The last thing he remembered for sure was being at a bar called Greeley's, the same place where Zochi and Len had found him the night after his mother's body was discovered. Greeley's was maybe two miles west of Holly's apartment, between her apartment building and Joe's house. Zochi had a couple of Six-One guys head out to Greeley's to check this out. An hour later, she had the answer she expected. Yes, he had been at Greeley's. But they had him leaving there around 11:00 or 11:15 p.m. Surveillance video there would confirm it.

Holly's last communication, Zochi said to Joe, had been long after that, although she didn't tell him exactly how long, which was around an hour. So, she explained, it would have taken him thirty-five, maybe forty, minutes to walk from Greeley's over to her apartment, assuming he didn't take a cab or a car. And if he did, they'd figure it out eventually.

So, Joe, really? You don't remember anything?

No, he did not, and there was no guile about him. No shifting eyes, as if searching his head for something that might be helpful. None of the opposite either: the vomiting of scenarios, possibilities, and stories in hope that something will hit the wall and stick.

Maybe you walked by her place, though, or just in that direction? Maybe you were in her neighborhood, just for old times' sake. I mean, you had just seen her. So maybe you wandered? It happens. I mean, if there's video of you on those streets, Joe, we're going to find it.

Rather than flatly denying any of that, which she had expected and which she probably would have done herself in his shoes, he had just shrugged. No, he didn't think he had. He never walked very far to begin with, and he certainly didn't make a habit of going by his ex-girlfriend's place. He respected her decisions and her distance. Yes, he had loved seeing her after Lois's body had been found. He had been grateful for their time together that day. He knew what it was, though—an act of friendship, nothing more—and he had no intention of trying to follow up, let alone walk over to where she lived.

But could he swear to it? Well, no. He just didn't remember. The whole night was black. Most of Thursday night was gone also. He knew a few things he had done on Friday, earlier in the day. He had been hungover. He had gone to the liquor store. By evening he was deep in a bottle, then headed over to Greeley's just for a change of pace. Next thing he knew, he was waking up on his boat. That, he maintained, happened regularly during the months the boat was in the water. If he was going to wander, that's the direction he'd go in, and apparently he had. That was all he could say.

In a way, Zochi felt that she shouldn't have been surprised. Joe DeSantos was not her typical interviewee. He was not a gangbanging kid trying to sound tougher than he was or some fuckhead wife killer or baby shaker, figuring his bullshit and swagger would work on her like it did helpless family members. Joe was a veteran criminal practitioner. He had seen both sides, and he knew cop psychology. She tried to adjust for that. She wasn't acting like she was still on his side, trying to find the murderer of the woman he seemed to refer to only as Lois. Instead, she went at him as neutrally as she could muster. It boiled down to this:

We talked, you and me. We had a moment, even, while digging through your boxed-up childhood. But let's not bullshit each other. I have a job to do. I'm focused on you now, and you know it. So one of two things happens. Either you crack and fold—start sobbing and tell me you snapped and murdered your ex-lover, maybe even your mother too—or you at least allow for the possibility. And then things start to unravel. Maybe you try to play crackerjack attorney and outfox me at my own game. I'll see that, though, and take note of it.

The highest hope from the division on down was that Detective Xochitl Hernandez would close two major murder cases that day. She would break the drunken middle-aged lawyer suspect and reveal him to be some unhinged rage machine under his sad-sack exterior.

That had not happened.

Right. So why I am not more pissed off?

It was a fair question. Zochi was humble. She worked to live and not the other way around, but she had an ego like anyone else. If Joe was the guy, she would have *loved* to have broken him into confessing. She'd be more than the Queen of Brooklyn South for a few weeks, soaking up attaboys from inspectors and deputy chiefs. She might actually be in line for a promotion to first-grade detective—the very top—or at least to some plush assignment. In NYPD parlance, it was "the Door," the case that took you to the next level. Today had not opened the Door, but she wasn't entirely sure that was a bad thing.

Why? Because she wasn't certain, not 100 percent, that Joe was the guy. It looked right, sure. She understood why everyone was so excited to nab Joe for both Lois *and* Holly. It wasn't just a rush to close a case; it made sense. The vast majority of murders are committed by perpetrators who know their victims. In this case, two women with clear connections to Joe—and possible conflicts with him as well—were dead. Both women had their heads wrenched back, their necks broken. And, Joe could offer no alibi for either murder.

It's just a matter of time, Gallagher had said, patting her on the back after Joe had finally gathered his belongings from the desk sergeant and scuttled off. *We'll scour his phone. We'll look at a million fuckin' cameras. We'll nail him, Hernandez. You did good today.*

Yeah, maybe.

The last thing she had gotten from Joe was a DNA "exemplar," meaning a sample of his own genetic material. Joe had given it willingly. He knew the process anyway and didn't pretend like it was a mystery. She handed him the swab, about seven inches long and tipped with cotton. He ran it along the inside of his cheek, then dropped it into the evidence bag she held with gloved hands.

That process, Zochi thought, might have produced some fresh doubt or anxiety in Joe as a suspect. Plenty of guys talked tough and seemed as carefree as songbirds throughout a long interrogation, only to start sweating and backpedaling when it came time to provide what most people assumed was better than magic. Providing a DNA sample was as good as turning your entire identity over to the police. But like pretty much everything else that day, Joe had done it without hesitation or any hint of rancor.

The long day finally over, she stood out in front of the Six-One, a forgettable square brick building that looked like a '70s medical office. She texted her daughter, telling her she'd be home in an hour. Today had been rough, but tomorrow would be worse. There was one thing Zochi had told Joe that, for all his stoicism, produced a look of horror and almost startling grief. Holly Rossi's mother and father were back from Paris. Zochi would be meeting with them in Mimi's office the next afternoon.

CHAPTER 31

"We were waiting for room service," the man was saying. He was Sal Rossi, Holly's father. He and Holly's mother, Linda, sat in two chairs facing Mimi Bromowitz's desk while Zochi sat a few feet away, her hands between her knees. Mimi was behind the desk, and before the couple had arrived, she had taken everything off it—other than a box of tissues—so that she wouldn't be tempted to look away from them. Zochi admired that.

Sal looked older than Zochi expected, although part of that was probably shock and exhaustion. From what she knew, they hadn't really slept since the news reached them in Paris on Sunday morning.

"There was a knock on the door. That's what I thought it was, you know?" Sal let out a slight chortle that Zochi sensed could have evolved into a full-throated sob, but it was cut short. "Room service. Instead, it was a Parisian detective in a yellow windbreaker, there to tell me that my daughter had been murdered."

His eyes, swollen and red, searched Zochi's with a combination of disbelief and desperation. She held his gaze and waited, unsure if she was projecting some measure of empathy or just blankness. Eventually, Sal's gaze moved to Mimi, who could only do the same thing. Sal had a large, rounded nose and a bushy gray mustache. To Zochi he looked kind, the type who once laughed easily. Linda looked younger and had been pretty once, with small, delicate features and light hair. She clutched the arms of her chair and sat portrait still, as if moving would shatter her like an ice sculpture.

"Do you think she suffered?" Linda asked, her voice low and raspy. Her eyes, dark pools of suffering, moved back and forth between the two women.

"Lin, don't—" Sal started.

"Let me ask, please." The eyes bore into Mimi's. "There was an autopsy; you must have an idea." Mimi paused, and Zochi held her breath. It was an easy question to answer with a lie, but Mimi didn't look like much of a liar.

"I think she was very frightened for a few seconds," Mimi said. "There was an initial blow to her face, but then her neck was broken. To the medical examiner, it looked like it happened very fast." Zochi let the breath go. Mimi had handled that about as well as possible.

"Do you think he . . . did sexual things to her?" she asked, this time to Zochi. Sal put his hand on her arm, but she pulled the arm out from under it, moving something other than her mouth and eyes for the first time since she'd sat down.

"No," Zochi said. "There was no evidence of that. Like ADA Bromowitz said, it happened very fast. She was surprised by the intruder, probably. He left quickly."

"She was all alone," Linda whispered.

In the end, aren't we all? Zochi thought.

"I guess I'm not sure why we're here," Sal said, breaking the silence. "If there isn't a suspect yet, there isn't a court case, right?"

Mimi nodded. "There isn't an arrested suspect, but we think your daughter's case could be related to another case."

"Oh my God," Linda said, the last word almost a sob. "Oh my God, another one?"

"We don't know if they're connected," Mimi said. "If it's determined that they are, we want to know early so we can respond in a coordinated way."

"What connects them?" Sal asked. "Was the other person a young girl also?" The "girl" came out just short of *goyl*. Mimi glanced at Zochi.

"No, she was an older woman," Zochi said. "There's no obvious connection between her and your daughter, but . . . there is a man who knew them both."

"A man?" Linda asked. "What man?"

"His name is Joseph DeSantos," Zochi said. "We believe Mr. DeSantos's mother was the older woman who was found . . . the way your daughter was found."

"Oh my God," Linda said again. She looked a little faint. "Joe?"

"Did you know him?" Zochi asked. She took out a notepad.

Sal looked foggy and confused. "Joe? He was her boyfriend for a time." He looked at Linda. "Not for a while now, though, right?"

"Yes," Linda said. Clearly she was the parent who was closest to Holly. That wasn't surprising, but there were mother-daughter relationships that were closer than others. It was heartbreaking but obvious to Zochi that Linda had been very close to her daughter. The two had talked probably every day. She could just tell.

"Do you remember when they stopped seeing each other?" Mimi asked.

"It was early October, last year," Linda said, confirming everything Zochi had suspected. *They talked all the time. Like friends.* "We didn't approve. Joe was much older, but he seemed like a nice man. She always went for men who were older."

"I see," Mimi said. She also seemed to sense that mother and daughter were tight. "Mrs. Rossi, did your daughter talk to you about the relationship?"

"She did, yes. Like I said, we didn't approve. He was very good to her, but . . ." She trailed off.

"It's okay to tell us," Mimi said. "I hope you understand why we need to know."

"Joe drank," Linda said, as if throwing a phrase aside she no longer wanted to think about. "She tried to help him with it, but it didn't get better. She ended the relationship last fall because of it. She said Joe took it very well, though. I can't imagine he would hurt her. I mean . . ."

"We don't know anything for sure," Mimi said and gave a nod to Zochi, as if to hand things off to her.

"That's right," Zochi said. "We're looking at everything. Did you ever meet Joe in person?"

"Once," Linda said. "He came to the house for a Labor Day block party. He was nice."

"Respectful," Sal said to no one in particular, as if he had reflected on it for some time.

"Yes," Linda said. "It was awkward, though, and he knew it. He's closer in age to us than he is to—" she lurched forward and gripped her stomach. For a moment Zochi thought Linda might throw up, but that didn't happen. She just doubled over and sobbed.

"It's okay," Mimi said, just above a whisper. Sal put a hand over his eyes and heaved quietly. "It's okay."

Linda seemed to pull herself together and sat up straight.

"I'm sorry," she said. Sal swiped his face with a big hand, as if wiping the tears back into his head.

"Please don't be," Mimi said. "We're so sorry to be asking these questions. We just want to find the person who did this to your daughter."

"This other case," Sal said, "Joe's mother? We don't know anything about her, but has it been in the news, like our Hallelujah's case?"

"Not prominently, no," Mimi said, and Zochi could tell she was stepping carefully. No one in KCDA or the NYPD wanted the press to connect the two cases yet, but it was inevitable. There had been some small takes already from crime-beat writers in the local papers about an old woman, probably homeless, found on the beach at Coney Island.

"But . . . an old woman?" Sal asked. "I mean, the city isn't like it used to be. That kind of thing doesn't happen much, does it?"

"Well, no," Mimi said, "but—"

"Was she at home?"

"She wasn't," Mimi said, looking to Zochi like she was unsure of what to say. "We don't know where she lived. She was estranged from Joe. I'm not sure if you knew that. They had not seen each other in many years."

"We didn't know much about him," Sal said with a shrug. He looked over at Linda for confirmation.

"No, not much," she said. "Halle talked to me about Joe but not about his family. Really what she told me was that he didn't have a family. He had an uncle he was close to, but he died a long time ago."

"That's our understanding also," Mimi said. "He has a brother, a few years older. We're talking to him too. Again, we don't know if the cases are connected, but we'll do everything we can to find out,"

"Thank you," Linda said. Her brow knitted, like something had just occurred to her. "There was a message left, right? Something written on the wall above her bed?"

"There was," Zochi said. Another thing clear to her was that Linda, not Sal, led this couple in everything they did. "There was her name and then some letters. The spelling of the name, though—"

"You mean 'Holly,'" Linda said. "Like the Christmas plant."

"Yes. H-O-L-L-Y. I've been referring to her that way."

"Everyone called her Holly," Linda said. "She didn't like her real name. People had trouble spelling it, even saying it, sometimes. Hallelujah."

"I know that feeling," Zochi said.

"Well, we shortened it to Halle, like H-A-L-L-Y, but she goes by Holly. Her friends call her that. Well . . . called." She swallowed audibly and stared as if into the barrel of a gun.

"Do you know if Joe called her Holly?" Zochi asked. Her detective haunches were up. She didn't want to seem like she was interrogating Linda, but this seemed important.

Linda seemed to mull it over. "You know, he didn't. He liked calling her by her real name. I remember Halle telling me once, he thought it was special. Hallelujah. We thought so too."

"It's a lovely name," Mimi said. "Different."

"It was in my family," Sal said. "She had a hard time with it, I guess."

"For almost everyone, it was Holly," Linda said, as if to close off any reminiscing or discussion about the naming of Hallelujah or what it could possibly mean now. "For Joe, though, it was Halle. There was a difference in how he pronounced it."

Zochi was about to speak but then clamped down on it. She had some thinking to do about the name thing. Better, for now, to just think.

CHAPTER 32

Bay Thirty-Fourth Street
Bath Beach, Brooklyn
10:50 p.m.

Joe had worked with a couple of people who had kicked heroin over the years. One was a witness in a gang case, the most high-profile one Joe had handled in the Bronx DA's office. It was a murder-for-hire prosecution, and the nineteen-year-old eyewitness—Hector—had been the bagman between the gang leader and the hitman. Hector was willing to testify, but he had to "kick" first, and Hector was intent on "kicking" in his own way. It was the old-school, neighborhood way.

That process, Joe learned, was a horror in and of itself, and he hadn't been certain Hector would survive it. Rather than something hospital based and methadone driven, it happened in an abandoned apartment building in the Four-Two Precinct with the doors and windows boarded up. The attending "medical" person was an old woman who sat outside and heard the screams and the curses, and came in to clean up puke and shit and maybe dab a forehead with a wet towel. The old woman was a legend in the South Bronx neighborhood but had no friends. She looked and spoke like a witch, and people stayed away from her. But when it came to kicking, if a person was serious, that person went to her.

Joe's issue was alcohol, but still he wished he had that woman by his side. He had emptied or broken every liquor, wine, and beer bottle in the house, down to a couple of forgotten bottles of bitters. He had gone down to the boat and done the same thing, pouring anything that was left over the side and into the bay. Some of it, the breaking of whiskey and wine bottles that were collectible, expensive, and—in some cases—of real sentimental value, felt like self-injury. He felt a bad tingling in his hands at times as he poured out the contents and smashed the bottles, sweeping up the glass. His stomach clenched at the thought of it, but now there was nothing to drink in his immediate reach.

The really scary thing was not knowing what came next, after three or four days. He knew you weren't supposed to think about it that way. *One day at a time.* It was nearly impossible, though, not to play out a string of them in search of the other side of this, whatever it would be.

Sobriety, goddamn it! Once and for all.

Whatever comes next, it's got to be that.

That was true. Dry had never been enough; it was time to push back against the ancient juggernaut of drunk logic at last. No more spinning them in his own head, those soothing, serpent-at-the-tree arguments, the kind he could effortlessly shut down if he heard them made in a courtroom.

He thought again about Hector, the skinny, smiling kid who had done what he said he'd do and kicked heroin. Joe never got to meet the witchy woman Hector had gone to, the one he credited with getting him across that miserable first line. But Joe willed that woman to his side now in the form of an angel, a saint, his own dead mother, whatever he could summon. He might end up needing her very much.

CHAPTER 33

"W-who are you?" *Robbie said. Joe fell behind him.* "Why are you in the woods?"

"We're on a path," *the voice said. Robbie didn't seem poised to run, so Joe stayed put also. The voice was steadying and reassuring.* "It's okay. There are quite a few paths through here. This is Riverside Park. We're almost to where you are. Give us a few seconds. We can lead you out."

Joe saw the dog first. It was a big, dark creature with ears that pointed up. The dog's eyes were round, bright, and alert, even in the darkness. Joe could make out a harness strapped to the animal, and attached to that was a short leather leash. The leash was wrapped securely around a man's hand. The man was white and balding with bushy eyebrows and a big nose. He looked a little goofy in a sweaty Hawaiian shirt, baggy shorts like Joe and Robbie's father once wore, and loafers with black socks. He had dark glasses on.

"I'm Bertie," *he said.* "This is Penny." *He paused a few feet from the boys. Beside him, the dog sat and stared at them. Joe could see it now, the black path the man was on that led into a wood. "How many of you are there? I heard two of you."*

"Just us two," Robbie said. "We're trying to get up to the street."

"Broadway," Bertie said. "That's where the traffic is moving. Yes, it's your best bet. I can show you out. You boys sound young. Are you lost?"

"Not really," Robbie said. Joe was terrifically glad he wasn't having to call the shots about whether to engage with this stranger or run from him like the coughing, screaming thing in the tunnel. The man in front of them seemed okay, though, just a funny-looking older man out for a walk. He was clearly blind; Joe had learned about "Seeing Eye dogs" in school, and this poised, sculpted-looking animal was definitely one of them.

"Is Penny a German shepherd?" Joe asked. He had seen pictures of those in school too. Fearsome, strong-looking dogs.

"Good guess," Bertie said. "Yes, Penny is a shepherd." At the sound of her name, Penny looked up at Bertie. Her tail wagged minutely. "She's sweet, but she can be tough. She takes care of me out here." Now he tugged on the leash just a tiny bit, toward the top of the hill where the traffic was moving. Instantly, Penny stood and began walking at a relaxed, easy pace along the path. Robbie and Joe looked at each other and then fell in behind the man and the dog. It got darker as trees closed in on the path.

"Uh, sir?" Robbie said, his voice hesitant. "Is that a Seeing Eye dog?"

"Bingo," Bertie said, speaking to the side as they walked along. "I'm as blind as a bat. Have been all my life."

"Wow," Joe said, barely a whisper. Bertie chuckled, and Joe was surprised and embarrassed to think he'd heard the remark. Off the path, there were sounds from time to time, mostly human. Coughing, laughter, curses. Joe kept his eyes on what he could make out of the path, his heart thumping. He was able to see more than before, though, and slowly he was getting a sense of where they were. It was a park between the river and the city, he figured. There wasn't much use in peering much farther ahead, so he kept pace behind Robbie, Bertie, and Penny.

"How old are you boys?" Bertie asked. "I don't mean to sound pedantic, but it's dangerous out here. I mean all the time, not just tonight. Especially tonight, though."

"I'm fifteen," Robbie said. "Um, my name is Robert. My brother, Joseph, is ten. We . . . we lost track of our mom. We're trying to find her."

Bertie turned his head to the side. "You lost track of her?"

"Kind of," Robbie said. "We're hoping we can find a police officer, maybe. To help us look for her." In front of them, Penny paused as they came to a street at the end of the path. Bertie lifted his chin a little, then tugged on the leash, and Penny got moving. Joe looked with wonder as Penny deftly stepped off the curb and onto the dark street. Bertie did the same while the dog seemed to wait for him.

"That's a good idea," Bertie said, "but there's a blackout happening, and they're going to be busy." He turned back toward them. "You know what I mean, right?"

"The whole city?" Robbie asked.

"That's what George Michael is saying."

"Who's—" Joe started and then stopped himself. For some weird reason he felt awkward and silly around the man and the dog, but he was deeply impressed with both.

"He's a radio broadcaster," Bertie said. "WABC. Lovely voice. They don't need that echo, though. He sounds like he's in a tunnel. Anyway, yes, the whole city, apparently, and some of Westchester. It's going to be a long night. This is Riverside Drive, by the way. We're going to walk to the corner of Seventy-Ninth. My building is right there. You will walk up the hill to Broadway from there."

"Are you out here helping people?" Joe asked, a sudden burst of courage encouraging him to speak. They walked past ornate, old-looking buildings with thick stonework and curved windows. To Joe they looked like something out of an old, scary storybook.

"Well, we are, sort of," Bertie said. "We don't usually go into the park after dark. It's just not very safe down here these days. We heard the news,

though, and we decided to take a walk and see if anyone was just kind of stuck down here in the dark." It took Joe a few seconds to realize that when Bertie said "we," he meant Penny and him. Up ahead, he could make out a dead streetlamp, overhead wires, and equally dead traffic lights. They were near the corner. "It didn't take us long before we heard you two. Was there someone there under the overpass?"

"Yeah," Robbie said, his voice low. "A really scary guy. I don't know how you can walk around out here, mister."

"Oh, we don't, generally, at night. Light and dark are nothing to me, of course, but I know what it's like when the sun goes down. Frankly, it's not much better during the day. I think tonight will be very scary, though, for people who can see and now all of a sudden just can't. How about you two? Is it better now?"

"It's getting better," Robbie said. "When a car goes by, we can see stuff, but then it's harder to see after."

"I can see a lot more stuff now," Joe said, wondering if he was talking out of turn.

"You're closer to ambient light and car traffic now," Bertie said. He stopped at the corner of Riverside and Seventy-Ninth Street, and Penny sat. "You'll be okay. The parks are the worst, especially that one right by the water. When there's no light out there and no moon? Forget it. You're as blind as I am."

"We were," Robbie said. "Um, I mean, thanks for helping us."

"Penny loves to do her part," he said and smiled. The smile faded. "Go straight up this street. It's a major one that goes both ways, east and west. When you get to Broadway, you'll probably see people, hopefully some police, and there should be plenty of traffic, so enough headlights to see by. But what Robert says is correct. They ruin your night vision. Or so I'm told."

"We'll remember that," Joe said. His heart was swelling a little bit. He imagined telling the story of the dark night and the man and the dog to his classmates come fall. Then again, he couldn't picture what that would look

like, because he had no idea where they would end up. "Thanks, Bertie. And Penny."

"Yeah, thanks again," Robbie said.

"Good luck finding your mother," Bertie said. "Be careful and stick together, whatever you do."

"Are you going home?" Joe asked, looking around at the dark buildings.

"We're going to take another pass through the park, but I'm not sure how much I want to press our luck. At least this far west things are mostly quiet. The park is rough, though. Don't come back this way, if you need to, until morning, okay?" With that, he tugged gently in the direction of the park, and Penny was on the move again, looking over at him from time to time. The two crossed the street, turned into shadows on the other side, and disappeared down a path.

CHAPTER 34

Wednesday, August 2, 2017
Surf Avenue and Twenty-First Street
Coney Island, Brooklyn
12:45 p.m.

Zochi knew that although homeless people usually lacked structured and scheduled days, unhoused locals often had reliable patterns that could be divined, spots they frequented at similar times during the day. One was the Brooklyn Medicaid Office and Department of Social Services building on Twenty-First Street, just south of Surf Avenue. A square brick structure on an otherwise flat, featureless street. There were no trees, so there was no shade. Wilomena had found some, though, inside a little alcove near the front entrance. She was seated on a plastic milk crate, one heavy arm resting on her shopping cart.

"Wilomena, how are you?" Zochi asked, hiking up her waistband as she walked over.

Wilomena rolled her eyes but otherwise did not make a move to leave. "Who killed Lois? Why ain't he in jail?"

"We don't know who it is yet," Zochi said. "We don't know if it was a 'he.'"

"It's always a 'he.' Wake up."

"Usually, yeah. So, listen, there's something we found."

"Yeah, just not who did it. Here you are anyway, hassling old Wilomena."

"Nah, not hassling. So you know what's weird?"

"What?" Wilomena said, suddenly without guile, like she'd been taken off guard, and genuinely curious.

"The bra that was wrapped around Lois's neck that night," Zochi said, looking down at her cell phone to avoid direct eye contact. "The thing is, we don't know if it was really hers."

"Oh yeah? Why not?"

"To the medical examiner, it didn't look like it would have fit her," Zochi said. She made eye contact but then flicked her eyes down the block toward the boardwalk. "And there was something else. On the bra strap, there was an inscription." For a fleeting moment, Zochi thought about quickly defining "inscription," then thought better of it.

"What was the *inscription*?" Wilomena asked, stressing the word to acknowledge that she knew what it meant.

"Six letters. F-W-Y-D-T-M." The next line was a fib, but such was detective work. "We found those letters on other clothes Lois had on too. It was like a label or something that she put on her stuff. You know, like maybe some combination of letters that meant something to her. Did she ever talk to you about that? Those letters? Their meaning?"

"F-W-Y-D-T-M. That's it, right?"

"It is," Zochi said, concealing a grin. Wilomena was many things that Zochi would never understand, but intellectually compromised was not among them.

"Right. Six consonants, not even a goddamn vowel. And yeah, I know—'sometimes Y.' But this ain't the sometimes. So, no, I don't know what the fuck it means. But see, to me, that ain't the point anyway."

"Okay. What's the point?"

"She didn't have no bra on that night."

"What?"

"You heard me."

"How do you know?"

"How would you know something like that? You look at a woman. You're not blind, yo. So you can see nipples stickin' out and titties swingin' back and forth. That clear enough? Lois didn't have no bra on that night."

"Gotcha. Thank you, Wilomena."

CHAPTER 35

Mermaid Avenue near Twenty-First Street
3:00 p.m.

"Where you at?" Zochi said into her phone when Len Dougherty picked up. She was in her city car, slurping the last of an iced latte and watching a hand-to-hand drug deal proceed near an old storefront church on Mermaid Avenue. She could not have been more apparent to them as a cop had she pulled her sunglasses off and waved her shield, but both men seemed unconcerned.

"Avenue X, by the train."

"Way up there? Did you get lost?"

"I'm under the El; there's shade at least." As if to confirm this, the roar of the F train sang through the phone. "What're you up to?"

"Watching a buy."

"Where?"

"Between the Beulah church and a deli."

"Gonna do anything about it?"

"Yeah right. You talk to Robbie DeSantos?"

"Yep. Drove out there last night. Found him at work."

"Does he have an alibi for either body?"

"Yeah, but they've gotta be confirmed. There's a guy from the One-Two-Two who's helping me run them down." The 122nd was the precinct that covered most of Staten Island's South Shore. "They're similar, so it shouldn't take long."

"Similar how? Was he with someone? Girlfriend?"

"This guy ain't got a girlfriend," Len said. "Unless she charges by the hour."

"Sounds like a charmer."

"He's just . . . I don't know what the word is. Hostile, but it's all bottled up. I don't think he has friends either. For both cases, though, his alibi is that he was at work until ten." She heard the roar again, probably the F going the other way. "That checks out. He does a 1:30-to-10:00 p.m. shift most of the time, unless he's filling in for someone. After work on the thirteenth, he says he parked his car at home and walked over to a sports bar on Hylan Boulevard. Says he's a regular there, keeps to himself. Says he was there past midnight. He gave me the same story for this past Friday, when Joe's ex-girlfriend got clipped."

"Gotcha. Does he use credit cards?"

"He says he did on at least one of the nights. There're probably cameras, too, at the place I went by. It's a neighborhood place, not a dive. Maybe the bartenders can help. That's what my guy over there is running down. I'll have it all sorted before I come back on."

"And no activity with the car after the time he says he parked? For either night?"

"Nope. No tolls. Nothing on the license plate. No evidence he left the island on those nights, at least not in his car."

"Okay. What do you think?"

"I don't know," Len said thoughtfully. "Could this guy Robbie have a motive for the mother? Sure, same as Joe. The girl, though? I don't see it. He says he only knew her as Joe's old girlfriend. Saw her once, never talked to her. That was the day after we found Joe, when she went over there and the two of them went to ID the old lady."

"So he didn't seem to know anything about the girlfriend? Holly?"

"Not at all, but maybe that's bullshit and he was fixated on her or something. Just talkin' out loud here."

"That's all we have right now," Zochi said. "We'll see what we can confirm on his whereabouts. I'm with you, though—Joe's a better suspect in terms of motive. Definitely opportunity."

"We gotta rule the brother out," Len said. "The DA's gonna want that. I like Joe for both, though. Kinda sad. He seems like an okay guy. Like a sad sack, not a killer, you know?"

"I know, right?" she said, her eyes drifting back across the street. The dealer was on the move again, walking toward a car stopped in front of the deli. Zochi cursed under her breath and gave her siren a quick squawk, something cops called a "whoop." The seller looked up, and she gave him a double thumbs-up to shoo him away. He shrugged and walked in the other direction as the car sped off. "He seems decent, but maybe he goes psycho on the bottle and doesn't know he's doing it."

"Oh yeah, like on the murder channel!" Len seemed cheerful at the thought of it. "My wife loves that shit."

"We'll grab it eventually. You know, I thought one thing was weird."

"What?"

"Wilomena, the homeless woman, noticed it."

"Yeah?"

"I found her earlier today," Zochi said. "By the Medicaid office on Twenty-First. I was asking about the bra. The inscription on it."

"Oh, yeah, to see if she recognized it or anything. Long shot."

"Yeah, she didn't know anything about the letters. She did notice something, though. She said Lois didn't have a bra on that night."

"Okay."

"Well, it's weird, right?"

"What, no bra?"

"Yeah, think about it. An old lady is found on the beach, bra wrapped around her neck. So it looks like a strangulation thing, but then you get closer and realize someone snapped her neck. Then you find out from an eyewitness that she wasn't even wearing a bra. And that's backed up by the fact that the bra wouldn't have fit her anyway."

"Right. So why's the bra there?"

"That's the thing. If Wilomena is right, Lois DeSantos wasn't wearing a bra that night, and the one found wrapped around her neck wasn't hers."

"It had those letters written on it, though," Len said. It sounded like he was munching on something.

"Yeah, so I'm wondering if someone placed it there." She put a stress on *placed*. "I mean, if that's the case, then it changes things, right? It's not really a crime-of-passion thing. It's not some keyed-up psycho who snaps and finishes her off with her own clothes, like pantyhose or a bra."

"Whoa," Len said. "When you say 'placed,' you mean the bra was put there, like a staged kind of thing?"

"Staged," she said. "Yeah, that's the word I was looking for. What if it *was*?"

"Shit," Len said. "It complicates things. I mean, why stage something if you're Joe DeSantos and you're out of your mind on booze and you just want her dead?"

"No idea. Maybe it sends a message? There was an inscription on the bra—those letters we found. Maybe Joe didn't just want her dead. Maybe he also wanted to leave something behind for someone to make sense of."

"For who to make sense of?"

"No idea. Let me know when you confirm Robbie's alibi. We'll go from there."

CHAPTER 36

New York State Attorney General's Office
Lower Manhattan
6:55 p.m.

Joe brought one Jameson whiskey box to pack up the things he was going to bring home from the office. He had never kept much there. No framed photos. No degrees on the wall. Just a paperweight, some extra ties, and a spare pair of dress shoes. It was a little before seven in early August, so the office was empty. That was good—the last thing he wanted was awkward goodbyes or good lucks from any of his coworkers. The few he was closest to had anticipated his exit and sent him some nice thoughts. It was an office he would dearly miss, and the work had given him another couple of years he never believed he'd get. But it was over. He was about to start filling the box when he heard an all-too-familiar voice talking on a cell phone and projecting from down the hall. He sighed.

Craig.

As the bureau chief, Craig came down to the city for meetings regularly, but Joe always knew when. Except for now. A few seconds later, Craig rapped his knuckles on the doorjamb.

"Anybody home?" he asked.

Joe gave him a tired shrug. "I'd ask why you're down here, but I know."

"It was last minute," Craig said. "I should have called, but I knew I'd find you here."

"Let me guess. A meeting with the chief of staff. At least one minute of it on me, and how fast I'm leaving."

"He mentioned you," Craig said, as if conceding a point. "But nothing's been decided."

"I've decided. I just signed it." He plucked a stiff piece of AG letterhead amid the mess of papers on his desk, hoping his hand wasn't shaking. He'd been without a drink for four days.

"What the hell?" Craig asked, settling into a chair across from the desk. His face morphed into an exaggerated "confused" expression—his brows furrowed, his lips bunched like he was making a duck face—and then he glanced at the letter.

"I won't accept this."

"You have to."

"Why? I'm five years from retirement. What's the worst that could happen? They send me to defend the tax department? What the hell do I care?"

"Craig, please. We've got to get serious. I can't work here, and you know it. I have a feeling you came down here today for me. To accept my resignation, ultimately, but also to try to talk me out of it. Because you're loyal. Thank you."

"Yeah, well, I'm not accepting it."

"You are. It's better for everyone. For you, for the bureau. It's better."

"The bureau is doing fine. Better with you in it."

"You're the best boss I've ever had," Joe said, checking the emotion rising up inside. "When I first got to the Bronx, years ago, I was lucky to end up in your unit."

"I like to think I was lucky," Craig said.

"Whatever. I was a kid. I was a really screwed-up, really broken kid."

"You were," Craig said, making another exaggerated expression. Joe knew what this was. It wasn't that Craig wouldn't go deep, emotionally. It was just that he wouldn't go there easily. He pointed a finger at Joe. "But you had talent."

"Craig." Joe spoke with dead evenness, as if to expiate any further funny faces, regardless of what a balm against the truth they were. "You saved me back then. And again a couple of years ago. You can't save me now. It's okay." There was a pause, and then Craig's face went blank, like the signal feeding it had died.

"You didn't kill anyone."

Joe's face fell. "I don't think I did, no."

"You didn't."

"I—I don't think . . ."

"Hathorne," Craig said. He said it slowly, accentuating each syllable.

"Hathorne what? He's locked up."

"He's *been* locked up. Think about how much he's pulled off from the inside, just with the computers he's had access to. That was one of your better arguments for confinement, remember? The guy can get through a firewall like it's a paper bag. He runs circles around the IT guys at the psych hospitals—forget about corrections staff."

"Well, sure, that was part of it. Hathorne's family would have left him alone with a laptop and an internet connection."

"Right," Craig said. "And you argued that was intolerable. The guy is dangerous, no matter where he is. It's a cyber issue."

"Yeah, but he's not escaping by use of a computer and then killing people."

"He doesn't need to escape. How much damage did he do to you while this case was playing out?"

"They didn't know as much about him then," Joe said and sighed. "Anyway, whatever he got, he used on me already." This was true, and if Joe had a family or even a wife still, it would have bothered him much more. Hathorne, hacking the nearly obsolete computers available to him in prison, had gathered quite a bit of information on Joe: his address, his driver's license history, and a bunch of other stuff, including psychiatric and medical records. He had filed a bar complaint against Joe, citing an untreated drinking problem, which wasn't entirely untrue. The complaint went nowhere, but Joe had had to go through a "voluntary interview" with a counselor about his drinking habits.

"That stuff about the drinking that he pulled up?" Craig said, as if he'd read Joe's mind. "That would have kept me up nights. I don't want anyone knowing how much I put away, least of all my wife."

"She knows. And, yeah, that hit home. Mostly because it had some truth to it."

"Whatever. You're functional."

I thought I was, Joe thought. *Obviously, I overcalled that one.* "Okay, he collects information. I'm sure he's thrilled about what he's seeing now."

"Collects information? How do you know he isn't *sending* information?" No more funny faces. Craig was dead serious.

"Sending it? You mean communicating with someone?"

"Of course. Jesus, he did that from behind bars for years!"

"Yeah, but . . ." Joe trailed off and ran his hand through his hair. "I mean, yeah, he made contact with a few other assholes like him. So?"

"He's behind this somehow. He's setting you up. I know it. And I know *you* know it." There was a long pause.

"But even if . . ." Joe trailed off.

"Even if what? Find out."

"Find out how? I'm about to be indicted. I need a lawyer, boss, not a conspiracy theory."

"I have an idea about a lawyer."

"Me too. I've got plenty of names in my head, but—"

"Aideen Bradigan," Craig said. Joe was taken aback. Joe hadn't spoken to her, other than via the occasional text, since the long process of her husband's death and funeral the previous fall. She seemed to be doing well, but as far as he knew, she had no plans to return to legal practice, let alone as a defense attorney.

"Aideen? What about her?"

"She needs something to do. Like defending you and getting to the bottom of this." Craig said all this as if he were proposing that Aideen pick up groceries for Joe on the way home. "And she's better than both of us put together."

"She's in early retirement. The city gave her a good settlement."

"She says she is, but she doesn't want to be. She needs this. Have I been wrong before? I mean, you know, about really big stuff?"

Joe sighed. "Not that I remember, no."

"There you go." Craig met Joe's gaze, all the clownishness dropped. "Look, I know you didn't do these things. Fight like you didn't."

"I have to believe it really *wasn't* me before I can do that." It was almost a whisper.

"It wasn't. I know it wasn't."

"I wish I believed that," Joe said. He was breathing in gulps, trying not to crack. "I wish I believed it like you do."

"My youngest," Craig said after a long pause. Joe pictured Craig's son Victor, who at eleven lived with a host of complex disabilities but was still a loving, mostly happy kid.

"Victor? What about him?"

"He's a mess."

"He's a good kid."

"He's a mess," Craig said. He pointed a long finger at Joe. "But he's a great judge of character, and he's always liked you. And don't blow this off. He may be intellectually delayed, but his intuition is off the charts. He knows things. He's always liked you."

"I bring him candy. And I'm nice to your wife, and the cat, and—"

"Plenty of people do those things. But Victor likes you. He always has, since he was a toddler."

"So?"

"So you're not a murderer—of your mother, of a young woman, of anyone. Victor knows it. I know it. Prove it to the world."

"Here's the thing," Joe said. He felt hope—an annoying sensation as much as it was life affirming—rising in his chest and pushing other things aside. He was set on staying miserable, and this was complicating matters. "Let's say you're right. Somehow, someway, Hathorne is behind this. If that's really the case—that Aaron Hathorne has his tentacles out in the world, killing people—then I don't want Aideen anywhere near him. I don't want her in his sights, Craig. I don't want that."

"That would be her decision. Let her make it."

"She's in mourning!"

"She's a grown woman," Craig said. "She did this job, just like you. She's seen all sorts of terrible things. And, anyway, I'm not sure Aideen mourns for long. About anything."

"Oh, come on."

"You come on. You know her as well as I do."

"I know she's . . ." Joe trailed off. He was looking for a retort, but, frankly, he didn't have one. Yes, he knew Aideen. She was as tough as nails, but that was kind of a cliché. And, anyway, so were a lot of people who had come up in, and navigated, the New York legal environment. Still, Aideen's strength was different. She was oddly nontemperamental. Nothing seemed to rattle her, but it went deeper than that. Her highs and lows were strangely close to one another. To Joe's knowledge, she had grown up in a functional family, give or take. She had married a good cop who was now, tragically, dead. But through it all—the marriage, the shock of 9/11, the birth of the kids, and then her husband's illness and death—she really hadn't vacillated much up or down. It was like she had been born with a baseline emotional state and didn't deviate from it.

So maybe she is the person to take on someone—something—like Hathorne, he thought. It was a tantalizing argument but one that another part of his mind wanted to demolish.

No, God, no. Don't put her in his sights. If you go down for this, at least Hathorne will probably stop whatever he's doing. He'll be satiated.

"I can't," Joe said finally. "I can't do that to her."

"Okay, you'll infantilize her instead," Craig said with a mocking tone. This was the side of him that wasn't pleasant. At worst, it was bludgeoning.

"Don't . . . just don't."

"This is your life, Joe." Craig leaned forward and tapped his finger on the desk. "I'm an asshole, I know. I'm also usually right. Aideen can make her own decisions. If she thinks this is too much, she'll tell you."

"She's got kids."

"She's well aware of what's on her plate." There was another long pause in which neither man spoke. They just stared at each other, a clock ticking on the wall.

"You know what I really learned from that case?" Joe asked finally. "The Hathorne case?"

"What?"

"I learned how random this . . . this level of cruelty is." He looked away for a second and then cut his eyes back to his boss. "I mean the type of cruelty a guy like Hathorne dishes out. You see, that's the thing. You don't hope to win against Aaron Hathorne. You don't hope to put him away. You just pray to God you never *meet* Hathorne. You pray you don't cross his path.

"No bullshit, Craig, I mean it. I could say he's like a shark, but it's worse than that because he can make choices. You hope—if you're smart—just not to be where he is. You know, there were a couple of mob cases Jack and I worked. We weren't the lead attorneys; they just picked us up to run some witnesses down and do some legal errands. Anyway, I met a few mob associates. I mean, I grew up in Staten Island; it's not like I didn't come up with one or two of them. And they can be exactly what you see on TV, these 'wise guys' everybody laughs about and who seem so much like your own goombah relatives. But if you get too close, you see what they really are. The big players. They're plea-sure seekers. They're not funny. They're not comical stereotypes. They're just hunters, things that tear apart whatever they encounter. Maybe it's immediate and bloody. Maybe it's over time, and there are papers peo-ple sign. But that's what they do. They destroy. Everything they touch."

"You're not wrong," Craig said, shaking his head and lowering his eyes, as if to acknowledge Joe's points. "If you talk to Aideen, you tell her that, so she understands. Make it clear."

"That's the thing," Joe said. "I don't know if I *can* make it clear. Because Hathorne scares me more than any wise guy I ever knew, Craig. He really does."

CHAPTER 37

Thursday, August 3, 2017
FDR Boardwalk
Midland Beach, Staten Island
12:58 p.m.

"Please, sit down," Joe said to Robbie, motioning to the empty park bench next to his. It was brutally hot on the boardwalk, but a reliable breeze flowed in from the ocean. A few kids were making sandcastles and playing at the water's edge, their calls bright on the salty air. Robbie hesitated for a moment, as if deciding whether to just walk away, then sat down.

"Okay, I'm seated. What is it you want with me?"

"I don't know," Joe said, now staring at his hands. "I really don't know, but . . ." He trailed off.

"That girl, the one I saw at your place a few weeks back—they're looking at you for that, aren't they?"

"Of course they are," Joe said, shaking his head. He wore torn khaki shorts, an old T-shirt, and boat shoes. Robbie had on slacks and a button-down shirt, but he looked far less overheated than Joe, who was sweating profusely. "I'm afraid, Robbie. I really am."

"So, what, you want to run?"

"No, I don't want to run. That's not what I'm afraid of." He forced himself to look squarely at his brother. "I'm afraid of what I can't remember. I'm not just talking about Halle. I'm talking about Lois too. That's what I'm here about."

"Lois," Robbie said, almost wistful. "You know, you don't help yourself when you refer to her that way. She was our mother. You won't call her that, though. Even when we were kids. You made that decision right after it happened. Uncle Mike never corrected you. Maybe he should have, but you were his favorite. Like you were everyone's favorite."

"She forfeited that right. Anyway, you ditched Uncle Mike and me. You were never a part of that family, not really." Joe clamped down on whatever he might say next. He had not come out here to antagonize his brother or rehash old hurts, as easy as that was to do. For once, Robbie didn't fire back.

"Whatever. It's about appearances. You're a suspect in her murder, but you can't bring yourself to call her what she was to us. Yeah, I know what she did. Doesn't fuckin' matter. Smarten up, man."

"I'm trying," Joe said. "That's why I'm here." This was harder than he thought, humbling himself to Robbie. *Well, in some fucked-up way, maybe it's his turn.* "Did she ever reach out to you? Our mother?"

"No," Robbie said. He looked away, out over the water. The "no" was definitive. Flat.

"Think, please. Has anyone approached you? Or seemed like they've been watching you, maybe? Any strange messages? Anything, in the last month or two?"

"I told you. No. What is this, a spy movie? No one's watching me."

"She was around Coney Island for a few weeks before they found her, but . . ." Joe trailed off.

"But what?"

"I remember the DA telling me about a witness. A homeless woman who knew Lois, for a while. She told a cop that Lois wanted to get over here. To Staten Island."

Robbie let out a little chortle. "Yeah, well, she didn't look me up."

"Not that you know of," Joe said. He felt like he was lecturing Robbie. "That's why I'm asking these—"

"I know why you're asking. You can stop. I just don't know, no more than I know where she was all the goddamn years before that." He smirked. "You know, it's kind of funny—you don't seem to care about those years, just the last few weeks before she was capped."

"I cared at first."

"Yeah, funny way of showing it. You had her relegated to a first-name basis before that first summer was up."

"Jesus, that was a defense mechanism. Come on." He knew he shouldn't say the next thing, but out it came anyway. "You know, I get the feeling sometimes that it wasn't the same for you. The abandonment, I mean."

Robbie made a *tsk* sound.

"You're oh so wise. Look where it's gotten you."

"Nothing then? You just have no idea how she ended up here?"

"All I know is, she didn't end up *here*." He lifted his chin toward the Brooklyn side. "She ended up *there*. I guess that's why this is your problem. There were notes with her, right? Like shit she had just written? To you?" Joe looked away. He was hearing something in his brother's voice. Something angry but underneath pained.

"She knew I was in Brooklyn, I guess," Joe said, quieter. "I think the idea was to find you too."

"What, you're in her head now?"

"It's not that. The homeless woman the DA told me about. Whoever she was, Lois was talking to her about trying to get over here. She was looking for a way. So maybe she knew about you too."

"What did she look like when you saw her at the morgue?"

"Why?"

"I dunno. I didn't get to see her. You did. What did she look like after all this time?"

"Old. Worn out. What would you think?"

"Did she look like our mother?"

"Just an old woman."

"Man, you're a cold fish," Robbie said, shaking his head. "You should listen to yourself, how you talk about her. No wonder they think you tried to rip her head off."

"If I did, I want to understand why!" He couldn't believe he'd just said that out loud. And really loud. He put his hands over his mouth in prayer formation.

"You're sober at least," Robbie said. He stood and lit a cigarette. "Maybe that'll help you, 'cause I can't. I've got work in thirty. I've got to go."

"That rehab place," Joe said, his brow knitted, "on the hospital grounds, right?"

"Yeah."

"How long have you been there? And how the hell did that happen, anyway?"

"A buddy of mine knew about it," Robbie said. He drew on the cigarette and glanced out over the water. "I've been there three, four months, I guess. Pays well. Plenty of overtime."

"Well, I hope you can keep this one," Joe said. To himself he didn't sound judgmental, but frankly there was no other purpose for the remark. He could feel himself slipping toward snark. If he wasn't going to gain anything from Robbie, he needed to walk away. He had enough to fear and regret. Still, the words kept rolling out. "That's all I'm saying."

"That's never 'all you're saying.'" Robbie accentuated the words. He fixed Joe with a dull gaze. "You should've been a judge. That's all you do—judge people. Now it's all catching up to you."

"Then I'll face it. I'm looking for answers, not redemption." He lowered his voice. "I'm sorry, okay?"

"Sorry for what? You're just being honest, looking at me like something you'd scrape from your shoe. It's always been that way."

"It wasn't always that way," Joe said, shaking his head. The foot was slipping off the brake now. Stupid or not, this is what always happened between them. "You made your life what it is. I've bailed you out. I've paid off your victims, for Chrissake."

"What victims?" Robbie threw his hands up. "Some breathing skeletons whose families said I took money from? Family members who were pretending their aging loved ones were dead anyway? Let me tell you something—whatever I took didn't exist for those kids until they started sniffing around and wondering what was left for them. That makes me public enemy number one?"

"It was more than just found cash. You manipulated accounts. You think I don't know? You took money that wasn't yours; it doesn't matter who you think was entitled to it."

"I didn't have the head start, remember? I missed out on the trust you had."

"That went to my education and nothing else," Joe said. "Anyway, you separated yourself from Uncle Mike. From both of us, the only family you had left after that night. I've done what I could for you in the face of that, Robbie. You know I have."

"Yeah, well, you should have saved yourself." There was an odd gleam in his eye, something foreign to Joe and a little frightening. "All those years, you were so fuckin' strong. Of course, she was just 'Lois' to you. You could handle it all; you just put it in a neat little box. Like that poem you wrote in school that one year. Fuckin' Uncle Mike was so proud. 'Look at Joey! Coming to terms with his grief!' Yeah, you had it all figured out. Except it was still in there, wasn't it? You just didn't know where to put it until a bottle showed you—"

"Don't—" Joe started, cutting him off. Robbie plowed on.

"It's worse than that, though, isn't it? Maybe you did murder your fucking mother and your ex-girlfriend. This is what happens when you stay in the dark and don't look at things, Joe! Everyone looked down on me, but I *looked* at our mother leaving us. I let it sink in. If it fucked up my life, at least I dealt with it. I didn't walk around pouring liquor on it until it went off inside me like a time bomb."

"We've both kept things in the dark," Joe said. He spoke low enough that Robbie had to lean in to hear him. The next thing he said was more than a snipe. The gloves were off. The string that held Joe just above hate where his brother was concerned snapped. He had never said anything like it. "For me, yeah, maybe it was the full impact of her leaving. But I know what it was for you, Robbie. It was that night. I still remember what happened, and what it did to you." Robbie opened his mouth, then shut it again. Joe felt cold satisfaction slide through him. It wasn't right, but it would shut his brother down. Then Robbie's mouth turned up in a mean little grin. The weird gleam was back too.

"The light has been looking for you, little brother," he said. He drew the last half inch from his cigarette and pitched the butt in between Joe's legs. "Get ready to be blinded by it." He turned and walked off. Joe felt like he'd been punched. The satisfaction was gone. There was just the coldness. It was bitter and dark and deep. He put his head in his hands and thought about drinking.

CHAPTER 38

Wednesday, July 13, 1977
West Seventy-Ninth Street
Upper West Side, Manhattan
10:38 p.m.

The first intersection west of Riverside Drive was up a little hill to West End Avenue. It was eerily quiet but otherwise nonthreatening. The heat pressed on them both; it seemed to be getting even hotter, the air heavier, as they moved into the city. The buildings on either side were huge and stately, with stone or brick facades and balconies. Windows were open and dim; flickering candlelight emanated from most of them. They could hear radio broadcasts from a few of the windows, echo-laden male voices announcing details that meant nothing to them: street closures here, hospitals dissuading new patients there, admonitions against using the telephone for anything other than emergencies. Joe figured one of them must be George Michael.

It was as they approached Broadway, where more cars and people seemed to be moving up and down the street, that Joe heard heavy breathing behind him. He and Robbie spun around in unison, ready to scream. A young man with a dark, sweaty face was carrying a parking meter over his shoulder.

"Out of the way!" he bellowed and ran past them, turning south on Broadway. Parked at the corner was a station wagon, its tailgate down and another shirtless man standing beside it. The parking meter was thrust into the back of the wagon; the men jumped in and sped off.

The next thing that drew their attention was straight ahead, across the wide two-way boulevard on the east side of the street. It was the unmistakable murmur of a crowd: people talking over each other, laughter, shouting. There was the tinkle of breaking glass. At first, they couldn't tell what they were seeing; in the intermittent glow of passing cars, it looked like people in throngs were trying to muscle their way into the same door all at once. There was the screech of metal and then more breaking glass. A cheer went up from the crowd, pressed against the building like a writhing mass. Then a young man in gym shorts and knee-length tube socks wiggled his way out from the scrum. He was carrying an appliance box. Another guy in a pink shirt and a white fedora followed with a load of clothes over his arm.

"They're, like, breaking in," Robbie said. "Stealing stuff." On Broadway, cars drove by in both directions, a few of them honking horns and yelling out open windows. A fat man in a tank top was standing some distance from the crowd, scratching his chest and screaming at everyone. He wasn't the only one. There were shouts and screams from the windows above them.

"It's a Woolworth's," Joe said, pointing at the sign above the mess. It was a neon sign, grayed out and lifeless. On the second floor there were windows behind the sign with mannequins and display cases. From time to time a flash of light or a flicker of flame could be seen in them. Figures moved about up there, upending things.

"Let's get out of here," Robbie said, motioning toward the south side of the intersection. "This way."

Then Joe's heart leaped into his chest. A really big car, like an old Cadillac or an Imperial, moved past them going east on Seventy-Ninth and crossing Broadway, which had become a four-way stop, and cars just waited their turn. As the big car moved away, its headlights illuminated a bar on the left with a massive sign in the shape of a harp that hung *suspended over the sidewalk. There was a little stoop with iron railings in front of the entrance, and people were milling about in front, raising glasses, talking, and singing. A few feet from them, a woman stood alone, smoking a cigarette in her left hand. The scene was at least a football field's length away from him, across the big intersection and up the block, but in the glow of the headlights, she looked like she was tapping on the cigarette butt with her thumb. Also, her right hand seemed perched on her hip. It was a familiar pose.*

"Mom!" Joe screamed with everything he had, but the din of the intersection—the screams, the rumble of engines, and the laughing and shouting—seemed to swallow the sound. He could hear Robbie yelling for him to stop, but he was bolting across the street before he was even aware of it.

Light seemed to come from everywhere and nowhere at once. There was a flash of yellow in front of him and a screech of tires. It was a taxicab with a triangular sign on top. Joe's thighs collided with the front fender on the passenger's side, and he tumbled up onto the hood of the car. Now his elbows were on the hot surface of the hood, and his sneakers were up by the windshield. Joe saw two things at once. One was the triangular sign, announcing that BankAmericard was now Visa. The other was the image of the driver's face: bearded, dark, and shining with sweat. The driver's eyes were wide with terror and rage. He was shaking his fist.

Joe rolled off the cab and onto Broadway. Robbie was calling from behind him somewhere, and more cars were screeching to a halt, but he couldn't stop now. He dodged another car, this one a small, egg-shaped Datsun, and then reached the corner. There was a subway staircase, a hole in the ground going down to blackness. In between the subway railing and the building entrance was the mass of people breaking into the Woolworth's. A man with an armful of clothes on hangers rushed past him, breathing hard. Joe peered east down Seventy-Ninth Street. There were pinpricks of headlights way up the block but almost nothing around the bar entrance. He could make out figures and saw a few cigarette cherries here and there.

He whipped his head around, desperate for a car to turn left or come straight along Seventy-Ninth, but none did.

"Mom!" he called again. He ran east up the street, past the group of smokers and drinkers. The door to the bar was open. Weak, flickering candlelight spilled out. He whipped his head back and forth, looking for the smoking woman on the street. On the south side of Seventy-Ninth were more storefronts. One was a liquor store, also with the door open, and two men standing on either side. "Mom!" One of the men seemed to stare at him, but he could barely see anything at this point. He plodded forward, reaching the sidewalk a couple of doors east of the liquor store. "Mom! Please!" He felt his way along a wall, still moving a few feet at a time. Then he thought he saw a flash in front of him and a figure behind it. A flame, maybe. It disappeared to the right.

Where the wall ended there was an opening to a narrow alley. A damp, garbage-y smell wafted from it. He turned and screamed into the space. "Mom!" He staggered forward, kicking at some rubbish and then slamming his foot into a trash can. "Mom, where are you?!" A few feet farther he was suddenly seized with terror. There was a metal clanging sound a few feet away. Joe stared in that direction but saw nothing.

Literally, nothing.

He was as blind as Bertie. He looked up, where the sky should have been. Nothing. Nothing in front of him. Nothing behind. He was in total inky blackness. He remembered a nightmare in which he was in hell. It was endless black space like this, a concrete floor beneath his aching feet. He felt sweat running down his back. The air was still and thick. It was difficult to breathe.

Wait. Could he breathe at all?

He couldn't. He was gasping and felt like he was trying to draw hot, fetid air through a tiny straw. Maybe it wasn't air he was in anymore. Maybe he had turned a corner and was now trapped forever. He opened his mouth to scream, but nothing came out. The dark pressed in on him, strangling him. He fell to his knees and then collapsed on the hot pavement.

"Kid! Hey, kid! Look over here!"

Joe was in a ball on the ground, mouth opening and closing like a fish out of water. A cone of dirty light washed over him. The voice was low and growly. "Kid, what the hell? Get up. Come back here!"

"Joe!" It was Robbie, next to the first voice. "Joe, walk toward the light! Come on, get up!"

"Walk toward us, kid," the first voice said. "Come on. Get out of there."

Joe made it to his feet, which he could see now in the flashlight beam. When he reached the mouth of the alley, he saw that he'd only been about ten feet inside. It felt like miles, though. The first-voice man had a cigarette dangling from his mouth and a shiny aluminum flashlight in one thick, hairy hand.

"Joe, for God's sake," Robbie said. His voice sounded exhausted and frightened.

"I saw her!"

"You didn't, Joey. Come on."

"Get outta here!" the first-voice man said. He waved the flashlight like an usher at a performance. "Get off this block; you can't see shit. You're gonna get killed out here!"

Neither Joe nor Robbie got to thank the flashlight man, but he didn't wait around anyway.

"Don't run from me like that!" Robbie said. His face was very close to Joe's. "You hear me?! Don't ever!"

"Robbie, I swear, I saw her!" He was about to say more when Robbie did something that Joe didn't expect. Robbie slapped him. Not hard, like their mother sometimes did, but firmly. It burned and hurt anyway, deep down.

"Stop saying that," Robbie said. "Stop saying it, because it isn't true! Stop it. Just stop it!" Robbie opened his mouth again, but then it was like he was about to hiccup or even throw up. Joe knew that look. Robbie was about to cry. Instead, he spun Joe around and pushed him forward. "Walk," he said, a croak. Joe did as he was told, back toward the intersection with Broadway. He didn't dare turn around.

CHAPTER 39

Thursday, August 3, 2017
Sixtieth Precinct
Coney Island, Brooklyn
6:13 p.m.

"How's my suspect?" Mimi asked over the phone. Zochi had it pressed between her cheek and shoulder as she settled into her desk. She had just begun an evening tour, the so-called turnaround detectives did on revolving shifts, meaning that the evening tour "turned around" to a day tour the following morning.

"On ice," Zochi said. "He resigned from the AG's office yesterday."

"I heard. Not surprised. Any travel?"

"He was in Staten Island today." She pulled up the screen that allowed her to monitor license plate activity. "Went over the bridge around twelve forty. I'll bet he went to see the brother."

"Robbie," Mimi said, as if confirming it to herself. "That guy's alibis check out, though, right?"

"They do," she said, sifting through reports. Len had written up a DD5 on both. "Len had a guy over there chase them down. Robbie wasn't in Brooklyn either night."

"Hmm. Okay, so not him. He's kind of a creep, though, right?"

"A little yeah," Zochi said. "Shady. He's got a job, though, and an apartment over there."

"If the alibis are tight, that's all I'll need," Mimi said. "I don't want a defense attorney playing a look-at-the-weirdo-brother angle to the jury."

"Yeah, I get it. Don't worry; we'll lock it down."

"You know I'll want a motive," Mimi said, "if it goes to the mats. I mean, why did he do these things?"

Zochi nodded as if Mimi could see it over the phone. She had been thinking about this also, and it was related to a couple of other things that had been nagging her where this case was concerned. "Something was bottled up, right?" she said. "Something he never let out, and then—bam!"

"Yeah, the backstory," Mimi said. "That's probably it. The blackout, their mother leaving them like that. It seems like he came out of it okay, but you never know. It's got to be anger, right? Anger he could no longer control after all this time. But what released it?"

"Blackout," Zochi said. While Mimi was speaking, she had been thinking, and she'd scribbled that word on a stickie pad and underlined it three times.

"What?"

"Blackout. That's what happens to him when he binge drinks. He's lost whole days. Maybe once he got far enough in the bottle, something took over. Something in his core. Something he doesn't even know about."

"I can see that," Mimi said. Zochi could tell she was also taking notes.

"It's just a hunch, but I get the feeling that he might come clean if the DNA comes back and it's him. I didn't get much when I interviewed him at the Six-One, but I didn't get a lot of noise either. He just seemed confused. Kind of like he just wants to . . . know what happened. Does that make sense?"

"Sure," Mimi said. She was silent for a few seconds. "The name thing with the girlfriend, Holly—that seemed odd to me."

"I know. The spelling difference."

"Yeah. The killer left 'Holly' on the wall. H-O-L-L-Y."

"Right."

"Joe doesn't seem to have called her that, though. The mother says he used her real name or the short version, like H-A-L-L-Y but ending with an E."

"I remember," Zochi said. "Joe refers to her that way too. He says it like that. *Hally.*"

"That could be an issue. If my motive is that he snapped—blew like a volcano—and killed her out of rage, then why did he use a different spelling of her name on the wall? I mean, if it was coming from deep down, wouldn't he have stayed consistent with how he usually acted, deep down?"

"Yeah, but it might have been an insult," Zochi said. "Like, okay, here's what everyone else called you, and now I'm no different to you than everyone else."

"Wow, that's good," Mimi said, her voice rising on the last syllable. "I can use that."

"There's one other thing." Zochi told her about finding Wilomena again and hearing about how Lois was braless on the night of her murder.

"I'm okay with the idea that he planted the bra with her body," Mimi said. She sounded confident, as if she'd thought it through already. "We knew the size was way off. It seems like he was leaving a message with it. That's what the inscription on the bra was about, just like the letters he left over Holly's bed."

"Right. So it was rage, but—"

"Controlled rage," Mimi said. "Remember, whatever state he was in, he had to make an effort for each woman. He had to find Lois on the beach or arrange to meet her. He had to make his way over to Holly's place. There would have been planning no matter what. That could happen even if he *was* in some Jekyll-and-Hyde blackout state and doesn't remember doing it. I need to be careful with that, though, because it's a possible defense."

"Oh. Insanity or something, right?"

"Yeah, but that's a tough sell to a jury. Personally, I don't think DeSantos is crazy. I think he's deeply angry. Alcohol doesn't make us anything we're not already. It just lets things out that were there in the first place."

"Good point," Zochi said. She was feeling better about it. "Where's the DNA, anyway?"

"In process. We put a rush on it after Holly Rossi. I should know something early next week. Keep eyes on him until then, okay?"

"Like a hawk," Zochi said and winked at a dark-skinned little boy peeking at her from behind a desk. He was there with his mother, talking to another detective about a missing person's case. "Like a hawk."

CHAPTER 40

Saturday, August 5, 2017
St. Lawrence Psychiatric Center
Ogdensburg, New York
Midnight

A thrashing thunderstorm had passed over the hospital, but the night was cool and breezy in its wake. Hathorne was lying in bed, a stack of books next to him and the iPod Touch in his hands. He had opened the messaging program on his end, which he knew opened it up on the other end—Reaper's end.

A few minutes had passed, though, before he'd gotten a response. His first message to Reaper was just:

So close.

Finally, the response:

What is?

Everything. How does he look, now that the walls are closing in?

Cornered. Like a rat. They know he did her, the ex-girlfriend . . .

Don't say her name, Hathorne punched out. Don't use names, ever. There is no need. There is only you, and me. And our work is almost done.

Whatever. He looks like he saw a ghost, haha. They're all over him.

It will get much worse for him, Hathorne wrote. The time to collect is very near. In all respects.

My money?

Yes, your money. You'll be paid. Handsomely.

Yeah, what about the guy who brought me the computer? Who is he? Is he getting paid?

Hathorne stared at the screen. What a churlish little prick Reaper was being tonight! No matter—it was all but finished. He wouldn't need Reaper much longer. Hathorne was not a man of honor, but he would arrange to have Reaper paid, just as promised. There was little satisfaction in this, as Reaper was too pathetic to know that Hathorne could disappear at any moment, utterly untraceable, and Reaper would get nothing. Still, sometimes it was best to keep one's promises and just move on. He would placate the dumb, single-minded Reaper, and he would move on.

None of that is your concern. You'll likely never see him again.

Why? I know how to contact him. Is he the person who will get the money to me?

The money will arrive in the manner I choose. Do not be troubled. You should know by now, I will do what I say I will do. Hasn't every single thing I told you come true so far?

Yeah, so? I want my money. Anyway, what's your name?

Soon.

Then, before some boorish reply could appear, Hathorne shut the program down and turned in bed to sleep.

CHAPTER 41

Monday, August 7, 2017
Tappan, New York
7:45 p.m.

She wasn't supposed to, but Zochi took Joe's worn-out box of memorabilia home with her. She was distrustful of working from home; home and work had to be rigidly separate in a job like hers. Still, she could concentrate better in the basement while her daughter, Lupe, sat with her *abuelita* upstairs, the fat tabby in between them, watching *Beat Bobby Flay*. Her town house was on a quiet street in a darling town about an hour northwest of the city. The choice of where to live was purposeful. It was the opposite of South Brooklyn.

In the finished basement where Lupe rarely went anymore, her girl toys and art projects mostly forgotten, Zochi could spread things out, be they photos, documents, or objects, and get a feel for each piece. More than that, she got a feel for how they *fit* together, and not just in some linear, puzzle-like way. Her dark eyes moved between the things laid out, rearranging them from time to time. *This* went before *that*—maybe in time, maybe in prominence, maybe in relevance.

In the case of Joe's memory box, she wasn't getting much in terms of a coordinated vibe. The photographs were typical, vaguely sad '70s prints of people forcing smiles during a time that valued a happy pose more than an honest feeling. Beyond them were the faded keepsakes, the graduation cap and tassel, the two baby rattles, a coffee mug with the Monsignor Farrell High School logo on the side. They spoke nothing to her outside of what they were: the keepsakes of an average man, nothing more, nothing less. Then there was that literary journal. She kept coming back to it, and to Joe's heart-wrenching poem.

The title and year—*LIT, 1979*—were spelled out in smoke curls from a cigarette burning in an ashtray. *Wow, is* that *not something you'll see anymore,* she thought, just as she had when she first beheld the thing. She chuckled, thumbing through the yellowing pages again. Two staples held them together where the fold was. A group of nerdy kids had hand-pressed them, hot off whatever machine was used to produce them.

A few pages before Joe's poem, there was a tribute to a teacher who had died the previous school year. There was no photo of her, just one of a tree with the sun behind it. The inscription read, *To Mrs. Friedan: the students in Section A missed you this year.* On the pages after was a two-dimensional drawing of the city skyline, apparently penned by *Spencer Clancy, 8th Grade, Mrs. Mobi's class.*

Zochi flipped over to page twelve and beheld Joe's poem again. The page opposite, page thirteen, was blank. There was no illustration accompanying the poem. It was just the block type: five lonely stanzas on the white page. The title and attribution—*"For Lois," by Joey DeSantos, 6th Grade, Mrs. Benedetto's class*—were no bigger than the text.

This is who he is, it occurred to her. *Not big, not small, but deep.* It was an odd, almost intrusive thought.

So what's in here?

Sadness. Betrayal.

Anger?

She read through each stanza again. All five had the same . . . meter? She knew nothing about poetry, but she believed that was the word. The rhythm of the thing—it was the same in each stanza, but the last two were a little different, like a song building to an end. That was odd, though, because the poem didn't wrap itself up. It ended with the desire to ask its subject—Lois—something.

Lois, that's what he calls her.

Yeah, but Mama, that's what she was. The mama who walked away from him on a terrible night in a dead, hot car.

Zochi's eyes drifted back to the first two stanzas, the ones that seemed more concise, snappy.

There's that line he repeats.

"For what you did to me . . ."

She blinked, looked up at the old, opaque light fixture on the ceiling, then back down.

Scars.

Mute.

Dull.

Not kissed.

For What You Did To Me.

Zochi felt her heart seize in her chest.

F. W. Y. D. T. M.

At that moment, her cell phone buzzed. She wanted to throw the journal down, expel it from her hands like a snake at first believed to be a toy, but instead she closed it very carefully. The number coming up was Mimi's.

"DNA's back," Mimi said, a little breathless. "Clear as a bell."

"I know," Zochi said. "It's him."

CHAPTER 42

Wednesday, August 16, 2017
Anna M. Kross Center, Rikers Island
East River in the Bronx
12:45 p.m.

The week or so between Joe's arrest—on Tuesday, August 8—and now, as he was led into the attorney visiting area to meet Aideen Bradigan, had been blurry and dim, like something lived underwater. The motions he had gone through on the day of the arrest—from his initial placement in handcuffs at 6:45 a.m., to the long wait at Brooklyn Central Booking on Schermerhorn Street, to the few minutes in the echoing courtroom—had been staid and mechanical.

Aideen had not been there for any of it, as Joe hadn't retained her. Joe appeared without counsel, and a date was set for him to return with a lawyer. In the meantime, as he expected, no bail was set. He was in custody for the foreseeable future.

It was only when the rear doors of the DOC bus closed that Joe, with his hands cuffed behind him, began to feel his life unraveling like a spool. He was the only white man on the bus; the other guys were all Black or Latino, and he looked to be the oldest by five or six years. One of the Black guys asked Joe if he was an attorney, and if he was, why the hell he was sitting in a DOC bus on its way to Rikers like a regular crackhead. Joe just shrugged and stared straight ahead. Airplanes from LaGuardia passed low overhead as the wheels whined over the bridge connecting the island to Queens.

Rikers Island was a squat, ugly disk of land in the East River named for a Dutchman—Abraham Ryken—who gained it in the city's infancy and created a slavery-based empire around it. Were Ryken, or one of his Rikers descendants (the name was Anglicized by the early 1800s) to return in a time machine to the island, they might be fooled into believing not much had changed. Rikers was still mostly populated by men of color, living and working in captivity.

Joe had spent a fair amount of time there, both as a prosecutor and a defense attorney. Like most people in his line of work, he never imagined he would see it as a defendant in shackles. As the bus squealed to a stop in front of the reception building, he felt the last bit of hope leak out of him like pus from an infected ear. He would be at Rikers for a few months, depending on whether, and how, he pleaded guilty to two counts of murder in the first degree. The Brooklyn DA's office would offer nothing in terms of a plea deal, not with a DNA match on two bodies. He could throw himself upon the court's mercy and see what happened. In all likelihood, that meant "life without the possibility of parole," a sentence he had seen meted out to only one of his clients over the years. It meant life upstate, maybe Sing Sing in Westchester County. More likely Dannemora, near the Canadian border, or Attica out by Buffalo. Gray walls, endless winters, and God only knew what kind of daily violence and other horrors.

If I can kill myself in here, I might, he thought as he made his way off the bus and fell in line with the others.

Now, a week later, he reached the assigned attorney cubicle and beheld Aideen, her grin tight but warm. She was in a dark suit and a white blouse, her plump little hands folded on the desk. At Rikers, even for a lawyer, she stood out simply by being a short woman with blonde hair and blue eyes.

"Sit down, Joe," she said gently, as if she knew it was a strange request.

"Aideen, I can't."

"You can't what?"

"Bring you into this," he said, sighing heavily and sitting down at last. There was a tug at his groin, and he winced. His orange jumpsuit was scratchy and badly fitted. It grabbed at his body in odd places. "By the way, I hate this thing."

"Oh, the jumpsuit?"

"Yes. How are you, anyway?"

"I'm fine, thank you."

"The kids?"

"All good. Have you been okay in here?"

"So far, yeah," he said, his eyes widening as if he knew that was a lucky break. There had been a few bad looks and one shoving incident, but for the most part Joe had been left alone. For the first few days he was mystified at this. A middle-aged white guy could expect trouble, at least a shakedown if not a beatdown. A younger Black inmate had explained it to him, though, on the third day as they made their way back from breakfast. *You ain't got a short-timer's look,* the guy had said. *That's why no one's messing with you. Never seen a white man in here who didn't have a short-timer's look—scared, like it's a dream they can't wake up from. But not you, old man. You look like you just got home.*

"Do people know you're a lawyer?" she asked. "That can cut both ways."

"I don't think anyone cares."

She nodded. "Well, I hear you need counsel."

"I'll find someone. Look, if Craig put you up to this, I'm sorry. It's not that I wouldn't want you to represent me—"

"I know," she said, cutting him off lightly. "You don't want me wrapped up in it."

"Correct. I don't."

"I wasn't sure about it either. Believe me, though, that Craig didn't put me up to anything. I mean, sure, he's playing us both. I could see that. It's what he does." The last word was higher and accented. "But he does it for the right reasons, most of the time."

"Craig told you what he thinks?" Joe asked. Aideen's blithe, almost throwaway line about Craig "playing" them both—as if this were some kind of game and not the most serious thing imaginable—had not escaped him.

"Yeah," she said. "Aaron Hathorne setting this all up? I can see it. You can't?"

"I can see it, but . . ." He trailed off and was quiet. Aideen seemed to wait patiently. He opened his mouth to speak, then clamped down. He wanted more than anything not to say the next thing. He had never said it aloud. It was horrifying to contemplate. He looked at her with red-rimmed eyes. "Let me ask you a question. What if I think I *could* have done it?" He held eye contact with her, willing her not to look away. She did not look away.

"What if I don't care?"

"Oh, come on, Aideen, this isn't you."

"It is now. I represent you."

"It's not that simple."

"When you were a defense attorney," she said, "did you ever ask your clients if they did the thing they were charged with?"

He thought for a moment and answered truthfully.

"No."

"In fact, you kind of did the opposite, right? It was like, 'Don't tell me if you're guilty or not. Just tell me everything you know about the case.' Am I right?"

"Basically, yeah."

"Okay, so let me do my job. The government has its job, and I have mine. That's how this goes."

"You know, Craig might be seeing things," Joe said, shaking his head. "I'm sorry, but it's true. I know he doesn't want to believe it could have been me, but this Hathorne theory, or whatever it is, sounds weird. I mean, really."

"Doesn't mean it couldn't fit. Hathorne went after you hard. I saw it coming."

"I don't have the resources to take on Hathorne. I don't have the methods. Even if I thought this whole thing was somehow being spun by him, how would I uncover it? How would *we* uncover it?"

"Not sure yet," she said. "You need to be a little more patient; we're just getting started."

"Why? Really, Aid, why are you doing any of this?"

"Maybe Craig's right," she said. "Maybe I just need something to do. Something new."

"You've got three kids."

"They're fine."

"I'd much rather that Aaron Hathorne never have an inkling about you. Or them. I'm not kidding."

"I know you're not," she said. There was no trace of a grin on her face. It was dead set and stony.

He sighed. "So now what?"

"Now we begin. Tell me everything you know about the case."

"But not if I'm guilty."

"I wouldn't necessarily believe you anyway, whatever you said."

"You're a pisser, Aideen Bradigan. Craig's right about that."

"We'll see." She took out a yellow legal pad and clicked a pen. "Go."

CHAPTER 43

2:35 p.m.

"So the last contact you had in any way with Hathorne was a few weeks ago, right?" Aideen asked. Joe glanced up at the clock. They had been talking for almost two hours. The afternoon count took place at three, so they would need to wrap things up soon. Anyway, he was exhausted. He assumed she had to be also, but she seemed brimming with energy. She had written pages of notes as they spoke.

"Um, yeah. It was the yearly confinement review, right before Lois was killed. That week, in fact."

"Did he say anything to you directly?"

"No, not to me."

"He didn't go rogue, say anything threatening?"

"No, he was a little smarter this time. He didn't even look at me, and with the judge he was polite, calm, and collected. He's still acting like an asshole in the hospital, though. That's what kept him in."

"You mean at St. Lawrence?" she said.

"Yeah, that's where they're treating him. Whatever that means."

"Right, okay." She sighed and scrunched up her lips as if trying to recall something. She thumbed through her notes, then looked up at him. "Did he ever go after your brother?"

"Robbie? No, I don't think so."

"Have you ever mentioned Hathorne to Robbie?"

He shook his head.

"Robbie and I don't talk much. We've spoken more in the last month than in the forty years before that. But, no, I've never discussed work with Robbie."

"When did you see your brother last?"

"Last Thursday," he said and sagged.

"Where?"

"I went over there. Staten Island. He works in Midland Beach at a long-term rehab facility."

"For kids or adults?"

"Adults. Severely disabled. It's not the kind of job I would have imagined for Robbie, but working with vulnerable people has allowed him to rip a few of them off over the years, so I'm not completely surprised."

"Was he ever arrested for that?" she asked, raising an eyebrow.

"No. He was fired from a couple of places, or left under suspicion, but that's it."

"I ask because your uncle Mike was involved in human services too, right?"

"Well, yeah, but . . . he died in 1985, and Robbie was barely around when we lived with him. I don't think my uncle inspired him to work with disabled people. I think it was just a job he came by. And then it became an opportunity to steal."

"Do you know what he does at the current job? Security? An attendant?"

"Like an orderly, I guess. He cleans up, assists the staff."

"And he works afternoons, mostly? I think that's what you mentioned." She flipped back a few pages in her notes.

"Yeah, lately, that's been his shift. Like a one thirty to ten or something."

"Any idea if his alibis check out for the nights in question? I won't get discovery for a while, but I assume they told you something."

"They check out," he said and sagged lower. "Everything checks out except for me." He dropped his eyes to the floor, linoleum scratched and faded in the shadow of the chair.

"Joe, stay with me," she said.

He lifted his eyes and nodded. "I'm sorry."

"Don't be. I know it looks hopeless."

"And maybe it should." He sighed but pressed on. She needed to hear this. "My brother is an asshole, but he told me something the other day that resonated. I never really faced what happened to us as a kid, Aideen. Not really."

"The abandonment by your mother."

"That, yes. The whole process. The blackout. I just ended up rolling the horror of that night into more of them."

"More of what?"

"More blackouts," he said. His mouth went dry. He had a feeling that his eyes looked hollow, on the edge of madness. But he hoped she understood that he was saner at that moment than he had been in years. It wasn't just kicking the booze. He felt more *present* than he ever had. He could make a dark joke and say it had taken jail to do that to him, but it was so much worse than that. Maybe, in fact, it had taken two innocent lives.

"You have a drinking problem," she said. "It sounds like you're dealing with it better than most who go cold turkey. That doesn't make you a murderer."

"I'll tell you what I told my brother."

"Oh, Christ, please tell me you didn't confess to him!"

"No, no. I just . . . I told him that if I did do it, I needed to understand why."

"Dear God," she said and sighed. She dropped her pen. "If they call him as a witness—"

"I'm sorry, okay? Yeah, I said a dumb thing. I meant it, though. I need you to understand that, Aideen. If you're serious about seeing this through with me, I need you to understand it."

"I get it," she said. For a moment it looked like her energy was flagging, but then it seemed to roar back. Her eyes lit up, crackling with blue fire. "Just talk to *me* from now on, okay? No one else. No one in here. Not your goddamn brother. Just me."

"Of course," he said. He felt chastened and childish. A little nauseous also. "I need to face something ugly, though. I need to grapple with the possibility that I retreated into liquor in a way that made me something else. Something I couldn't imagine. That first blackout? In '77? That was on the universe. The ones that followed are all on me. I let them ruin my life. I need to understand what else they might have made me capable of." For a long moment, neither of them spoke.

"Can you do this 'grappling' without confessing to me?" She put air quotes around *grappling*.

"I suppose so."

"Good. Just don't go down that road. I mean, a blackout drove you to *black out* and commit murder? It's poetic to the point of being silly."

"Now that's the Aideen I know and love."

"Whatever. Just . . . don't stew too much, okay? I know that's hard to avoid in this place. You've got nothing else to do but stew. But don't lose heart. Not yet."

"The DNA . . . ," he started, then trailed off.

"We need to know more," she said. "Of course, it's bad. It's why you're in here, but it's not a ray gun that points at you and says, 'Guilty.' I'll know more when I talk to Mimi Bromowitz. She seems decent. I think she'll be up front with me. What else should I be thinking about? Has anything else unusual happened since the fourteenth?"

His thoughts circled for a few seconds: Robbie, Halle, Hathorne, the misery of it all. Then he remembered. There were two things, actually. The first was the sand he had found in his shoes the morning after he learned that Lois was dead, but he pushed it back below the surface. It was foolish to withhold information from one's lawyer, but that was just too frightening to mention, at least for now. The other thing, he was ready to tell her about.

"There was something I found, late last month, in a case file. It really freaked me out. I have no idea how it got there, but I think it was in my possession beforehand."

"What?"

"A baseball card in a plastic bag. Not just any baseball card. It was a Reggie Jackson from 1977." He explained its significance and what had become of it on the night of the blackout. How he had given it to Lois just before the car broke down. Aideen's face scrunched up in confusion.

"Wait, are you sure it was the same card?"

"It's been a very long time. I guess I can't be sure. I remember having it, though. I remember it disappearing into my mother's back pocket right before she herself disappeared."

Aideen's face smoothed. Now she seemed mystified.

"I know, it's weird."

"And . . . it was in an accordion file?"

"Yeah, just sitting in there."

"No idea how it got there?"

"At some point I'm sure I dumped the file on a table, probably at home, to look through it. I was . . . ah, shit, I was probably bombed. It was the same week Lois's body was found. If I did dump this file out on the table, and I was out of it, then other stuff on the table could have gotten mixed up with papers from the file. It's happened before."

"It's happened to me too," she said. "I've found my kids' school papers in the occasional case file. It just means it was in your possession. So maybe you don't remember digging it up from somewhere."

"Yeah, but that's the point. I didn't have it! I hadn't seen the damn thing in forty years!"

"That's where you may be wrong," she said. She tapped the side of her head. "Distorted thinking. That's a thing, you know."

"I don't think my thinking on this is distorted. Then again, I haven't been thinking very clearly."

"No, you haven't. Where's that card now?"

"It's in the box of stuff I brought home from the office. At the house someplace."

"Okay. Look, you must have found it someplace. It would make sense. You had been reliving that night, especially around the fortieth anniversary. Maybe looking through old stuff. Combine that with binge drinking and who knows? For now, it's a footnote." An announcement came over a loudspeaker. Visitors needed to exit.

"Thanks for this," Joe said as she gathered her materials. He waited until she made eye contact to be sure that sank in.

"Just stay with me."

"I am. I'm not giving up yet. I could have refused to meet with you, then gone back to court next week and just told them I wanted to plea straight up. I'm a lawyer; they'd let me."

"Yeah, well, you'd have a fool for a client. Anyway, I'm glad you didn't do that. So, for now, the usual advice: keep quiet and let me do a few things."

"Things like what? Please don't tell me you're going to talk to Hathorne."

"I'm going to do my job. I was married to a cop most of my life. I'm plenty paranoid, and I'm well armed. Don't worry; no one is coming to get me."

"Be careful," he said, standing up as a guard shouted out the second order. Around them, chairs screeched across the floor. "Don't say I didn't warn you."

CHAPTER 44

Thursday, August 17, 2017
Kings County District Attorney's Office, Sex Crimes Unit
Brooklyn
1:45 p.m.

"You'll get full discovery," Mimi said as Aideen looked over the final results page of the OCME report. In essence, she was looking at DNA results that perfectly matched Joe's genetic profile to the blood found at both of the crime scenes. "The match is clean in both cases, I'm afraid."

"You're not the one who should be afraid," Aideen said and raised her eyebrows. "So, to be clear, the biological material from both crime scenes was blood?"

"Yes. A spot was found on the bra that was wrapped around the neck of the first victim, his mother. For the second victim, Holly Rossi, an amount was found under a fingernail. She had some serious fingernails."

"Brooklyn girl," Aideen said, mostly to herself.

"Through and through," Mimi said. "She seemed like a sweetheart, you know? The kind everyone loved. And her parents, oh my God. They're devastated."

"Joe loved her too," Aideen said and sighed. "Of course, here we are."

"I take it you're not here asking for a plea offer yet," Mimi said. "I know it's a little early."

"A plea? I was an ADA for a while. I wouldn't offer anything for this if I were you."

"There's no death penalty here anymore," Mimi said. "So, you're right, there isn't much to talk about. Trials are expensive, though, and nothing is one hundred percent certain in front of a jury. The girl's family has been through hell already. We could talk. I doubt I could offer him anything that wouldn't realistically amount to life, but you never know what my boss might agree to."

"We'll see," Aideen said. "I've got to run down a few things."

"Can I ask you . . . ," Mimi started, then trailed off.

"How I got this dog of a case?"

"Yeah."

"I've known Joe a long time. We worked together, and he helped pull me through a bad time when my husband was dying. It kind of fell into my lap otherwise."

"I'm sorry about your husband."

"Thanks."

"I'm sorry about your client too," Mimi said, as if also commenting on a person who had died. "He seems like a likable guy. I don't know if I was surprised when the blood came back to him, but he doesn't seem like the type who would do these things."

"I'm hoping he isn't."

"He is," Mimi said with a polite but cold air of finality. "He's a nice guy; he held it together for a long time. But there was something underneath. Something undetonated but ready to go off. Twice last month, it did."

"Like a time bomb, I know. I've heard that."

"I can't look at evidence like this and think anything else."

Aideen nodded and slid the DNA report into her briefcase. "Understood."

"I hope he's paying you, at least."

"He's doing what they all do when they're white and middle aged," Aideen said. She was a bit unsure if that was appropriate, but Mimi had a reputation of being pretty down to earth.

"Borrowed against the house," Mimi said.

"Yep. His only asset. So, yeah, I'm retained. He could do better, though. I think half the reason I'm on it is because it looks so hopeless."

"Oh, I know a few hustlers who would take it on. They'd really clean him out, though."

"It's a hell of a way to start a defense practice," Aideen said. "Thanks again. I hope we can keep it this friendly."

"Do what you have to do," Mimi said and offered her hand. "Discovery will be on time. I don't go in for tricks."

"Probably no need for tricks on this one, but thanks. Listen, would you hold off on an indictment if I waive 180.80?" By this, Aideen meant waiving the statutory requirement that a defendant in custody be indicted within roughly five days.

"As long as he stays at Rikers, sure. Just get me the paperwork today or tomorrow."

"Thanks. It'll buy me some time."

"Good luck with whatever that time is for," Mimi said as Aideen stood to leave and gathered her briefcase and purse.

"Hope springs eternal. Take care."

CHAPTER 45

Friday, August 18, 2017
Anna M. Kross Center, Rikers Island
East River in the Bronx
10:17 a.m.

"Yo, DeSantos," a familiar voice, low and smooth, called out. Lying on his narrow bed on the common floor of the dormitory, Joe set his book down. It was Marcus Aurelius's *Meditations*, which, among other things, advised that suicide was an honorable end in certain circumstances. Joe wasn't suicidal, though. He was further from suicidal than he had been in weeks.

"Hey, Kamal."

Kamal was about thirty-five, muscular and dark complected with strong features and quick, smart eyes. He was the closest Joe had to a friend in Rikers. He sat down on the next cot over and intertwined his fingers. Like many Black inmates, he wore a do-rag. "What do you know about educational law? I mean . . . things kids should be entitled to if they're disabled."

"I know a little," he said, sitting up to face Kamal in a mirrored position. There were ways of showing respect in Rikers, and Joe had picked up on them with an ease that surprised him. "If it's okay to ask, is this about your nephew?"

Kamal nodded, a cloud over his face. "Yeah. My sister's getting him screened, but it looks like autism."

"I'm sorry."

Kamal shrugged. "Just a thing. She'll get through it."

"How old is he again?"

"Three."

"Early intervention is important," Joe said. "There are resources—more than the schools will admit having if you don't push it. Give me a day or two and I'll give you some ideas and some people she can talk to. My uncle raised me, and he was a city social worker. He had ways of navigating the system that still apply."

Kamal seemed to absorb this, then gave a clipped nod, which Joe took as a communication of thanks. He lifted his chin in a "so long" manner and turned away.

Contrary to what Joe had thought when he first met with Aideen, guys at Kross did care that he was a lawyer, and for the most part it was working to his advantage. He wasn't cozy with the inmates who seemed to run the place—shadowy figures on the upper floor who seemed to come and go from cells at will and at all hours—but he was visited regularly by men asking for help with motions and appeals. Joe obliged and asked nothing in return. Mostly Black except for one or two Latino men, the inmates were folksy and plainspoken. The Latino guys stuck together and took counsel mostly from within. Some of the guys he helped reminded him of old clients. Some of colleagues. Some of cops.

With the fog of his first miserable days in Rikers receding, he was finding himself able to do more than simply endure. It's not that he could or would make light of the terrible things all around him, or the horrors he only heard echoes of from the shadows. There was incessant noise: talking, screaming, jailhouse rapping, fighting sometimes. If he slept at all, it was mostly during the day. The food was awful. The boredom was stifling. In short, it was bleak, but he was quickly learning that all states of mind could be products of perspective as much as circumstance.

It was strange to think that he had never learned something so profound in his fifty years, half of that as an attorney. But with mixed feelings of guilt, stupidity, and acknowledgment of privilege, he was internalizing it. He had been a prosecutor for most of his career, an arbiter of punishment for codified gradations of evil. A professional finger-pointer. Now the pale finger of the law was pointed at him. That reality cracked him open like an egg, but it allowed in truths he had never been forced to contemplate. For all the legal help he could provide, and that the recipients seemed grateful for, the truth was that the inmates of Rikers were teaching Joe more than he could have possibly imagined or could ever repay. Among those things was the reality that a man—any man—inside this terrible place was more similar than different from any man outside it. This realization was painful but freeing, and he was beginning to embrace it.

CHAPTER 46

Wednesday, July 13, 1977
Broadway
Upper West Side, Manhattan
10:57 p.m.

Joe calmed himself by counting things.

He counted vintage Checker cabs as their headlights cut through the gloom. He counted triangular Marlboro signs atop the newer ones. Robbie had directed that they walk south on Broadway, on the west side of the avenue, so he counted the streets as they reached each corner. The signs were a pale yellow, grayed out in the darkness, but there were enough passing cars that he could make them out.

The streets were filled with trash and debris. People on the sidewalk, thankfully, paid the boys almost no mind. Old men stood smoking in doorways. Kids, many of them shirtless and in high striped tube socks and short shorts, congregated on front stoops down the side streets. Their laughter was mostly cheerful, not foreboding. Joe counted the types of storefronts also. Two coffee shops so far, one a Chock full o'Nuts and one with a Hot Bagels sign in the window. A candy store. A hardware store. In front of the hardware store, two men with undershirts and hairy backs stood outside and casually swung baseball bats.

Steel gates were down on most of the stores, many of them covered with graffiti. The boys had seen people on the street with merchandise, even pushing shopping carts full of items, but had encountered no looting since Seventy-Ninth Street. The term itself—"looting"—was not familiar, but now the men on the radio were using it regularly and talking about areas of the city where it was happening. Their echoed voices seemed to come from everywhere.

At the corner of Seventy-Fourth Street was a massive, beautifully carved building that seemed to disappear into darkness above them. Like most of the buildings they were passing, there was candlelight in many of the windows but little activity. On the street, though, was something like a block party. At first Joe thought it was another store being looted, but the mood of this crowd was very different. There was no shattering glass, no whooping or grunts, no pushing and shoving. It was a happy gathering of young men, most of them shirtless, arms flung over each other's shoulders. They huddled in groups and passed around bottles and cigarettes.

"Queers," Robbie said flatly as they passed the crowd. Disco music was playing from a big box radio on the sidewalk—"Boogie Nights," a song Joe recognized because on the radio it began with a dreamlike harp-plucking sound. The men seemed to move in unison to the driving bass beat that followed the intro.

"How do you know?"

"You see a single woman over there?"

"So? They don't want girls around."

"Queers," Robbie said. "Uncle Mike's a queer, you know."

"Is not."

"Is too. Mom told me."

"You don't . . . you don't even know."

"No, you don't know," Robbie said. "You were, like, barely born. And guess what? If we can't find Mom, we'll have to live with him."

"We'll find Mom," Joe said. The likelihood of that was slipping further and further behind them, though, like the counted street signs in this smelly

city that felt more and more like a steaming graveyard. "We will, right?" The sense of dread and abandonment was bewildering, but Joe had no way of expressing it. The thumping music in his ears just made him feel colder inside.

"I don't know," Robbie grumbled. They walked another block in silence. They could see more traffic at Seventy-Second Street, a big intersection a couple of blocks ahead with a square or a little park in the middle. Across its expanse, people stood around in small crowds, lighting cigarettes and tilting up bottles.

"Is he nice, at least?" Joe asked when they reached Seventy-Third Street. "Uncle Mike, I mean?"

"For a queer, yeah," Robbie said. This meant nothing to Joe, and he had a feeling it was little more than something for Robbie to say. He tried to picture his uncle Mike. He had seen a photo, a yellowing one in a drawer in the living room. Joe pictured Uncle Mike smiling, as he was in that long-ago photo with his sister, Joe's mother, at Christmas and tried to pin some hope on that.

Then a plump, curvy woman in an apron called out to them.

"Where are you going, you two?" Her voice was high, delicate, and accented. She had one hand on her hip and a long, thin cigarette in her mouth. She stood in the open doorway of a small restaurant. There was a plate-glass window to her left with painted letters in a semicircle. La Quenelle. More candles than they had seen anywhere burned inside, and a small group of people sat at the bar fanning themselves.

"We're just walking," Robbie said, looking straight ahead. Joe knew he should follow Robbie's lead, but the woman's face was soft and inviting. Everything about it seemed round—the curve of her chin, the red of her cheeks, the pug nose. Her mouth was like a little red target with a cigarette in it.

"Are you hungry?"

"Us?" Robbie asked. "No, I mean—"

"Kind of," Joe said. The fact was, they were both famished but hadn't had a chance to think about it. There had been no food since lunch, and

Lois had quashed any requests for dinner on the road. It was "wait till we get to your uncle's" and nothing else.

"We don't . . . we don't have any money," *Robbie said to the sidewalk.*

"Money, what's money? Everything we have goes bad if we don't serve it. Come in." *The words came out in a funny string, each syllable stressed like the one before it.*

"It looks like adults only, though," *Robbie said. Indeed, there were no kids inside, just drunk, sweaty grown-ups, mostly at the bar. At the tables, couples leaned in close.*

"Et alors? *Come in.*"

CHAPTER 47

Aideen had learned from psychologists over the years that, in the presence of psychopaths, a decent percentage of people actually felt something physically distressing, like hair going up on the back of the neck. For her, though, there was none of that, and she had been around her share of psychopaths. That morning she had hopped a quick flight from LaGuardia up to Ottawa, Canada, rented a car, and driven over the International Bridge back into New York State in order to reach the psychiatric center where Aaron Hathorne was confined for at least another eleven months.

The center itself was just on the US side of the bridge. The grounds still held some terrifying stone buildings from the nineteenth century; one could almost hear the screams of the chained patients who had been housed there. The modern facility, though, was clean and friendly. From the outside it looked like an elementary school, with a circular driveway in front and a little portico. She signed in and was searched, then followed a pleasant female attendant with a Nigerian accent to the room where Aaron Hathorne had been directed to wait for her.

He was seated at a plain wooden table, his hands clasped neatly in front of him, dressed in a plaid shirt, khakis, and loafers without socks. The room was a small library, like one found in a law office, with book stacks, a copier, and some office supplies on a table. For a fleeting moment she pictured the Hannibal character from *The Silence of the Lambs* and wondered how many things in the room Hathorne could kill her with. That passed.

"Hello, Ms. Bradigan," he said, looking up at her as she walked in. His speech was soft but clipped and clear, the diction of a well-educated person. He stood to his full height, which was a good foot or more above Aideen's. He was whippet thin and wiry, with long hair, gray and gathered around a narrow face.

"Aideen Bradigan, yes," she said. He motioned to an empty chair opposite him, then offered his hand. He seemed hesitant, as if he expected her to reject the gesture. Instead, she thought, *I guess if I'm going to feel creeped out, this is how it'll happen.* She shook his hand firmly, and it went limp like a damp rag. It wasn't a pleasant feeling, but it didn't sick her out either. So the guy had a terrible handshake? That was the least negative thing about him.

"Please, sit down," he said, doing so himself. She set her briefcase on the table. Opening it, she pulled out a legal pad, a pen, and some notes she had taken previously.

"Thanks for agreeing to speak with me, Dr. Hathorne," she said. "I'll try to make this quick."

"I've got nothing but time, Ms. Bradigan," he said, a little grin turning up the corners of his mouth. The lips were thin and purplish. "But I won't blame you if you don't want to linger in my company."

"I've met all kinds," she said, a breezy quip relayed with an elevated tone and a jaunty lift of one shoulder. Neither damning nor affirming, it was exactly the tone she wanted to convey.

"And you're wondering if I'm the kind who could destroy Joseph DeSantos with some astonishingly elaborate scheme from behind these walls."

"I'm just gathering information that might be relevant."

"And what could I possess that's relevant? DeSantos is a serial murderer with volcanic rage impulses. It's simple."

"I'm not sure it's simple, actually. That's why I'm here."

"Well, it's no inconvenience to me," he said, lifting his right hand a few inches and then flipping it, palm up, "but I can assure you, I am not relevant to what's wrong with your client. If you want ideas, I could offer a few. I've forgotten more psychology than the people who try to treat me here. But I'm guessing you're well advised."

"Well, you sued my client, Dr. Hathorne. Far more than that, you made attempts at uncovering facts about his personal life. Serious attempts, and some were successful."

"And I never," he said, leaning forward, "thought I'd uncover what DeSantos has now exposed about himself." His eyes widened a little, and she almost nudged her chair back.

"The lawsuits were all nuisance suits," she said. "You also have access to money, money you've used to interfere with Mr. DeSantos's life. Maybe worse. You've got to acknowledge that."

"What if I do? I've sued plenty of people, as I'm sure you're aware."

"Yes, pretty much everyone who's been involved in your life professionally," Aideen said.

"Which suggests even less of a motive on my part to somehow create a far-reaching conspiracy against Joseph DeSantos involving murder. As you can see, I'm an equal-opportunity legal bully. I have used the system that's been stacked against me for two decades. I've used it as liberally as it's been used against me. DeSantos was a bitter drunk whom I went after because I found it worthwhile. He's now revealed himself to be a monster. That has nothing to do with me. And quite frankly it doesn't concern me either."

"He broke you, though," Aideen said at low volume and then wondered if she should have. But it was out, and Hathorne seemed unmoved. "The process that put you in here after so many years in prison—I think it pulled you apart. I think you've been focused on DeSantos since then."

"I was broken long before that dispositional hearing, but perhaps that kind of thuggish, police-like braggadocio is what DeSantos engaged in, with you and others? You worked with him, after all."

"I've been studying up on you, Dr. Hathorne. I don't mean any disrespect, and I really don't judge, but I think maybe there's something you could add as far as what's happened to Joe. You don't have to have been behind anything. Maybe you just know something about it."

"This conspiracy, you mean."

"If that's what it is, then yeah. You have a network. 'Elaborate' is a word you used earlier, and the fact is, the network you've developed from in here and from your time in corrections is very elaborate."

"How powerful you imagine me," he said, sounding almost wistful. "And how magnanimous, as if, assuming I did know of some scheme to tear apart Joseph DeSantos's life, I'd share it with you in order to save him."

"I do believe you have power," she said. "I believe you have free will and a soul. So maybe you'll search yourself and tell me if there is something Joe deserves to know. Or not, but it's my job to ask."

"To ask, or to beg, on his behalf?"

"Just to ask. He wouldn't want me to beg."

"Understood. So if we are asking things, Ms. Bradigan, may I ask you something?"

"Of course."

"Why are you defending DeSantos?"

"Everyone deserves a defense."

"But why you? I know for a fact that you did almost no defense work before this."

"So he probably deserves better than what I can offer."

"He chose you, though."

"He did."

"Yes, and you're fighting for him."

"I'm doing my job."

"Ah, but I think you're doing more than that," he said, his eyes brightening. "You're fighting for him, and I admire that."

Aideen found that the longer she was in his company, the less creeped out—weirded out—she felt around him. She made a mental note to never be unmindful of that, because it seemed dangerous. "That's why I'm here," she said, having little else to say.

"Of course, but has anyone ever fought for *you* that way, Ms. Bradigan?" For a moment, Aideen was taken aback. She was fairly certain that she'd never been asked anything of the sort. Hathorne seemed not to notice.

"I'm sorry, fought for me?"

"Yes. Not in a dramatic sense, necessarily. Has anyone ever really stood up for you? I don't mean your parents or siblings, in the roles they played in your upbringing. I mean beyond that. Has anyone struggled against others, or a system, so that you'd be more successful or more secure? More comfortable, even?"

Aideen hesitated, the pause less about being uncertain and more about how much she was revealing to a guy like Aaron Hathorne. She gave a more or less honest answer.

"No. Not really."

"Then perhaps you can understand a person like me," Hathorne said. She almost opened her mouth to say something time honored and publicly defensible, like *God forbid I ever understand a person like you,* but stopped herself. Most people might think a thing like that. Some might say it. But it was neither productive nor professional.

"I can understand feeling separated from the world," she said. "Undefended. I doubt I could fathom what it's like to be judged by it so thoroughly."

"You certainly could not. And you may be the only person I've met in twenty years willing to even contemplate the idea. I admire what you're doing for Joe DeSantos. I've never known devotion like that. You referred to the money I control through a trust. It has bought me legal competence. It has never—not once—bought me devotion. My lawyers have treated me much like my family always has. Like a filthy thing, a rat or a cockroach they were nevertheless responsible for."

"I'm sorry for that."

"It would be very appropriate not to be, but thank you. You're a noble lawyer, it seems."

"An honest lawyer is what I shoot for, that's all."

"Yes, like a fishmonger. One in ten thousand."

"Maybe," Aideen said. A tight grin. Hathorne had quoted *Hamlet*, but she couldn't remember wherefrom. "I know you don't cooperate with the doctors here, but there are good people in this environment, men and women who do care, at least about making you healthier so the rest of us feel safer." He scoffed, and she sensed his contempt.

"The doctors fall into two categories. The first are naive or just foolish and think they can get close to us without being compromised. The second are wiser and harder. They last longer, but they're equally worthless."

They're afraid of you, she thought. *All of them.* But she said, "It's a tough job, I would guess."

"I would also." He let that hang in the air and then said, "The least among them, though, could explain Joe DeSantos to you. He's passed as an enlightened, mostly healthy person for decades, and yet all that time he stewed in a darkness he didn't even realize existed. Now the light has found him. He'll soon be blinded by it."

She scribbled a few more notes, then rose to leave, and Hathorne rose with her.

"Again, Doctor, thanks for your time."

"I was happy to oblige. I have enjoyed your company, Aideen Bradigan," he said, his eyes narrowing, and for a fleeting moment Aideen felt some queasy fear rush back at just the idea of this man knowing her full name. "You shook my hand when you came in. It's a simple gesture, but you might not understand how powerful it is for a man like me to be treated like a human being by another."

"I'm glad for that."

"You also didn't make it a point to tell me you got the *Hamlet* reference. But I know you did." The corners of Hathorne's mouth turned upward, and there seemed to be a gleam in his eye.

"Good day, Doctor."

CHAPTER 48

6 Iroquois Way
Yorktown Heights, New York
11:31 p.m.

Aideen's oldest child, Máiréad, walked into the master bedroom and sat down glumly on the end of the bed. Aideen was on her laptop under the covers, even though it was still hot and the AC was roaring. She was exhausted from her trip to St. Lawrence, but her mind was racing after meeting Aaron Hathorne. Around her was the case paperwork and her notes.

"Knock much?" Aideen said, frowning. She removed her reading glasses and set her laptop down.

"Sorry," Máiréad said. She was fourteen and the physical picture of her father, dead now a little less than a year. Unlike Aideen, Máiréad was thin, tall, and dark complected, with deep brown eyes. Next to her, in a ball at Aideen's feet, was their mutt, Finster. "I can't sleep."

"Try harder."

"What are you working on?" She reached over to rub Finster's belly, and his tail thumped against the comforter.

"New case."

"But . . . you're, like, not working I thought. Is this why you were gone all day?"

"Yes. I am working again. I'm a defense attorney this time, though."

"Huh? What kind of case?"

"It's a murder case, actually." She gave her daughter an abbreviated version, hopefully suitable for her age, but that was getting very hard to gauge anymore with teenagers. Máiréad seemed to be listening closely, more closely than she usually listened to her mother.

"So you know the guy?"

"We worked together."

"Did Dad know him?"

"Yep."

"Did Dad *like* him?"

"Yeah, he did."

"Well, I mean . . . this case. Did he do it?"

"I don't think so. The evidence against him is really strong, though."

"Huh," Máiréad said, this time not a question. Now she scooted up and sat cross-legged next to her mom, looking over the notes.

"Hey, that's confidential."

"Let me help."

"Mair, you're a freshman in high school. You're very smart, but you can't help with this." There was some back and forth, but eventually Aideen gave up, and in fifteen minutes she was going over the facts with her daughter and discussing next steps. Part of it was that she was too tired to object, and Máiréad was stubborn. The other part was that Máiréad was grieving in a different and, in some ways, deeper fashion than her younger brothers. Aideen had been worried about it. The fact that Máiréad seemed interested in something, while appearing positive and focused to boot, was a bit of a relief.

"So, like, his DNA was found on these women?"

"That's what it looks like," Aideen said. "I don't have the reports yet."

"And your guy—your client, I mean—doesn't know where he was on these nights? No one can help him with that?"

"Not so far."

"Because he was really drunk."

"Yep."

"Whoa," Máiréad said. "That's bad."

"I know."

"And you still don't think he did it?"

Aideen sighed. "I don't have a crystal ball, hon. I can't say for sure. I think I'll have a better understanding once I see the scientific reports. Maybe we'll get lucky and an alibi will come up."

"An alibi?"

"Meaning a place where he was when these crimes happened. If we can show that he was somewhere else—"

"Gotcha. Just seems weird he can't remember anything."

"It's sad. Joe is what you would call a functioning alcoholic. That means he can hold a job, but he is drunk a lot. I mean, like, out of it for a day or two at a time. So I need to figure out where he might have been if he wasn't at these crime scenes. I don't know if I'll ever find out, but I have to try."

"Okay. But if you start to think he *did* do it, what will you do?"

"I'll defend him anyway. You know that's how it works, right? I'm his lawyer now. I'm stuck with him."

"What if he *tells* you he did it?" she asked, her eyes widening. It was like she was commenting on one of the *Twilight* movies. *Good to know she's still a teenager under there,* Aideen thought.

"If he *tells* me he did it, then I can't put him on the witness stand, since I know he would lie under oath. I would still have to try to stop the prosecutors from doing their job, though."

"I don't think Dad would see it like that."

"Dad was a cop; it's different."

Máiréad nodded and seemed to accept this. "So this old guy," she said, looking at a printout of a security photo of Aaron Hathorne, "he's the pedophile guy?"

"Yes."

"So if there was some setup, you think he's the person behind it?"

"Maybe. Yeah."

"And these guys," she said, pointing to a list of names Aideen had scribbled in one of the five or six legal pads on the bed, "they used to work for Mr. Hathorne?"

"Dr. Hathorne, yes. They were investigators who worked for him." Aideen knew this because she had started her investigation at the AG's office. The office had several files on Aaron Hathorne, including a big one about how his legal team and investigators had gone after Joe DeSantos over the past two years. Craig Flynn had made sure that Aideen had access to all this information.

"You're gonna try to talk to them, then?"

"I'll try. Not sure if they'll talk to me, though."

"Were they cops once?" she asked. "'Cause if they were, I'll bet they don't like him."

Aideen looked over her glasses at her daughter. She was impressed. "Yeah, probably. That's a good point."

"Dad said a lot of retired cops become private investigators. You should tell them Dad was a cop. If they were city cops, maybe they knew him."

"Well, let's not use your dad's memory that way," Aideen said, although that was exactly what she planned to do once she knew more about the backgrounds of the investigators.

"Dad was smart," Máiréad said. "He'd want us to be smart too." Her eyes softened. She was probably tired—it was nearly midnight—but she was getting a little misty also.

"We'll be smart," Aideen said. She stroked her daughter's hair and smiled. "It's time for bed. And if there are nightmares because of this, no whining!"

"I don't get nightmares," Máiréad said flippantly, like it was just a plain fact. She noodled for a moment with Finster, then hopped off the bed with a nimble, balletic twist of her legs. Aideen was amazed by how dexterous her daughter was, how effortlessly graceful. And she would never appreciate it at her age.

"I love you, Máiréad."

"Love you too, Mom."

"Check on your brothers."

CHAPTER 49

Tuesday, August 22, 2017
Anna M. Kross Center, Rikers Island
East River in the Bronx
9:24 a.m.

Bleach and shit were the two paramount scents of his environment. Joe had no idea those two things could coexist in an atmosphere, but that was the daily perfume. He no longer smelled them, really, but he noticed their absence as he rounded the corner, the walls changed color from gray to green, and he was led to the attorney consult area, where Aideen was waiting for him, her briefcase at her feet.

"I can't believe you went up there," he said, sitting down. They had spoken over the phone about her field trip to see Aaron Hathorne.

"Eh, he's not as creepy as I thought he'd be."

"I don't want you anywhere near him. Don't say I didn't warn you."

"Relax, I know where they keep him," she said. "Listen, that's not why I'm here."

"Okay. I was wondering why you insisted on an in-person visit. Is there a plea offer or something?"

"No," she said. There was a bit of a sardonic look on her face, but she wasn't smiling. "I've been doing some digging. Internet searches. Some criminal databases."

He tugged at his jumpsuit, trying to get comfortable. "Okay. And you found something you needed to tell me about in person?"

"I did," she said and sighed. Then it dawned on him.

"You found her."

"I believe I found the last place she lived before she came back here. I also found a trail, or bits and pieces of one, from the early '80s until a couple of years ago."

Joe felt a coldness slide through him. Through the echoes of decades, across thousands of miles, somehow among the cobwebs of cyberspace, she had found Lois DeSantos. This was like pulling back a curtain on something he wasn't sure he wanted to see. "But how? I never had a social security number for her. I wasn't even sure of her birthdate. Was she in a database somewhere?"

"No. The ME's office uploaded her DNA into a national missing and unidentified persons database, but nothing came up. Lois never had her blood pulled for DNA. It's not surprising. She had an arrest record—I'll get to that—but it ended before they were taking DNA samples the way they do fingerprints now. The DA may try to establish that she was your mother, which helps them with motive. They don't need to prove that, though. They have a human body, and they have evidence as to who, well, you know."

"Right. They don't need to prove that she was Lois DeSantos to prove that I killed her. Anyway, you found her."

"It took some doing, but ultimately it wasn't very hard." She looked up at him. "I didn't cheat either. No help from any of Ben's friends still on the job. I did it the civilian way—on my laptop late at night."

"I should have done this," he said. "Years ago, I should have."

"She was born Lois Ann Carroll," Aideen started, as if she hadn't heard him. "Born March 7, 1944, in Staten Island."

"The Staten Island part I knew."

"Sure. And the details of her early life—her marriage to your father and the births of you and Robbie—are things your uncle Mike probably filled in for you, right?"

"Some things. We really didn't talk about it very much, to be honest. But, yes, I saw some wedding photos, and I knew some of the background by the time I left for college. My uncle acted like there was more to tell me, actually. He had some things he planned to show me when I turned eighteen, is what he said. We never got the chance, though."

"We'll talk more about that," she said, jotting a note down. "For now, I'll tell you what I found. I also printed out a few things to leave with you. Are you ready?"

He shrugged. "As I'll ever be."

"She was really dark for a while after she left you two." From her briefcase, Aideen drew a yellow envelope stuffed with paper. "I mean, untraceable. The first thing I found on her was in Reno, Nevada. That was 1980. She was a waitress for a while. And she drove a cab."

"Huh," he said. He could think of nothing else to say. His last image of her, cold and dead at the OCME, was still in his head, but now he was picturing her at thirty-four, driving past sleazy little casinos with a jaunty cabbie's hat and a Winston Red between two fingers out the window.

"She was in Reno until around '85, then she went dark again. I picked her up in Las Vegas. She was in jail for a while on drug possession. She was in a rehab program and graduated, but she was arrested a few times after that. Mostly, she held a job, though. Different stuff."

"Any other family?" He had always wondered if he had a half brother or sister out there someplace. It was a hopeful thought.

"No, not that I found. No marriages, no other children. Just work records and signed leases. A car purchase. Some criminal records. That kind of thing all through the '90s. She was mostly in Nevada. Around ten years ago, she relocated to Sacramento, California. Same pattern. There were drug arrests and . . . a few for prostitution. I'm sorry, Joe."

"She was lost to us a long time ago." The word sank into him anyway. *Prostitution.* He had been certain that no detail about Lois could hurt him, but that one did. He knew what prostitution was, at least much of the time: a desperate, addicted woman working the parking lot of a motel or a truck stop, always for someone else. He closed his eyes.

"Things got a little better a few years ago," Aideen said, as if rushing in to make up for that detail. "She found a woman's program run by a church and got involved. She turned seventy there, in 2014. I think she had friends there."

"Well, I guess she was too old by then to—" He stopped himself. What was the point?

"She went dark again earlier this year." Joe watched her eyes as she spoke. They narrowed when she described hitting a "dark spot," or when she couldn't pinpoint an event, and brightened when she was describing something definitive. Despite the circumstances, his heart swelled. Not since his soft-spoken, fastidious beanpole of an uncle had helped him with college applications had anyone expended so much effort on his behalf. "The church group home was the last place I found information on her. I think she did good things there, though. I think she helped younger women. Um . . . I found one photo." She looked up at him, her mouth pursed. "Do you want to see it?"

"Sure."

"I think she looks happy," Aideen said encouragingly. It struck him as curious, this almost tender side of Aideen he hadn't seen in a dozen years of friendship and professional association. She was many things, but not much of a comforter. Still, she looked as if she hoped he would find this uplifting. She handed him the webpage printout.

He studied it for a long moment, then whispered the name to himself.

Except this time he said, "Mom."

It was a newspaper photograph of a living, breathing, healthy-looking Lois DeSantos—she was still using her married name—with a group of women outside a church. A local section of the *Sacramento Bee* had covered an event that took place at the Tahoe Park Grace Lutheran Church on a Sunday in 2013. A group of women "living and working" at the church had started a community garden and were raising vegetables and herbs for the area's needy population. In the photo, six women stood around the freshly planted garden on a bright, sunny day. The women were a mix of ages and races. All but one was smiling.

The woman on the left was their minister, Pastor Suzanne Nelson, the caption stated, with a white clerical collar above a long black dress. Second to the end on the right was a pale, tired-looking old woman with a thin mouth, a slightly crooked nose, and flat hair parted neatly in the middle. She was not smiling, but she looked content. Even a little self-satisfied. The names of the women were listed under the photo, which was how Aideen pinpointed the image in the first place.

"I enhanced the photo and compared it to the crime scene and ME photos," she said. "I won't be sharing this with the prosecution, but that's her."

"She does look content," he said, "Not happy, exactly, but content."

"I agree, but I think she also thought she had one very important thing left to do. As far as I can tell, it was soon after this that she decided to come back. I think she hoped to find you, Joe. Maybe Robbie too."

"Nothing more recent on her, though?" he asked. "Nothing in New York?"

"Just what the police found. She was in and out of a shelter in Coney Island the last few weeks. She might have also gotten services from another women's shelter in Brooklyn. Most women in her circumstances move around. I couldn't find anything, though."

"So she *was* here," Joe said, shaking his head. "Maybe I ran into her in Brooklyn someplace. I mean, I don't know. Maybe she tried to talk to me? Maybe I was . . . mean to her?" He looked at Aideen, tears forming in his eyes. He was shocked at them. It had been decades since he'd cried about her. *Decades.*

"You wouldn't have been that way," she said, her mouth firm. "That's not you."

"When I was drinking? I mean, *really* drinking? I have no idea who I was."

"I think I do," she said. "I know a little about alcoholism. You don't do things drunk that you wouldn't do sober. You're not a murderer. Whatever happens, I'll never believe that."

"DNA says otherwise."

"I know, but . . . let me ask you something. This talk you were supposed to have with your uncle—I know it didn't happen, but did you ever go through his papers after he died? Did you save anything?"

"Almost nothing," Joe said, picturing the square box of childhood memories that he assumed was now in an evidence locker somewhere with Zochi's name on it. "I was a kid, just floating in the middle of it all. I signed a few things just before he died. Everything about the cremation and the service was already taken care of. Mike knew he was dying long before I did. He set up a trust for me. It carried me through law school."

"Right. And Robbie was bitter about it. We know that. What happened to your uncle's house?"

"No idea," Joe said. "Someone on my mother's side of the family swooped in. They sold it at some point. There was no money in it, though. My uncle was mostly broke. He had borrowed against it. Some of that was medical bills, but it was mostly for me."

"Was there anyone else around? After the blackout, when you were living there? Other than Robbie, I mean."

"There was one man, yeah," Joe said. He felt a sudden rush of memory, colors, sensations, darkness. He had to shake his head to clear it. "We met him the night of the blackout, before we reached my uncle.

I haven't thought about him in years, but . . . he helped us when we were stuck in the city."

"Helped you? How?"

"We were able to call my uncle at one point. He had a friend who lived in the city and was willing to help. Mike had us meet him at a coffee shop. Things went a little sideways, but . . . in the end, he followed through. He brought me all the way to Staten Island."

"Okay, so a friend of your uncle's."

"Actually, he was more than that. I just didn't know it then."

"What was his name?"

"Nate, but that's all I remember." He closed his eyes, picturing him again. "Black, about my uncle's age. Tall, lanky. Great voice, like a DJ. Anyway, he was a godsend. He got me to the ferry and rode with me to the other side, that morning of the fourteenth. The lights were still out, but the ferry was running. God, it was hot."

"Where was Robbie?" Her brow knitted, she reached for a yellow notepad and began to scribble. "You said, 'He got *me* to the ferry.'" Joe wasn't sure that he had noticed this about her before. She was a marvelous listener.

"Robbie disappeared late that night. We got into a situation and . . ." He trailed off and sighed. "It's a lot to go into, but Robbie ultimately blamed Nate for it, and he left us in the city. Robbie showed up at my uncle's a day or two later, but he didn't stay long."

"We've talked a little about this," she said. He saw her scribble the name Nate and underline it three times. "Robbie was gone long before your uncle died, right?"

"Yeah. He never accepted Mike as a caretaker, or us as a family. Maybe he didn't want to let go of Lois, I don't know. Or maybe he was just pissed off. He broke all of Mike's rules, and there weren't many. He turned sixteen that December, and Mike couldn't control him. After a while he was just gone. We were lucky to see him at holidays."

Aideen was writing, then stopped and looked up. "So what happened with Nate, the guy who helped you?"

"I have no idea," Joe said, shaking his head. "He was a friend of my uncle's, as far as I was told. Then, one day, I just didn't see him around. I guess I should have known it was more than friendship, that something had broken down between them."

"Most guys hid being gay then," she said. "I'm sure your uncle felt he couldn't tell you."

"Probably. It wouldn't have bothered me, though. I hope he knew that."

"I'll bet he did." She wasn't exactly smiling, but her face was warm and glowing. For a moment he wondered who had body snatched the Aideen he had known for so long.

"So what now?"

She blew out a breath, finished a note, and underlined something a few times. "I keep digging."

"I'll never be able to thank you for this," he said. "I know the money isn't enough. Not for what you're doing."

"The money's not bad, actually." She grinned, and the spell seemed to be broken. She was Aideen again. Still, he could see this other oddly hopeful person underneath. "Anyway, don't worry about me."

"I do, though. Please don't let this consume you, Aideen."

"I need this too." Her eyes went cold, her jaw firm. "It's not important why, not for now. But I do. Anyway, I'm more interested in how you're holding up in here. Where your head is. How you're doing without alcohol."

"Better than I expected." That was true, and he'd expected everything from night sweats to tremors. Nothing like that was happening. It was uncomfortable. He craved the taste. The pleasant burn. The spreading, calming glow of liquor. It was painful to reflect on it sometimes, and his hands shook. It was working, though. It wasn't like he could walk into a liquor store where he was, but there was alcohol at Rikers, and by now he could have established the connections to get it if he needed it. He didn't. He was dry, and he was staying that way, at least for now. "Honestly, I'm okay."

"Normally I wouldn't believe that. I sort of see it, though. You look better. It makes no sense, I guess, but . . ."

"I'm wiser, a little. This place . . ." He looked around as if seeing it for the first time. "It's miserable, but it's been—I don't know how to put it. 'Educational' sounds stupid. 'Enlightening'? Maybe that's it. I feel a little more *whole*, even if it's too late to do me any good."

"Don't give up yet."

"I'm not," he said, and meant it. But he also meant it when he said he was doing better, the tranquilizing bottle behind him. It was hard to explain, and it needed to sink in further, but he was clearer than he had ever been—about Lois, about Robbie, about what was behind him, and even about what lay ahead. He was strangely centered and calm. He only wished Aideen wasn't going too far, wading too deep into his and his family's fucked-up pathologies. Aideen was all in, though, and not even he could pull her back out. He stood and met the gaze of the guard who was supervising them, then brought his eyes back to her. "Thank you for this. Now please get out of this awful place."

"Just until next time. Hang in there until then." She looked determined, almost pouty. He wasn't sure, but he had an odd feeling that she would fight this like the devil, even if she believed he *was* guilty. He smiled and turned away.

CHAPTER 50

The place was called Jamie's Juice, and Aideen went there whenever she was in the neighborhood. It was a hole in the wall that served up wonderful green juices and healthy drinks. She was walking out and sticking the straw through the top of the plastic cup when she heard her name.

"Aideen Bradigan?" The voice was thick with all the things she had married, built a life with, and then buried. NYPD, through and through. She turned toward it and saw an older man, maybe fifty-five or sixty, in a pair of gray slacks and a simple white golf shirt. He had a generous gut and a short silver crew cut.

"Who wants to know?" she asked, lifting an eyebrow.

He walked over. "So I wasn't gonna return your phone call."

"Well, you didn't return it. You found me." She recognized him now. It was one of Aaron Hathorne's former investigators. Sean something.

"I did, yeah. I mean, it's what I do."

"Okay."

"You were married to Ben Bradigan." It wasn't a question.

"I was, yes."

"I'm Sean Hogan. I knew Ben; he was a good cop. I was really sorry when he passed."

"Thank you, Sean."

"I was down there too—9/11. Fuckin' still coughing."

"I get that," she said. He nodded and dropped his eyes.

"Anyway, that's why I looked for you. Because of Ben."

"Can you help me?"

"This guy, DeSantos, did he do it?"

"I don't think so," she said. His eyes met hers, and she held his gaze. "Even if I thought he did, though, I'm stuck with him. I'm his lawyer. You need to know that."

"I can understand that," he said. "I can respect that."

"You asked, though, like it might make a difference."

"It's an old habit, okay?" Finally, a smile broke, toothless and slight, over his ragged face.

"I get it. So you were a PI hired by the Hawthorne family? I know that Hathorne himself spells it without the 'w.'"

"Yeah, but I reported to him. I gathered info on stuff he wanted. He wanted a lot of stuff on your client."

"Can you give me the time frame in which you worked for him?"

"About eighteen months, up until about two months ago."

"What'd you think of him? Hathorne, I mean?"

"Gave me the creeps."

"He has that effect."

"That wasn't the thing, though," he said.

"No?"

"No. He's a prick. I've dealt with plenty of psychos. This guy? Just a prick."

"Gotcha. You must know a lot about my client."

"Yes and no. I know stuff that happened to him. Probably stuff *he* doesn't even know, or at least doesn't remember. I don't know anything about him as a man. Not really."

"His brother too?"

"Some stuff on him, yeah."

"I'll take whatever I can get, if you're willing to share it."

He pulled a thick manila envelope from a canvas briefcase slung over his shoulder.

"There're some records here from when Joe and his brother were born. Some other stuff too."

"I appreciate this."

"It's for Ben," he said. "Good cop." He took a step back, gave her a quick, slight nod, and then turned away.

CHAPTER 51

The boys were asleep, and Aideen's king-size bed was again a loosely organized surface of papers, reports, photos, and files. Sharing this makeshift war room, bathed in soft, yellow lamplight, were Máiréad and Finster. Máiréad was seated cross-legged beside her mother. She yawned and stretched, clasping her hands over her head, then picked up the mysterious baseball card, still in the plastic baggie.

"Who was this again?" she asked.

"Reggie Jackson," Aideen said. She had gone to Joe's house to retrieve the card from his box of work stuff. Joe didn't know it, but she had also done some light cleaning and aired the place out. The house had never been particularly comfortable or inviting, but it was musty and foreboding in his absence.

"That mustache is terrible," Máiréad said, frowning. Jackson's photo was of him in a tight, rounded Yankees cap and sunglasses. Below it was his name in curved red letters and then NEW YORK YANKEES, OUTFIELD below that.

"They were popular then. I don't know what to tell you."

"Huh." She flipped it over and scanned the stats on the back, then set it down carefully in front of them. "Where did Joe say he found this again?"

"In a work file. A case file, like the ones I have."

"I know, but where was he when he found it? In the office?"

"He was in court. He had the file with him for a hearing."

"What kind of hearing?"

"You know, a hearing for a case. A guy, I guess, who was up for civil management. They call them respondents."

"Wait," Máiréad said, her eyes squinting, "like . . . a criminal, right? A guy who had been in prison already?"

"Yeah, that's what respondents are. They're people who have been convicted of sex crimes, and they're back in court because of their mental health."

"Okay, but who was the guy? The *respondent*."

"I don't know, Mair," Aideen said with an air of impatience. She was making notes from another report and straining to read someone's bad handwriting. "Why?"

"Because he's a *criminal*, Mom!" Máiréad's tone accused her of being even more obtuse than usual. "I mean, was this guy, like, anywhere near Joe during the hearing?"

Aideen looked at her daughter over reading glasses. "What do you mean by *near* him?"

"You know, like, were they close together?"

"There are different tables for prosecution and defense."

"I know. I've seen *Law and Order*. What about after? How does Joe know that this guy—whoever he is—didn't slip this baseball card in a file he was carrying around? Has anyone thought of that?"

Aideen stared at her, then down at the card. Indeed, she had not thought of that.

CHAPTER 52

Thursday, August 24, 2017
Anna M. Kross Center, Rikers Island
East River in the Bronx
10:11 a.m.

"Evan Bolds," Joe said. "It was a case I was working just before I left."

"It was the Bolds file you found the baseball card inside of?" She looked down at some notes.

"Yeah, why?"

"Máiréad had an idea," she said, frowning. Then she glanced up with a you-got-me look.

"Wait. *Máiréad?* Your daughter? What does she know about any of this?"

"Well . . . actually, quite a bit," she said. The guilty look stuck to her face. "I tried to keep her out of it, but, you know. She comes into the bedroom. She sees me working. She asks questions. She's getting older."

"Older? She's what—fourteen?"

"She's an old fourteen, and she needs something to focus on, just like me. She thought she could help, okay? And maybe she has. Look, I'll apologize later. For now, please help me think this through. Is there any way that Bolds could have slipped that baseball card into your file?"

"I can't imagine how—" he began and then stopped. He could hear something in his head, a bang or a boom. He closed his eyes.

The door to the courtroom.

Fuck you, Vera! This shit ain't over!

The wretched pregnant woman who had come out after him, trying to scoop up whatever papers he had thrown.

Joe and Ben Yang, both on their feet trying to help her.

Behind them, Bolds, seated on the heavy wooden bench like an orphan waiting to meet with potential adoptive parents.

The files, sitting right next to him.

"What?" Aideen asked. "What are you seeing?"

"There was a moment. Only a moment, but . . ." He explained it to her.

"Security video," she said. "We might get lucky if that area is surveilled, and I'll bet it is." She scribbled a note. "What was the appearance date? I'll check it out."

"Um, the last Thursday in July. The twenty-seventh, I think."

"Okay. One other thing: I need to go through the details, but I got some information on Hathorne from an investigator who worked for him for a while."

Joe's eyes widened. "Wow. How did that happen?"

"He was a cop; he knew Ben. I reached out to him and didn't hear back, but then he found me in Midtown. There are account records in the materials he gave me. Stuff about how Hathorne accesses money, how he moves it around, and how he gets things like computers and electronic devices."

"Are family members helping him?" Joe asked. "I didn't think any of them were inclined."

"Not that I know of, but he doesn't need them as long as he has money to spend. This investigator—Sean Hogan is his name—was part of a team with some lawyers at the top, directing things. Hogan seems like a straight arrow. I don't think anything illegal was done. But there's evidence they dug deep into your past."

"We know about that, though, right? All the stuff he knew about my professional life. The cases I worked. The drinking, even."

"Yes, but they found more than that. They had information on Lois. They found a lot of the same stuff I did, even more of her criminal history. There was a photo of Robbie and details about his job history. Notes about Holly Rossi too—times you two were together at her place and on your boat last summer. You were followed, Joe."

He sighed. This felt utterly intrusive and terrible but unsurprising. He felt like a fool. "Yeah, I guess I should have known. Remember last winter, before Ben passed away? You tried to warn me. Craig did too."

She seemed not to register his last comment and instead stared intently at yet another notepad she was filling up. "We also need to find out if there was a connection between Bolds and Hathorne in prison. I'll start with DOC records and see if they were ever confined together."

"Craig can help with that," Joe said. "He's got connections at DOC. Remember, though, Hathorne is very good at covering his tracks. Be ready to find nothing."

"He may be clever," she said, raising an index finger, "but he's only as clever as his weakest link. I'm going to find it." She paused, her lips pursed, and scribbled a few more lines on the page. "Evan Bolds has a PO, too, right? I'll talk to him as well."

"Bolds? Yeah, absolutely. Craig will get you his contact info. But . . ."

She looked up at him. "But what?"

"Where does this all lead?" He raised his hands in frustration. "Regardless of who found whom or who communicated with whom. Let's say that Bolds somehow got ahold of a piece of memorabilia from my childhood and was able to pass it to me. What does it mean?"

Aideen spoke slowly, her eyes on his. They were bright again, that brilliant blue. "You said that the last time you saw that card, it was going into your mother's back pocket." She flipped back a few pages. "If Bolds, or someone he knows, got that card from your mother before she died? I'd say it means a lot."

"How would he know the significance of it, though?"

"Aha," she said, scratching out more words. It was remarkable how quickly she could write and how many pages she could fill at one sitting. She switched back and forth between yellow pads. "That's where the connection between Hathorne and your brother, Robbie, comes into play. And I *know* there is one. Robbie knew what that card meant to you, didn't he?"

"I would guess so, yes. We fought about it, just before the lights went out."

"Tell me about that. Close your eyes if you have to."

"I can see it like it was yesterday. That card was everything to me that summer; I couldn't put it down. We were in the car, going down the West Side. The sun was down, and it was getting dark. I had it in my hand, and Robbie swiped it. It was a kid thing—he was messing with me, holding it out the window, letting it flap in the breeze. Then something happened, and he let it go. I think that was the moment the lights went out. I started screaming; Lois pulled over. I jumped out and went running up the side of the road for it."

"What?"

"Crazy, I know. It was a miracle that I found it. There was no wind to blow it away, though. There was nothing but heat. Once it landed, it just lay there in a pile of road trash. I ran back with it, and Lois took it from me. By that time, we could tell the lights were out."

"And you're certain," Aideen said, each word deliberate, "that you never saw the card again before she left?"

"Yes. I'm certain it disappeared that night. Just like Lois."

"Right, and just like Lois, it ended up here again. So maybe she brought it with her, and it got taken from her. Then it got handed back to you. Do you understand what I'm saying, Joe? What if she planned to give it to you herself but got stopped? And by stopped, I mean murdered?"

"I guess it's possible. Or maybe Lois *gave* it to someone else, like someone whose job it was to drive me crazy. Someone who hoped I'd see it and think I was being haunted by it. Someone who wanted me to see her as a ghost, as something I'd feel compelled to get rid of."

"In a way she was a ghost," Aideen said. "I don't think it was her doing the haunting, though. Stay with me. We're getting somewhere."

CHAPTER 53

Wednesday, July 13, 1977
La Quenelle Restaurant
Upper West Side, Manhattan
11:19 p.m.

Twenty minutes after being hailed inside, Joe and Robbie were perched at the bar drinking watery Coca-Cola and tearing through the most delicious hamburgers they had ever tasted. There were french fries too, big baskets of them, and two salads neither boy was interested in. The tastes were decidedly different from McDonald's or Burger Chef; the fries were peppery, and the cheese was sharper. It was all mouthwatering.

The curvy woman's name was Geneviève, they learned, and the man behind the bar, running in and out of the kitchen, was her husband, René. René had a dark mustache, was thick and barrel chested, and drank endlessly from bottles of red wine. Geneviève's face gleamed a little with sweat, but it was more like she glowed. The revelers at the bar had a few bottles between them and seemed to go back and forth in conversation, speaking a mixture of a slippery-sounding language and English.

French, Joe guessed. He was good with languages.

"This was really nice of you," Joe said to Geneviève, concealing a burp. He was smiling for the first time he could remember. It was remarkable, he'd

think much later, what food and light could do to keep fear and despair at bay. Like wolves from a fire.

"We gotta go, though," Robbie said. Geneviève was on a barstool beside them, another cigarette and a wine glass in her hand. Her elbow was on the bar, and her head rested against her fist.

"What are you two doing out here?" she asked with a tired smile. It sounded languid, like it really didn't matter. Neither boy was used to adults speaking to them that way, casually, like they were equals. "You're not neighborhood kids; I would know."

"We're trying to find our mom," Robbie said. He hesitated and then said, "We got, like, separated." Joe frowned at this. The disquiet was creeping back in, the protective fire dying.

"You have a phone number for her? You call her?"

"She wouldn't be at home," Robbie said. "We're supposed to go to my uncle's."

"Where's does he live?"

"Staten Island."

"Whew!" she said, the sleepy eyes widening. "That's like . . . New Jersey. So you can call him? It's not a good night for boys to be out. We hear crazy things."

"We don't have money for the phone," Joe said.

"Money, again with money! René!"

"What?" he called from the kitchen.

"Apporte-moi le telephone." They both caught the last word. René emerged, gleaming with sweat. He fished out a heavy black dial phone and set it with a clang on the bar.

"Pourquoi?" he asked.

"For them." She looked at Robbie and said, "Staten Island. That's two-one-two. You know the number?"

"Not by heart," Robbie said. "I'm really sorry."

"Un instant," René grumbled. He dug behind the bar and pulled out a massive phone book, by far the largest they'd ever seen. Geneviève barked

something at him in French, and then René dug further and found a slimmer version. "Staten Island" adorned the cover in lifeless black Arial font.

"Take a look," Geneviève said. She stood up and sauntered over to the group at the end of the bar, joining them in a song.

"Michael Carroll," Robbie said. "Greeley Avenue—that's all I know." He grabbed the book and pushed his plate aside.

Robbie got to make the call. For a fleeting second after Robbie started talking, Joe was seized with hope. Maybe their mother, somehow, had made her way to Uncle Mike's already! All was well, and there was a perfectly reasonable explanation for why she had ditched them.

That was not the case, though, and Joe heard a one-sided conversation as Robbie explained their situation.

"Yes, we're safe. No, we don't know where she went. The car? It's, like, right near a park but on the side of the road. Seventy-Ninth Street. Yeah, near the river."

Joe was glad this was Robbie's job. He didn't remember his uncle, and in any event, he didn't want to get on the telephone with a grown-up and start hammering out plans. At some point in the conversation, Robbie asked Geneviève for the number to the restaurant, and she wrote it out.

"What's going on?" Joe asked when Robbie hung up. "Is he coming here?"

"He said to wait by the phone," Robbie said. He looked sheepishly to Geneviève. "Is it okay if he calls us back here?" Instead of answering, she just smiled and swished away, back to the singing group at the end of the bar.

"Why?"

"Just wait."

A few minutes later the phone rang, a metallic bell that startled them both. Robbie looked at René, who shrugged and poured more wine. Robbie answered. This time, Joe heard little other than Robbie acknowledging that he understood whatever he was being told. There was some back and forth, and Robbie insisting that he could do something on his own because he was fifteen. There was more discussion, and then an agreement was reached about who was allowed to do what. Then Robbie handed the phone to Joe. The heavy black receiver was nearly longer than his head. He had not spent much time on a telephone ever.

"Hello?"

"Hi, Joe. How are you?" The voice was calm and kind, exactly like Joe would have wanted it to sound. He felt himself relaxing and calming. He didn't understand why Robbie would be frustrated with this person.

"I'm okay."

"That's good. Listen, Joe. Can you hear me okay?"

"Yeah."

"Okay. I know you probably don't remember me, but I remember you, from when you were really little. We'll get to know each other again, but right now, I have a friend in the city, and I want you and Robbie to go to where he is. He would come to you, but, well, Robbie and I spoke, and I know Robbie wants to walk and maybe check around up there for your mom. My friend is waiting for you, though, and he'll keep you safe until I can get there or he can bring you to me. Is that okay? Robbie knows where to go. It's not hard to get to, but you need to stay where there are people, and the most light. You need to keep each other safe. Okay?"

"Yeah, I guess. Did my mom call?"

"Not yet," he said brightly, as if her call was imminent. "But I'm right here, so when she does call, I'll tell her what's going on. When you two find my friend Nate, Robbie knows to call me again. Make sense?"

"I guess."

"Okay, good. Be careful, okay, Joe? Listen to Robbie, and be really careful."

The phone went back behind the bar, and Joe and Robbie in turn went to the restroom, a tiny closet with a candle burning inside. When they paused to thank their hosts, René grunted something at them and tipped his glass their way. Geneviève seemed to study them in the flickering light.

"You know where you're going?" she asked, lighting another cigarette. She seemed to smoke nonstop, more than their mother even.

"Yeah, we know where to go," Robbie said. He hesitated. "Thank you for dinner and the phone and all. You have a . . . really nice restaurant." In that moment, Joe remembered a swatch of French, something he had heard on a TV show.

"Bonsoir, Geneviève!" he said with a little flourish. He beamed, expecting a great show of appreciation for this. Geneviève only grinned, sleepy and content, as if she expected Joe to begin speaking French like a native.

"Bonsoir," she said as she drew on her cigarette and sent a plume of smoke out of the side of her mouth. She gave a little three-finger wave and winked.

It would be many years before Joe realized something about that interlude. He would never forget Geneviève and René for their kindness and hospitality. It just seemed odd that neither one ever asked their names. Not once.

CHAPTER 54

Friday, August 25, 2017
Riegelmann Boardwalk, Coney Island
Brooklyn
3:40 p.m.

"Hi, Wilomena?" Aideen asked. Wilomena went rigid and shot a glance to the side but then seemed instantly to calm. Seated on a boardwalk bench, she turned her eyes, in a dark nest of wrinkles, back to the ocean.

"I shoulda been this popular in high school."

"I'm sorry to bother you," Aideen said, her tone neutral and tentative. "Do you mind if I sit down?" Wilomena shrugged, and Aideen smoothed out her skirt and sat, setting a thin leather briefcase to the side. "I'm looking for information about a woman who died near here. I'm not a police officer."

"No, you definitely are *not*."

"Well, I'm a lawyer, you should know. Not one who works with the police, though."

Wilomena kept her head pointed toward the waves but gave Aideen strong side-eye for a few seconds. "Yeah, I see the briefcase. I figure you're not selling watches out of it. You say you ain't a DA, though? You sound like one."

"No, I'm not." She paused. "I was for a long time, though."

"Yeah, I can *hear* it, yo. Cops in your family too?"

Aideen grinned a little. Whoever Wilomena was, she was not slow on the uptake. "I was married to one, yes." She paused again. "Wilomena, the woman I'm here about, I think you knew her. Her name was—"

"Lois," Wilomena said heavily, as if uttering the name was exhausting. "Funny how everyone and their aunt Jo all the sudden takes a serious interest in this woman. She had to turn up on a beach with a seagull's beak buried in her cooch first, though." Aideen had never heard that fact, and for a split second her face froze in horror. Wilomena looked back at her apologetically. "I saw that shit. It was nasty."

"I'm really sorry."

"So did they find him?"

"You mean the killer? They arrested someone, yes."

"He did it." Wilomena said it with casual certainty.

"Well, he's who I represent, Wilomena. I'll understand if you don't want to speak with me knowing that. I will say that you're right about Lois. I've found out a few things about her. No one really paid her any mind until she was dead. That's awful."

"You're trying to get him off, then? Or plead him out?"

"Right now, I'm just trying to figure it all out. I believe that something's wrong, and that Joe's a good man. That's why I'm representing him, and it's why I'm here."

Wilomena's eyes had been dulcet and sleepy but now lit up sharp again. "He's a good man? Strangled his mother like that? That's the word on the street."

"I don't think they arrested the right person."

"Oh, I got a headache comin' on."

Aideen sighed. "Yeah, I know that feeling. Did the cops ever show you Joe's photo?"

"Didn't see no photos from the cops."

"Do you mind looking at one?" Again, Wilomena just shrugged. From the briefcase Aideen drew a manila envelope and then from it a photo of Joe, taken from his law firm's website. He and his old partner, Jack Abrams, stood side by side in sharp suits against a dark background. "He's the one on the left." Wilomena studied the photo for a few seconds. She seemed about to speak but then stopped herself, her eyes still on it.

"He's a lawyer too?"

"He is, yes."

"Lois mentioned him," Wilomena said matter-of-factly. Aideen felt her heart pick up a beat. "She said she knew where he lived, even."

Aideen was taken aback. "Were you able to tell the police this?"

"Police didn't ask. Anyway, I didn't remember it until I saw that picture. Wilomena's tired, yo."

"Sure. So Lois knew that Joe was her son, and that he lived nearby?"

"Something like that, I didn't grab it all. Sad-ass story's what it sounded like. Old lady wandering around out here, living in shelters and looking for her lawyer son? What's that about?"

"They were estranged for many years," Aideen said.

"Sad-ass story."

"It is. It's very interesting to me that Lois was looking for Joe."

"Yeah, maybe Joe didn't want to be found."

"Maybe. Can I show you one other photo? This one is of Lois, but it's from a couple of years ago." She held up the printout of the *Sacramento Bee* article, the one with a photo of a group of women posing with Pastor Nelson in a community garden. Wilomena hesitated, then looked over.

"Yeah, that's her. The old lady on the right side."

"Did she look much different when you met her this summer?"

"Not really. A few pounds lighter, maybe."

"That photo was taken in California, before she came back here."

"California. She should have stayed there."

"That's the thing. Based on what you're telling me, I'm wondering if she came back here to maybe look for family, like Joe. They were apart for many, many years, but . . . I get the sense she might have wanted to reconnect with him."

Wilomena released a heaving breath, like she was tolerating a particularly annoying child. "If you or anyone else had ever talked to her before she got strangled out here, you wouldn't have to *get the sense*, yo."

"It's what she told you, then? I'm sorry to sound thickheaded, Wilomena, but these details could be everything."

"Wasn't much. She hadn't seen him in a long time, just like you said. I think she took up here because she found out he lived in one of these neighborhoods, off the beach."

"He does," Aideen said. "But from what I understand from reading the police reports, Lois was trying to get to Staten Island. That's where she's from, orig—"

"She needed a lawyer, first," Wilomena said, interrupting.

Aideen's fingertips were tingling. "She needed a lawyer?"

"That's what she told me. This guy, Joe? As far as I know, he's the person she wanted to connect with. I don't know what she planned on after that. Pick up the pieces somewhere else. Staten Island, maybe, whatever was over there."

"Right," Aideen said, as if confirming it aloud helped her put it together. "So Lois knew her son Joe was an attorney, and she needed his help. It would have been hard for her to approach him. I have an idea of how long she was away from her sons. And how she left them."

"She never said nothing to me about that," Wilomena said, as if warding off another person's problem. "Chitchat, that's all we had. I don't know if she ever found him, or if he found her. I hope he didn't do that shit to her, though."

"Me too." Aideen was sweating with the sun on her back, but a welcome breeze swept in from the ocean and lifted her hair. She was hesitant to ask the next thing. "So if police wanted to know about this, would you talk to them?"

Wilomena frowned. "The one lady cop. Spanish lady. I guess I'd talk to her. You know who she is."

"I do."

Wilomena looked satisfied for a moment, then scrunched up her face. "How the hell'd you find me, anyway? I know what goes in those reports. 'No fixed address.' That's what they write. I've seen that shit. You found me anyway."

"Finding people, I learned from my husband," Aideen said. "It's harder to do it without a badge, though." There was a gleam in her eye—part pride, part fresh ache—and for a flash she thought she saw it reflected in the other woman's. "Take care out here, Wilomena. Thank you again."

CHAPTER 55

Tuesday, August 29, 2017
Anna M. Kross Center, Rikers Island
East River in the Bronx
9:45 a.m.

"You ever walk through a crowd," Joe mused, "like anywhere in this town, and even though there are hundreds of people, you see how one person is looking at you?" Seated across from Aideen in an attorney interview room, he seemed subdued and unusually sad.

"I'm not that perceptive," she said. "I can imagine that, though, sure."

"I can't remember where I was." He scratched the back of his neck where the jumpsuit collar was itching him. "I was probably half-drunk. I know I saw her, though. I'm positive."

"Tell me what you remember."

"I just told you, I don't remember where I was."

"That's not what I asked you," she said patiently. "Just tell me what comes to mind."

"There was no expression," he said after a few seconds. His eyes dimmed. "She wasn't afraid. She wasn't hopeful. She wasn't . . . expectant. She was just watching me. Like clocking me."

"Okay."

"It was dusk, or just after dark. Everything was a mess, like trash every . . ." He trailed off and snapped his eyes to Aideen's. "Yes, trash! I remember now. It was right after the Fourth of July, because the whole boardwalk was a mess."

"Ah, so it *was* Coney Island. Makes sense. It looks like that's where she took up residence."

"Yeah, it was on the boardwalk," Joe said. "I walked there from the boat, right next to Calvert Vaux Park. It's a good half-hour walk. I probably walked down to Surf Avenue and hung a left, east to where the beach bars are. I can see it now. Things were slow at work because of the holiday. I'd been half in the bag all week, to tell you the truth." He paused, and Aideen fanned herself with a manila envelope. There was AC running, but the air in the room was hot and thick. Murmurings of attorney-client conversations droned nearby.

"Tell me more," she said. "Close your eyes if you have to. Tell me what you saw."

"It was just a moment." He shook his head. "She was looking at me, though, from the beach side, near one of the bathhouses—you know, those brick buildings you walk through to get onto the beach. I was still walking east, toward the aquarium. There were plenty of people out: families, kids, the usual weirdos. Then there she was, following me with her eyes. Like a cat."

"Was she standing? Sitting?"

"She was standing." His eyes went dim again, like he was hypnotized. "Just by herself. She had a long dress on, kind of like in the newspaper photo you found." His brow knitted. "There's something else I noticed. She was smoking a cigarette."

"Okay."

"I can see it now, in her right hand, between the first two fingers. And she was . . . tapping on the butt with her thumb." He made the motion himself, then swallowed hard and looked at Aideen with eyes raw. "Lois smoked like that. All the time. That tapping. It was like a nervous tic. I didn't recognize her, though. I mean, even seeing that, it didn't register."

"It did though," she said. "You remember it, so it registered somewhere. It just had to be drawn to the surface, like something in a well. I have moments where I remember things about Ben that way. Little things, like how he twirled his cell phone or flicked beer bottle caps into the trash. They sneak up on you."

"But . . . forty years?"

"I don't think it matters," she said with a shrug. "I know your memories are distant, but . . . I think it works the same."

"Maybe I should have talked to her, even if I didn't know who she was, if she was looking at me like that." He stared at his hands.

"That's not what most people do," she said. "Particularly in this town. Look, you have to process this. I don't think you can second-guess what you should have done. But I think what I got from the homeless woman, Wilomena, makes sense: Lois came back here for a few reasons, maybe, but at least one of them was hitting you up for legal help."

"I can't imagine why, though. You said you found no charges against her, right? No judgments?"

"Correct, nothing. That Lutheran church really cleaned her up. She was in the clear in terms of her own legal problems. So what else, then?"

"I don't know, I just . . ." He trailed off and seemed to sag.

"It's okay." She was in a particularly driven mood, but she had to remember to go a little easier on Joe sometimes. This was important to her, but it was life and death to him. She softened her tone. "Anyway, I'm sorry you didn't get to talk to her. I really am."

"I wish she had said something. Anything. I don't even know how I would have reacted, but . . ."

"She wasn't ready to approach you," Aideen said. "She found you, and she was watching you. Look, it was she who made the choices that put so much distance between you two in the first place. I don't mean to sound harsh, but if Lois thought it would be difficult to approach you again, out of the blue, then she was right. Maybe she was trying to work up to it."

"The DA's gonna say I saw her first and decided for both of us."

"The DA doesn't know about this sighting on the boardwalk."

"I mean in general. They'll say I saw her out there. Targeted her. Hell, they can ask the jury to speculate, to an extent. They'll imply that I found out she was back in New York. They'll say that maybe she *did* try to talk to me. And then I snapped."

"Even if that was true, how does it explain what happened to Holly Rossi?"

"Mimi will want them to believe my cork popped. Decades of pent-up anger, hatred, whatever. Once I crossed the line, it was easier for me to start settling other scores."

"That's a lot of conjecture."

"It goes down easier with DNA evidence," he said. "It's how I'd sell the case, anyway."

"You're *not* selling it," she said. She was heating up again, sensitivity be damned. "We're getting somewhere, so stay with me. Lois isn't the mystery she was a few weeks ago. We've got her whole criminal history. Hogan's team also tracked Lois, right down to a string of bus tickets a few months ago. She got here mid-May, just when it was getting warm. Also remember that Hogan was working for Hathorne when he picked up her trail. That means *Hathorne* knew that Lois was here."

Joe seemed to react to this, his eyes darting quickly back and forth. That was good; she needed him operating on her level of effort, not bogging down with frustration and anguish. "You know," he said, speaking slowly, "it's possible he put her in my way." His face darkened, and he shifted his eyes to her.

"How do you mean?"

"I don't know much at all about who Lois was before she died, but I know Aaron Hathorne. When he's on his game, he can charm anyone. He can make them believe almost anything."

"Okay, so . . ."

"So what if Hathorne did reach out to her? If you found her at that church, maybe he did too. Maybe he reached out, presented himself as someone who cared. He has the skill, believe me. Except that could just mean . . ." He trailed off again.

"I do believe you," she said. "Except that could just mean what?"

He sighed and ran a hand through his hair, then looked up at her. "It could mean he *led* her to me. Maybe that was his goal, to sort of . . . put her in front of me right when . . ."

"Right when what?"

"The anniversary was coming up." His gaze was still on her. "I'd been thinking about it. I'd been fucked up about it for weeks. He probably knew that, or he assumed it. It's the kind of thing Hathorne would do. He'd find her, reach out to her, ingratiate himself to her. A stranger with a long-lost message of hope. He could have lured her back here and dangled her in front of me somehow."

She scrunched up her nose in confusion. "So what are you saying? Hathorne lured your mother to your environment, just hoping you'd snap and kill her?"

"What I'm saying is, I didn't know who I was until very recently. I've learned more in here than I thought possible."

"Ugh." She sighed. She was losing him again. "Joe, you're dry for a change. That's what's bringing this on. There are alcoholics in my family; I know the progression."

"Maybe. Look, I don't want to say I told you so, but I told you so. I'm as hopeless as this case is. I don't even know if I want to beat it."

She would not let this go unchallenged. "Yes, you do, and maybe you still can." They were quiet for a long moment. Joe seemed far away, doubt and hopelessness in his eyes.

"There's still an Occam's razor thing going on here, you know," he said. "We can come up with all kinds of elaborate theories, but at the end of the day, I've got no alibi and my blood at two scenes."

"You know, if I have to convince *you* that you didn't do it, maybe that'll be perfect practice for the jury."

"Jury." The word in his mouth sounded like it was weighing him down. "Where are we with that, anyway? Even with me in here, Mimi Bromowitz won't wait forever to indict."

"This Thursday will be two weeks since I asked her to hold off," Aideen said. "Friday starts Labor Day weekend, so it won't be this week, but after the holiday I'll probably hear something. You're right; she won't wait much longer."

"Go get ready for the weekend. Have some fun with the kids, and forget this for a few days."

"Don't worry about us. We'll be out at my parents' beach place all weekend."

"You should stay there," he said. "You don't need any of this. If I ever see Craig Flynn again, I'll clock him for pulling you into it."

"It's keeping me occupied," she said and smiled weakly. She felt herself deflate a little, coming down from the intensity of the last few minutes. "Craig was right. I've needed this—more than he knows, even."

Interestingly, that was something Aideen hadn't told anyone the truth about since signing on as Joe's counsel. Yes, the case was a nightmare, agonizing and hopeless enough without a client going through some half-assed recovery and believing he could have committed the crimes. Yes, she was consumed with damning DNA evidence, bloody crime scene photos, and now four decades of some fucked-up family's dirty laundry.

She was occupied, though, and that was a blessing. Her bills were paid. The kids were missing their dad and processing his death in the ways they would, and she could only do so much to steer that process. Her own grief was still there, as present as the smell of Ben's aftershave when she dared to pull it from the medicine cabinet.

Beyond that, though, there had been a hole in her days that needed filling. When it was really over—the flag-draped burial complete, the whiskey downed, the bagpipes silent, the endless casseroles eaten, the headstone in place—there was a terrible nothingness, another type of suffering she hadn't expected. She had found it worse than grief, which she understood. This other thing had been stalking and relentless, in her head like the mocking tick of an old clock. She simply hadn't had enough to do.

And then it had happened. Their old boss, Craig Flynn, had rung her up one day.

Hey, Aid, I've got an idea.

Smiling, joshing Craig Flynn, except his smile stopped under his eyes in most cases. The eyes remained deadly serious, cauldrons of conflict and calculation. Thankfully it was largely benevolent calculation. Craig was a complex man but a decent one. For whatever reason, he had calculated that Aideen and Joe needed each other. He'd had an idea.

You sure did, you son a bitch, she thought. *You sure did.*

CHAPTER 56

Thursday, August 31, 2017
Harbor View Rehabilitation Center
Staten Island
7:59 p.m.

The wooden door to the room at the end of the hallway was thick and closed with a sturdy *chunk*. On the outside hung a small whiteboard with the name "Caleb Evermore" written in dry-erase marker. It seemed a cruel irony that Evermore's name was scrawled that way, as if he might soon be up on his feet and released, a new patient's name written on the board. In fact, no one had taken Caleb's place in that room in fifteen years. And he had not walked a single step on his own since birth, decades before that.

"Do you know him?" Miguel asked. They were both in the room—he and Robbie. Miguel was resting his huge hands on a mop handle, the mop swishing in a dirty yellow roller bucket. He grasped the handle like a knight with a mighty sword. Robbie scoffed.

"Oh yeah, we play cards."

"I don't mean nothin' by it," Miguel said. "I've seen you in here looking in on him. I just thought there was a connection. Some people take jobs in here 'cause they had people in places like this, you know?"

"Too depressing to think about."

Robbie couldn't stand Miguel. He was one of those always-smiling guys. Friendly but a subtle know-it-all. If you had a story, he had a better one.

"If you got depression, coma services ain't where you need to be," Miguel said in a low, paternal tone, like he was delivering anticipated wisdom. Robbie didn't respond at all, so after a few seconds Miguel went back to talking. "No one comes to see him. I mean, it's good that you're in and out at least."

"I'm in and out because he shits a lot."

"It took me a while to get used to the persistent ones up here," Miguel said with a meticulous punctuation of "persistent." He meant the people in coma services, like Caleb Evermore, who were in a persistent vegetative state, or close to it. Robbie had seen the notes that described Mr. Evermore. He was not totally comatose, but most descriptions of him culminated with "reacts inconsistently and nonpurposefully to stimuli in a nonspecific manner."

"It beats the screaming I hear in other parts of this place."

"You know," Miguel said, lowering his voice and glancing toward the man in the bed, "he was a Willowbrook kid." And there it was. The story Miguel knew that so few others knew. He was like that one local tour guide all the websites tell you to ask for when you visit some place.

"Oh yeah?"

"Yeah, man. They brought him over in the early '70s. He got lucky, I guess. They didn't close that place until the late '80s."

"The coma lottery," Robbie said, staring at Caleb's half-closed eyes and partially open mouth. "I guess that is lucky."

"He wasn't always this out of it," Miguel said. "He's gotten worse over time."

"Sucks to be him."

"You working all weekend?" Miguel asked. The next day was Friday, the start of Labor Day weekend.

"Most of it."

"Time and a half, I'll take it."

"Yeah." Robbie had shown about as little interest as possible in anything Miguel had to say. "Cigarette break," he said, and left the larger man poised atop his mop handle before he could open his mouth again.

From his cage in the employee locker area on the ground floor, Robbie strolled out into the warm, muggy evening and sat down on a concrete bench outside the ground floor entrance. The sun was down, and the last of the light was melting in the sky, receding in a brilliant mix of red, orange, and purple. New Jersey's "chemical coast" wasn't much on scenery, but it did produce some fabulous sunsets. Summer sunsets reminded him of that long-ago July night. He remembered sweating in polyester shorts on slick vinyl and dodging his mother's occasional cigarette cherries when she ashed out the window, the dirty air rushing through his hair. He remembered the boredom that drove him, at intervals, to fuck with his whiny little brother.

And underneath the mundane memories, in a way he couldn't quite express to himself, he remembered the powerlessness. That shrugging sort of helplessness. Wasn't that what being a fucking kid was, ultimately? All you had were the grown-ups who carted you around. You wondered. You worried. You counted the endless minutes in the hot, vibrating car. You weren't in control, though. Not of anything. All you could do was sit there, propelled through whatever someone else had decided for you.

"Hi, Mr. DeSantos?" he heard. He was slumped over but now sat bolt upright. Before him was a short, heavyset, and attractive woman with bright eyes and blonde hair.

"Who's asking?" he said, and was proud that he had thought of it on the fly like that. Truth was, he was startled. Wearing a pantsuit with a white blouse and carrying a briefcase, she had walked over from the parking lot. His eyes narrowed. "Wait a minute. You're my brother's lawyer."

"Aideen Bradigan," she said. "That's right. I am."

CHAPTER 57

8:13 p.m.

"You don't have to speak with me," she said, but without waiting she took a seat on the bench next to Robbie's. "I hope you will, though."

"My brother is toast," he said. "I'll talk, but I can't help you, lady. I hope he's paying you."

"Do you mind if I take notes? I'm not recording anything, but I like to jot things down." A lamppost over their benches cast a sodium glow on the notepad, and she readied her pen. Robbie seemed to stiffen, then relaxed. He looked older than in the one recent photo she had seen of him. There were dark circles under his eyes. She wondered if the fortieth anniversary of the blackout had gotten to him also.

"Whatever."

"I know Joe asked you already about your mother. Like if you had seen her right before she was found at Coney Island."

"Yeah, no," he said, muffled, as he lit another cigarette. He looked up and grinned, the cigarette pointing upward between his lips as he sucked it to life. "I'd say the last time I saw my mother was the same night Joe last saw her, but I guess that's not true, huh?"

"Correct," she said. "Joe did see her, or he believes he did, before she was killed."

"Yeah, that's not what I meant." His eyes, a little beady—which was strange, as Joe's were so big and expressive—narrowed on her. "You don't live in Staten Island, do you? You look like you drove a long way to hear me tell you nothing."

"Westchester," she said truthfully. "It's a long way, but I've traveled farther to hear less. I assume you don't have much to say about recent events. I'm actually curious about what you remember from the night your mother disappeared."

The cigarette in his hand seemed to twitch. "The blackout?"

"Yes. Do you mind if I ask you a few questions?"

"What the hell for? That was forty years ago; what's it got to do with anything now?"

"Honestly, I'm not sure," she said. She punctuated this with the ghost of a smile, a kind of golly-gee expression to lighten things up. "You never know what might be relevant, though."

Robbie looked unmoved. He seemed completely guarded now. "I don't talk about it much," he said. She expected stubborn or awkward silence to follow, but instead he started talking rapidly. "There isn't much to talk about, and I'm not about to repeat a bunch of shit my brother probably already told you. She ditched us. We got through the city on foot. A bunch of shit happened, and then Joe and I made it here separately, about a day apart. We never saw my mother again. Forty years later, I'm still here. Joe's in jail. End of story."

"Joe told me some details," she said. "It sounds very frightening, being left in the city on your own. Especially then, and in a blackout."

"We did okay," he said. "She ditched us, and we still did okay on our own."

"Not completely on your own, though, right?" she said. She saw him stiffen. He drew hard on the cigarette. "You had help at some point, right? Joe mentioned someone."

"Who, my uncle Mike?"

"Well, yes, but before that. A friend of your uncle's. A man named Nate. He was able to help you, right?"

Robbie opened his mouth as if to speak, then shut it again. The emotion that spread across his face was one of pure hate, she was certain of it. "Nate was . . ." He trailed off but then seemed to collect himself. "Nate was some guy my uncle knew. He was in the city. He helped Joe, maybe. He didn't help me. We split up, like I said. I got here on my own."

"I understood that also," Aideen said. She was a little nervous; the man next to her suddenly seemed like an overinflated tire about to explode. She glanced around. It was almost full dark, but there were plenty of cars still in the parking lot and some foot traffic on the grounds. "I guess what I'm asking is, can you explain that to me? What happened between you, Joe, and Nate?"

He flicked the cigarette away and glared at her, his little eyes like lasers. "No, lady, I can't. How about that?" He stood up, and she set her pen down. "How about none of this shit matters? How about—sorry, but how about *fuck you*—and you get out of my face?" He seemed to catch himself then and walked back into the building.

CHAPTER 58

July 14, 1977
Forty-Seventh Street and Eighth Avenue
Midtown Manhattan
12:22 a.m.

"Who is Nate?" Joe asked. They were roughly following Uncle Mike's directions, which were to stay along Broadway as they walked south, since there was likely to be more car and foot traffic. The place where Nate was to meet them was near the Port Authority Bus Terminal, just off Eighth Avenue on Forty-Third Street. When they were near Times Square, they were to look for a safe street to move from Broadway over to Eighth Avenue and then follow it south against the traffic to Forty-Third. There was a coffee shop near the corner where Nate would meet them.

"He's a friend of Uncle Mike's, I guess," Robbie said. "Probably a queer too."

"Will he help us find Mom?"

"Stop asking about Mom." Robbie's voice was cold and flat. Joe sniffed, and Robbie looked over like Joe was about to throw up on the living room rug. "Don't cry."

"I'm not."

"Don't," Robbie said. "We need to look cool, okay? We need to look in control." Joe nodded and wiped his eyes. He had taken to counting pizza *places. Four so far since Seventy-Second Street, all with guys in aprons standing out front, talking to passersby. One pizza maker with a flashlight was simultaneously illuminating and giving the finger to a huge rectangular sign above his store that said* ReElect Mayor Beame.

It turned out that Broadway wasn't very easy to follow. A few blocks south of Seventy-Second Street was Lincoln Center. The wide plaza and quiet fountain in front were surrounded by well-dressed grown-ups who smoked in the dark and tried to hail taxicabs. There was another weirdly shaped intersection at Sixty-Fifth Street. The darkness made it difficult to determine which corridor to follow. Absent headlights, they were left navigating vague spaces between buildings and tended to move in the direction of more activity if it didn't seem threatening.

That was a gamble also. Some groups were laughing and chattering until Joe and Robbie passed by, then became eerily quiet. When that happened, Joe felt his breath catch in his throat. They would hear the occasional taunt, but so far no one had pursued them. Once, just north of Columbus Circle, they passed a rowdy group of boys who threw insults at them and then a bottle that shattered just behind Joe's heel as they quickened their pace.

Things got less scary as they reached Fifty-Eighth Street and moved south toward Times Square. There was more car traffic, so more ambient light and more people on the street. Many looked cheerful, sweaty, and a little drunk. Broadway had narrowed to one lane, and bars and restaurants on either side had open doors and candles burning inside. People were dressed better than the shadowy figures they had seen earlier. Many men were in loosened ties and damp dress shirts. Women had their hair tied up and patted their necks with handkerchiefs.

The activity increased as Joe spied the sign for Fiftieth Street and declared they had advanced another ten blocks. Now they were dodging people on the sidewalk, including an increasing number of shady guys making "psst" sounds and flashing things for sale. Across the street at Forty-Eighth was a massive video store—the word "video" and silhouetted graphics of men and women in sex positions were unmistakable even in the dark—with a crowd milling around in front.

At Forty-Seventh Street, Robbie looked to the right and decided to walk west to Eighth Avenue. People were plentiful, including a raucous crowd singing and carousing below a cluster of garish theater and marquee signs. The only one Joe could read in the gloom was tall and rectangular with Oh! Calcutta! in cursive, which meant nothing to him. Along the street were other theaters, including some that looked like they probably showed dirty movies, and several cramped-looking bars. Westbound vehicles lit their path; there was a general flow of foot traffic going the same way.

"Eighth Avenue," Robbie said when they reached the corner. "This way." Joe hesitated as Robbie turned south. The strip they were leaving, even in the dark, was gay and lively compared to this darker, wider thoroughfare. Then a creepy guy was talking to him about where there was a girl he could see, and Joe hoofed it to catch up to his brother.

He took to counting dirty movie theaters. They had seen them along their route since Fiftieth Street, but on Eighth Avenue they were on every block. Under each deadened marquee were at least two or three restless-looking men and boys watching the traffic pass. Hollywood, Capri, Eros, Peepworld. It should have been more entertaining, but Joe felt strangely exposed and nervous walking by these places. The marquees, when he could read them, said things that made him feel mushy inside. SEXational. The Swedish Way. The Devil in Mrs. Jones. All Male Action.

"There are buses, you know," Joe said as they passed Forty-Sixth Street. The darkness around him seemed to thicken. "I kind of wish we had taken one."

"We don't have the money for that."

"Geneviève gave you money. I saw it!" That was true. Joe had seen Geneviève reach into a cash drawer while he was coming out of the bathroom and hand Robbie some coins and a couple of crumpled bills. Robbie's face looked forlorn upon accepting it, which seemed strange to Joe. Wasn't that what grown-ups did for kids when they were left on their own?

"That's for emergencies," Robbie said. "I wouldn't have taken it otherwise."

"Why can't I have some?"

"What did I just tell you? It's for emergencies."

"That's not fair; you're not the boss! That was for both of us."

"Yes, I am the boss," Robbie said. "Without Mom here, that's exactly what I am. I almost told Uncle Mike he could piss off too. He didn't want us to walk down here by ourselves. You know what? We're fine."

"I don't like this street," Joe said. Robbie continued on like he hadn't heard him.

"And you know what else? If Uncle Mike tries to put a bunch of rules on us, I'm not following 'em. Why should I? I've gotten us this far. He's not even here."

"I wish there were more cars," Joe said. There were vehicles from time to time, but the boys were walking toward oncoming traffic, so headlights would blind them momentarily, making figures and faces harder to see afterward.

"It's like three more blocks, just—"

"Three blocks to where?" a voice asked. It was raspy, and the word "where" was drawn out.

Joe looked back. The man was short and skinny, in cutoff jeans and a dirty T-shirt with the car from Smokey and the Bandit on the front. He had a mustache, and his jaw moved in a circular motion like he was chewing gum. His eyes were wide circles in the dark.

"Nowhere," Robbie said to the side. "Joe, come on."

"Joe, is that your name? You don't gotta listen to him. Come on, hang back."

"Chino, get the fuck away from them boys!" someone called out from the other side of the street. The voice was deep and booming, but the person behind it was swishing across the street in a long, tight-fitting yellow dress and a pink wig. Whoever it was was easily twice Joe's size, with makeup *obvious even in the murkiness—thick, bright lipstick and winged eye shadow. And then to the boys: "What the fuck are you doing out here?! Run!"*

As if the word was a starting gun, they ran. Joe and Robbie sprinted down the avenue past doorways, theaters, smoke shops, and piles of trash. Joe strained to see his steps pounding the pavement, but fear wouldn't let him slow down. He could hear Robbie huffing and puffing next to him, and then Robbie pulled ahead. He jumped over a little pile of stinking garbage next to a fire hydrant. Then Joe tripped on an empty forty-ounce bottle. The bottle didn't break, but it rolled under his right foot, so he spun around, his left foot scraping for purchase on the sidewalk. His arms were doing pinwheels as he staggered backward. Then something hooked into the right pocket of his shorts and dug into his hip. He boomeranged forward and then felt searing pain as something pressed into him. There was a tearing sound as his shorts came almost all the way off.

"Joe, what happened?" Robbie yelled, heaving to catch his breath. Joe still had no idea what had happened, but now he saw it, the scaffolding he had run under. A thick bolt was sticking out from one of the scaffolding poles. It had caught on his pocket and prevented him from falling backward, but it had also torn his pants open, as well as left a scratch.

"I got caught on something," he said. He reached to pull his shorts up, but they were torn all the way open. The next second he was just holding them in his hand.

"Oh no."

"Oh my God," Robbie said, still breathing hard. "We're almost there. What the fuck?"

"F-word."

"Oh for . . . who cares? What happened?"

"I told you, I got caught on something." He looked down at his body, covered only by white Fruit of the Loom briefs below his T-shirt. The ruined shorts were still in his hand. "Where are we?"

"Almost at Forty-Third," Robbie said. "Come on, I guess."

"I can't be out like this!"

"What else can you do? Pull your T-shirt down." Robbie turned away and started walking. Joe looked around him. There was no one following them. There was no one at all on the street. Still, he felt like he positively glowed with his shorts gone. His T-shirt was a little oversize, a thick-striped maroon and brown. He pulled it down as far as he could and stomped forward.

At the corner of Forty-Third and Eighth Avenue, Robbie dashed across the street in front of a black limousine and a city bus. Joe hung back, petrified of the headlights, but then got moving. Going west, Forty-Third Street was swallowed in darkness. But there on the right, just a few steps down from the corner, was the open door of a business with a corona of yellow light and the tinny sound of music. The music was the kind Joe heard where people spoke Spanish. He fell in step behind Robbie, wanting to stay within his shadow as they approached the door.

When Joe peeked in, the first thing he saw was the fattest man he had perhaps ever seen. The man was surrounded by candles and sat on a wooden chair in front of a darkened pastry counter. The candles were placed along the counter, on the floor behind him, and on shelves on the wall. The man was sweating profusely and bulging out of a tentlike baby-blue T-shirt. He wore shorts that ballooned below the belt line between his legs. On a table next to him was a transistor radio that played the music, with lots of horns and harmonious voices.

"Mira, Nate!" he called out, his dark face breaking into a toothy smile. "Tu corillo!" From the left side of the store, a tall, lanky man stood from a table and set down a tiny cup of coffee. He brushed his hands on his jeans and walked over to the door. He was dark skinned and long limbed, with sad, expressive eyes. Joe liked him instantly. He seemed kind and knowing, which was exactly what Joe craved in that moment.

"Joe and Robbie," Nate said. His voice was deep and smooth, like a DJ's. His lips turned up into a smile. "I'm Nate Porter. Welcome to New York."

CHAPTER 59

Nate Porter opened the outer door to his East Village apartment building and sighed. At sixty-eight, he was getting too old for this. He had been away for Labor Day weekend with friends on Fire Island and had returned early to get a fresh start on the week. Now instead of relaxing, doing laundry, and maybe reading a book, he had a mini crisis to deal with.

There was a little vestibule between the outer and inner doors of the building. The lock on the inner door had been broken for months, with a quarter-size hole where the lock housing should have been. Just inside the inner door, spread out in the dimly lit hallway, was a clearly homeless man with terrible body odor and blackened bare feet.

Nate was not surprised. This was just the latest in a string of impositions, hardships, and insults being hurled at the residents by their landlord, among the most notorious in the entire city. The landlord was determined to clear the building of its rent-controlled tenants and convert their apartments to what would be multimillion-dollar condominiums. Nate had moved into the building as a younger man, when the corner was dangerous and trash strewn. By 2017 it was a playground for the rich, and do-gooder old queens like him were just in the way.

He was the building's unofficially appointed advocate against the landlord's tactics, and so tasked with dealing with things like this: the landlord's thugs planting homeless men in the hallways, along with heroin addicts and prostitutes. Nate was well suited to the job. He was a retired social worker and had dealt with vulnerable populations for decades. It was through city social work, in fact, that he had met Mike Carroll, the man who would become his lover not long before becoming a father figure to two young boys in July of 1977.

"Sir," Nate said, "you can't be in here." Age had grayed his hair and stooped him a little, but he was still tall and slim, neat and fastidious, with the same kind face and knowing aura. His voice retained its DJ quality, sonorous and calming.

"Fugginlivehere," the man mumbled into the floor.

"Sir, that's not true. There's a nearby men's shelter I can point you to up on Thirtieth Street. They'll assist you, but you can't stay here."

"Fugginlivehere," he said again, slurred really, so the words would have been unintelligible had Nate not just heard them. "Leave me the fuck alone."

"You need to get up," Nate said more forcefully. "Get up and get out, or I'll see to it that you're escorted out." He was careful not to threaten to call the police, as he was certain the guy had been allowed in by someone connected to the landlord.

For a moment the man was silent, as if he'd fallen asleep. Then he turned toward Nate, exposing broken teeth behind a leering grin. When he spoke this time, there was no slur in his voice. His eyes, surprisingly alert and cruel, narrowed on the older man. "Back off, asshole. I got a right to be here."

Nate clenched his fists and gritted his teeth but then slowly unclenched them and grinned back. "Five minutes." He made a five with his left hand. "I'll be back." The lobby was small and rectangular, maybe twenty feet wide, with a brass mailbox panel on the right side and two elevators straight ahead. The guy stretched out across the lobby floor so that his head was just under the mailboxes. Nate walked around him toward the elevators. Just before the elevator bank, on the right, was the door to the stairwell.

"Come back with an army," he heard. "See if I give a shit!"

The building had two elevators, only one in service. The other, on the right if you were facing them, had been broken for months, with no signs of being fixed. The steel doors on the lobby level were stuck in a partially open position, with a rectangular piece of plywood covering the bottom half of the doorframe. The plywood was screwed into the wall on either side, and blue painter's tape created a big X over the entire frame. Before the weather turned in April, cold wind whistled up the shaft, blowing hard enough through the lobby that a letter might fly out of a person's hands at the mailboxes.

Nate stepped into the working elevator and hit the button for the fifth floor. As the car rose with jolts and squeaks, he pictured his fellow residents as the lower floors passed underneath. The widow, Mrs. Horowitz, on the second floor had a hole in her ceiling after "construction" had been started but never completed. On the fourth floor was a Pakistani family with twin toddlers who had been subjected to a rat infestation that began when someone dumped a box of them out of a makeshift trap in the hallway.

Nate wasn't particularly angry at the homeless guy; he was just a tool in the landlord's hands. He didn't know exactly what he would do when he went back downstairs, but he knew he had to return, and with a weapon. Hopefully, he'd only need to brandish it. A tire iron had done the trick the last time he had to chase someone out. There were helpless kids and old people in that building. An aggressive vagrant could be dangerous.

He found the tire iron in his front closet. The elevator creaked like a Spanish galleon as it moved slowly back down to the lobby. Nate hoped the noise of it approaching would encourage the guy to move on while the getting was good. When the doors opened to the lobby, though, the man was still there.

And something was very wrong.

He was still curled up on the floor facing the front door, but his head was turned back toward the elevators. The angle wasn't right, though. His head wasn't just turned back, it was *wrenched* back, the expression on his face no longer a dirty grin but a hideous grimace. His eyes were glassy and frozen open with something like astonishment. Nate took a few steps toward him and dropped the tire iron. It made a dull thud on the softened linoleum. Beside him, on his left, was the door to the stairwell. He took another step and kneeled down before the body. Now it was clear. The man's head had been twisted in some horrid display of force, his neck snapped like a bundle of dry twigs. The neck was already starting to purple, with pools of blood under the skin spreading like blossoms. A second later, a prickling sensation moved up his spine, all the way to the hairline.

Someone's behind me.

He rose and turned just in time to see a figure eclipse his vision. A big, bare forearm clipped the left side of his jaw, spinning him back the other way. Then a thick, heavy hand came down on his right shoulder, grasping like a pincer.

He's behind me! He's behind me! He's going to tear my fucking head off!

Nate threw his head back as hard as he could, connecting with a satisfying thud against flesh behind him. As he hoped, he had struck the attacker's face. There was a terrible howl and then a string of curses and hard, heavy mouth breathing.

"Motherfucker, motherfucker . . ." The words were garbled and thick. Nate ducked, stepped to the right, and turned around. The tire iron was just a step away, but the attacker was reaching for it also, even while he belted out curses and blood poured from his nose and mouth. The man was sizable and sturdy, dressed in khakis and a dark T-shirt. Nate couldn't see his face, as he was staring at the floor. He was white, at least middle aged, and moving his arms back and forth as if sweeping the surface in search of the tire iron.

Nate was spry and his vision was good, even in the dimness of the lobby, so the grab for the tire iron wasn't much of a contest. He snatched it up and swung it sideways at the man, still bent over and bleeding from his mouth and nose.

"Owwww!" He clutched his midsection and stumbled backward toward the stairwell door. Nate raised the iron again. He didn't want to knock the guy's head off, but he wanted him prostrate, on the ground and neutralized. The man demonstrated some interesting acrobatics, though, ducking the blow by hitting his knees and then scrambling away. He started out in a crawling position but rose and ran toward the elevators.

"Stop!" Nate yelled. "I don't want to hurt you, just . . ." He trailed off as the man lunged toward the broken elevator like a rodeo bull from a chute. He grabbed the plywood piece and yanked it backward. The screws, the blue tape, and everything else gave way like a popped balloon. The man plunged two thick arms between the stilled open doors of the elevator and grunted. They moved apart, and he squeezed between them. Nate watched, horrified, as the man flung himself into the black space.

There was no car behind the lobby elevator doors. The car itself was stalled between the eighth and ninth floors. Behind the doors was just the shaft space, with one thick cord bundle reaching upward toward the car. Under that was the bottom of the shaft, two levels below in a sub-basement, maybe twenty-five feet from the lobby level. At the bottom of the shaft, surrounding the cord bundle, were four heavy springs. One of the springs was damaged. In an abandoned repair attempt, it had been left partially uncoiled so that a stiff, daggerlike spike pointed upward.

It was on this rusting, thick metal prong that the attacker's chest landed. Because of a hideous display of physics, he not only impaled himself on the exposed end of the spring but also twisted a three-quarter turn as the spring bored farther into his body. Behind the rib cage, the metal dug into his heart and lungs like a wine cork. He was dead before he stopped moving.

CHAPTER 60

The body of the man impaled on the elevator spring was bathed in the harsh glare of three aluminum-cased floodlights. NYPD's Emergency Services Unit, or ESU, had responded around the same time as the Ninth Precinct detectives and commanders. The ESU was something like a SWAT team within the NYPD, but in addition to those kinds of duties, it also responded to structural failures, cave-ins, fallen debris, and things like this—a body at the bottom of an elevator shaft. ESU responders extended a ladder to the bottom of the shaft, checked the stability of the elevator car above them, and ran lighting equipment down to the bottom. Meanwhile, the Ninth Precinct detective catching the case waited patiently before being invited down the ladder. Around Zochi's age, she was an athletic, youthful-looking Black woman named Letitia Clark. She went by Letty.

Now at the bottom, Letty hunkered down to look at the dead man's face, a flashlight in her gloved hand. Even though light was everywhere, there were still tricky shadows cast by the body itself. She rested on her hamstrings so as not to place her knees on the concrete floor of the shaft. The floor was filthy, coated with dust and grime, as was the bottom apparatus itself, the massive iron springs and cables that fastened to a steel plate and ran up into darkness.

Above her, another Ninth Precinct detective and a police captain looked down on the scene, their faces gauzy in the glow of the lights. With her—and Letty was thankful for this—was a sturdy and extremely handsome young ESU cop named Will Perry. She wasn't freaked out by the body, but the idea of being more than twenty feet underground in a cramped and dank elevator shaft was a little unsettling. Perry stood a few feet from her, poised in the corner in an "at ease" stance, as if awaiting orders. He was over six feet tall with light hair, broad shoulders, and big, piercing eyes.

Handsome white boy, she thought, knowing it wasn't what she should be focused on but allowing a moment's recognition of it anyway. *Yes, and also very young.* Well, they were all getting younger compared to her, weren't they? She shook her head and grinned to herself, then steadied the flashlight on the dead man's face. The grin disappeared, replaced by an ear-to-ear, squinting grimace. She was grateful it wasn't her job to pull the body from the deadly spring, the top of which was burrowed into the man's chest.

There were growing spots of purple on his chin and nose, the result of blood starting to pool in those places. Under the nose was a bushy, graying mustache. He was facing downward, his head not quite touching the steel plate where the spring was attached. His eyes were wide open and pointed upward so that the tops of the irises were under the eyelids. They looked almost cartoonish, the way dead people's eyes were presumed to be focused if encountered still open. The mouth was agape, and a wide tongue poked out. A quantity of blood had come out of his nose and mouth, she noticed, but the stream had long since stopped. The blood flow from his face looked like he'd been struck somehow. To Letty, it looked he'd been punched or headbutted, something that must have happened before he took the fall.

She shined the light at the wound. Blood was still dripping from the spot where the spring had torn through his shirt. The dripping had slowed, so there was no longer a steady *pat-pat-pat* sound as the drops hit the steel.

"Perry," she said. Her hams ached. She stood up, arching her back and stretching. Perry snapped to attention.

"Yes, ma'am?"

"I think we know what killed him."

"Seems clear, yes."

"Were you in the military before this job?"

"The Marine Corps, yes ma'am."

"Good on you," she said with a clipped nod. "I'm going back up that ladder. MLI should be here anytime, and this is their job now, but you shouldn't have to wait down here alone with him. If you want to take a break and come up after me, no one will have a problem with that."

"I'm fine, ma'am, but thank you. I'll watch as you go up. Please be careful. Hold on to both sides." Now she felt a little self-conscious about her backside as she made her way up the ladder with Perry looking after her. Up top she described what she had seen, and the captain made a similar cringe face. He was red faced, heavyset, and completely bald.

"The witness says the guy ran toward the doors," the captain said, "tore the plywood off, and jumped in. Maybe he thought there was an elevator car there."

"The witness—the old Black guy?"

"Yeah, he says he had a tire iron. Says he was gonna scare the homeless guy with it, but then this other dude came out of nowhere and attacked him. Says he was able to whack the dude with the tire iron once or twice, then the dude ran for the elevator. That's it."

"And he says the homeless guy was already dead?"

"Looked dead."

"Do we believe him?"

"So far," the captain said with a shrug. They glanced in unison toward the homeless man's body, with its blackened feet and clearly broken neck. Crime scene photographers and MLI techs were prepping it for transport.

"Where's Ito?" she asked, referring to her partner, Kevin Ito.

"He's canvassing in the building. He situated your witness. Nate Porter is his name."

"How's he doing?"

"Shaken up, but that's about it. Looks like a tough old guy." He shook his head and stared down the shaft again. "Is that ESU kid okay down there by himself?"

"He's just fine," Letty said, pursing her lips and tugging the blue gloves off. "Just fine."

CHAPTER 61

1:03 a.m.

Letty's witness, Nate Porter, was sturdy looking and wiry, with a thin layer of silver hair and big hands. The hands looked especially large given that he was thin and tall. He had a deep and lovely voice but was soft spoken, as if he knew the voice had power and needed to be reined in. She met him downstairs from the lobby in what was probably the super's office, although it was dust laden and stuffy and didn't look much used. Looking a little spaced out, he sat on a sweat-stained swivel chair with a bottle of water. Nearby were two patrol officers, one male and one female.

Letty had the feeling that Porter was a gay man, though not because he seemed effeminate or carried himself in any particular way. There was just something in how he settled into a chair or moved his hands and arms to stretch or adjust his posture. Maybe it was the way his eyes passed over the scene, the responders, or Letty herself. She could be wrong, and it didn't matter anyway; it was intuition, nothing more. But after twenty years on the job, intuition had become second nature. It was impossible to silence and sometimes strangely valuable. Other times, lifesaving.

"How are you, Mr. Porter?" she asked, pulling up a cracked plastic chair and sitting down. Letty had bright, almond-shaped eyes; a smooth, broad nose; and generous lips. Her hair was bobbed, with short bangs over her forehead. Her stylist called them "fringe."

"I think I'm okay," he said, offering a weak smile.

"I'm sorry about how long this all takes. Soon, we'll move to the precinct. I'll take you over there."

"Thank you."

"I understand that you don't believe you know the man who attacked you. Sometimes, things become clearer, though, after time passes. Does anything ring a bell?"

"I can't even picture him," Nate said, shaking his head and sighing. "It all happened so fast. He looked to me to be white. Younger than me. A big guy. Honestly, that's all I know."

"And the homeless man? You encountered him first?"

"I did." He gave her a play-by-play of what he had seen, heard, and done from the time he walked in until the time he saw the fat guy push his way into the shaft.

"So the homeless man insisted he lived here," she said, taking notes. "And he was pretty aggressive?"

"He was. I really wasn't all that angry; I just had to get him out of here. This sort of thing happens quite a bit—the introduction of homeless or intoxicated people by the landlord. There are children and old people in the building." With that, he explained the conflict.

Letty glanced around the dilapidated, neglected super's office and thought about how the lobby had looked, not to mention the death-trap elevator bank. She had little reason to doubt Porter. They were a few minutes into that backstory when a landlord "representative," escorted by another patrol officer, appeared in the doorway.

"Detective Clark?" the officer asked. He was young, white, and fresh faced.

"Yes?"

"This is, uh, Mr. Cana. He works for the landlord."

"It's pronounced *konna*," he said, flashing a disgusted look at the cop. "Yeah, I work for the landlord. This is our building, so I got a right to be here. What did this guy do, anyway?" He nodded toward Nate, who stared back at him and said nothing. Cana was a swarthy, paunchy man with thick, black eyebrows and a couple of days' growth of beard. His expression, the upper lip slightly curled, was that of a man smelling something unpleasant.

"Some terrible things happened here tonight, Mr. Cana," she said, standing up. "We have a lot of work to do, and it's going to be a long night. I'll speak with you when I can." She moved her eyes to the young officer. "Take him upstairs, please."

"I'm responsible for this building. I'm not going anywhere," Cana said, flashing a threatening look at the cop. He stood back to give command of the scene to Letty.

"What's back there?" she asked Cana, gesturing with her thumb to his left.

"Trash room. Boiler."

"Come with me."

When they had gotten to the boiler room, which reeked of garbage and mildew, Letty crossed her arms and stared at him. "Do not interrupt my investigation or you'll end up in jail tonight."

Cana's face scrunched up in frustration. "Lady, it's my building. And that guy Porter is a menace. Do you know anything about him?"

"See, that's what an *investigation* is," she said, trying to keep her tone a step up from mocking. "That's what I'm doing. Investigating. And please stop saying it's your building, because it's not. I've got an idea of who owns this building, and if I were you, I'd be cooperating with us so that we can go about our business."

"We got lawyers."

"So do we. Plenty." She eyed him keenly. "You know anything about how that dead homeless man got into this building?"

"What? No!"

"So if I go back a few hours and look at surveillance video from two or three points on this street, I won't see someone with a key opening the door for him?" Cana opened his mouth to speak, then shut it again. "That's a good instinct, staying quiet. What about the other guy?"

"What other guy?"

"The guy at the bottom of the elevator shaft."

"I don't know anything about that," he said, his eyes widening. "What happened to him, anyway?"

"That's what we're investigating." She looked closely at him. He was an asshole, but about this, she did not think he was lying. "Someone let the homeless guy in. I'm not sure how the other one got in, but this building is an encyclopedia of DOB complaints, so I'm guessing it wasn't hard. You're going to be answering for quite a few things, so be cooperative."

Cana left with the cop, but before Letty could restart the interview, her partner, Kevin Ito, called down the stairs. Of Japanese descent, Kevin was slight with a crewcut and round glasses. He motioned her up a few steps.

"What is it? I'm trying to get through this interview."

"A couple of things," Kevin said. "The body in the elevator shaft? MLI found a photograph of your witness, that old Black guy, in his pocket."

"Wait. My witness downstairs?"

"Yes." He pushed the John Lennon glasses up his nose. "One other thing—they found ID on the body. His name is Evan Bolds."

CHAPTER 62

"I was sorry to call so late," Letty said to Zochi upon her arrival to the Ninth Precinct. "Your duty lieutenant said you were on the turnaround and might not be sleeping anyway. He gave me your number."

"No, it's fine," she said. She didn't know Letty, but she already respected her as a detective. Once things had calmed down and she was back at the squad room, Letty had done the right thing—dug up data on Bolds and also the mechanism by which it seemed the homeless victim had been killed. By connecting a few dots through the NYPD online system, she was able to see that a Detective Xochitl Hernandez from the Sixtieth Precinct was working on a case with a similar mechanism of death. On top of that, the deceased in Letty's case, Evan Bolds, was the subject of a court case that Hernandez's suspect had been working on right before he himself had been arrested. The connection was enough to attempt late-night contact with Hernandez.

Zochi wasn't sure what to make of Letty's case. DeSantos was in custody, so he wasn't the perpetrator. The details were intriguing, though. One person had been killed in the same way her victims had.

The other body had been a legal target of her suspect when he was still with the AG. She didn't expect much, but who knew? Maybe DeSantos was still involved somehow and not working alone. Maybe he was still pulling strings from Rikers. She had seen that before. There was also a surviving eyewitness she could interview. All things considered, it was worth coming in early for and checking out. Letty was right; she didn't sleep much on the turnaround anyway. She suited up and sped down to the city through warm night air with no traffic. Now in the squad room, the two women stepped away from the flurry of activity for a cup of coffee.

"What time did you come on?" she asked.

"Nine o'clock," Letty said. "The bodies are packed up and the scene is secure, but there's brass everywhere and everyone wants to be briefed. I doubt I'll get out of here in under twenty-four hours."

"Well, overtime."

"Yep. First double homicide we've seen in a while." Letty blew on her coffee. "I feel bad for this witness, Nate Porter? Seems like a nice old guy."

"I don't know anything about him," Zochi said. "What he knows could shed some light; you never know. You sure he's ready to talk to me?"

"He's shaken up, but he seems okay to me. Less spaced out than most people who went through what he just went through."

"So you think that Bolds—the dead guy in the elevator—killed the homeless guy, then attacked Porter, right?" Zochi was trying to keep it all straight. "That's what I'm going on, so far."

"Pretty much." Letty glanced at her notes. "It looks like the homeless guy was just in the wrong place at the wrong time. One of the landlord's thugs let him in. We've seen it before at that building. Homicide guys are looking at video from the street and talking to the landlord's man about that. It depends on where the street cameras were placed, but we might be able to see when the homeless guy and Bolds entered. No cameras in the lobby, though, so we can't see what happened inside."

"One of the sergeants mentioned the 'placement' of the homeless guy," Zochi said, putting air quotes around "placement." "My understanding is that Porter found him first, on the way into the building. Tried to get him to leave, got some noise. Went up to get something to wave at the guy."

"Exactly," Letty said, nodding. "But when Porter got back downstairs, if what he says is true, the homeless guy was already dead. Head wrenched back. A second or so later he encountered the attacker—Evan Bolds."

"Right," Zochi said, picturing it. "Brief struggle, then down goes Bolds."

"You should have seen him," Letty said. The original grimace was back. "Bolds, I mean."

"Yeah, I heard that too." Zochi made a corkscrew-turning motion with her right hand. "And the head-wrenching thing with the homeless guy—is that really what it looked like? That's important for my case."

"That's what it looked like, yeah. Back to Bolds for a second. He was what—a probationer for your suspect, DeSantos?"

"No, DeSantos is a lawyer. He was at the AG's office. Bolds was his case, one of those sex offender civil commitment things. DeSantos's mother turned up dead, then his ex-girlfriend a few days after. The DA authorized an arrest after DNA came back a match."

"That's why I called you," Letty said. "Those two women out in Brooklyn. I heard about those cases. You've got a DNA match for both bodies, though, right?"

"I do, but I haven't put it all together yet. If nothing else, this feels like a box I should check off. Maybe this guy Porter can shed some light."

"And this homeless guy," Letty said. "Just a troublemaker? Any idea what he has to do with all this?"

Zochi sighed. "No idea, but the head-wrenching MO in that death matches the ones in my cases, so . . ."

"Overtime," Letty said with a shrug. "He's in an interview room. Get a refill, and I'll take you to him."

"Thanks," Zochi said. "So Evan Bolds—you know why he went to prison in the first place, right?"

"I don't."

"He nearly beat a woman to death in an elevator. He raped her first, then chased her into the elevator and—bam! Just went crazy on her. Did, like, twenty-five years for it. My suspect, DeSantos, brought a civil commitment case a few months ago because his probation was almost up."

Letty stopped and looked at her. "No way. The guy I just found at the bottom of an elevator shaft?"

"Screwed to the bottom," Zochi said, and winked. Letty grinned. "Classic."

CHAPTER 63

3:39 a.m.

"Hi, Mr. Porter," Zochi said, "I talked to Detective Clark, and I understand you've been up most of the night already. I appreciate you waiting around for me." Nate looked at her and smiled, his long, slender fingers wrapped around a coffee mug. His eyes looked raw and red rimmed but alert.

"It's okay. I wouldn't be sleeping anyway. I don't think I'll sleep well for a while."

"I'll be as quick as I can be," she said, sitting down and taking out a notepad. "This could be relevant, though, so again, I'm thankful for you waiting up. The reason I'm here is because I'm investigating another case, out in Brooklyn. I have a few questions, probably not more."

"Okay, sure."

"Does the name Evan Bolds mean anything to you?" She stated the name slowly and clearly. No one had told Porter that Bolds was the guy corkscrewed down there.

"Evan Bolds?" He seemed to ponder it. "No."

"You're sure?"

"Uh . . . yeah. I can't think of anyone I've ever known with that name."

"Okay. And the two men you encountered tonight, the homeless man and the one who attacked you—I know this is covered territory, but I'm confirming—you had no prior connection to either of them that you know of?"

"That's correct," Nate said. "The homeless man was no one I'd ever seen or worked with. The other one, well, I really didn't get a look at him, as I told the others. There was no sense of familiarity, though, nothing that made me think I knew him or had any idea who he was."

"Okay. I also understand that you were the person in your building who was playing point with the landlord, dealing with those issues?"

"Yes," he said. "I was informally appointed once the hardball stuff started happening. I'm not sure how else to put it. I'm older. I'm alone. I was a career city employee, and I have experience dealing with agencies and the like. I guess I seemed like a logical choice."

"Makes sense. So, in connection with that, did you ever feel threatened personally? What I'm getting at is whether anything that happened to you last night was something you expected. Does that make sense?"

"It does," he said firmly. Zochi was impressed. Whoever this old man was, he seemed to be as sharp as a tack, not fuzzy or spacey at all, which so many people were in the wake of trauma. "The building manager is a man named Daniel Cana. He's the guy I usually butt heads with. He's not violent, though. It's been kind of a test of wills between us, but not much else. I don't think Cana sent a killer to attack me, if that's what you're asking."

"Basically, it is," she said. "Thank you. There's just one other name I need to run by you—Joseph DeSantos. Does that name mean anything to you?"

She didn't expect that it would, and at first that's how it seemed. Then recognition sank through the man's face, his eyes slowly brightening with it.

"Joey DeSantos?" He shook his head like he needed to clear it. "I mean, that's the only Joseph DeSantos I can think of, but this was many, many years ago."

"How many, Mr. Porter?" Her heart picked up a beat.

"Well, he was a little boy. I knew him and his older brother through their uncle, Mike Carroll."

"That's interesting," she said. Porter did look a little spacey now, as if recalling a dream.

"Joe was ten when we met. I'd guess he'd be around fifty now."

"He's exactly fifty, yes."

"Wait," he said, lifting his hand. "That isn't Joe down in that elevator shaft, is it?"

"What? No." For a moment she wanted to kick herself. This was the dangerous thing about interviewing witnesses shortly after traumatic events. Nate Porter might seem completely together, but he was still rattled, whether *he* knew it or not. She needed to be patient and take things slow. "Uh, that person hasn't been officially identified, but it's not Joe DeSantos. I'm afraid Joe was arrested for murder a few weeks ago. Two murders, actually."

"Oh," Porter said. He appeared confused, not necessarily shocked, but not fully processing it either. "I'm sorry to hear that." He paused and looked down, then wrinkled his brow and looked up at her. "I think I understand. Evan Bolds is the man at the bottom of the shaft, isn't he?"

"That needs to be confirmed," she said, feeling like she should wink at him. "I can tell you Bolds is a person who's relevant to the case against Joe DeSantos. That's really why I'm here."

"Okay."

"Let's back up some to your connection with Joe. I have some information on Joe's backstory, including how he was raised for a while by his uncle. I assume you knew the uncle as well? Mike Carroll?"

"Of course," Nate said. It was as if the first mention of Joe's name had brought the whole time period back to him. Now he seemed confident, not dreamy.

"Can you tell me about him?"

"Mike Carroll and I were lovers. I mean . . . there were thousands of men in this town who could have said that about each other in the '70s, but . . . we were a thing for a while."

"A couple."

"Yes."

"For how long?"

"Oh man." He sighed. "I met Mike in '76; I remember *Rocky* came out later that same year. We were both in social work. He was in Staten Island. I was in Chelsea. We met at a city conference. The New Yorker Hotel."

"Were you dating when the blackout happened the following July? That's a subject Joe and I discussed before his arrest."

"We were dating, yes. That was a very strange night. It was how I met the boys, Joe and his older brother. I think he went by Robbie."

"Robbie is how Joe refers to him," Zochi said. "I know it was a long time ago. I'm not sure how much detail I need, but what can you tell me about that night?"

"Well, the phones were working. I was in the city with a mutual friend of ours who owned a coffee shop near Port Authority. Mike reached me there. He said he had two nephews in the city who had gotten separated from their mother. The police were telling people to stay off the phone except for emergencies, so I didn't ask a lot of questions. He said the boys would come to where I was. He asked if I could guide them to Staten Island. About an hour later, they showed up. I remember that Joe had torn his shorts really badly. Poor kid was basically in his underwear."

Porter smiled for a moment, as if seeing it all again. Zochi could almost picture it herself: jumpy candlelight, two sweaty kids, some guy's coffee shop with the door propped open. Other than the propped-open door, her vision was spot on.

"Anyway, we went around the corner to see if we could find some shorts for Joe. Things went sideways there. We got into a tight spot with the owner of the store, and . . . well, Robbie got angry and left. I got Joe home, but I didn't see Robbie again that night." He looked genuinely troubled at this, as if the event had happened recently and not forty summers ago. "After that, Robbie wasn't around much, but I saw Joe. Mike brought him into the city a few times. We ice skated in Central Park around Christmas. Mike and I broke up, though, about a year later."

"And there was no contact after that?"

"No, we needed a clean break." He shook his head and smiled wistfully. "Mike wouldn't come out of the closet. I wasn't a radical, but I was way out compared to a guy like Mike. I lived in Chelsea. I was active in politics. That kind of thing. Mike couldn't be that way."

"He was from Staten Island," Zochi said with a shrug.

"That was a part of it, sure. We all had our reasons in those days. I didn't judge Mike. I just couldn't go on that way. He liked the island too. He was provincial that way. He had his delis, his diners. He didn't want to live in Manhattan. My life was here, and his was there, raising two boys."

"Did you hear that he had died?"

"I did, but . . . honestly, I couldn't tell you what year."

"It was 1985. Joe was a senior in high school."

"That makes sense," he said, nodding. "It's just all a blur."

"You've been through a lot tonight."

"It's not that," he said, appearing defensive for the first time. He seemed to catch himself. "Mike and I broke up about two years before AIDS hit New York. I don't know how to describe what I—what we—went through next. By 1985, I had lost dozens of friends. Maybe hundreds. I became numb to the news after a while."

They spoke for a few minutes longer, but Zochi wasn't grasping much in terms of puzzle pieces fitting together. Evan Bolds was a guy Joe was connected to. Bolds had attacked Nate, whom Joe was also connected to. But why? She needed to think on it, but for the time being she needed to let this poor old guy get some sleep.

CHAPTER 64

Thursday, July 14, 1977
Forty-Third Street and Eighth Avenue
Manhattan
1:15 a.m.

"*Cabrito needs some new pants,*" *the fat man said, looking sideways at Nate. Joe blushed and pulled his shirt down lower. The man's name was Ricky, and it was his shop. He had given Joe and Robbie each a grape soda.*

"*I don't know where we'd find any clothes right now,*" *Nate said to Ricky. "Do you have anything extra here?*"

"*To fit him? Fuck no.*" *The "him" came out* heem. *There was no one else in the store, but a couple of guys had poked their heads in to give greetings and share gossip. Nate explained to the boys that he was a friend of Uncle Mike's who lived a few blocks down, in a neighborhood called Chelsea. The plan now was to call Uncle Mike and figure out the next move. Buses were a possibility, but they were harder to plan for in the middle of the night, let alone in a blackout. The Staten Island Ferry wouldn't run until 5:30 a.m. The clock on the wall said it was a quarter after one.*

"*I think we'll just have to get you to your uncle's with what you have on,*" *Nate said, frowning. "I'm sorry, Joe.*"

"*I can't go like this!*" *Joe said, trying to keep the whine out of his voice.*

"Let's call your uncle," Nate said with a honeyed voice. "We'll be here a while anyway."

"Well, if we have time, can we look for a store?" Joe asked.

"A store?"

"To get me new pants!"

"Joe," Nate said, "there's a blackout. Anyway, it's the middle of the night. No stores are open."

"We saw places," Robbie said, speaking for the first time in a while. He had seemed despondent since they got there, pushing his grape soda around like it was a booby prize. His hair was long in front and hung over his eyes. "Stores with glass broken, where you could just take stuff. We're not trying to cash in, just get a cheap pair of shorts."

"That's really dangerous," Nate said. "I know it sounds easy, but—"

"My brother needs a pair of shorts," Robbie said, his voice deeper. His chest swelled. "We can find some. There's a whole city right out there. Someone will sell us some, if they're watching their own store."

"There's a guy on Ninth," Ricky said, raising his voice on the last word, as if noting an option. "He's got athletic wear—shoes and stuff. He might be watching his place. Maybe if you offer him a buck or a two, he'll give you some gym shorts."

"Ninth and what?" Robbie asked.

"Forty-Four, right there. East side of the street. Carmelo's."

"Let's go," Robbie said, as if the next move was obvious.

"Wait," Nate said. "We need to call your—"

"My what?" Robbie said, standing up. "My uncle Mike?" He put a whiny stress on the words. "We barely even know him!"

"Robbie, please," Nate said. "I'm responsible for you."

"No, you're not! Who are you?! Some guy! Some fucking guy in the fucking dark! We don't know you! We don't have to be here!" With that, he swatted the bottle off the table, shattering it on the tile floor. "Joe, come on!" Joe sat paralyzed in his chair for a few seconds, then flashed an apologetic look toward Ricky.

"I'm sorry," he said. "Is there a mop or something?"

"I'll get it," Ricky said with a shrug. "S'okay."

"Joe!" Robbie called from outside.

"Can you come with us?" Joe asked Nate, his lower lip trembling. He knew the request was impossible, stupid even. There was no way this guy would do anything for them after Robbie had acted like that. Nate was sitting with his hands between his knees in a sweat-stained white polo shirt. He stared down at the leather sandals on his feet. After a moment, he looked up and nodded.

"I'll go with you," he said. "I can't control your brother, and you know what? He's right; I shouldn't be able to."

"He'll calm down. Maybe we just go to that one store around the corner. If there's nothing there, we come back." Joe moved his eyes to Ricky. "Robbie will say he's sorry. I think he's just . . . like . . ."

"He's under a lotta pressure," Ricky said. He stretched his arms forward, his thick fingers clasped, and cracked his knuckles. "It's cool."

"We've got to call your uncle," Nate said. "I'd much rather do that when I have you both here for him to talk to."

"I know, but I don't want to lose Robbie, like if he wanders. Please. We'll call as soon as we get back."

"Gimme the number, and I'll call him," Ricky said. He hefted his bulk out of the chair and reached for an order pad on the counter. Nate wrote it out for him. He knows it by heart, Joe thought. He wondered how this city guy would know his uncle's phone number in Staten Island.

"What will you tell him?" Nate asked.

"La verdad—you went around the corner, and you'll be back in a minute. Go ahead."

Nate frowned and said, "I can only go as far as that one corner. I want to help you both, Joe, but that's as far as I can go. One way or the other, I have to let your uncle know what's going on."

"I know you want to help," Joe said, his heart pounding. "So please come with us."

CHAPTER 65

Monday, September 4, 2017
East Seventh Street
Manhattan
4:30 a.m.

Back in his apartment, Nate undressed to boxers and a tank top and sat on his bed, a creaky, old full-size he had slept alone in for years. From outside the door, his cat, Disco, whined until Nate got up and shook some fresh food into her bowl in the little galley kitchen. Disco munched in her bowl, lapped up some water, and then rubbed against his leg.

He knew he needed to sleep—to try, at least—with the AC droning and the blinds drawn. His mind was racing, though. And now memories of Mike Carroll, painful and tender, were reaching through the decades like scarcely any time had passed at all.

Under his bed was a dusty plastic storage bin that he had found at Bed Bath & Beyond: one of the wide, flat ones. Disco dodged the dust balls, and Nate squinted as he drew the bin out and flipped open the top. It was filled with photographs, many still tucked into the Kodak-colored envelopes that held them when you picked them up from the drugstore.

He dug around until he found a nine-by-fourteen clasp envelope with the city seal in the upper left corner. The New York City seal had been modified in 1977 so that the Dutchman and the Native American man standing astride the windmill were in color. The Dutchman wore blue whereas the Native American man was barely clothed and kind of a mustard color. The envelope had been given to Nate by Mike with a Christmas present inside—tickets to a play he could no longer recall. Later, Nate would put all their photos into that envelope. There was a joke attached to it in the "to, from" message on the front.

Mike was deeply closeted, the thing that ultimately drove them apart. So much so that Mike had provided a fake name at their first meeting. It seemed silly, as they were both city employees meeting at the same conference, but such was Mike's confession to Nate after their first intimate evening. He told Nate that he hadn't planned to lie. But then he had looked into Nate's eyes and felt a spark, then the old familiar fear. The safest thing in the moment had seemed to be a fake name.

Nate's eyes grew misty as he thumbed through the twenty or so photos of him and Mike Carroll together between '76 and late '78. There were two or three from Central Park, and sure enough, one with little Joey DeSantos, grinning up at the camera with a Mets cap on, a bowl haircut nearly covering his eyes. There were a few summer photos from Fire Island, the place Nate had just returned from. In one from 1978, he and Mike were arm in arm at a backyard barbecue at a friend's house, a friend who was now long dead.

So many were dead.

He slid the photos into the envelope and flipped it over. The inside joke was written across the front in Mike's neat, girlish handwriting. There it was, the fake name Mike had provided that first afternoon. It was distinct and interesting. Nate had bought it completely, believing it captured well the sweet, sad-faced man who offered it. He moved a forefinger over the writing and smiled.

To: Nate, Christmas, 1977, with all my love

From: Caleb Evermore

He was about to stuff the old envelope back into the box, then looked it over again. He glanced over at Disco, keeping her distance from the mini dust storm from under the bed. Then he went looking for his cell phone. There was one more thing he needed to tell the detective. He wasn't sure if it had any meaning or not, but it suddenly seemed important to tell her. It seemed ridiculous after so many years, but it was like a weight he wanted off his chest.

CHAPTER 66

Ninth Precinct Squad Room
West Village, Manhattan
4:37 a.m.

"Hernandez," she yawned into the phone. A desk sergeant at the Ninth Precinct had put Nate through to her.

"Detective, this is Nate Porter. I'm sorry; I thought of something else. It might be nothing, but—"

"It's okay. I'm falling asleep at a desk. What is it?"

"Well, it's just . . . you mentioned the two brothers. Joey and Robbie."

"Right."

"Did you know about the third brother?"

"The what?"

Fifteen minutes later, she was at Nate's door.

CHAPTER 67

East Seventh Street
4:53 a.m.

"Yes, there was another brother," Nate said, putting a cup of coffee in front of Zochi. "He was a big part of Mike's life, long before Joe and Robbie came on the scene." Zochi looked back at him with her notebook in hand but hadn't yet written a word. She was sort of dumbfounded. Outside, blackness was giving way to a smoky blue, and birds twittered on the fire escape. Nate's cat eyed them greedily.

"Do you know his name?"

"Charles," he said, as if it were obvious. "I have no idea if he's still alive. I'd guess not, but . . . wow, I just don't know. Mike made a lot of sacrifices for him too." He paused, his tired eyes moving back and forth as if searching yellowed files of memory.

"Charles?"

"Yes. Charles is the person Mike's life revolved around, before Joe and Robbie. I knew about Charles before I knew either of them."

"But . . ." Zochi paused and squinted. "I don't know anything about a third brother. I haven't met Robbie, but I've spent a fair amount of time with Joe. I asked all kinds of questions about his family, and he's never once mentioned a Charles." At this, Nate's face seemed to bloom with something between shock and embarrassment.

"Wha . . . you mean?"

"What?"

"You mean Joe doesn't know who Charles is? *Still?*" The word "still" seemed to ring out like a bell.

"I can't be sure what Joe knows," Zochi said, quieter. She clicked her pen and readied the notepad.

"He didn't know in 1977 when he came to live with Mike. Neither of the boys knew; I'm sure of it. I assumed, though, at some point that . . ."

"That what?"

"That Mike told Joe he had a twin brother!"

"A twin brother," Zochi said, as if the fact was weighing down her tongue. "Identical or fraternal?"

"Identical," Nate said, again as if it was obvious. "Wait, I mean . . . no one knows about this?"

"Well, *I* don't," she said, a frustrated tone creeping into her voice. She checked it. She was tired. They were both tired.

"Okay," Nate said, as if it could all be rationally dealt with—this chasm of a knowledge gap between the distant past and now. "So maybe Mike didn't tell him? Did he not *get* to tell him?"

"I don't know," she said, genuinely bewildered. "You mentioned the AIDS thing earlier. I know Mike died of that, and—" She held up a finger as if to ask him to wait, then fished for another notepad in her bag. Her heartbeat quickened as she thumbed through it. She had experienced maybe two or three moments like this in more than twenty years on the job. It was different and more powerful than that golden "gotcha" instant when a perp gave himself away with something dropped from his mouth like windfall fruit. It was better than the eminently satisfying moment in a good, fair interrogation when the poor bastard just broke down, sobbing, and admitted to what he'd done—diddling his niece or offing his boss. Nate was not a guilty party. Still, Zochi was feeling that same electrifying, game-changing sensation.

"Joe told me his uncle died before they could speak," she said, scanning the older notes. "He was away on a trip and was called back. His uncle was in a coma and died a day later."

"Oh, dear God."

"Let's go back a bit," she said, switching notepads again, "because I need to hear as much of this as possible. Charles is an identical twin to Joe?"

"Yes. Joe and Charles were born at the old Staten Island Hospital, on Castleton Avenue. The boys' mother was Mike's sister, Lois. What Mike told me was that there was some terrible *in utero* thing that happened. Charles, in the womb, was struggling somehow, and Joe kept growing. The doctors didn't know. But at the moment of birth, it was obvious. Joe came out first and looked like a healthy baby. Charles came out next and was underweight. Sick. Cyanotic, I think, like they had to revive him? I don't know every detail. From what Mike told me, they had to do all kinds of tests. The child made it out of intensive care but never out of institutional care."

"Do you know where he was institutionalized?"

"Eventually? Willowbrook," he said. She raised her eyebrows, and he said, "Yes, that Willowbrook. The state school. It wasn't far from the hospital."

"The one they shut down," she said. "The one that . . . whatshisname did a big story on."

"Geraldo Rivera, in the early '70s. The *Staten Island Advance* covered it earlier than that. It was known that conditions were bad there, but not everyone knew how bad. Mike Carroll was one of them."

"Then why would the parents put him there?"

"From what Mike told me, Lois's husband made that decision. Lois fought it, but there wasn't much use in fighting that guy, or so I heard. He more or less abandoned the kid to Willowbrook, then moved the family out of Staten Island. Charles was about three. He would have been left at Willowbrook, but . . . Mike took action."

"Action? What action?"

"He got Charles out of Willowbrook under an assumed name," Nate said. He shrugged, as if this sounded so crazy it needed that kind of gesture to follow it up.

"What?"

"I can only relay what he told me, but Mike Carroll knew people. I mean, Mike knew everyone. If you were in social services, in the Staten Island medical community, in the disability community, whatever—Mike knew you. Staten Island was a lot smaller then."

"So what are you telling me?"

"That Mike Carroll did something illegal—really illegal—although I think he was right to do it. It was before my time with him, but this is what I remember. Lois's husband—the boys' father—was a cruel man. He wanted Charles behind him, in state care, and he wanted a new life. He wouldn't let Lois visit Charles. It was like he was dead. That's how Mike described it to me. As far as the father was concerned, there were two boys, not three."

"Okay."

"So Mike worked his connections. By '71 or '72, the family had moved away. That left Mike to do what he could for Charles. I have no idea if he's still alive. If he is, I'm sure he's under the assumed name."

"Which was?"

"Caleb Evermore," Nate said. He spelled out the last name. "I was reminded of it a little while ago, going through some old photos."

"I don't get it, though. How did Charles become someone named Caleb Evermore?"

"Mike knew staff at Willowbrook. Good people, exhausted people. He also knew people at a much better rehab facility. It was more appropriate for Charles's disability, anyway. Mike knew the boy needed round-the-clock care, and probably always would. So he made things happen. Records got changed. Names. A kid who was Charles DeSantos, maybe, probably got listed as deceased. Then another kid around the same age popped up with this other name, Caleb Evermore. Orphaned. He was in one facility, but he really needed to move to this other facility. That's all Mike needed. He couldn't have changed things for a kid with involved parents, but he could do all sorts of things for a kid who was alone."

"This can't be," Zochi said, barely above a whisper. It was just a verbal reflex. She had a feeling it was all very doable, and that Mike Carroll, whoever he was, had done it.

"You might think it's crazy, but you had to be there," he said, as if he'd read her mind. "In the early '70s, when the city was broke, the state was cutting staff, and it was all just coming apart. Getting a severely disabled boy named Charles DeSantos from one place to another with a new name would have been difficult but not impossible. There were all sorts of things you could pull off, particularly if the kid was left for dead."

"Dead," she said, looking up from her notepad. "That's how Lois viewed him by the time he was five or six, I guess. Dead."

"I don't know. Mike said Lois wasn't the one who wanted to walk away from Charles. It was the father, Reggie. I never met him."

"It was Lois who abandoned the other two, though. Just a few years later."

He nodded. "I know. I never understood it. Mike never understood it. He never heard from her again that I know of. He just made do and hoped she'd turn up one day. I guess she never did."

"What about her bringing the boys to the city in the first place, the night of the blackout? Did Mike know she was coming?"

"It was very short notice. Lois called him that morning, I think. I hadn't heard from Mike most of the day; it's not like we texted back then. All I knew was, the lights went out. Then I'm getting a call from my boyfriend in Staten Island, like, 'Hey, can you give these two kids a hand and get them to the ferry?' It was crazy. The whole night seemed like a dream. Then it just wasn't discussed. It was Mike's secret to tell, not mine. And our whole lives were secrets back then. We presented ourselves as friends. I think Robbie knew better, but he never said anything. Joe was just a nice kid. They missed their mother, and Mike and I didn't know what to say. What do you tell two boys when their mother just disappears like that? We talked about all sorts of things. Maybe she got sick. Or a bump on the head."

"Sounds awful," Zochi said.

"Sometimes I wish that I would have stuck it out with Mike and been easier on him. I wish I had known Joe was still in the dark about his twin brother."

"Wait," she said quietly. Her pulse was thrumming in her ear. She had never felt so tired and yet so energized at the same time. "If Charles was in state care, it would have been in Staten Island, right?"

"Yes, that's where Mike had all his connections. The facility was a small one. Private, but they took state funds."

"Do you remember the name?"

"I don't," he said. "You could probably track him down, though. If I had to guess, I'd say that Mike kept his birthdate the same. The facility would have records, even if he's deceased."

"I've gotta run." She looked at her watch. It was a little after 6:00 a.m., nearly sunrise. Nate's cat was on the windowsill, silhouetted against the pink dawn. "I'll follow up when I can, but . . . thank you."

"Is Joe a murderer?" he asked as she packed up. The question was blunt, dropped into the little living room like a stone. "I guess maybe you can't say, but I had to ask. It's the one thing we haven't talked about."

"Maybe not," she said. "If he isn't, he might have you to thank."

"I don't know what for. I feel like I held back something terribly important that seems to have ruined his life, one way or the other."

"Actually," she said, "if it's what I'm thinking, it might save his life."

CHAPTER 68

6:22 a.m.

Zochi stooped under police tape on her way out of the building. Out front, with her butt resting on a bike rack and looking red eyed, was Letty Clark.

Letty yawned. "Anything good from my witness?"

"I think so," she said. "I'm trying to get my head around it, but . . . I don't even know how to explain it."

"Give it a try. Do you think our cases are related?"

"It's possible, yeah." With that, she gave Letty the shortest version she could manage about her suspect, Joe DeSantos, who had been prosecuting a case against Letty's victim, Evan Bolds. DeSantos was in jail on unrelated murder charges, but now the case was getting stranger with an identical twin out there who maybe Joe didn't know about. The twin was severely disabled, though, and Zochi had no idea if he was still alive.

Joe also had a brother, Robbie. Both Robbie and Joe had an ancient but powerful history with Nate Porter, Letty's surviving witness. Now, if Zochi could connect Robbie to Evan Bolds? Then yes, her and Letty's cases could be related.

"Wow," Letty said after Zochi had spit that all out. "Okay, so it *is* likely Bolds came here looking to kill Nate Porter."

"I think so," Zochi said. "Unless we figure out some other history between Bolds and Porter, I think it was my suspect's brother Robbie who set it up."

"So this guy, Robbie, wanted Nate Porter dead?"

"I'm just guessing, but that's what's gelling for me, yes."

"Well, it's consistent with Porter's description," Letty said. "Porter doesn't know anything about Bolds, but he was attacked by him anyway. There was also this homeless guy who Porter tried to shoo away."

"Yes, the homeless guy," Zochi said. "That's the kicker for me. He was killed in the exact same way that the victims in my Brooklyn cases were killed. The two women? The perp twisted their heads back and snapped their necks, just like how this guy died."

"Ah," Letty said. "Right. So maybe Bolds is the killer in *your* cases, and last night he showed up to kill Nate Porter."

"Yes, and the homeless guy was in the way. Bolds took him out, because why not? Otherwise, he's a witness. Then he waited for Porter, but Porter fought back. The elevator shaft was just bad luck for Bolds."

"Okay, but your suspect's DNA is on those bodies in Brooklyn, right?"

"That's the crazy part. DeSantos's blood was found on both bodies. But if there's an identical twin out there in a comatose state? If someone drew blood from the twin and left it at a crime scene, it would have the same genetic profile as my suspect."

"Whoa." Letty scratched her forehead and seemed to mull it over. "You mean, your case could all be a setup?"

"Maybe, yeah. When I drove down here, I didn't expect this, but . . . now? I think it's possible that Evan Bolds killed DeSantos's mother and ex-girlfriend. And somehow Bolds had blood from an identical twin to plant as evidence against him."

"Good God," Letty said, crossing her arms. Around them, birds were tweeting, and delivery people were on the move. The neighborhood was waking up. "So if you can connect Evan Bolds to your suspect's brother, Robbie, then you've got it. Robbie made the whole thing happen."

"I wouldn't bet on it yet," Zochi said, "but I'll be following up on it." She looked eastward, down the narrow, tree-lined street. A magnificent sunrise was lurking just behind the Jacob Riis houses, barely visible in the distance beyond Avenue D, where the island ended. Reds and oranges streaked through high clouds. "I need to call back to my command and see who's on the day tour. Oh, Bolds parked a van down that way, right?" She thought that was the case, but her head was churning with so many details, it was hard to keep them straight.

Letty nodded. About an hour before, with keys from Bolds's pocket and information from his PO, they had located his panel van, parked down the street. "It'll be towed to the CSU impound in Queens."

CHAPTER 69

6 Iroquois Way
Yorktown Heights, New York
6:30 a.m.

The phone rang, waking Aideen up. It was the landline beside the bed, which she didn't use nearly as much as when Ben was alive, more specifically when Ben was on the job. She sat up and cleared her throat. She had no idea who was calling, but it was unusual. Ben had kept their number very secret, not listed anywhere.

"Bradigan," she said.

"You answer your phone like a cop."

She frowned and then smiled. She recognized the voice. It was Anthony Marcos, a detective Ben had worked with for years. He was still on the job, now a lieutenant in Manhattan at the division level.

"Tony?"

"The very same. I'm sorry it's so early. And it's a holiday, right? Days run together for me. Anyway, I'm sorry."

"It's okay. What is it?"

"You're still working that case, right? The guy from the AG's office who was arrested for the homicides out in Brooklyn?" By "working that case," Aideen knew that Tony meant defending it.

"Yeah, Joe DeSantos. He's my client."

"Right. Well, this is weird, but his name came up late last night."

"His name?"

"There was a double in the East Village," he said. Aideen stiffened. She knew a "double" to generally mean a double homicide. "I know your guy is at Rikers, but his name came up in connection with one of the victims."

"Wait a minute," she said. Then the door opened, and Máiréad walked in, her face puffy with sleep and fresh concern. She mouthed *who is it*, but Aideen put up a finger. "Do you have the names of the victims?" Máiréad's eyes widened. Aideen pointed to the bed, and she sat down.

"One looked like a homeless guy, and they haven't ID'd him yet. The other one was a guy named Evan Bolds. Does that ring a bell? From what I understand, the AG's office was charging him under the civil management law. Your client had the case."

Aideen could feel the color drain from her face. Máiréad looked ready to burst with curiosity. Thankfully, the boys were still asleep. "Evan Bolds. You're sure it was him?"

"This is all unofficial, Aid, but yes, I'd say that ID will stick. His probation officer was alerted. Not sure if he has family."

She looked at Máiréad and pointed at her briefcase. Máiréad brought it over and pulled out a notepad and a pen for her mother. "Wow, okay. And the homeless victim—not ID'd yet?"

"No, but they'll figure out who he is. They may have already."

"Any other details? Any witnesses? Arrests?"

"No arrests. There's some chatter. No fives written up yet. I can only say so much, but it's starting to shape up like Bolds might have been the principal assailant. There's also a surviving witness. They're thinking Bolds might have killed the homeless guy, then attacked the eyewitness, then ended up falling down an elevator shaft. His death is still considered a homicide, for now. That's why they're calling it a double."

"This eyewitness? Got a name?"

"Um . . . Nate Porter. Black male, older. Lives in the building where it happened."

She started writing the name, then froze. "Nate Porter?"

"Yeah, Nate. Or Nathan. He's fine from what I understand. That's all I've got for now. And, listen, you didn't hear it from me, okay? I shouldn't be calling you, period. But . . . you know, Ben's memory and all. I figured you'd want to know."

"Mom, my God, what's going on?" Máiréad said, once Aideen had thanked Tony profusely and hung up. Her daughter sat cross-legged in her nightgown. Finster was beside her, looking concerned at the tension in the air.

"I'll explain," she said. "Right now, though . . ." She trailed off, her mind racing. There was something she was forgetting to check, something that had arrived recently.

Bolds! Video from the courtroom lobby!

That was it. After weeks of staying after them, the Office of Court Administration had mailed Aideen a tiny flash drive with time-stamped video on it from the day of Joe's July 27 court date with Evan Bolds. It was still sitting in the unopened mail downstairs. Máiréad went to retrieve it while Aideen got her laptop ready.

Four minutes later, and after some back and forth with the keyboard controls, mother and child were watching the same thing over and over again. The video was a surveillance clip from the 111 Centre Street courthouse. The wall-mounted camera footage showed Joe and Ben Yang, fuzzy but recognizable, running to assist a woman in distress. The time was exactly 2:48 p.m., July 27, 2017. A few feet away was Evan Bolds, drawing a baggie from his slacks and deftly placing it into one of Joe's accordion folders.

"O-M-G," Máiréad said. "Like . . . O-M-G."

"I know." Aideen ran a hand through her hair. There were pillows and bedding everywhere. She was wearing an old T-shirt of Ben's and granny panties. And Finster was acting like the world was ending. She needed to get organized. There was more to what was happening than just this series of revelations. The video was big news, but on its own, it could have waited for her to act on. It wasn't even 7:00 a.m., and it was Labor Day.

She couldn't wait, though. There was something else afoot; she could feel it. Bolds turning up dead was one thing, but Nate Porter being involved? *The* Nate Porter? Máiréad helped her make the bed and calm Finster. Then she sat dutifully next to Aideen, handing her notepads. At one point, she went downstairs to make coffee. By the time the coffee was ready, Aideen had it figured out. When Máiréad walked in with a mug for her and a glass of juice for herself, Aideen had four notepads spread out on the bed, all flipped to specific pages.

"What do we know?" Máiréad asked quietly. She hopped up on the bed and waited. Aideen had her reading glasses on, a little lower on her nose. In her gut was a glowing feeling of satisfaction, but also fresh anxiety.

"We know," Aideen said slowly, "that Evan Bolds was part of setting Joe up, or at least making him think he was crazy. We also know that Evan Bolds is dead. It looks like he probably killed one guy first and was maybe trying to kill another man named Nate Porter when he died. That man, Nate, was someone Joe liked and was grateful for." She looked over at Máiréad, unsure if she'd grasp it. "And someone whom his brother Robbie hated." Máiréad seemed confused, waiting for an explanation. "The thing is," she went on, "what does any of this have to do with Aaron Hathorne?"

"I was gonna ask that," Máiréad said. "I think I'm a little behind, though."

"I'll catch you up, hang on." Aideen shuffled through the notepads until she was able to compare what she needed. In one set of notes, about Joe's recollection of his talk with Robbie at Midland Beach in Staten Island, she had written what Robbie had told him.

The light has been looking for you, little brother. You're about to be blinded by it.

The other set of notes was from her visit to Dr. Hathorne at the St. Lawrence Psychiatric Center. She had taken note of a comment Hathorne had made because it sounded almost lyrical.

The light has found him. Soon, he'll be blinded by it.

"That's the link," she said to Máiréad. "You see? It's kind of a cryptic phrase, like a weird thing to say. And both of these men said it almost exactly the same way and about the same thing."

"That's not, like, courtroom proof, though, right?" Máiréad asked.

"No, not at all. And it could just be a coincidence, but . . . I don't think so."

"So you think this means that Joe's brother was doing something bad for Aaron Hathorne? Maybe Evan Bolds too?"

"Yep," Aideen said. "If I'm right, Evan Bolds has already paid for whatever he did. Now it might be Robbie's turn. It's Hathorne I really want to connect this to, though."

"Wow. Do you think Robbie knows?"

"I don't know. Someone with a badge needs to talk to him, though, preferably today. I'll make a call in a few minutes." She smiled and looked over at her daughter. "So do you think you want to do this for a living?"

"Oh *hails* yes," she said, altering a swear word she wasn't supposed to use.

"Good," Aideen said, pulling her close. Finster whined with jealousy. "You're good at it."

CHAPTER 70

Joe and Nate rounded the corner at Ninth Avenue and turned north. There was southbound traffic on this street, about as sporadic as what they had encountered on Eighth. Between Forty-Third and Forty-Fourth they caught up with Robbie, staring at a storefront. The entrance door was intact, but the plate-glass window to its left was missing, only jagged pieces of glass in its place. The shards sparkled like diamonds in the wash of headlights. There were big pieces of plywood leaning against the building.

"Robbie?" Joe called as they approached. He looked over and frowned.

"It's been hit already."

"The owner's been here also," Nate said. "That's what the plywood is about. He'll be back."

"He's not here right now," Robbie said, peering into the shop. "I see stuff inside, clothes on the racks. It's worth a shot. We just need a pair of kid's gym shorts." He looked over to Joe and Nate. "I can see where the clothes are; I'm going in." He stepped over the glass pieces onto a short display shelf, then into the shop.

"Come with us," Joe said. "Just for a few seconds, so I know he's okay."
He took Nate's hand, a gesture he would remember as being so strange for a
ten-year-old boy and yet so appropriate in the moment. Nate hesitated, then
folded his bigger hand around Joe's, and they stepped inside.

Passing headlights moving south on the avenue provided the only light,
but there was enough that Nate and the boys could make out the basic layout
of the store. There were the usual circular racks of clothing and platforms
here and there. Most of them were bare, although a mess of discarded items
and plastic hangers were all over the floor. Robbie scooped through them,
pulling up shirts, socks, or individual shoes. Nate and Joe tracked Robbie's
path through the store.

"Over here," Robbie said as a truck rumbled by and a wide stripe of
yellow light passed over them. "Against the back wall, there's stuff." They
followed Robbie mostly by feel, waiting for the next injection of light from
the street. Robbie reached the back wall and found metal rods attached with
rows of athletic shorts. Joe was a few feet behind. They felt their way through
the remaining merchandise and found a pair of nylon running shorts that
seemed the right size.

"Let's go guys," Nate said. "Hurry."

"These are fine," Joe said, stepping into them. He reached back and tore
the little tag from the back. "Let's—"

There was a scraping sound and then the sound of glass tinkling from
the front of the store.

"You motherfuckers!" It came out slurred and accented. Yoo
Muthafuckas. Joe froze. His eyes were adjusting, and he could see a figure
moving swiftly around the racks toward them. In his peripheral vision he
caught movement—it was Robbie, leaping toward a door he had pointed
out earlier, a swinging door that led to a back room. Joe also caught sight
of Nate, raising his hands and mouthing a whoa sound. Then the figure
took shape as two cars passed the store, spreading light from right to left. It
was a man, stocky and compact, wearing a pastel-colored shirt with a wide

*collar. Joe saw that he held a stout rifle, like a shotgun. The man snapped
back a part of the gun with his left hand. It made a thick* clack-clack *sound.*

*The next thing Joe heard was like an explosion. The entire world lit
up with it. The store. Nate, his eyes wide. Even the street out front. There
was a ringing in Joe's ears—he had never heard a sound so loud. He felt
dust and debris rain down around him. For a long, terrible moment he felt
blind and deaf.*

*The next few seconds seemed to pass in slow motion. Joe felt an arm
land between his shoulder blades. It was Nate, pushing him in total blackness in the direction of the door through which Robbie had disappeared.
Joe could feel Nate's breath on the back of his head. Nate seemed to envelop
him as they moved forward like one person, Joe carried along like something
in a basket.*

*"Motherfuckers!" he heard above the screaming in his ears. It was
tinny and distant. Nate pushed them both through the door, and for a
few awful seconds they were enveloped in total darkness. Then there was a
click, a spark, and a little halo of yellow light. Behind it was Robbie's face,
ghostly and pale. Mom's lighter! Robbie held it up for a few seconds, and
the storeroom began to take shape. In front of them were two narrow aisles
formed by H-frame shelving units, stretching back into darkness. Most of the
shelves were empty, but there were boxes and folded clothes on some of them.
Robbie's whole body was shaking. After a few seconds, the light clicked off.
By that time the three of them were gathered tightly together.*

"The lighter gets hot," he whispered.

*Nate said, "That's fine. Give it a rest, Robbie. Let's move this way. Stay
together." Like three men tied together, they moved forward in awkward,
dragging steps, with Nate in the lead. At one point he bumped one of the
H-frame storage racks and corrected course. They seemed to walk ten or
twenty feet, then Joe sensed a wall ahead of them. Nate did, too, and paused.*

*"Robbie, can you light it again?" Robbie did, trying to keep his thumb
back on the red clicker. Sure enough, they had reached a wall. The light
wasn't much, but Robbie managed to turn the level up all the way with*

the little metal wheel on the side—a favorite pastime of the two boys when lighters were left unattended—and the flame rose, dead steady in the still air.

"What do we do?" Robbie asked, his eyes huge in the dirty glow. All three could hear the man with the gun, cursing and making his way toward the storeroom door. He was almost certainly the owner, which meant that he probably knew the storeroom as well as any room in his own home.

"Move that way, toward the back," Nate said. "I think I see a back door. If so, go through it. I'll be right there." They hesitated for a split second. "Go!"

As they moved down the narrow space between the H-frame and the wall, Nate disappeared back into the darkness and made a racket. Joe wouldn't know this until later, but Nate was grabbing whatever he could find in the dark—boxes, piles of clothing, pieces of wood—and tossing them toward the storeroom door. There was an old metal desk that he managed to push in front of it. He was still snatching items and throwing them toward the doorway as Joe and Robbie reached a steel door to the outside. Then there was a heavy thudding sound at the storeroom door.

"YOO MUTHAFUCKAS!"

Another thud, then a series of crashes and curses as the man with the gun tried to pound his way in. Nate stumbled through the mess while Robbie held the outside door open for him. Nate slammed it shut and leaned against it, his chest heaving.

The night air was hot and still, but a welcome change from the stagnant interior. Above them was only the inky blackness of the sky—no sodium glow, no lights from windows. All three looked around as Robbie again clicked the lighter. They were in a small courtyard bounded by brick buildings on every side. Joe had expected that there would be an alley running right behind the building, maybe a parked car or a couple of trash cans. That's not how midtown Manhattan was laid out, though. There was just brick and concrete around them.

"We're trapped!" Robbie said in little more than a whimper. Nate's eyes darted around the cramped space of the courtyard, blinking as they adjusted.

To Joe, his movements seemed oddly purposeful, almost as if he had been in a situation like this before. Joe quivered. Robbie was right; it did seem like a simple, awful trap—like a pit from a Bible story where Christians were thrown to lions. Nate was reaching for a cinder block, a few of which lay strewn about the otherwise empty space.

"There's a stairwell over there," Nate said, hefting the cinder block with one hand and pointing to one side of the courtyard with the other. Both Joe and Robbie followed his eyes. Robbie was closest to it. "Robbie, can you see down there?" Robbie walked over to the steps.

"It's dark," he said, peering down.

"Take a look, please," Nate said. "Use the lighter; just be careful. There might be a way out down there." With that, he dragged a cinder block and placed it in front of the exterior door to the shop. Inside, the owner was still thrashing around and cursing. At the top of the stairs a few feet away from them, Robbie clicked the lighter on and stepped down into the dark. Joe saw him disappear, and then Nate whistled over to him, indicating that he should grab a cinder block. They were heavy, but Joe could heft one. He set it against the steel door as Nate had, and Nate stacked it. Then Robbie's voice floated up from the stairwell, weak and weirdly contorted, like through a tunnel.

"Hey. Hey, what . . ."

Then a bunch of things happened at once. First, Nate was lifting a cinder block to stack it on top of another one. Then the steel door burst open like a battering ram had been used against it. Both Nate and the stacked cinder blocks went tumbling away from the door. At the same time, a flashlight beam shot outward from the doorway, spreading a garish stripe of white light.

"YOU MUTHAFUCKAS!"

Joe pictured one of the army guys on a Hogan's Heroes *rerun, the light sweeping over the camp fence but missing him. Instead, it fixed on Nate, who had landed on his butt and was shielding his eyes from it with one hand. Joe heard the* clack-clack *sound again, satisfying and solid. His* heart froze. *The stocky man with the pastel shirt stepped through the door. The flashlight was crammed between his left arm and his side. The rest of the arm steadied the shotgun. A finger on his right hand cradled the trigger. He stepped forward and fired, tripping on a piece of cinder block as the gun discharged.*

The muzzle flash was blinding, the sound earsplitting. Joe screamed. On the opposite wall over Nate's shoulder, there was a shattering of brick and mortar. The man yelled as he began to trip, the sound barely audible over the ringing in Joe's ears. He was careening forward and off balance, headed for the ground and trying to break his fall. The flashlight went spinning and clattered on the ground. The shotgun did too, smacking the cracked concrete and pinwheeling toward where Joe was cowered.

In his peripheral vision, Joe could see Nate scrambling backward, trying to stand. The man let out a slew of curses and grunted as he tried to make it back to his feet. The flashlight was still lit, sending a broadening pipe of milky light through smoke and dust. The door stood ajar, with cinder blocks and pieces scattered about, like a hole had been blown in the building. In the air was a sharp metallic smell. Joe looked down.

The shotgun had stopped right in front of him.

The man was working his way to his knees, his eyes on the gun. Joe saw this and reached for it. Nate cried out something, but Joe couldn't understand it. Joe stood up with the shotgun and felt for the trigger. It felt like warm lead in his hands. The man was soaked in sweat, one side of his shirt collar flipped up and stuck to his cheek. His eyes were positively mad.

"Leave us alone," Joe said. His voice sounded like it was coming from somewhere other than his body. The man wiped the collar away from his face and grunted. He was not tall but sturdily built and had hair like a clown: two dark patches above his ears and not much on top. His mouth was open, and a fat pink tongue swept around his lips. He spit blood to the side.

"Gimme that."

"No. Let us go. I needed shorts, that's all. We have money."

"Gimme it, you little fuckin'—" He took a step forward. Joe grabbed the lower part of the gun and squeezed backward. The stock moved more easily than he expected. Clack-clack. The man stopped.

"You don't even know how to fire that, you little shit."

"I just saw you do it twice." Joe could feel his heart thudding like a bass drum. The man fished more blood out of his mouth with the slimy, restless tongue and spat. Then there were noises from inside the store—a muffled crash and a tinkling of glass. The man gave Joe one more baleful look, then screamed something unintelligible and stomped back through the open door into the darkness. His voice echoed back and forth between the courtyard and the storeroom.

"Joe, let me have it," Nate said softly. Joe hadn't noticed that Nate had moved over to him. He hadn't noticed anything, really. All he could see was the man's face—the wild eyes, the lolling tongue. *"Joe?"* Joe let Nate take the gun. There was hot silence for a moment, the air still angry with the shotgun blast, the strange tunnel of light still emanating at ground level from the flashlight.

Then there was a scream from down the staircase, where Robbie had gone.

"Robbie!" Nate yelled, still holding the gun and darting that way. *"Robbie!"* He turned to Joe. *"Grab the flashlight!"* Joe's heart was thudding again; it was a wonder that it didn't just slam out of his chest. The scream came up again, and Joe's blood curdled with it. It was Robbie, but it almost sounded like a girl's scream.

Without words, Joe and Nate worked in concert, Joe knowing that he needed to hold the flashlight and shine it down the stairs while Nate went down. Nate bounded down holding the shotgun, but with the butt forward instead of the barrel. Between Nate's body and the shadow it cast, Joe couldn't see much. There were people down there, though, arms and legs shuffling and skittering on a hard surface. A face turned directly toward the light, and Joe almost dropped the flashlight. The lips were peeled back, *exposing dark teeth. The face was covered in facial hair or dirt or both. The eyes were squinted shut. It turned, and the mouth opened.*

"Fuck! Go!"

Joe heard a door swing and hit a wall. More skittering, shoes scraping on gravel. Nate had reached the bottom of the stairs. Joe tried moving the flashlight around, but Nate's body and shadows were obscuring everything.

"Robbie!" Nate yelled. "Oh God, Robbie, are you—"

Another scream came up, echoing into the dank stairwell. Joe took a few steps down. Nate set the shotgun aside and knelt down. Now the flashlight found Robbie. He was on his side, curled up and covering his head with one hand. His clothes were on, but he was clutching his shorts with the other hand, like someone was trying to pull them down. Joe almost clicked the light off. He moved it over to a corner so as not to shine it right on Robbie.

"Robbie, can you move?" Nate asked. "Let's get you up, come on." Robbie wouldn't budge, though. He stayed balled up, not moving except for his hands, clenched in tight fists. They were shaking. "Joe, come down here, please." Nate had found Lois's lighter and was staring into the open doorway at the bottom of the stairs. It was the doorway those two people had disappeared into, one of them with the horrible face.

"Is he okay?" Joe asked.

"I think so," Nate said, but his voice sounded terribly pained. "Wait here." He hefted the shotgun, again with the butt in front, and walked through the door with the lighter on. Joe knelt beside Robbie who still wasn't moving except for the terrible, shaking fists. The flashlight felt like an accuser, a glowing wand exposing Robbie somehow, but he didn't want to turn it off. After a few seconds Nate was back.

"There's a basement through there. It's a storage area for a deli or a restaurant. There's a ladder leading up to the street. Let's get him up."

"But . . . those guys," Joe said.

"They're gone," Nate said. "It's okay; we can go out this way." Robbie screamed again. "Robbie, please, let's get you out of here. Can you hear

*me?" Robbie made a gurgling sound. Nate turned to Joe. "Shine the light
in there."*

*Joe did as he was told. The area beyond the door was a small pantry-like
place with big cans on shelves and a few huge plastic barrels. Joe could hear
squeaking noises and scurrying in the corners. Rats, oh God. Joe let out a
tortured little moan. He moved the beam around the room. There was a
tiny puddle of light coming from above. Below it was a wide, slanted wood
contraption that looked like something between stairs and a ladder. Above
it and standing open to the air were two big steel doors that folded together
and locked. They were the kind that sagged under your feet if you walked
over them on a city sidewalk.*

"Robbie," Nate said, "can you hear me?"

"Why isn't he talking?" Joe asked. "He's like . . . frozen."

*"He may be in shock; it's okay. Robbie?" Then, like he'd been hit with
a bolt of electricity, Robbie came alive. He uncurled himself and screamed
in Nate's face.*

*"Why did you send me down here? WHY?!" The sound echoed up the
stairs.*

*"Robbie, I'm so sorry," Nate said. "Let's get you out of here, okay? It'll
be all right."*

*"It won't be all right!" Robbie's eyes were wide and tear filled. He
scrambled up, then fell to his knees again and threw up. Vomit splattered
on gravel and concrete. Joe cringed. It was the really good dinner from the
little French restaurant. And some grape soda.*

*"I'm so sorry," Nate said again. "Robbie, please believe me. I should
never have asked you—" Before he could finish, Robbie sprang to his feet,
pushed past Nate, and rushed through the door. He would not look at Joe
but followed the flashlight beam to the ladder. Joe shined it after him, not
knowing what else to do.*

*"Robbie, wait!" he called out. Robbie didn't answer, just scrambled up
the ladder and out onto Ninth Avenue.*

Nate and Joe followed, Nate holding the shotgun in scraped and bleeding hands. On Ninth Avenue, he cleared the gun of its remaining cartridge and then found an old Asian couple sitting on a stoop and smoking. He offered them the gun. They smiled and took it—this from a Black man who looked like he had been in battle and an equally scuffed and scarred little white boy—without saying a single word.

Nate and Joe looked up and down the avenue and in both directions on Forty-Third Street. No sign of Robbie. Joe's ears were still ringing, and there was that sharp burning smell he couldn't get out of his nose. The new shorts fit fine, but they were really dirty after all the ruckus. Nate looked terrible, his shirt torn and covered with dust, the collar bloody. He crouched a little as he walked and rubbed his neck.

"I'm really sorry," Joe said. "About everything."

"None of it is your fault," Nate said. "It's okay, Joe. I'm just really worried about your brother."

"What happened to him? Do you know?"

"I think the men who were down there attacked him," Nate said. "Robbie is probably very traumatized by it, whatever they did. Do you understand? That's why we have to find him."

"Like, he's scared and stuff? And freaked out?"

"Yes. Freaked out for sure. It's not his fault, though. You know that, right? Whatever those people did to him, it wasn't Robbie's fault."

"I know. I feel bad for him."

"I do too, but . . . when we find him, we have to be really careful about how we talk to him. Okay?"

"Sure."

"It might be very hard for him to think about, let alone talk about. So we'll be really careful." He paused. "And maybe it's best if you don't bring up what happened, even after Robbie seems okay. Does that make sense? Let him mention it, if he wants to, but it's best not to bring it up. No teasing or anything. It's too serious for that."

"I understand."

"Okay." He patted Joe on the back, and they began walking up Forty-Third toward Ricky's.

"Were you in a war?" Joe asked. He was thinking of how Nate had created obstacles behind them as they ran into the shadows.

"I was in the Vietnam War, yes."

"Is that where you learned that stuff?"

"Stuff?"

"Yeah, like throwing things behind us to stop that guy from chasing us. And how you carried the gun and stuff."

"Maybe. I don't really know." He sighed. "Let's look around a little more. We still have the flashlight. We'll walk by Ricky's also. Hopefully, he went back there. If not, we'll wait for him. We'll be there until morning."

Robbie didn't come back, though, not the entire night long, even after Joe had fallen asleep in a booth at Ricky's coffee shop. Nate stirred him as the first light was visible in the sky, and the two caught a city bus going downtown.

On the first ferry to Staten Island, as dawn painted the harbor a smoky rose color, Joe gazed back at the twin towers, looking chalky and stiff like chimneys. He wondered where Robbie was, and where his mother was. He would never see his mother alive again. He wouldn't see Robbie until a day later. And although he followed Nate's advice and never said anything to Robbie about what happened in the courtyard, it didn't matter.

Robbie never, ever looked at him the same again.

CHAPTER 71

Robbie never learned Evan Bolds's name. That hadn't been given to him, so Robbie made up a name for him, Wally, because for whatever reason, Robbie felt it suited him. He had expected to hear from Wally by midnight. Maybe 1:00 a.m. It was now after seven, and Robbie had heard nothing. The blinds were drawn. His single-room apartment was dim. And the AC unit was droning its numbing *wah-wah* sound.

His palms were sweaty. A knob at the back of his neck ached from the tension through his shoulders. He was lying on his couch a few feet away from the computer desk, trying not to reach for the burner phone every few seconds. Wally had given him both that phone and the laptop with the creepy old-school messaging application. Just as Robbie only used the laptop to communicate with one person, he only used the cell phone to message Wally. No one else was ever involved with either device.

Wally was very good about getting back to him when he was supposed to, but now he was totally AWOL, and Robbie was freaking out. For a while during the night, he had turned off the notifications because he couldn't bear the wait, but that only pushed him to grab for the phone more. Eventually, he tossed it to the dirty carpet and stared at the ceiling.

At 7:14 a.m., he reached for it again, clutched it in his fist, and pounded it against his chest. *Where the fuck is he, where the fuck is he, where the fuck is he?* He fell into an uneasy half sleep. A minute later it went off, sliding from his chest onto the floor. He scrambled for it and swiped it open.

Computer

He stared at the word. Wally never used the term "computer." Wally didn't write anything other than simple words, often misspelled, or addresses and times.

His hands shook as he wrote back. **What? Where are you?** He hit send and waited.

Computer

A coldness slid through him. The computer was not how he communicated with Wally. It was how he communicated with the Other One.

The Other One was the only name Robbie had come up with. He had never seen the Other One, like he had seen Wally, so no nickname or descriptor occurred to him. The Other One was the guy with the payoff, the reason he had been doing all this strange shit. There had been some money already, but much more was promised. All Robbie had to do was torment his brother Joe. Well, that wasn't all of it. He knew he was part of making some other terrible stuff happen, like what happened to their mother, Lois, and Joe's ex-girlfriend. Those things weren't Robbie's problems, though. He had been given simple tasks to perform, and he had done so.

There was a problem, though.

Robbie had "gone off the reservation" a little.

There was one thing he—and he alone—had sent Wally out to do that the Other One didn't know about. Wally, Robbie figured, was the real muscle, the guy willing to snap necks. As it happened, Robbie had one particular, long, skinny neck *he* wanted to see snapped. Wally knew that Robbie was expecting a big payoff. A lot of money. Robbie had to promise a good bit of it to Wally in exchange for this one task. It would cost him plenty, but it was worth it. As for Wally, he just seemed like a robot with thick glasses and a dumb mustache. He acted like he'd do anything for money, and Robbie was about to get some. *Get this done,* he had told him, and *I'll make it worth the effort out of my end.* Wally had seemed fine with the arrangement, even though an exact dollar amount hadn't been settled on. It didn't seem to matter. For one, Wally seemed to enjoy his work. And anyway, Wally was responsible for transporting whatever money was promised to Robbie. Wally knew he'd get paid. Robbie had sent him on his way with a photo and an address.

Simple.

But then Wally had been gone all night without answering him back, until now. And now it seemed like maybe there was someone else messaging him from Wally's phone.

The Other One.

Oh, please, no.

He felt the phone buzz in his hand. Another message had come in.

Computer

Robbie swallowed hard and pulled himself off the couch. He was in a T-shirt and shorts, both damp with sweat. He grabbed for his cigarettes and sat down hard at the computer desk. The laptop whirred, blinked awake, and went through its motions. After a few seconds, the home screen appeared. The wallpaper was what Microsoft had assigned, a crisp photo of a mountain field in Switzerland. He drew deep on a cigarette and blew out slowly. He had figured out over time that something on his end alerted the Other One when he was online. After a few seconds, the black box appeared. Inky-green text slid into view.

What did you do, Robbie?

Robbie stared at the text, his fingertips pulsating. The Other One had never used his name. Not once. He never really referred to him at all. He just gave directions and answered questions.

What?

You sent my man on an unauthorized errand. My man betrayed me, and I know he did so at your direction. You betrayed me, Robbie. Now that man is dead, and you are the one who will suffer for it.

What? I don't know what you—Before he could finish the sentence, another line appeared.

My man is dead, but the man you sent him to kill is just fine, and talking to the police, perhaps still as we speak. I have eyes and ears everywhere, Robbie, and I know what you tried to do and what happened. Now you will pay.

Whose dead? What the fuck?

My man is WHO'S dead, Robbie, you ignorant, perfidious worm. Stop writing and read.

Robbie stared open mouthed, the cigarette burning to the filter in an ashtray. His hands went limp.

> I know everything, and with that knowledge, I tried to protect you. I offered you the best possible outcome and a considerable sum of money to boot. You threw it away.

Robbie managed to punch out you dont, but then text started streaking across the screen.

> Of course I do, Robbie DeSantos. I know what you wanted. I know what you've always wanted. You wanted your mother punished. We accomplished that. I groomed her and cosseted her back to New York, a reformed whore from a storefront church, and she was punished. You wanted that, and I gave it to you.

> And Joe. You wanted Joe to suffer also, and we accomplished that, didn't we? Lois first, Joe's fat, perfumed girlfriend next, and both of them so perfectly pinned on Joe. All we needed was blood, Joe's blood for all the caring world, and I directed you to it. For once, for all time, I allowed you to wipe the sanctimonious grin from his face. Now you have pissed on all of it. Alas, I should have known.

Robbie's mouth went dry. He felt imprisoned in the black desk chair.

> Known what?

That what I offered wasn't enough for you. You wanted one last person punished, didn't you, Robbie? That's why news reached me this morning, news more complete than I'd guess you could imagine. News brought to me by men I pay to keep six steps ahead of worms like you. You only knew one of the men I direct, Robbie. You turned him against me and sent him out to murder. Well, my man did murder a person, a vagrant. That vagrant is of no consequence. The man who survived, though? You knew that man, likely from your past, didn't you, Robbie? You hated that man.

Robbie's mind raced. "Vagrant" meant nothing to him. The deal with Wally wasn't about killing some vagrant. Robbie had tracked down Nate Porter to his address in Manhattan, a task as easy as thumbing through the white pages. All Wally had to do was case him, get in, and get it done—just like he had with Robbie's mother and Joe's ex-girlfriend. The only difference with this job was that he didn't need a vial and a dropper to leave blood behind. Joe was already on his way to prison for two murders. Wally was no one. He would never be suspected of Nate Porter's murder.

I didn't

He paused, shaking, then wrote

I don't know what this guy did.

Maybe not, but you knew what he was supposed to do—what you bribed him into doing, I suppose. You, Robbie, needed something else. What did this

old man do to you, Robbie? That is the only thing
I don't know. I can imagine many things, though.

Robbie felt like he might throw up. For months now, the whole
thing had seemed unreal, a show he was watching rather than really
being a part of. In some ways, he was doing the will of the Other One
before he was fully aware of it, going through the motions. It had all
been laid out so perfectly. The job at the rehab center was one of a
string of similar ones he had done most of his life. The Other One had
instructed him on the best way to obtain employment there. It was easy,
even with the cloud of complaints and accusations that had followed
Robbie over the years. He was a US citizen without a criminal record.
There was a labor shortage. He was in.

Also surreal but smoothly accomplished was his introduction to the
man he was to draw blood from: the breathing husk in room 728 with
the name Caleb Evermore. Only one blood draw was needed. That's
all the Other One demanded. Robbie was squeamish about the needle
Wally had given him, but he used it well enough. The man in the bed
jerked a tiny bit when Robbie inserted the stout syringe and pulled
blood from his left arm, but otherwise didn't react. The arm went limp
again, a thin, pale appendage barely different in color from the sheet it
lay on, running down to a hopelessly idle hand that grasped nothing.
After that, there was a trick or two, like pouring sand over his brother's
shoes. It was madness, aimed at Joe and delivered one step at a time.

Robbie wasn't stupid. Caleb Evermore was really Robbie's brother.
More importantly, though, he was Joe's identical twin. The Other One
hadn't offered much in terms of how that had come about, but Robbie
got the gist, and it rang very true. His parents, for whatever banal or
complex reasons, had left a boy to die. What Uncle Mike had pulled off
was an elaborate trick on a failed, dying system. The machinations and
sleights of hand were unknown, but Robbie could imagine them. He
was no stranger to changing names, creating identities, shifting realities.

Institutional bureaucracies were soft underbellies for deceit. Uncle Mike was clever. Clever and meddling.

Meddling Uncle Mike couldn't leave well enough alone on the night of the blackout either. Their mother was gone, but Robbie was handling it. Uncle Mike had to butt in, though, pairing the brothers with some other gay man. A smooth-talking savior, a usurper. That man had led Robbie blindly into an unspeakable violation. He would never look at Joe the same again. He would never look in a *mirror* the same again.

Robbie's chest heaved. He wished he could reach into the black square and pull the author of these words back through. Yes, Robbie wanted something else. He wanted that bastard Nate Porter punished along with his mother and brother. It was so little to ask after the killing they had already done.

He swept the ashtray off the desk in a rage. He wanted one last thing for himself—a bit of control, the ability to step off the path the Other One had placed him on. Who did that person think he was, anyway? Why did *he* get to direct everything? Why was Robbie trapped in the back seat, marched around in the dark like a dog on a leash? As if that miserable, fetid, terrifying night hadn't been bad enough? They had been *abandoned*, and Robbie had been left to fend for his little brother. He had been *brave*. He had been *steadfast*. But then he had been ordered down a staircase and

they jumped me I couldn't stop them

Robbie hit send before he knew he was doing it.

What?

THEY JUMPED ME TWO OF THEM I COULDN'T STOP THEM I COULDN'T STOP THEM THEY

JUMPED ME THEY JUMPED ON ME THEY WERE ALL OVER ME

He slammed his fists against the keyboard, sending letter caps flying. Ghostly white light emanated from underneath, exposing the hardware. The keyboard looked useless, but maybe that was best. If this whole, strange trip had been just above a dream, then it could be snuffed out like one too. Maybe, down the road, he would find Nate Porter himself. A sweet thought for another time. Now it was time to walk away. His mother was dead. His brother was trapped, just like Robbie had been in that black stairwell when there was breath in his face, and laughter, then that terrible smell, then hands all over him . . .

I see you.

Robbie gawked. The screen was still lit, the black square in place.

That's right, I see you. I don't care about your reasons, your tantrums, about who tortured you, or who you blame. But before I leave you, know this.

Words flew across the screen.

The truth is, your mother discarded you both and never looked back, but as you can see it was me who was able to convince her to come back. It wasn't for you, though, Robbie. It was Joe she loved. It was Joe she came back for. It was Joe she wanted help from: legal help, financial help, and stable, strong assistance to reorient herself and find Joe's twin brother and maybe even start over.

It was never you, though. She had no regard for you. She never mentioned you. If you hated her, you had good reason. I harnessed that hate. I used you as a tool to see her murdered, and to see your preening, drunk bastard of a brother blamed for it.

Yet you've soured that.

You're a worm. A blind worm destined to spend your miserable life in the dark. You'll get nothing now, Robbie; you are done. They're coming for you, and only for you. All roads, the blood, the bodies, the man I sent.

They all lead to your door.

I am no one. You will never find me, and they will never find me. I will destroy this computer, the one I gave you, from the inside out. Blank, all of it.

Now there is only you, Robbie, you and your miserable, worthless word, when they come for you.

All darkness. All night. Forever and ever. It's all you deserve.

You filth.

You failure.

You maggot.

Robbie threw up. All over the remains of the keyboard and up onto the screen, vomit sprayed, pixelated light streaming through milky stripes of it. He pushed himself back from the table and vomited again—bitter bile. Then the computer was making a noise.

There was a series of beeps, and then the black square disappeared. The screen flickered, and a blooming burn mark, like something emerging in a film reel, grew from the center outward. It consumed the mountain field wallpaper. The screen went black.

Robbie walked into the bathroom and turned the water on in the tub, then poured in some old bath salts. He couldn't remember the last time he had sat in a bath, but the rubber stopper was in there, leashed for all time to a rusty chain. When the water was high enough, he went back to the living area and found the small portable heater he used in the winter months. It was cube shaped, eight inches square, and black. There was a screened fan on the front and on the back a cord and UL specifications.

He had an extension cord in the coat closet. He ran the cord from the living room into the bathroom, then powered up the space heater, which slowly whirred to life. He set it on the toilet, gripping it with his left hand. Then he drew a deep breath and plunged his head into the cold water. He gritted his teeth and swept the purring unit into the tub. For a split second he felt an enormous jolt, as if his head was being kicked open from the inside out. Then Robbie DeSantos knew no more.

CHAPTER 72

Sixtieth Precinct
Coney Island, Brooklyn
7:11 p.m.

"It was that line from the poem," Zochi said. She and Len Dougherty were sitting on the hood of Len's car outside the Sixtieth Precinct building, a three-story brick-and-concrete monstrosity brightened only by the red garage doors of the firehouse, which took up the northern end of the edifice. "It's where the inscription came from, the one they found on the bra and on the wall at Holly Rossi's place. That's what sealed it for me. Even before the DNA. All that, and I was wrong."

"The DNA sealed it for everyone," Len said, yawning and glancing south toward the subway station at the end of the block. Kids were pouring out of it—late summer stragglers stretching the holiday weekend a little further. "It looks like a brilliant setup, period."

"I mean, if I had it do all over again, I'd still have asked for the collar. It scares me, though. Being wrong like that."

"We were wrong," Len said, looking sideways at her. "We weren't sloppy, though." The day had been hot and bright, but the evening was mellowing out nicely. Early September in New York City loosened summer's grip in fits and starts. Cooler nights were coming. "There's no way anyone saw this coming."

"If Evan Bolds hadn't taken that dive, we might not have seen it."

"He did, though," Len said with a shrug, as if the universe was properly ordered after all. "And they found his car down the block, right? Impound searched it?"

"It was a panel van, yeah. He used it for deliveries to dry cleaners. It was a great search. They found the blood vial and an eyedropper. Some personal papers, too, from Joe's mother. Remember that planner thing we found on her? It looks like he rifled through it and took some stuff. I'll look at it tomorrow. Right now, I'm seeing double and can't think straight."

"No shit. You need to rest."

"Robbie's place, though," she said, as if she almost forgot to ask, "they didn't find anything?"

Len crossed his arms and shook his head. "Other than a couple of cell phones, not a thing. No weapons. No drugs. No paraphernalia about his brother or his mother. No notes, nothing."

"The computer, though," she said, "that's weird."

He raised his eyebrows. "Yeah, it was." The police response to Robbie's apartment that morning—when he was found electrocuted in the bathtub—began as a fire department call. A laptop computer on a desk had caught fire, apparently from inside the device itself. A computer forensics examiner would have to see if anything was salvageable, but at the scene it didn't look likely.

Robbie was found half-submerged in the bathtub, dead of electric shock in what was either a strange accident or an apparent suicide. To Len it looked very much like the latter. It was a bold move, taking oneself out like that, but probably quick. The bathwater had absorbed most of the energy, even as it shocked Robbie DeSantos into oblivion, but the extension cord he used to avoid the ground fault interrupter in the bathroom had melted all the way back to the living room wall. At the wall outlet was a huge black spot. Between that and the smoldering guts of the laptop, smoke alarms had gone off.

"There's one more connection to make sense of," Zochi said. "The phones will connect Robbie to Evan Bolds, even if they're burners. We can establish that Robbie provided Bolds with blood from Joe's twin, the guy at the rehab place. Bolds was the hands-on killer, the one who left the inscriptions behind and dropped the blood."

Len crossed his arms over his chest and shook his head. "Fuckin' unbelievable."

"Yeah. There's a link missing, though."

He looked over. "What?"

"I don't think Robbie found Evan Bolds and got him to do all of this stuff. I think it's more like Evan Bolds found *him*. That doesn't make any sense, though. I mean, why? Why does a loser ex-con like Bolds look up some *other* loser and then agree to set up a murder spree with him?"

"Maybe DeSantos knows something, since Bolds was his case. He's getting released, right?"

"Yeah, this week sometime, as long as everything checks out. I'll talk to Mimi Bromowitz in the morning."

"You should catch a few hours' sleep here, before you drive back."

"Nah, gotta get back to my kid. Traffic's light; I'll be all right."

"It's one for the books, Zoch," he said, putting out his hand. She shook it and grinned at him, the reddish glow of the declining sun in her eyes.

CHAPTER 73

"I have two last things to show you," Aideen said after explaining the remarkable events of the previous forty-eight hours. "I'll start with the easy one." She handed him her cell phone, teed up to play a ten-second video from the 111 Centre Street surveillance clip. Máiréad had compressed it for her and loaded it onto her phone. Joe watched as Evan Bolds slipped the baggie into one of the thick brown case folders.

"The Reggie card," he said, just above a whisper.

"Yes."

"And . . . he got it from Lois?"

"Almost certainly, yes. When she was found, she was carrying that leather-bound planner thing. I'll bet it was in there. Hathorne probably knew and told Bolds to look for it. It would have been a great way to psych you out."

"It worked." He was quiet for a few seconds. "Hathorne. We can't prove he was behind this, can we?"

"Not yet, but I'm onto that son of a bitch."

Joe was taken aback. There was fire in her eyes, more than he had ever seen before. In a way it was funny; as angry as Aideen was, his heart felt lighter. He was disarmed by the love and support that still surrounded him, even when he seemed to deserve it the least.

"Hathorne's hard to pin down," he said.

"I'm sure he thinks he is. The burned-up laptop isn't searchable, but I'm sure Hathorne gave it to Robbie through Bolds."

Joe nodded. "It's something Hathorne would know exactly how to do—cause it to self-destruct like something out of a James Bond film. He'll get away with this, believe me."

"Hmm, we'll see," she said, her voice rising in pitch. The fire had been replaced, in a flash, by something wicked and conspiratorial. It was the prankster side of her he hadn't seen in a long time.

Joe gave her a questioning look. "What am I missing?"

"Nothing," she said, feigning ignorance and innocence. "Craig's been working on something. Let's let him work on it."

"Craig? What is it? What's he doing?"

"Don't worry about that right now," she said, shaking her head and waving away the topic. "You've got other things to think about, Joe." With that, she paused for a long moment, then reached for an envelope in her briefcase. "I received something from the pastor who worked with Lois in California."

The cream-colored business envelope was addressed to Aideen Bradigan, Esq. In the upper left-hand corner was a cross logo beside the return address: Tahoe Park Grace Lutheran Church, Sacramento, CA. Joe's hands trembled as he removed the contents. There were two letters, one neatly typed on church stationery in the same cream color as the envelope and one that was handwritten on ruled paper, the kind schoolkids used.

The letter from Pastor Suzanne Nelson to Aideen Bradigan, Esq., was clipped and brief—not particularly warm. She wrote a few kind things about Lois and made it clear that she and the other women at the church would miss her dearly and were devastated to hear of her loss. The letter went on to say that the substance of her interaction with Lois—the things Lois felt, spoke of, and sought counseling for—was confidential and privileged and therefore could not be discussed with anyone. However, there was a handwritten letter she was in possession of from Lois to her son Joseph. The letter had started off as an assignment of sorts, a writing project for Lois to work on as part of other therapeutic work, the details of which could not be shared. The pastor was satisfied, however, that the message was now enough of an independent writing for it to be offered to Joe. "I am gratified to hear of your client's apparent exoneration in this matter," the letter concluded, "and I trust you will direct this final message to him and him alone." It was signed "Yours in Christ."

Joe unfolded the next page and beheld his mother's large, loopy cursive. This was the only time he could remember seeing it outside of the few bits and pieces that Aideen had shown him from the crime scene materials. It was undated.

> Joey:
> I write this to you in hopes of finding you again in New York when I have the strength and the will to leave here. I am happy in this lovely, simple place after so many years of misery and wretchedness, most of which I caused to myself. I must come home, though. If I dare try to forgive myself, then first I must attempt the impossible. I must find you, my darling boy. I must pray that you'll allow me to explain myself to you and Robbie, and I think I will need you to reach Robbie, as I believe I scarred him even more than I did you. And there is another brother, Charles, whom your father and I abandoned, even before I abandoned the two of you.

The tears on this page, if you can see their marks, may be the only evidence of sincerity that I can offer you. I feel guilt like a fire in my bones, and it has all but consumed me. I wish I could tell you the darkness that overcame me that night the lights went out. I say this because they went out in me too. There is no excuse. There is no apology I can offer for the madness and the call of death that I answered and that led me away from you, along the dark blocks lined with people like ghosts that I just kept following and following until it was morning, and then I was on a bus and I was hoping that you had found Mike and that you would be okay.

You would not be okay, though, not really. I know that you and Robbie found the strength and courage to go on without me and find your uncle in that blackness. I know that Mike gave everything he had to make your lives as whole as possible before he died too, another thing I chose not to be there for. I know the gifts God gave me—in you, Charles, and Robbie—and I know how I not only squandered them but also rejected them and spit on them. On you. On our lives together and what was left of them.

I lost my nerve when the lights went out, Joey. And then I lost my mind.

I deserve nothing, but I am praying that the pastor is right and that being a child of God means I can seek redemption in this life as well as the next. I want nothing for myself, Joe. Please understand that. Every debasement of my body and soul over the years is one I deserved. Pastor Suzanne and I disagree on this, but it's how I feel, and I don't lie anymore. But maybe if I can see you and talk to you, maybe I can win your assistance in finding Charles and perhaps the same with Robbie and perhaps . . . I just don't know. There is no wholeness, I know that. There will be no family life for us. Maybe there can be life for us, though. Something brief and beautiful that you can hold. Maybe.

I've watched you from afar, Joe, and I know you've done good things, even with your struggles. I've been corresponding with a man whom I really do not know, but he tells me he's worked with you, and he believes I can find you. He has provided a few details to that end, and he's asked nothing of me in return. That is difficult for me to accept, as I have never, ever, received anything from a man that didn't have strings attached.

I don't know that I will see him when I arrive there, but I am hoping to find you. I wish I could just pick up a phone or a pen and write you, but that isn't possible. I can't explain it, but if I see you, it will be because I have the courage to actually physically approach you. I will look into your eyes. We will see each other, and if you are willing to hear me, then I can admit to you—you first, before Robbie and Charles—the things I am guilty of.

I say these things because I have hope, my darling.

God, through Pastor Suzanne and my sisters here, has given me many things, but none more important than hope.

I hope.

I love you.

If God wills it, I will find you.

"I don't even know where to start." His eyes wandered around the room, and his hands shook until he squeezed them together. It was more than overwhelming. It was impossible to fully absorb. He looked back at Aideen. "What happens now?"

"You should be released from here tomorrow, maybe Friday. The case won't be formally dropped until KCDA submits a motion, but you'll be out, pending that."

"No, Aideen, I mean, what do I *do*? I can't even . . ." He trailed off and felt his eyes brimming with tears. "What the hell do I do now?"

"You have to process this," she said. "After everything else, now this. I'd say one day at a time."

He ran a hand through his hair. "I had no idea she even had thoughts like that. I had no idea she could express them."

"It sounds like she couldn't for many years. I'm glad she did, and that this pastor was able to share them with you."

"These crimes, Aid, I thought I committed them. For a while there, I really did."

"I know you did."

"So . . . how did you . . . I mean, *why* did you . . ." He was fighting breaking down and sobbing.

"Why did I what?"

"*Believe* in me? That's different from believing me, you know what I mean? No one had done that since Craig Flynn. Before him, it was Uncle Mike."

"Plenty of people believed in you. I did too, for the most part."

He felt himself grinning. "For the most part?"

"I like to hedge my bets."

"Do you think Craig knew I was innocent? I mean *really* knew it?"

"I don't know how Craig's mind works," she said, her eyes strangely suspicious. They seemed to clear and she shrugged. "He thought we belonged together, fighting this thing. I don't know what else."

"Halle," he said. "Her parents. I hope they'll see me. I think about her more than anyone. I mean, the letter from Lois . . . it's a good thing. I'll treasure it, and I'm glad she found peace. She was right, though. It would have been a stretch to turn her intentions into anything real. But Halle? Jesus, Aideen, she was so innocent. She was just a kind and decent . . ." He couldn't hold it back anymore. Across the table from his attorney, he bawled. Aideen sat quietly as it worked through him. He was embarrassed at first, then it occurred to him how silly that was. Some things, men just never got past.

"Knowing what they know, I think Halle's family will see you," she said. "But one day at a time, Joe. There's a lot to go through before this is over and you can get on with your life."

"My life?"

"Yes. You have it back, whether you want it or not."

"Nothing I do will bring Halle back. Or even Lois, for that matter. Hathorne made sure of that."

"Lois kind of made her peace," she said. "She did what she set out to do. That's what the pastor says, and that's what Lois was able to tell us too. She got straight, and she came back, looking for you. She died hopeful. That's better than nothing."

"Yeah, like Robbie. He died with less than nothing."

"I'm sorry about that."

"I lost Robbie the night of the blackout. In a different way, but he was still gone." He looked up at her. "He got hurt that night. It was a sexual attack of some kind, down in a stairwell. Nate asked him to go down there and check, to see if there was a way out of where we were. We heard him scream. We got to him. We stopped it. But . . . wow, I've never said this out loud."

"I'm sorry that happened."

"Robbie blamed Nate, or maybe both of us. Or maybe he just couldn't stand the thought of us around anymore? I don't know.

Hathorne fed on it, whatever it was. That much I know. He's got claws. That's why I didn't want you near him, Aideen."

"I understand. I always did. For now, let Craig worry about Hathorne. Robbie? Well, I think you have to bury your thoughts about Robbie with him. I know that's cold, but . . ."

"No, it's smart. Anyway, I've got another brother to meet." He sighed. "That's the future."

"I think it'll be good for you to meet him. It sounds like things are in place in terms of his care, but now you can make sure. You can be there for him, finally."

He shrugged, suddenly exhausted. "I'll try."

"I'm going over to see Mimi now. I'll be in touch, and I'll pick you up when you're sprung."

"I can cab it."

"Don't be ridiculous. It's a defense attorney's dream—driving her client away from Rikers after the case has been dropped." She grinned and snapped her briefcase shut.

"Aideen?"

"Yeah?"

"Thank Máiréad for me, okay?"

"I will. Your fee might send her to law school. Well, a public one."

He smiled, then searched for her eyes. "And thanks for living this with me."

She smiled toothlessly, her eyes sad. "Thanks for choosing to live, Joe."

CHAPTER 74

Tuesday, September 19, 2017
St. Lawrence Psychiatric Center
Ogdensburg, New York
3:14 p.m.

Craig Flynn thrummed his fingers on an empty desk as wind-driven rain slashed against the windows. Here on New York's sloping Canadian frontier, summer was over. He was set up for the day in an unoccupied office at the psych center, taking meetings with a couple of doctors and some admin staff. He was looking forward to the last meeting, though, one he hoped would be a surprise.

"*There* he is," he said cheerfully as Aaron Hathorne appeared in the doorway. Behind him was a hospital attendant who took a quick look around the office, then told Craig he'd be outside the door and that they had about ten minutes. Hathorne did look surprised, but the look shifted to contempt.

"I can't possibly imagine what would keep me here for ten minutes," he said. Craig hooked his hands behind his head and flashed an exaggerated, rubbery smile.

"Have a seat, Doc."

"I'll stand if I can choose."

"That's not your only choice," Craig said. The smile disappeared. "You could do some good for yourself and talk to my investigator about your relationship with Evan Bolds."

"That name barely rings a bell. Where is this investigator, anyway?"

"No need to waste his time if you're gonna act that way."

Hathorne flared his nostrils. "What way?"

"Ignorant, which is the one thing I know you aren't."

"If you are here about a man named Evan Bolds, I can assure you I'm quite ignorant. As I said, I can barely remember the name."

"Then you might be slipping a little," Craig said, pulling on a confused face. "My friends over at the corrections department created a fairly intricate trail between you and Bolds—the facilities you were in together, the sex offender sessions you both attended. You talked. You knew each other."

"This proves a marriage?"

"You were working together, and I'll find out how. Yeah, he's dead, but it's given us a chance to do some deep dives on his van, his house, his phones. You could short-circuit that, though. You could come clean and tell me what the arrangement was. It might do you some good."

Hathorne had been standing arrow straight, but now he seemed to relax, and he offered the slightest hint of a grin. "I really can't help you, Mr. Flynn."

"I had to try," Craig said. He leaned forward and intertwined his fingers on the desk. "Thankfully, there's Elaine Benedetto."

"Elaine . . . I'm sorry, who?" Hathorne's eyes gave nothing away, but his posture went rigid.

Craig smiled. "Don't be coy, Doc. You're *really* no good at that. Elaine Benedetto taught English at Joe DeSantos's middle school in Staten Island. She's retired now but still active—keeps in touch with a bunch of her former students, healthy as a horse, all that stuff. But you knew that, didn't you? You knew when you called her to see if you could track down the poem Joe wrote. The one that wowed them all. The one that made it into the school magazine."

Hathorne snorted. "This is absurd."

"I assume it was his brother Robbie who told you about it, but I'll bet he didn't have a copy of it. It intrigued you, though, didn't it? The idea of that poem, and what he wrote. You saw it as something cryptic. Something you could use."

"I won't dignify this any longer." He called out for the attendant.

"The phone call you made was recorded," Craig said. Hathorne stopped in his tracks. "Darndest thing. It had nothing to do with you. Elaine's husband, Arthur Benedetto, has been wrapped up in some litigation with a guy who owns a beach house next to theirs, down on the Jersey Shore. Can you believe that? It got nasty a couple of years ago, so old Mr. Benedetto started recording all incoming calls."

"You expect me to believe this?"

"I don't really care, because we got lucky. Elaine definitely remembered talking with you. A nice old man, she said, who told her he was an old friend of Joe's. This nice man wanted to see if he could round up a copy of the literary magazine where Joe's heartbreaker of a poem was published, way back when. He said something about a presentation for Joe's fiftieth birthday. Elaine keeps archives of the literary magazine going back to the '60s. You knew that too."

"This is a fantasy," Hathorne said, but his eyes were wide and his face pale.

"I can't remember the name you gave her or the address near Saratoga to send the copy to. The amazing thing was that—sure enough—your call to her was one of the seventy-five or so that old Arthur recorded and stored on a hard drive that year. I've heard the call, Doc. It's you, and I'll be able to establish your voice pattern." The attendant, a stocky Black guy about Craig's age, was at the door now. He gave Craig a questioning look. Craig put up a finger as if to ask for one more minute.

"This is utter nonsense. Try to scare a younger man, Mr. Flynn. I know what can convict someone in a court of law and what cannot."

"It's not about convictions anymore, though, is it, Doc?" Craig asked, again feigning the exaggeratedly confused face. "I mean, it's a lesser standard now, isn't it? When it comes to how long you'll stay in here, it's really about whether you're *mentally ill*." He paused for effect. "And dangerous."

Every muscle in Hathorne's frame seemed to freeze. His hands shook minutely. Craig stared back at him. The attendant moved a little closer.

"Let's go, Doctor," he said.

"You're an ugly man, Mr. Flynn," Hathorne said, his rigid mouth finally spreading into a leering purplish smile. "An ugly man with a tragic face." The attendant looked at him with alarm, but Craig just grinned back.

"My dog loves me anyway," he said. The grin disappeared. "You'll die in here. I'll see to it." His eyes shifted to the attendant. "Get him out of here."

CHAPTER 75

Monday, April 15, 1985
Bayley Seton Hospital
Staten Island
9:15 p.m.

Lady Blue *was the ABC Monday Night Movie playing in Uncle Mike's room. A cop movie with a redheaded woman as the star. The sound was off, but Joe got the gist. He was following it mostly because he had no idea what else to do.*

He was standing between his uncle's bed and the window, still in the rumpled shirt and tie he had worn on the flight from Dublin. He felt guilty for not paying more attention to the figure in the bed, but it hurt just to glance. His uncle looked skeletal under a white sheet, his arms like matchsticks tethered to bags and machines.

"Hi, Joe?" In the doorway was a thin young man with a clipboard in his hands. He was neatly dressed in jeans and a collared shirt with a knitted maroon tie. "My name is Stephen. I work with the hospital." He had kind, softened eyes under wispy blond hair. It looked like he'd been crying not long ago.

"Oh, hi."

"I understand you were traveling. Have you been home yet?"

"No. I came straight from the airport. I was on a school trip. Um . . . my uncle has been sick for about a year." He pictured Mike's crowded night-stand at home—pill bottles, tissues, the plastic thing he threw up into some-times. His uncle had never—not once—asked Joe for help. Still, Joe felt he should have known better.

"Your uncle's condition deteriorated rapidly. He lost consciousness before you got back, but he was in a lot of pain."

"Do they know how long he has?"

"Hours. Maybe a day." There was a pause. *"Do you know what your uncle is sick from, Joe?"*

"AIDS. I mean, I know they have other things on the charts. Pneumonia. But I know what it is."

"You're not worried, are you? That you'll get it, just from living with him?"

"No."

"Good. It's important you know that."

"Thanks."

"Do you want to talk about your uncle's arrangements? I understand that you turned eighteen recently. You can help me get some paperwork signed. Would that be okay?"

"Sure, if I can help."

"Okay, come on over and have a seat." Stephen took one of the visitor chairs and Joe settled into the one next to it.

"He was really good to me. I shouldn't have gone on this trip. I knew he was sick, but . . . he said he wanted me to go." Joe burned with shame. *"And I wanted to go, so I just went. It was selfish."*

"I'm sure he wanted you to go. I'm sure he's glad you did."

"We were supposed to talk," Joe said, *"when I came back. That was this coming weekend, but the program put me on a plane this morning."*

"It's okay, really. The good news is that your uncle took care of almost everything."

As Joe would learn, that was an understatement. Mike Carroll had planned for his death long before Joe knew he was seriously ill. He was to be cremated; that was already paid for. There was no life insurance—Mike had already sold the policy—but there was a trust set up for Joe's education. There was no mention of Robbie or their mother.

Joe knew a little bit about the trust. He was attending Monsignor Farrell High School on an academic scholarship and would attend Fordham University in the fall. He was an excellent student, one of the most accomplished at Farrell. College was provided for, so Joe just had to stay on the path. It was so clear that he had given little thought to it, even as his uncle weakened.

How selfish I've been.

He lowered his head, wiping his eyes and choking back a sob.

"It's okay to be upset," Stephen said.

"It's more like . . . I never appreciated what he was doing for me. This whole time, he was just . . . setting things up for me. I mean, who am I?" He looked up at Stephen as if he might have a satisfactory answer. "I'm some kid who got dumped on his doorstep."

"He really loved you," Stephen said. Joe absorbed those words—the smooth, level tone—and something in him broke. Stephen was right, although Mike had never said those words. No one had told Joe that they loved him since his mother. For a terrible second he thought he was hyperventilating. Then Stephen leaned in and put his arm around his shoulder.

"Let it out, Joe," he said in the practiced, measured tone of a funeral director. It seemed strange, Joe would think later, for a person just a few years older than him to be so well versed in grief. "It's okay, just . . . let it out."

CHAPTER 76

"You never met him?" Joe asked. He was speaking in a low voice, although that didn't seem to matter. The supine figure in the bed hadn't seemed to register that anyone was talking at all.

"I never did," Nate said. "Mike told me all about him. He visited regularly, but I never went along."

"Was he ever more responsive than this?"

Nate shook his head. "Mike never mentioned it, if he was. I think he's been this way for quite a while. Most people in his state don't survive this long. He's been well cared for."

Joe leaned on the windowsill. He was between Charles's bed and the window. Nate was in the guest chair. He saw himself at Bayley Seton again, a gangly kid in a rumpled suit staring down with sadness and confusion at the shriveled man under a sheet. Charles looked far more peaceful than Uncle Mike had in the extremities of death. There were no tubes attached to his twin, at least for now. His head, which seemed much larger than his body, was tilted away. He had graying hair, like

Joe, and the same long lashes and heavy eyebrows. His eyes and his mouth were both half-closed. Joe noticed a bit of drool on his cheek and gently wiped it away with a tissue.

"I feel like I should have known," he said. "You know how they say twins have a connection? Or, when they're separated at birth, they still feel the other one, out there somewhere? I never felt that."

"I'm glad you get to know him now."

"Well, I get to know *about* him. I don't guess anyone can really know him."

"Love and affection are never wasted," Nate said. "I think of it this way."

Outside, the last of the day was fading into blue. The sodium lights of the parking lot bathed cars in amber. Joe looked over at Nate. "Thank you, Nate. I couldn't imagine who to ask to come with me, but you're the perfect person."

"I'm honored. I wish I had gone to see him with your uncle." He smiled. "How was the facility when you made contact? Were they afraid you'd sue?"

"Not that I could tell," Joe said and smiled back. "They were great, actually. The director offered to see if they could track down how it happened—what paperwork Mike shuffled around. I told them not to bother. He's Caleb Evermore now. That's okay with me, as long as he's taken care of."

"And what about you, Joe? Are you taken care of?"

A pause, then a shrug. "I'm good for now."

"Will you go back to work?"

"Eventually. My old boss wants me back. I was never indicted, so I guess it's possible. I'm gonna take some time, though, to stay near my brother. Stay dry."

"You said 'dry,' not 'sober,'" Nate said with an approving look. "You know your terms."

"Can't call myself sober yet. Working on it, though."

337

"I never told you how sorry I was about your mother. It was all so sudden, and then so unresolved."

"It's okay. Mike never said he was sorry either, but that was because he hoped Lois would show up, step out of a cab, and come straggling up to the house with a suitcase. I dreamed of moments like that for a little while."

"I hope you learned to dream about different things," Nate said. "We all have to."

"Yeah, we do. While we're at it, I never thanked *you*." Joe had been looking at Charles, who had fallen asleep. He shifted his eyes to Nate. "For what you did for us that night."

"I lost Robbie," he said, his eyes cast down. "I sent him down to something terrifying. Worse than that. I should have told your uncle, but I just . . ."

"It was a different time," Joe said, his voice gravelly. "We had different tools then. I don't know that it would have made a difference anyway. In the end, that night swallowed Robbie just like it did Lois." He paused, collecting himself. "You, though"—he waited until Nate looked up at him—"you led me out of the dark. I'll never owe a greater debt."

"Stay in the light, Joe. It'll be all the repayment I need."

In polishing this book and bringing forth a final product, I am eternally grateful to the amazing team at Thomas & Mercer, most especially Jessica Tribble-Wells, Jon Reyes, and Nicole Burns-Ascue, all of whom steered me so wisely through a crucial editing process. Your skill, patience, and dedication have transformed this sad but hopeful story into a published work of fiction. To the extent it genuinely reflects even one of the millions of such stories that play out on these streets throughout all time, I am deeply proud and grateful.

Roger A. Canaff
New York City
January 2022

ACKNOWLEDGMENTS

My love affair with New York City, where I was born and where my wife and I now call home, began in the fourth grade, the end of which unfortunately coincided with 1977, a year many consider the very nadir for Gotham in modern times. Between the stalking terror of the Son of Sam, the crippling fiscal crisis, and then the blackout, 1977 seemed to portend the city's permanent status as a moribund giant. But writing New York's eulogy has proven consistently premature. While far from perfect, it remains vibrant, intoxicating, and deeply relevant—an estuary in more ways than one.

It was those darker days that inspired this story, of course. I watched it from afar, a suburban kid in the outskirts of Washington, DC. For a while I wrote it off also, but then thrilled to the comeback and chased my own NYC dream when special victims prosecution brought me to the Bronx in 2005. The threads of that earlier time still weave in my mind, whether through Woody Allen movies, scars on old streets, or the memories of loved ones. As always, I am indebted to the men and women of the NYPD for the passion, resolve, and humor they bring to a Sisyphean task, and to my brother and sister attorneys on both sides of the uncertain criminal equation. In particular, thank you, John Harford, Kevin Gagan, Sally Crabtree, Larry Harvey, and Lulu Gonzalez for inspiring these characters and for being living light in my life.

ABOUT THE AUTHOR

Roger A. Canaff is a former New York City special victims prosecutor and author of *Bleed Through*, winner of the IBPA Benjamin Franklin Award and the second in the Alex Greco ADA series. Previous novels include *Among the Dead* and *Copperhead Road*. He began his prosecutorial career in historic Alexandria, Virginia, served as president of the board of directors of End Violence Against Women International, and is a charter member of CounterQuo, an organization challenging the way our culture responds to sexual violence. Currently Roger teaches undergraduate and law school classes and trains and consults nationally and internationally. He lives and works in New York City. For more information, visit www.rogercanaff.com/about.